# CODE BLUE

ATROUS SERIES, BOOK TWO

N.R. WALKER

# COPYRIGHT

# BLURB

Steve Frost had dreams of wearing the national championship belt in mixed martial arts, maybe even going pro, but instead, finds himself working as a security guard for the rich and famous in LA.

Quickly earning a reputation for his blunt and precise *people management skills*, he lands a position on the security team for an up-and-coming boyband, Atrous. Years later, he's head of security. He knows these boys, and with countless tours, flights, car trips, public events, concerts, he's closer to one band member in particular.

Jeremy's been a pillar for Atrous since day one, but even more so these last few months. Now the face of the band more than ever, he's also got himself the attention of a delusional stalker-fan.

When the fame and stress become too much, when Jeremy's health takes a hit, Steve becomes Jeremy's lifeline. But as Jeremy knows already, and as Steve is about to learn, not even the brightest star can shine forever.

# CODE BLUE

## N.R. WALKER

ATROUS

# CHAPTER ONE

THE PLATINUM ENTERTAINMENT offices took up the top five floors of executive levels of the Krüper building in downtown LA. Sleek polished concrete, expensive finishes and furniture, ergonomic everything.

It looked a billion dollars and probably cost that much.

I didn't particularly care for it.

What I did like about it was the security measures to get in. No one, and I mean no one, was getting within an inch of those five floors without the required credentials.

At least Platinum had used some of the absurd fortune Atrous had made for them implementing protection measures.

Now, *that* I cared for.

Being called into a meeting with the big boss, Arlo Kim, wasn't too unusual; all department heads would meet often. Nothing new about that. But an emergency meeting with all close-contact seniors, and *only* close-contact seniors, wasn't a frequent thing and it made me more than a little nervous.

Neil Ambrose, the band manager, was there. The three

personal managers to the band were there too. Roscoe Hall, Amber Seratt, and Ryan Morton.

And me, head of security.

We sat around the large oval desk in the conference room. "Anyone know what this is about?" Roscoe asked first. "Neil?"

Neil shook his head. "Not a clue. Just got told I had an hour to be here."

"Same," Amber added. Ryan nodded.

We had meetings all the time. And plenty that could have been simply an email. But an *emergency meeting*?

We were technically all at the end of one week off. We were due to come back to work tomorrow. We'd finished the *Code Red* tour. A massive eight-week international tour. Sold out every venue, great international press coverage, excellent publicity. Calling us back a day early for an emergency meeting wasn't good.

The sinking feeling in my gut got lower. "My feeling is this isn't good."

Roscoe offered me a smile but it was tight. "No offense, Steve," he said, "but you being here worries me."

I certainly wasn't offended. "That's why I think this isn't good."

Ryan, Amber, and Neil all stared at me and Roscoe as if we needed to elaborate or maybe we knew something they didn't. So I explained.

"If I'm here at first briefing, it means it's security related." I shrugged. "And it's something that affects the band. If it was a broader concern, everyone would be here. So I'm guessing this is serious and something to be kept on the down low."

Roscoe gave a nod, and I knew if any of them would think the same, it'd be him.

Before Neil could say anything, the door opened and Arlo came in, followed by a woman holding a laptop.

I'd never seen her before. She was maybe thirty years old, wearing a tailored suit, her long dark hair pulled back in a ponytail, her eyes sharp and focused. I didn't know who she was, but she clearly meant business.

"Thank you for coming on such short notice," Arlo said. He turned to the woman. "This is Hetty Reyes. She's a digital forensic security specialist. We've received some mail, both physical and digital, that relates to Atrous. It's—" He grimaced. "—concerning."

The hairs on the back of my neck stood on end.

Roscoe sat forward in his seat. "Excuse me?"

Arlo nodded but turned to Hetty, and she took her cue. "Good morning." She put the laptop on the table, opened it, and clicked some keys until the smartboard on the wall came to life.

On the screen were images of emails, letters, and packages. All focused on one member of the band in particular. It looked like something from a movie, a CIA film, or FBI.

Except this was real.

A cold sense of dread washed over me.

Hetty went through each one—clinical, detached, matter of fact.

The mailed-in letters began as most fan letters did. Expressing love and gratitude. Then they became angry at the lack of personal response. They grew in frequency, urgency.

Gifts of all kinds were returned to sender, unopened.

Then the emails to Platinum started.

From blame, accusations, responsibility, to downright anger.

There were links to social media, of course, with

publicity images from photoshoots and some taken by fans at concerts or on the street, getting into cars, at airports.

All images had been cropped, centering totally on one man.

Jeremy Dalton.

I felt cold from my scalp to my toes.

"Where is he now?" I asked.

"He's here. Upstairs," Roscoe answered. "Maddox and I flew back from Vermont yesterday. Jeremy came over, they had a few drinks, and he crashed at our place. He came in with us this morning."

I looked at Arlo. "Does he know?"

Arlo shook his head. "Not yet."

Jesus.

"If the culprit has used social media and an email, they're traceable, right?" Roscoe asked.

Hetty clicked through to another screen. "They're using screened VPNs. Multiple. All different. But we believe it's all the same user."

"The police have been notified," Arlo added. "We'll be meeting with them to share all the information we have."

I don't know why, but that didn't make me feel much better.

Arlo continued. "I wanted you guys to know first. Steve, you'll need to implement new security plans. You and I will go through that. But I didn't want to tell the boys without having some kind of game plan."

"How long has this been going on?" Ryan asked.

Ryan was Jeremy's manager. He looked a little pale.

Arlo paused. "The first letter arrived six months ago."

"Six months?" Roscoe and I cried in unison.

"We get letters and packages all the time," he explained. "Even some that border on concerning. It happens more than you'd think. But the emails started four weeks ago."

"Four weeks is still too long," I bit out. "What risk have we put him in in that time? Huh? Every day. Every time we leave here or take him home." Oh god. "When we were on tour . . ."

Arlo put his hands up. "The mail is postmarked here in the US. The emails are marked from a London location. That's why we never associated the two together. Not at first."

Hetty nodded, then scrolled through the smartboard pages back to the first physical letters. "This line here," she said, pointing to one in particular. "*Only the truest fan knows . . .*'" And then she scrolled through to an email. "From a VPN registered in London. '*Only the truest fan knows . . .*' It was too coincidental. So we began connecting dots and we found some other similarities, which make us think this is the same person. We're still working on connecting all the VPNs. There could be more, but this is all we have so far. And this is enough to warrant concern. I presented my findings to Mr. Kim this morning."

"The letters are postmarked from a US location?" Ryan asked. "Where?"

"All over," Arlo replied. "San Diego. Columbus. Seattle."

"We believe they're using a secondary postal service," Hetty said. "There are people who will receive any mail and forward it as directed for a fee. Makes it look like it came from somewhere else."

"So this is not a police issue," I said. "They crossed state and country lines, mail fraud . . . This is an FBI issue."

Both Hetty and Arlo nodded. "We're taking advice from local law enforcement first, as is protocol. Trust me,"

Arlo said sincerely. "We're taking this matter very seriously."

I ground my teeth together. This was bullshit, and this was probably something I should have saved for a private conversation with Arlo, but I was pissed off. "We should have known before now. You didn't just put Jeremy at risk or the whole band, but these guys." I gestured to Roscoe, Amber, and Ryan. "And me and my team as well. And you knew someone was sending this garbage while we were overseas on tour. At our most vulnerable." I tapped the table a little too hard. "Supposedly from London, while we were *in London*, and you never mentioned it."

"It turns out we don't believe they're in London," Hetty said.

"You didn't know that then," I replied.

"If they're not in London, if all the VPNs are scrambled or fake," Roscoe said, "then where are they?"

Arlo gestured to Hetty to answer. She looked at each of us. "We believe it's highly likely they're here, in the United States."

"Well, that's just fucking great," I mumbled.

Arlo's hard eyes met mine. "I understand your frustration. But we get mail from all over the world every day. We needed proof before moving forward."

I held his gaze. "You needed to tell us six months ago."

"Debating whether we divulge every piece of fan mail that comes through the system is moot," Arlo said dismissively. "We've concluded *today* that we believe the sender of these letters is one and the same, and there was a lot of mail to go through. We need to implement and action protocols and measures to ensure the safety of everyone."

Christ.

Roscoe glanced at me and gave me a nod. I knew he would be on my side with this.

Full security, full time. On all five of them.

As if he could read my mind, Arlo continued. "We don't believe there's an actual immediate physical threat But we'll let the authorities be the judge of that, and I promise everyone's safety is the highest priority."

Still, not a comfort.

I spoke to Arlo. Not exactly asking, but more telling him how it was going to be. "I'll feel a whole lot better when we've nailed down the details. We'll need more feet on the ground, private security, full detail day and night on each of them. Here, at home, wherever they go. They won't like that, but they'll just have to deal with it."

Arlo sighed. "Let's just tell them first."

Neil spoke next. "If I can suggest . . ." He made a face but shot a look my way. "Don't do anything without asking or informing them first. I learned that lesson, and well. We all know how that went. They're five grown men. They need to be a part of the decision process. This is about them. It's for them. They should be here."

Part of me wanted to tell Neil to fuck right off, but the part of me that knew he was right wanted to keep my job.

What had Roscoe called it? Looking after these five guys was like herding cats.

Arlo gave a nod. "Let's bring them in."

Fifteen minutes later, the five band members all sat, staring at the smartboard. Wide-eyed and a little pale, Jeremy sat in the middle. Maddox sat on one side, Wes on the other, and they'd both moved a little closer to Jeremy as the slideshow went on.

I hated seeing him so vulnerable. I hated that he'd been

at risk without my knowledge, and I hated that I couldn't even reassure him in a room full of people.

I'd always had a soft spot for Jeremy. But in the last two years or so, since the Maddox and Roscoe ordeal, I'd spent a lot of time with him, and the more time I'd spent with him, the deeper my feelings ran.

Now, every time I saw him, my heart did a double-knock. My belly tightened every time he smiled at me or looked at me.

Spending a week with him at Roscoe's family farm in Vermont over two years ago had sealed it for me. I had legit feelings for him, which I'd done everything in my power to ignore. And of course, since Maddox had taken time out of the spotlight and Jeremy had stepped in, I'd spent most days with Jeremy. I might even say we'd become kind of close.

I'd always remained diligent and professional. No one here even knew I was gay. It had all but ended my last career. I wasn't letting it ruin this one as well. No matter how much I wanted to say something, no matter how much I wanted to touch him the way he touched me, put his arm around me, jumped on my back, made me give him piggy-back rides when he was too tired to walk. All the little touches, the laughs, so casual, like it didn't mean anything to him.

Even if it did mean something to me . . .

Not that it mattered. Jeremy was straight, and he was a client. Those were two red-zones I didn't go near.

Amber, Ryan, Roscoe, and I stood at the back wall, and energy radiated off Roscoe. He was almost vibrating with anger, fear, and frustration.

"Maddox is gonna lose his shit," Roscoe murmured.

*And Jeremy was going to freak the fuck out.* "We'll take care of them," I replied.

Arlo explained the need for heightened security and how he'd divulge the full plans once the police and possibly the FBI had been involved. We would need to follow their advice, and we would need to not panic. These were all precautionary matters, Arlo said. He just wanted to keep the boys up to date. Being well-informed was part of the plan. No secrets, blah, blah, blah.

Like he was selling them insurance.

When he'd finished his sales pitch, he looked at me. "Steve? Anything to add?"

They all turned to me, and Maddox put his arm around Jeremy and gave his neck a gentle squeeze. When Jeremy's eyes met mine, I almost lost my nerve.

"To start with," I said, "there will be changes to daily routines, and you'll each have your own security detail, twenty-four seven, so you're gonna need to get used to that." I could see they didn't like the idea of that already, so I raised my chin. "I'll work out details and we'll go through them together, sort out any issues or questions. But Jeremy?"

He scrubbed his hand over his face, then looked up at me. Those blue eyes clouded with fear. "Yeah?"

"You're with me."

# CHAPTER TWO

I SPENT what felt like hours with the police. After being unable to decide if it was a cybercrimes unit job for stalking or if they needed to call the Detective Support Division for harassment, they decided it was a federal issue and handed it off to the FBI.

In the meantime, I'd called Robbie and told him to round up the entire team. Yes, they still had one day of vacation time left. No, I didn't care. I instructed them to bring a bag of clothes for a few days. Robbie never questioned why. He never did. His only response was his usual, "Sure thing, boss."

The FBI agent who turned up looked no more than twenty years old. Well, maybe twenty-five. Suit, blond hair, dark eyes, and I doubted he even shaved yet. His name was Miles Zielinski, and he diligently took notes and photographs, asked for copies of everything, all while sweating bullets as Arlo's legal team sat in the corner like vultures.

But the reports were filed, the case now open.

High profile stalking cases were all too common nowadays, though still taken seriously. The more high profile the person, the more traction, of course.

"This is to be kept secret. The press must not find out," Arlo had threatened.

Zielinski had collected his satchel, looked Arlo right in the eye, and said, "So don't tell them."

I almost laughed. Maybe the kid wasn't so bad.

We took a ten-minute break and I went in search of Jeremy. I found him on the third floor, in the dance practice studio with Maddox and Roscoe. Well, Roscoe was sitting with his back to the wall, studying his phone screen, while Maddox and Jeremy lay on their backs in the middle of the floor. They were sweaty and panting, as if they'd been dancing for hours. Knowing these two, they probably had.

"Hey," I said, walking in. I went to Jeremy and peered down at him to where he lay on the floor. "How you feeling?"

"I was just gonna call you." He lifted the hem of his shirt to wipe his forehead, revealing a sweaty six pack, which I didn't need to see.

"Why's that?" I asked.

"So you'd come protect me." He grimaced. "Maddox just tried to kill me."

Maddox snorted. "It was choreo, Jer."

He squinted at Maddox. "A form of torture. A crime against humanity." Then he turned back to me. "Notify the Hague."

Okay, so he was obviously fine.

Roscoe got to his feet and nodded to the door. "Got a sec?"

"Sure." I leaned over Jeremy again. "You're not allowed to leave without me."

He made a face. "Am I a prisoner?"

"Yes."

Jeremy rolled his eyes at me and whacked Maddox. "Notify the Hague."

Maddox laughed, rolled over, and pushed himself up to his feet. "Come on, get up. You've got more in you yet."

"Oh, fuck off. You made me drink last night," he grumbled.

"You had two beers!" Maddox cried as Roscoe and I walked out.

He wasted no time. "What did the police say?"

"It's an FBI matter."

"Fuck." He gripped his forehead. "Well, good. I guess."

"The agent in charge just got out of diapers."

Roscoe sighed. "Awesome."

I shrugged. "That's probably unfair. He might be okay. Given he's so young, he might have a better understanding of all the cyber shit."

His eyes met mine. "How bad is it?"

"I don't know. I'm guessing we'll find out more as time goes on. Hopefully the feds will trace this person and it'll all be over in a matter of days."

"God, I hope so."

"Me too."

Roscoe studied me for a second. "If you need anything, just let me know. If you need these guys to take it more seriously . . ." He shrugged. "I'm with you. Whatever you say we need or we have to do, I'll make sure they do it."

"Thanks."

He clapped my shoulder. "You looked pretty worried in the meeting."

I kept my expression neutral, my tone even. "It's my job to protect them. All of you."

He smiled. "And we appreciate that. And just so you

know, between you and me, Maddox is just distracting Jeremy right now. He was pretty shaken up before."

I gave a nod. "Where are the others?"

He pointed upward. "Lounge."

So they were all still here. "Good." I checked my watch. "I better go back. I'm meeting with my team now and we're going to work out detail. Robbie will more than likely be your security."

He grinned. "Maddox loves the big guy."

"I'll be having everyone's home security checked too. Just to be sure it's all up to scratch."

Roscoe's smile died. "Yeah, of course."

———

MY TEAM WASN'T TOO happy about cutting their rare vacation time short—they'd just finished an intense eight-week international tour after all. And they were cautious and curious as to what Mr. Kim and Neil Ambrose were doing sitting at the back of my meeting.

Until I explained why. Then they were all game-on.

I was with Jeremy, with Riko as my second. Robbie would take Maddox, and by extension, Roscoe. Ivan would have Wes, Jason would be with Luke, and Zoe would take Blake. Given Luke and Blake lived together, Zoe and Jason would double up.

The other eight on my team would rotate as needed, but there'd be two in each detail at all times, three in mine with Jeremy. Anytime they wanted to go out in public had to be planned and approved, with increased security numbers. If they went out as a group, it'd be all hands on deck. If it was a publicity or a promo shoot, we brought in additional private security.

"They have some scheduled briefings about the tour here at the head offices on Tuesday, which are still going ahead at this point. The only press event scheduled this week is on Thursday. It's a Billboard interview, which was to be on location, but that may change. So a lot of what we'll do will be at their homes," I said. *Thank god there were no press events.* "But that could also change. You know how it is. Robbie, Ivan, Jason, and Zoe, you will receive a full schedule of your guy. Whatever it is, be it chiropractor appointments, grocery deliveries, house maintenance, studio sessions. You'll monitor it all, and we'll keep in constant contact. We'll also get a list of any approved visitors to their house, and anyone not on the list does not enter."

They were all staring at me, growing more concerned with each thing I said. I sighed. "Look, honestly, in all likelihood, this will all be for nothing. The feds will catch this . . . person." I opted for no profanity. "For all we know, they're on the other side of the country and pose no physical threat at all. But I'm not taking any chances, and I'm not waiting for something to happen before we put plans in place."

They all nodded, and Arlo at the back also nodded, as if he approved of me playing it down a touch.

"Okay, guys, that's it. Robbie and Riko, a second please."

Robbie was a big guy. He'd once said that his dad's side of the family were Polynesian, which was why he was six foot three and his shoulders were three feet wide. He was big. Most fanatics or overexcited fans took one look at Robbie and backed up pretty fast.

If only they knew he was as soft as a baby kitten. Well, a soft kitten that I'd seen throw a grown man like a rag doll.

Riko, on the other hand, was a tall, sinewy Japanese guy.

Beautiful enough to be a model, his face was all sharp angles and I'd guess he had no more than eight percent body fat. He had the eyes of a hawk; the man saw everything, never missed a beat, and he had the reflexes of a cat. He also had a black belt in jujitsu.

Where I practiced the newer Brazilian jujitsu, Riko was trained old-school. As a test when he'd first started with us, he sent Ivan to the ground by applying pressure to nothing but Ivan's thumb. Zero force and effort, but by using Ivan's own body momentum, Ivan turned himself inside out and dropped to the ground while Riko never broke a sweat.

The fact I chose him to be my second, to be around Jeremy, spoke volumes about my trust in him.

"What's up?" Robbie said with a nod.

"You got Maddox, which means you got Roscoe as well. I'm suspecting Maddox is gonna want to be around Jeremy, so we'll double up a lot."

Nothing ever fazed him. "Sure thing."

"And Riko, we'll take Jeremy. If, for whatever reason you can't reach me, you call Robbie and you do what he says."

Riko nodded. "Got it."

"Between you and me, he's never alone. Day or night."

"Understood."

"That's gonna piss him off."

Riko almost smiled. "He'll get over it, boss."

I almost smiled. "He's gonna have to."

Neil Ambrose came over. "Steve? A moment, please."

I noticed then that Arlo Kim was gone. "Sure." I told Robbie where Maddox was and followed Ambrose over to the corner.

"I appreciate all you're doing," he said.

I knew that look. "You think I'm overreacting."

It wasn't a question. But I wasn't having anyone question why having Jeremy being the target of some stalker had me on edge.

"I think we need to use caution and not apply unnecessary stress—"

I wasn't getting into a dick-swinging competition with him. "This—" I gestured to the now empty room, where my team had just been. "—is what I do. I manage security and protection of the band. Particularly when one member of the band has a stalker that triggers an FBI investigation. What I did today was nothing. Basic, even. Textbook stuff."

"And I'm responsible for their well-being as well," he replied.

"Good. You worry about their mental health. I'll worry about keeping them alive. And at the end of this whole shitshow, we'll come out just fine."

He stared, and I stared right back until he backed down. Eventually he gave a nod, turned, and left.

Riko smirked. "Your people skills are awesome. You'll have to teach me how you do that thing with your eyes."

"What thing?"

"How to make people crap themselves with just a look."

I smiled. "It's a skill."

"It's a 'I will fuck you up, don't try me' skill."

"Exactly." I nodded to the elevator. "Let's go find Jeremy."

Jeremy was still in the dance studio with Maddox, chugging a sports drink, even sweatier now than he'd been before. His blond hair stuck to his forehead, his cheeks flushed red, and a V of sweat darkened the front of his T-shirt. It clung to his body, his defined chest, his narrow waist, his biceps.

He smiled when he saw me and I ignored the hold it

had on my heart. Like I had done for the last two years and then some, I feigned indifference.

Robbie stood by the door. I gave him a nod, then looked back at Jeremy. "Ready when you are, chief," I said.

Jeremy straightened up, his hands on his waist. He was still breathing hard but he threw the half-empty sports drink bottle to Maddox. "Gee. I'd love to stay and die some more, but I get to go home now."

Maddox laughed, put the bottle down, and threw a sweat towel at him. "Clean yourself up. Poor Steve has to stick to you like glue."

*I wish . . .*

"Like Steve'd care," Jeremy said, wiping the towel over his face.

*Oh, he cares. He wishes he didn't, but he does.*

Then he twirled the towel and tried to flick Maddox with it, which resulted in them both having a towel-flicking fight.

I went over to Robbie. "Where's Roscoe?"

"Meeting with Ryan and Amber."

"Okay."

I had no doubts they'd be in that meeting for a while, but for now, my meetings were over. If I needed to be updated on schedules or appointments, Mr. Kim or Ambrose would inform me. Or Roscoe would.

I wanted to get Jeremy's home security checked today. I glanced over at Jeremy to find him now shirtless. His trim and muscled torso glistened with sweat. Pale and perfect.

He had the body of a racehorse. Lean, powerful, strong.

Christ.

He pulled on a shirt, and I noticed two things. Riko's eyes went from Maddox to me, and Maddox was smiling at me.

I pretended I hadn't just checked out Jeremy, and I pretended Maddox hadn't seen, and I pretended Riko hadn't caught the whole thing. "Maddox, you good to wait for Roscoe, or did you want Robbie to take you now?"

"Oh, I'm fine," he said, smirking. "You?"

Yep, he definitely saw me looking at Jeremy.

I held his gaze. "I'll be a whole lot better once I check Jeremy's home security."

Maddox grinned, surprised, maybe even shocked. "I bet you will."

I glared at him, doing the 'I will fuck you up if you don't back off' look, but Maddox just laughed.

Jeremy threw his towel at Maddox. "Hey dickbag, what're you being a dickbag for? Like the guy doesn't have enough to worry about."

Maddox just balled up the towel and aimed a three pointer at the hamper in the corner, completely unfazed. "Yeah, sorry about that." Then he turned to us. "You two have a really fun first date tonight."

"Fuck off." Jeremy rolled his eyes. "Robbie, come put him in a chokehold or something."

Maddox laughed, but then his smile turned serious and he held his hand out for Jeremy. "Be careful. I'll call you later."

Jeremy did the brother handshake that they do and clapped Maddox on the back. "Will do."

Maddox gave me a pointed stare. "You look after him."

I raised an eyebrow as my reply.

"Yeah, yeah," Maddox said, rolling his eyes. "I know."

Ten minutes later, Jeremy, Riko, and I exited the elevator in the basement and climbed into the back of the waiting van. Me in the back with Jeremy, Riko in the front passenger side. These vans were huge, all black, with tinted windows. There were thousands of them in LA and no one turned an eye at them anymore.

I knew the Atrous offices and building were secure. Probably the most secure place on the planet for the boys to be. But leaving, being in traffic, and slowing down to enter Jeremy's house were when we were the biggest target.

I felt safer when we were moving.

"You feel okay?" I asked.

He drained a bottle of juice and shrugged. "About as good as expected. Have they found anything else on this person?"

I shook my head. "Not yet. You'll be the first to hear."

"And we don't even know where they are?"

"No."

He stared out the window for a bit. "Uh, where are we going?"

I smiled, pleased that he was at least aware of his surroundings. "I asked the driver to swing past my place. I need clothes and whatnot."

"Am I really getting a housemate for however long this takes?"

"You're getting two," I said.

Riko raised his hand.

Jeremy sighed again. "Look, I lived with four guys for a long time. So here are the rules." He counted off his fingers. "You pick up your own shit, do whatever you want in the kitchen because lord knows I don't use it, but keep it clean. And no snoring. Christ."

That made me smile. "You won't even know we're there."

He was quiet for a while. "I'll need to call my mom. If the media gets hold of this . . ."

I nodded. "Of course."

"Man, I just wanted to sleep all this week. The tour was brutal. Doing forty shows in eight weeks and six different countries was easy as taking a piss when I was twenty. Now I'm twenty-seven."

Twenty-seven . . .

With his head on the headrest, he turned to face me. "How old are you, Steve? You did the whole tour, every concert, every hotel, every car trip, every flight."

"I didn't sing and dance on stage for four hours forty times."

"No, but you still worked. On your feet, running around, managing a whole bunch of people, keeping us all together. That shit's not easy."

No, it wasn't.

"I'm thirty-five."

"Thirty-five?" He stared. "Wow."

"Is that a good wow, that I don't look thirty-five? Or a bad wow that you're surprised I'm not in a retirement home?"

Jeremy laughed. "A bit of both."

"Thanks."

He was quiet again for a few minutes. "And you still run five miles a day? At your age?"

At my age. Jesus.

"Run, swim, cardio, martial arts . . ."

He looked me up and down. "Explains the physique."

I kept my gaze out front. "I need to keep fit to keep you five in check."

Jeremy laughed. "Herding cats."

I nodded. "Herding cats."

Riko turned around. "ETA, two minutes, boss. No tail."

"Thanks." I looked at Jeremy then. "You'll come inside with me. Riko will stand point at the door."

"Like they do in the movies?"

"Kind of."

"Can't I just wait in the car? I'm so freaking tired. Maddox busted me with the whole keep-him-distracted choreo thing."

"You're not waiting in the car."

"I'm not a freaking child."

"I am not letting you wait in the car unprotected, like a sitting duck, while I'm inside and—"

"Riko can stand—"

"Jeremy," I said, my voice low. I glared at him, not breaking eye contact.

He looked away first and rolled his eyes. He stared out the window. "So this prisoner thing is a lot of fun."

I didn't reply.

The driver pulled up and I pointed to my place. "White stucco, tile roof, second floor. Wait for me to—"

Jeremy opened the door and got out.

"Fuck."

I scooted out after him, but he was already striding ahead and I quickly followed.

I pulled my key fob out and unlocked the front door and let him into the lobby, quickly closing the door behind us.

Jeremy grinned like he'd won the game.

"Not funny."

"You're fast for a thirty-five-year-old."

I wanted to throttle him. Or maybe kiss him. Possibly both. He had a smile that curled my insides. I'd ignored it for years. I could ignore it now.

"Stick to the plan, Jeremy."

I started up the stairs and he followed without comment. I unlocked my front door and went in first.

"I thought a gentleman held a door open?" Jeremy said behind me.

"Normally I would. But just in case there was a guy waiting in my apartment to shoot you, I thought I'd go first."

Jeremy stopped smiling.

I gestured to the small living area and kitchen. "Help yourself to a drink if you want."

I disappeared into my room and threw some clothes into a duffle bag. It helped that I'd only just got them back from the laundromat two days ago from when we'd returned from the tour.

That was my life.

Lived out of a suitcase, pretty much.

When I went back out to the living room, Jeremy was standing in front of my trophy cabinet.

"Division champion, MMA. California state winner, mixed martial arts. MMA Grand Champion."

"Yeah, there's a few."

"A few? There's like twenty."

"I was going to pack them away," I admitted. I wasn't sure why I was telling him this. "But they're a good reminder."

"Of what? That if someone broke into your place, they picked the wrong guy because you can kill people with your bare hands?"

I smiled. "The aim is to incapacitate or injure in a self-defense situation. Not kill."

He stared at me. "But you could?"

I shrugged one shoulder. "Yes."

"Jesus." He turned back to the trophies. "All the years I've known you, I never knew this. I mean, I know you're good at what you do, and we've all seen that one video of you in that tournament or whatever it was. The one you showed us that time."

"Regional titles."

His eyes darted to mine. "Yeah."

"That was a long time ago." And I hadn't set out to show the band and managers. I'd shown my team and they'd all heard about it and came to watch it.

Jeremy nodded slowly. "Do you like doing bodyguard work?"

"Sure," I replied. "When the person I'm looking after listens to me, it's great."

He snorted and a smile won out. "What's *that* like?"

"I don't know," I deadpanned. "You good to go?"

He looked around my place one more time. "Yep. You get everything you need?"

"Yep."

"Then let's go. I need a hot shower and food." Then he stopped. "Oh. I hope you like to eat out. Don't expect there to be actual food at my house."

"We won't be going out to eat this week. Too risky."

He seemed genuinely surprised by this. "What am I supposed to do for food?"

"We can order in. I can have one of my team go pick it up. I'd rather we didn't have a trail of different delivery people turning up to your place every day. Or we can have groceries delivered."

"I don't cook." He shook his head. "I mean, I used to. But I hate it, and I was never good at it. Just ask the guys."

"I've seen your grilling skills. Remember that week we spent in Vermont at Roscoe's uncle's farm?"

His mouth fell open. "Hey. I grilled that meat just fine."

"You charcoaled it so much I considered sending it for carbon dating."

Jeremy laughed. "Fine. Then you're cooking. But I'm telling you now, I don't eat that grilled tofurkey and quinoa shit. I like good food."

"Deal." I chuckled and paused at the door. "Stay behind me this time, and when we get outside, you go first and I'm behind you."

He waggled his eyebrows. "Sounds like a proposition, Steve. You trying to hit on me?"

There were so many things I could have said, wanted to say. A witty reply, maybe even the truth. Instead, I rolled my eyes and opened the door.

# CHAPTER THREE

---

JEREMY'S HOUSE WAS HUGE. I'd been to all the band members' homes at one point or another, and although they were all in the Hills of LA, each worth an absurd amount of millions, they were all different. Each home reflected their own personality, tastes, and lifestyle.

Maddox's home, which he now shared with Roscoe, was huge, with vast open spaces, lots of marble and glass. Like a museum, almost, but considerably warmer now, more lived in now that Roscoe lived there.

Wes's house was art-deco style. Huge, but designed and built by some famous guy in the '70s, now totally decked out with every modern thing you could imagine.

Luke's house was . . . well, Luke and Blake live together. Luke's house was in the Hills, and Blake owned a beach house in Malibu. The beach house was mind-blowing and great for weekends but a bit of a trek to downtown LA for work every day, whereas Luke's house was closer. It was also a prime party house, with its own movie theater, indoor half-basketball court, pool with a waterfall. Blake was there so much, he ended up moving in. According to everyone, they had bedrooms at opposite ends of the house and a constant stream of women in between.

The guys all spoke of many nights spent at Luke's place. I wasn't privy to everything that went on there, and I didn't want to be either. Seeing them let loose was great, but seeing them with women wasn't. Well, seeing Jeremy getting cozy with a woman wasn't fun for me. Not that I'd seen him do that lately…

But Jeremy's house was different. It was a Mediterranean-inspired Spanish Colonial mansion. The outside was white stucco over adobe brick walls, arched doorways, wooden beams, and a clay-tile roof. There were several tiled courtyards, the biggest off his main bedroom. Every other bedroom had a tiny balcony with decorative iron railings. The gardens were full of palms and vines and tall hedges.

Inside were white walls, terracotta floors, wrought iron, colors of rusty oranges and blues. Most of the artwork was wood or cloth, all textured and earthy.

Very warm and homelike.

Just like Jeremy.

The entire estate was outlined by tall stucco walls that, thankfully, boasted a canyon drop-off on the other side. If someone wanted to scale the outside walls, they'd need nothing short of climbing gear. Not impossible, but enough to keep most people out.

He had one neighbor with which his property shared a border. A tech celebrity who made his fortune making a social media app and selling it to Google. He sold his next one to Apple. Jeremy said once he'd never even seen the guy.

The house was also part of the Beverly Park gated community, meaning access to the front of the house was very limited. Visitors had to go through the community gates and *then* Jeremy's gate. No random person could easily even approach Jeremy's front gates. Not without some serious tech, serious connections, or an army tank.

Maddox and Roscoe lived just a ten-minute drive away, and I was fairly confident they'd be frequent faces over the next few days.

I was hoping this would all be over in a matter of days. As happy as I was to spend all this time with Jeremy, I didn't want it like this.

As we walked in, I went first, Jeremy behind me, and Riko followed. We entered into a foyer and through to a living space that opened to the kitchen. There was a formal living room to the left, complete with a grand piano, and from what I could see, a hall that perhaps led to the bedrooms. The place was huge, so it was hard to tell the immediate layout. It was quiet and a little dark until Jeremy unarmed the alarm system and hit a button on the wall and all the blinds began to rise.

The view was outstanding.

"I need a shower and food," Jeremy said. He went to the fridge and pulled out a bottle of flavored mineral water, then, ever so casually, went to a cupboard and retrieved a glass. "You guys want a drink?"

I resisted sighing. We weren't here for a drink or for *any* socializing. "Riko and I will do a perimeter check while you shower. I'll go with you first just to check your room and the rest of the house."

Jeremy began to smile and he quirked an eyebrow. "Very bold offer."

God, if only he knew . . .

That was his second insinuation in the hour of me

suggesting anything between us. Maybe he was just being playful.

Maybe I should just stop dreaming.

"Then afterwards," I added, ignoring his comment, "if you could show Riko to a guest room. I'm fine with a couch or the floor."

Jeremy swallowed half his drink but managed to give me an odd look. "Christ, Steve. I have five guest rooms. You're not sleeping on the floor."

Riko cleared his throat. "He has before. On tour or when you guys do those all-nighter film shoots. We'll crash on couches or on chairs. He takes the floor."

Jeremy appeared horrified by this. "Nooo. What the hell is Arlo doing not providing adequate arrangements?"

"He does," I said. "We always have adequate hotel rooms, but sometimes we work longer than usual and we need to get some sleep where and when we can."

"Well, it's still bullshit. And you," Jeremy said to Riko. "Letting the old man sleep on the floor. Jeez."

Riko fought a smile and I gave Jeremy a flat stare. "I'm not an old man. And as team leader, it's my job to look after them."

"You look after them. You look after us," Jeremy said. "Who looks after you?"

*No one.*

"I manage just fine." I looked around the large room. "Your bedroom?"

Jeremy hummed. "Slow down, big guy. You can at least buy me dinner first," he joked, but he led the way. His third insinuation . . .

Was I imagining this?

His bedroom, as it turned out, was up a set of stairs,

which meant it was away from all the other bedrooms, and as we reached the landing, I understood why.

His bedroom by itself was probably twice the size of my entire apartment.

His bed was huge and very luxurious looking. There was a sofa and a table before a massive arch with glass doors that I imagined were custom made. They opened out to a private terracotta tiled patio that overlooked the saltwater pool below.

His walk-in closet resembled a department store, and his private bathroom was enormous. Christ. Even his shower was about the size of an elevator.

Everything looked incredibly expensive.

"All clear?" Jeremy asked.

I turned around to see him toeing out of his shoes. He kicked his sneakers over toward the closet. Then he pulled his shirt over his head, leaving his sweatpants low on his hips. His abs flexed and moved, his V disappeared under the waistband.

"Ah, yeah. All clear." I turned back to the view. "Can we open the back doors to take a look outside? Any rooms you don't want us in?"

He stopped at the bathroom door. "You can go wherever you want. The panel to unlock the back doors is by the sliding glass door in the kitchen. The code is 0540."

"Thanks."

I left before he could get any more naked in front of me.

Riko and I did a quick check of every room, of which there were a lot: a gym, an office, a studio-looking music room, plus the guest bedrooms and the huge garage. We put our bags in a room each, and when that was done, I unlocked the backdoors and we did a perimeter check.

It was late afternoon, and the air was warm in the last days of summer. The sun was setting over the ocean, shades of orange reflecting off the pool, and if I wasn't here to do a serious job, I might've let myself take a moment to appreciate the view.

Riko let out a long breath. "Wow. Could you ever imagine living here?"

I snorted. "Not on my salary. Not in my lifetime." I went back inside, took out my phone, and checked in with everyone else.

I was finishing my call to Robbie just as Jeremy came out, freshly showered. He wore gray lounge pants and a plain black T-shirt, no shoes. His dirty blond hair was a bit longer than he usually wore it now, wavy when wet.

The smell of him, his deodorant or body wash, whatever it was, as he walked past me made me lose my train of thought.

"Everything okay, boss?" Robbie asked on the phone.

"Yes," I replied quickly. "Report in at 2200."

"Sure thing."

I ended the call and found Jeremy smiling at me. "Everything okay, boss?"

I almost told him to shut up, but then I remembered who I was speaking to. "We need to go through some things." I had my small notepad, which I flipped open, and clicked my pen. "Name of your security company and a phone number. I need to speak with them. Ideally, I'd like them to come around tonight, but that might not be possible. I also want you to make a list of any groceries or personal items you need so I can have them ordered—"

Jeremy put his hand up. "Stop." He patted his belly. "I'm starving. I'm actually starting to feel a bit sick because I need to eat."

"Oh, sorry. Of course. What do you want?"

His answer was immediate. "Korean BBQ. Grilled pork belly and spare ribs and that bulgogi stuff, with kimchi and japchae. Oh, and the rice. Gotta have the rice." He went to a cupboard and pulled out a tray that was apparently full of takeout menus. "This is my favorite restaurant and they deliver—"

I took the menu. "I'll order it and have it picked up," I said. "No one comes to the gate that we don't know."

Jeremy stared at me for a few seconds before obviously deciding not to argue. "Fine. Whatever. I need to call my mom." He left the menu with me, walked out the backdoor, and threw himself on a lounge chair by the pool. "Hey, Mom . . . Yeah, I'm fine. Listen, there's something I have to tell you and I don't want you to panic . . ."

I had Riko stand by the door, and I went and ordered enough food to feed a small army and had one of our company runners pick it up.

Jeremy came back in and went down the hall, coming back a few moments later with a folder and handed it to me. "Here's the security info." He went back to the kitchen. "You ordered food, right? I might have some crackers or something in here . . ." He opened a set of kitchen cupboard doors and pulled out a sliding vertical shelf. It looked pretty bare.

"Are you okay?" I asked.

"Oh yeah, sure. If I don't eat after a while, I feel a bit weird. It's a blood sugar thing. I'm not diabetic or anything. Been like this since I was a kid though. If I use too much energy and don't replace it, I get a bit shaky and nauseous." He found a box of wafers, inspected them with a grimace before opening them and shoving one in. "Fucking Maddox made me do too many hours of dance practice today, and I only had half a sandwich all day."

Opening his fridge, seeing it almost empty, I poured him some juice. "Drink this. How did I not know this about you?" I asked. "How much time have we spent together over the last however many years?"

I could recall him always eating or having some kind of snack in his hand, or someone was always passing him something to eat. I just assumed he ate a lot because of the workload. I knew it wasn't my job to make sure they ate, but still.

"When we were in Vermont that time, you never told me then," I added. "Or even mentioned it, to be honest." I wasn't sure why I was so hurt over this.

He took the juice but kinda brushed my concern off. "Because Roscoe's Aunt brought down so much food we did nothing but eat that week, remember?"

That was true.

"It's no big deal. I usually have something with me, or Ryan does. There's always food at the offices or on tour. But I stayed at Madz's place last night, and then we had to go into the offices this morning without notice." He shrugged and shoved in another wafer. "Then the whole stalker-video thing and FBI case . . . I wasn't up for eating much. I only ate half the sandwich because Blake made me."

"We're putting in a grocery order." I looked in his pantry shelves. "How do you not have food here?"

"Because I don't cook, and we just got back last week from a two-month tour. I slept most of last week, to be honest." He inspected the wafer box again. "I think these are expired. They're awful."

I took the box and checked the use-by date. They were fine. "They taste awful because they're whole wheat water wafers with 95 percent less fat." I handed them back. "Eat some more."

He shook his head. "I feel better already. But you ordered food, right?"

"Yes. How . . . how did your mother take the news?"

He rolled his eyes. "I told her not to panic, but of course she did. I told her it was nothing. The cops'll find this crackpot and nothing will come of it. This kinda shit happens all the time."

"Not to you it doesn't."

He shrugged. "I mean, you only have to read half of what they say about us on the internet."

I wasn't sure if he just told his mother this or if he truly believed that himself. But this wasn't about them as a band. This was about him, very specifically. Just him.

"I told her she can't tell anyone. If the press finds out, it'll be a circus."

I nodded slowly. "Good." I studied his face for a second. He looked a little better. "You feel okay now?"

He shoved in another cracker. "Yeah. Though these damn wafer things have the nutritional content of cardboard."

"Let's get started on a grocery list. We'll get it picked up and delivered first thing."

"They do that?"

I stared at him. "This is LA. You can get anything delivered." And I do mean anything . . . I took my notepad and pen. "What do you want for breakfast?"

"Iced coffee. Ryan usually gets it for me."

"I meant food."

He made a face. "Um . . ."

"Scrambled eggs? Or bagels? Corflakes?"

He laughed. "I haven't had cornflakes since I was like sixteen." He sighed. "I've missed cornflakes."

I scribbled it down. "Cornflakes goes on the list. You have soy milk, right?"

"Yeah. How do you know that?"

"I remember you joking about it with Maddox a few years ago. He dared you to drink cow's milk and they were gonna take bets to see how long it took to go through you."

He laughed. "God, my friends are such assholes. Just so you know, I can have some dairy, just not a great idea for me to have a lot."

"What about lunches and dinners? What would you like this week?"

"Uh, how about you suggest some things?"

"What about some tofurkey and quinoa salad shit?"

He peered at my notepad. "Can you write down a sense of humor? Do they sell those at the farmers market?"

I smiled. "I believe they do, yeah. What about some meat and salad wraps and fruit for lunch? Dinner we can have fish—"

"Not fish. Anything but fish."

"You ate three servings of that fish in Singapore three weeks ago."

Jeremy raised an eyebrow at me. "Because it was cooked with all those spices, wrapped in banana leaves, and didn't taste like fish. It was so good, so if you want to fly in that Singaporean street stall grandma . . ." He tilted his head. "Can we fly her in because she also made those chicken—"

"We're not flying anyone in, Jeremy. What about tacos?"

"Will they be as good as that Mexican place on Sunset that I like?"

"Absolutely not. But we can try." I nodded to the coffee machine on his kitchen counter. "Any kind of coffee pods you prefer?"

He looked at the machine, then at me. "Um . . . the kind that makes iced coffee?"

Dear god. I wrote down the kind I liked.

Riko cleared his throat from the hall and smiled. "Sorry to interrupt, but Elsie is at the gate with the takeout. Want me to go get it?" He was holding his phone.

"Oh, thank god," Jeremy cried. "Yes, please. That's the best news I've had all day. Literally."

"Yes," I agreed. "Feed him, please. And tell her I'll email her a grocery list for delivery early tomorrow."

"Sure thing." Riko put the phone back to his ear. "Yeah. Be there in a few."

Jeremy was quiet for a second. "Who's Elsie?"

"She's a company runner. Lunch orders, dry cleaning, documents, contracts. You name it, she'll deliver it, drop it off, pick it up. There are two runners at Platinum, but she's my favorite. You'd know her if you saw her."

He frowned. "There are so many employees at Platinum I've never met."

"You're not expected to meet them all."

He was quiet again while he chewed on his bottom lip. "Do you think it could be one of them?"

"The person who is fixated on you? Someone who works at Platinum?"

He nodded.

"Highly doubtful. Everyone is security-checked and fingerprinted. Arlo runs a pretty tight ship." I reassured him with a hand on his arm. "Everyone that you deal with on a daily basis, I trust. Everyone who has close contact with you, or even anyone who gets to walk past you in a corridor, I have no issue with. Actually, I think the Platinum offices are the safest place for you guys. Staff included."

He smiled, clearly reassured. "Well, good. I guess."

I gave his arm a squeeze. It was really the first hint of doubt I'd seen in him all day. "You'll be fine. Not only is the FBI after this person, but Arlo's also got his cyber team on it. They track all kinds of shit online, from the delusional fans who think you're going to marry them, to the haters. You've seen how good they are. Arlo's team is likely to find this person before the FBI does."

His eyes locked with mine in a way that made my heart react. "Thanks."

Riko came in carrying a box full of takeout containers. "I hope you're hungry."

Jeremy put his hands up in victory. "Yes! Fooood!"

---

AFTER DINNER, Riko went to bed early, ready to trade shifts with me at 3:00 a.m. I put in the grocery order, made some phone calls, and after speaking to the security system company, went through the folder Jeremy had given me.

Jeremy spent the night talking to Maddox, then Luke and Blake, and he texted back and forth with Wes. Neil Ambrose called me to discuss an updated schedule for the week. He emailed it, and less than a minute later, Ryan called.

"Did you get the new schedule?"

"Yep. You did too, I take it?" I asked.

"Yeah. It actually looks pretty good."

"It does." To my surprise, Ambrose had canceled almost everything. They were still expected at the offices on Tuesday to go over the tour footage, because the production team needed to get on it if there was any chance of having the new tour DVD and all the merch on sale in a few months, so I could understand the urgency.

The week itself was kinda quiet to begin with. First weeks back after a tour usually were. A lot of rest and recovery, but also a lot of meetings. I never actually sat in on those, but over the years, I'd picked up enough. They'd now be spending hours reflecting over the tour. What went well, what needed improving, what they needed more of, less of.

"I've still got Julio booked for Monday," Ryan said. Julio was the band's PT who even toured with us. "He said he's fine doing house visits instead, but I told him I needed to clear that with you."

That made me smile. "Sure thing. Can you send me his number and I'll line it up for him?"

Jeremy was now staring at me from the opposite couch. "Are you talking about me?"

"Yes," I replied. "It's Ryan."

Jeremy jumped up and rushed over, crashing onto the couch and half of me and taking my phone. "Ryan, you need to bring me coffee. Tomorrow morning, please. Steve's going to make me eat quinoa or fucking tofu. And he's threatening to teach me how to cook. I need real coffee."

I could hear Ryan say something and Jeremy sighed, closing his eyes. "Oh, thank god. You're the best. Not too early though, right?"

Jeremy handed me back my phone, but he stayed where he was. On the couch with me, a little too close.

Not close enough.

He tucked his legs up, clearly not going anywhere, and I pretended his knee touching my thigh wasn't burning through my jeans, setting my blood to warm.

It didn't mean anything.

"Sounds like you have everything under control," Ryan said with humor.

"Don't believe him," I replied. "He had a mountain of Korean BBQ for dinner. No tofu in sight."

Ryan laughed. "Sounds about right. I'll stop by in the morning and bring him his coffee. Just so you know, in case you *have* to know, he calls it 'iced coffee' but he actually has the iced Americano. Did you want anything from Starbucks?"

Far out. Jeremy was so insulated from the real world he didn't even know what coffee he drank.

"No, we'll be fine. Thanks." Then I remembered Jeremy's very bare kitchen. "Actually, two black coffees would be great."

"Sure thing. If you need me to get you anything, bring you anything, just shoot me a message. Or make me a list for when I get there around nine."

"Will do. Thanks again."

I ended the call and slid my phone onto the couch beside me. "He'll be here around nine," I said to Jeremy. "With your coffee."

He smiled, but it faded fast. "I'm tired," he mumbled.

"Go to bed."

He sighed. "Yeah, I guess."

I got the feeling he wanted to talk, or maybe he just didn't want to be alone.

"Are you just gonna stay up?"

"Yep."

"For how long?"

"Riko takes over at three."

He frowned. "That sucks."

"It's fine. I have a lot to go through." I gestured to his list of housekeepers, groundkeepers, the pool maintenance company, and anyone else who'd been to the house in the last six months. "It's a good time for me to write up my report. I'll check all the locks again, that kind of thing." I checked my watch. It was nine thirty. "And all teams will be reporting in soon enough."

He studied my face for a while. "For what it's worth, I'm sorry you have to go through this."

"It's certainly not your fault."

He sighed. "Yeah, but still. I'm sure you'd rather be somewhere else."

Not really.

"Jeremy, it's my job." I realized as soon as I'd said it that it sounded harsh, and I didn't want him to think I wouldn't be here if it weren't my job. Because I would. So I shrugged. "But your house isn't exactly shabby, and you're not terrible company."

He snorted. "Gee, thanks."

"Even if you can't cook."

Jeremy chuckled. "You're a hard man to please."

"I'm really not," I said with a smile. "But honestly, I don't mind. If I was at home, I'd be just watching some trash on TV."

"You don't go out much?"

I shook my head. "Nope. I don't drink, and I spend so much time either with my team or with you guys, I don't really have a thriving social life." Again, I realized how that sounded like I was blaming him. So I added, "But to be fair, even if I didn't work with you guys, I probably wouldn't be going out anyway. Not really my scene."

Jeremy's smile widened. "And I'm gonna be completely honest with you, Steve. You're not exactly a people person. To anyone who doesn't know you, you give off psycho vibes."

I almost laughed. "Psycho vibes?"

He grinned without shame. "Totally. You have that

'don't make me kill you' thing going on. But not with me. See, I know you might act tough, but you're actually a big ol' softy."

"A softy? I think I prefer the psycho vibes, if I'm being completely honest."

He laughed at that. "You do not. You just want people to think you're a meanie. But I know better."

This conversation was skirting into some very personal territory.

"Well, you'll just have to keep that to yourself. Can't have you ruining my reputation."

Jeremy chuckled, clearly tired, but his eyes were warm. He stared at me, too close, and still not close enough. It made my heart thump in ways it shouldn't have.

"I better go to bed," he mumbled just as his phone rang. He groaned and looked at the screen. I saw Maddox's name before he answered. "Hey, dickbag."

I couldn't hear exactly what Maddox was saying, but Jeremy laughed. "No, I'm going to bed. . . . Fucking tired, that's why." He hauled himself off the couch with a groan. "Say goodnight to Steve." He held the phone out and I heard Maddox.

"Night, Steve."

"Goodnight, Maddox," I said.

Jeremy held his fist out so I bumped mine to his. "Night, Steve," he murmured, his gaze locked to mine.

My stomach twisted in knots, my pulse quickened. "Night, Jeremy."

He smirked as he walked off to his room. I could hear him talking to Maddox until he was too far away to make anything out but the occasional burst of laughter.

*He said he knows me.*

*"You just want people to think you're a meanie. But I know better."*

I let out a slow breath and tried not to read too much into that. Or how he looked at me. How he smiled at me . . .

*Christ, Jeremy.*

My phone rang, startling me. It was Robbie.

"Hey, boss," he said. "All good here. How are things with Jeremy?"

# CHAPTER FOUR

I WAS UP BEFORE SEVEN. Three hours sleep wasn't my favorite way to live, but I could manage.

Elsie delivered our groceries, and Jeremy came down bleary-eyed, sleep-rumpled. He wore the lounge pants from last night, no shirt, and his blond hair was a mess. He was absolutely gorgeous.

He squinted at me. "What the fuck?"

Riko and I were putting things away, and I stopped and smiled at Jeremy. "Morning. Coffee's on."

"Iced coffee?" he croaked, still half asleep, and looked around. "Has Ryan been here?"

I managed to not laugh. "Not yet. You have a coffee machine."

He squinted harder at me. "Time is it?"

"Seven fifteen."

He groaned and scrubbed his hand over his face. "Does my coffee machine make iced coffee?"

"I'll see what I can do." I slid a carton of eggs onto the counter. "Want some bacon and scrambled eggs?"

He blinked one eye and sighed. "Yeah, that'd be great, thanks."

I did laugh at that. "Oh no. That wasn't an offer. You're making them." I gestured to me, Riko, and then to Jeremy. "Times three."

He stared at me, then cupped his hand to his ear. "I'm sorry. What was that? I didn't quite catch that over the declaration I gave yesterday that I do *not* cook."

I gave him my I'm-not-kidding glare. "You're going to learn."

He let his head fall back and whined. I half expected him to stomp his foot. Instead, he walked around the island and hugged my back, the side of his head against the nape of my neck. "But Steeeve."

This is how he was with Maddox and the other guys.

Not with me.

Sure, he'd touched my arm before, he'd even put his arm around my shoulder a bunch of times. I'd even had to piggy-back him when he complained of being too tired.

But he'd never hugged me. A back-hug, of all the things.

Every cell in my body ignited and butterflies flooded my belly. I tried to keep my body relaxed while simultaneously trying to ingrain this in my memory.

"Cooking lessons start today," I said, somehow managing to keep my voice neutral. "Do you have a frying pan?"

"I don't know," he mumbled. Then he pulled away and grabbed a few things out of the stack of groceries. "How about I put these away and you cook? I'll take notes. Mental notes. I'm not writing anything down."

I tried not to laugh but failed. "Fine."

I caught Riko staring at me before he shook his head.

"What?"

"You folded so easy," he said as he put a packet of pasta in the pantry. Then he shot Jeremy a disbelieving look. "He never folds that easy."

I glowered at him. "You wanna cook?"

"No, boss," he replied quickly.

Jeremy laughed and put his arm around my shoulder. "Everyone thinks you're a badass. You got them all fooled."

I gave him a playful shove. "Get off me and finish putting this stuff away."

Jeremy sighed but he did take his arm off me. "I thought you said there was coffee."

I rolled my eyes but decided to make coffee before eggs. Jeremy watched as I poured a few shots of coffee over ice and topped it up with a cold bottle of water. I handed it to him.

"Is that it?"

"What do you mean is that it?"

"Is that all that goes into it?"

"Uh, yeah. That's an iced Americano. It's what you have every day."

He sipped it and seemed genuinely surprised. "Even I could make this."

I snorted. "Yes, you could." I made two coffees next for me and Riko, and by the time I scrambled eggs and fried some bacon, Riko had everything put away and was making toast.

We sat out on the patio. The sun was already warm, and it was so easy to forget that this was work. And that was my fault. I was treating this like it was something more.

Something it wasn't.

Sitting across from a still-shirtless Jeremy as he demolished his breakfast, mumbling with his mouth half-full about how good it tasted, it was hard to imagine that anyone would want to hurt him. I knew the person responsible for the threats clearly had some issues with reality. Maybe they were harmless. Maybe the threats were empty and their delusions would remain fantastical. But, nonetheless, the threat remained.

I hated that it was Jeremy they wanted.

That anyone could want to hurt him made me feel all kinds of wrong.

"What's up?" Jeremy asked me.

"Nothing. Why?"

He rolled his eyes. "You need to work on your ability to lie." He finished the rest of his iced coffee. "You do this thing with your eyes. As though you don't like what you're thinking about."

I kept my face neutral, pushed my plate away, and looked him right in the eye. "Is that so?"

"Yep. You have a few tiny tells."

My stomach dropped. "Do you think?"

"Sure," he answered cheerfully. He turned to Riko. "Don't you think?"

Riko's eyes widened. "Uh . . ." He got to his feet and quickly stacked the empty plates. "I'll just go clean up."

Jeremy and I both watched Riko disappear inside, and then he grinned at me. "Why are they scared of you? Are you mean to them?"

I chuckled. "Not at all. I'm just . . . professional."

"Mean."

Why was I smiling at him? "No. I have high standards. I like things done in a certain way."

"Like the military."

"I'm not military. I had the wrong attitude for the military."

"You needed to enter as a general? Can't see you taking orders from anyone."

My smile widened. *He really did know me.* "Something like that."

"Wasn't Ivan in the military?" He shook his head. "I mean, he is the size of a tank. Maddox calls him a drill sergeant."

I chuckled. "Ivan wasn't. His father was."

Jeremy nodded. "Ah. That actually makes more sense."

"He would call his father *bojnik,* and I assumed that was his name," I said. "Turns out that it's Croatian for major."

Jeremy made a face. "Gawd. He calls his dad by rank? And I used to complain about my mom wanting the music turned down at midnight."

I chuckled. "Ivan's a good guy. I'm just glad he's on our team. I wouldn't like to go up against him."

"He's with Wes and Amy, right?"

I gave a nod. "Yep."

He grimaced. "Poor Amy. Her first security detail and you gave them Ivan?" He laughed. "Well, there's a baptism by fire if there ever was one."

That made me smile. "She'll be fine. Anyway, it's hardly her first. Do you not remember the first month of them dating?"

Amy. A sweet girl that stole Wes's heart about eighteen months ago. They met at a press thing where she was working as a make-up tech, and for Wes, it was love at first sight. Amy, not so much. At first she was absolutely not interested, which, of course, sent Wes into a bit of a tailspin.

How could someone not be interested in dating one of the world's biggest stars?

A few weeks after she turned him down, they met again

at another press thing. But he respected her original no, and so they talked for hours as friends, and lo and behold, she then asked him out for coffee.

They'd been inseparable ever since.

Their relationship hadn't been without its issues. First, Platinum tried to keep it secret, but paparazzi soon ended that. Then the nightmare of a few jealous fans who had said some shit online and, of course, the fucking papzz had tried to follow her every move.

We'd had to increase security on her and Wes, and I thought it might put an end to their relationship, but it hadn't deterred them. That was a year and a half ago and they were still together. They were now living together, so while Wes was our prime client, his detail now included Amy.

"Did she have a full detail back then?" Jeremy asked.

I was surprised that he didn't know. "Yes. Just to and from work, that kind of thing. No one staying with her. Just transporting."

Jeremy frowned. "I remember Wes being pissed off. Guess I forgot how bad it was."

I studied him for a second. His issue had nothing to do with Amy back then. His issue was that the band was changing. Their circle of five was growing.

First Maddox with Roscoe. Then Wes with Amy.

"It'll be you next," I said, aiming for a joke, even if it didn't sit right with me. It would happen eventually. "You'll find a girl."

"Me?" He looked kind of horrified. "Not likely."

One thing I had noticed on the last tour was that if there was a night or two off and Luke and Blake had wanted to meet up with some girls, Jeremy had opted not to. Not even once.

"Not interested? Even in something casual?"

He screwed up his face. "You know the saying you should make your friends before you make your money? How would I ever really know if they're with me for me?"

I nodded slowly. "Fair enough."

"I'd rather be lonely than taken for a fool."

God, that hurt to hear.

"I'm done with the stream of nameless faces, ya know?" he said. "It's all meaningless and it—" He shook his head. "Never mind. You don't want to hear this shit."

"You can tell me," I said gently.

He met my eyes. "We've been doing this a long time, right? And there's been women. A lot of women."

God, he didn't have to tell me that. I knew all too well.

"And this is gonna sound terrible. But I don't remember them. I couldn't tell you a name or a face. It was just meaningless. And I just can't do that anymore. It feels like I'm giving away a part of my soul every time." He shrugged. "I have nothing left to give."

Oh, Jeremy . . .

"It's taken a toll on you."

He nodded. "Yeah."

"Are you lonely?"

His eyes cut to mine. "Yes. There's a reason why Eleanor Rigby is my favorite song. I mean, apart from the fact it's a musical masterpiece." He gave me a weak smile and shrugged again. "This life is isolating. Remember what Maddox went through, how he said he felt like a circus monkey punished for wanting something outside the cage? And how he was just a commodity in a trade-off."

I nodded.

"It feels like that." Then he smiled. "Don't get me wrong. I love my life. Wouldn't change a thing. I *am* happy.

I just wish . . . some days I just wish I knew what *normal* felt like."

"Normal?" I grimaced. "It's work. And bills and rent and housework."

Jeremy gave me a rueful smile. "Stop selling it so enthusiastically."

"Sorry."

He shook his head. "I know I'm privileged. I know that. I don't have to worry about money. I don't have to struggle with that."

"Your problems are unique, yes," I said. "But not any less valid."

He finally smiled, albeit tinged with sadness. "I just want something real and genuine. And maybe that can't happen for me as long as Atrous is a thing."

"You deserve to be happy too," I offered. Even though the thought of him finding that perfect woman just about killed me inside, he did deserve to be happy.

And what right did I have being hurt? Jeremy was straight.

He snorted. "And subject them to this? Having a fixated stalker and an FBI investigation? No thanks. Not to mention the tours and the crazy hours, and my dedication to the guys. It's not easy to ask someone to be the fifth most important person in my life. Like saying, 'Hey, I think you're amazing and we could have something great, but here's the ladder of all the important people in my life—'" He held up one hand like a measuring stick, then the other much lower. "'—and this is where you are.' I can't ask someone to do that."

"The right person would understand. And Maddox doesn't treat Roscoe like that. Nor Wes and Amy," I tried. I held my hands up equally. "Maybe they're equal but separate."

"Well, even then," he replied, "I don't want to separate my life between the guys, the band being over here, and then some . . . one being over there. And the truth is, if they can't be part of my life with the guys, then what's the point?"

"True." I sighed. "I don't envy you guys."

He shot me a curious look. "No?"

"The house, sure. The private jet is nice. Not gonna lie. But I see what it costs you. The privacy, the intrusions, the demand. And the toll it puts on your health. Physical, mental." I shook my head. "I mean, we're both here right now because some deluded fan has got you in their crosshairs and instigated an FBI investigation."

He swallowed hard and took a moment to consider what I'd said. "Do you think it's a serious threat?"

I met his gaze. "I have no idea. But Arlo and Ambrose do, and until the feds tell me they've caught this person, we treat it like it's serious."

Riko joined us. "Boss. A Mr. Gerald Dubrowski is at the gate."

I checked the time. It was five to eight. Shit. I hadn't realized we'd been talking so long. "Good, let him in." I got to my feet. "He was in charge of the security system install here," I said to Jeremy. "I'll be awhile with him. Riko will have you covered. And don't forget Ryan will be here around nine. Knowing Ryan, he'll be early. And you have a physical therapy session with Julio as well."

Jeremy gave me a mock salute. "Understood." He stood up, and I quickly averted my gaze so I didn't appear to be checking him out. *Was a shirt too much to ask?*

"I'm gonna go shower," he announced. Then he patted

his belly. His very flat, very defined abs. "Thanks again for breakfast. You're gonna spoil me."

"No, I'm not. We're keeping it fair," I replied. "Because you're cooking lunch, remember?"

---

MY MEETING with Gerald Dubrowski went for about an hour. Jeremy's security system was a good one, and given the location—the gated community, the ravine drop-off on his property border—his house was well-protected.

I felt safe here, and Jeremy did too. But that wasn't any reason to relax.

"Can anyone access and watch this footage?" I asked.

Gerald frowned at first but then quickly shook his head. "Not without access through our servers. They'd need high-level security clearance."

"I'll need the name of everyone who has access to that information."

Gerald stopped and stared at me. "I can vouch for everyone on my team. I assure you—"

"Then you should have no problem with giving me the information." Then I changed tack. "Actually, it might be best to leave me out of it. I'll send you the contact details of a Special Agent Miles Zielinski of the FBI and you can forward it to him. Or would you prefer the request come *from* him, as in a formal request for information?"

"The FBI?"

"Hmm." I stared at the screen. "I'd like to get another camera here." I pointed to the screen. "And here. And I want better thermal imaging."

"This is industry-leading software."

"I want military grade. Multispectral, 4K, in-built

audios and illuminators. I want to be able to see their retinas."

Gerald scrubbed his hand over his face. He was quiet for a long beat. "There's a product. Not even on the market yet. It's been approved, but they're waiting on distribution rights or something. It has long-range detection capabilities, threat-assessment kind of thing. And it can read the identification signature of drones."

I grinned at him and clapped his shoulder. "Now we're on the same page."

"I'll have to make some calls. And I'll need Mr. Dalton to approve it, of course."

"Of course."

Jeremy wouldn't mind.

"Can you show me them online? If they're any good, I'll need five." I held up five fingers.

"They're not going to be cheap," he added.

I didn't care who was paying for it. Jeremy or Platinum. "If it keeps them alive, then it's worth it."

———

"HERE HE IS," Ryan said as I walked out. He held out a Starbucks cup. "Coffee?"

"Thank you."

I looked around the room, and before I could ask, Ryan nodded out the back. "He's out there."

Sure enough, he was on a shaded lounge chair with a notepad and pen. Riko was standing by, out of Jeremy's eyesight but close enough.

I sipped my coffee. "Sorry, I took longer with the surveillance company than I thought. What did I miss?"

"Schedule update," Ryan answered. "Week after next is all a go."

"All of it?" Meetings, interview, photoshoots, and an appearance on *Late Nights in LA*.

"Yep."

What the fuck had changed since yesterday?

Ryan clearly read my mind. Or maybe my facial expression. He shook his head. "Dunno what he's thinking," he said flatly. "Ambrose just confirmed it's all a go. I guess he assumes this FBI case will be over by then."

Maybe it would be. But why not cancel everything until we knew for sure? I resisted growling. "*Late Nights* is next Thursday, right?"

He gave a nod.

Ten days away. Ten days felt like a lifetime.

Yesterday Ambrose and Arlo were all concerned about safety and security, and today they just didn't give a fuck?

Not that I would say this out loud to Ryan. Or to anyone, really.

I took out my phone, read the update from Ambrose, and hit Call. He answered on the fourth ring.

"Steve."

"Just got your message." My tone was clipped, but that probably wasn't anything new. "I was in a meeting. Have you heard anything about the case?"

"No developments."

"And next week's all going ahead."

"Hm." And with that simple tone, I got the impression the order had come from Arlo Kim. "We have the award shows coming up. You know what that's like."

Yes, I did.

They were my least favorite events of the year.

Atrous had won at the Brit Awards and the Grammys

earlier in the year, and now Arlo Kim was pushing for a straight sweep with the AMAs and the Billboard Awards.

But they were weeks away. Surely this would all be over by then.

"How's Jeremy this morning?"

I turned to see Jeremy getting off the lounger with his phone pressed to his ear. He was coming inside.

"Yeah, he's fine."

"Good. Keep me updated."

"Of course."

"You're in tomorrow, 9:00 a.m."

"Yes, we are."

"I'll call you later with an update, if I hear anything or not."

"Good. Thanks."

I ended the call just as Jeremy came in. "Oh, hey," he said, smiling at me. He was now wearing swimming shorts and an old T-shirt, looking relaxed, a little sun-kissed, and extremely good looking. "Maddox is gonna come over."

As soon as he said it, my phone rang. Robbie's name came up on-screen. I answered, looking at Jeremy. "Robbie."

"Hey, boss," Robbie said. "You up for company."

"Yeah, of course."

Jeremy grinned.

So I added, "But warn Maddox and Roscoe that Jeremy is making our lunch."

Jeremy scowled at me, then spoke into his phone. "Whatever Robbie says about me making lunch is a lie. . . . Oh thanks a fucking lot." He laughed and pocketed his phone. "They'll be here soon."

Robbie laughed in my ear. "We're leaving here in ten."

"Call me when you get to the gate."

"Will do."

I ended the call and stared at Jeremy until I couldn't hide my smile. "You *are* making lunch."

"Then *you're* helping me."

Ryan cleared his throat, and both Jeremy and I turned to face him. He seemed a mix of amused and confused. "I'll wait till Roscoe gets here and catch up with him, then I'll be off."

"Don't want to stay for lunch?" Jeremy asked.

"Uh . . ." He looked a little scared. "No thanks."

"See?" Jeremy said to me. "Not even Ryan wants to eat what I make."

I laughed at that, just as Riko came in, his phone in his hand. "Maintenance is here to see you?"

"Good. Let them in."

---

IT WAS A VERY quick meeting with the gardening and housekeeping staff. Did I think they were possible suspects? Not one bit. But could they possibly be used as access points? Maybe.

I explained, without too much detail, that there was a need to upgrade surveillance and security. They all sat wide-eyed, and it wasn't my intention to scare them. But I wasn't going to sugarcoat anything either.

"Has anyone approached you in the last six months and asked you about your work here?"

They all answered no.

"Has anyone started working at your company in the last six months shown an interest in this address?"

No.

"Any change in suppliers?"

No.

"Have you noticed any suspicious activity in or around the house?"

No.

"Had anyone tried to deliver any packages in the time Jeremy was on tour?"

No.

I told them I understood they weren't at the house full time, and I appreciated them coming in on short notice. Then I gave them my number and told them if anyone does approach them, asks questions about Jeremy to please, please contact me immediately.

If they remembered anything, thought of anything, they were to call me. Any time, day or night. No matter how insignificant it might seem.

The head gardener, an older man by the name of Christian, stopped on the way out. He had rough hands and skin that had seen far too much California sun. "Is Mr. Dalton in any danger?" he asked, quietly. "He's a good boy." Then he made a face. "We do a lot of houses in this area. Some owners won't speak to us. But not Jeremy. Always smiles, always talks. Offers us drinks when it gets too hot."

I smiled at that. Of course Jeremy would be friendly to everyone. That's just who he was.

"He's fine. As I said, these are precautionary matters at this time."

He held my gaze for a while before he gave a nod. I didn't mind if he didn't believe me. If he drew his own conclusions that this was serious, then he might be more aware of every slightest issue in the future.

I walked him out just as Jeremy was coming down the hall, carrying a small keyboard. "Oh, hey, Chris," Jeremy said.

Christian smiled and gave a nod. "Mr. Dalton."

"You all good?" Jeremy asked him, slightly concerned.

"Oh, yes," Christian replied, but he did glance at me.

Jeremy's smile widened. "Don't let this guy fool ya," he said, giving me a gentle tap with the back of his hand. "He's a big teddy bear."

I rolled my eyes and Christian chuckled but said his goodbyes and left.

"You have to stop telling people I'm a teddy bear."

"And call you what? A marshmallow?"

A marshmallow?

I raised an eyebrow at him. "A what?"

Jeremy laughed, and when he turned and kept walking, I noticed that Ryan, Robbie, Maddox, and Roscoe were in the family room. Maddox was holding a guitar.

And they were all watching us.

"Oh, hi," I said. "Sorry, was in a meeting."

"Morning," Maddox said, a little too cheerfully. As though he knew I had feelings for Jeremy.

Fucking hell.

Jeremy made a beeline for Maddox and they went out to the patio. Riko and Robbie followed them. Never away from anything music-oriented for long, Jeremy and Maddox were clearly doing some kind of melody or lyric development, which they could do for hours.

And that suited me just fine.

It gave me a chance to speak to Ryan and Roscoe. I told them I'd met with housekeeping and the gardening team, and how it hadn't amounted to much. "I've also had a meeting with the security surveillance company who did the install here. I've requested an upgrade to include better night and thermal vision. This house is quite secure, but being on the canyon, it's also very exposed. Especially at night. It's pitch black on the boundaries. If someone *really* wanted to come over the back wall, they could. As it is now, sure, it keeps the less-determined people out. But those aren't the types I'm worried about." I looked out to where Jeremy and Maddox sat on the lounge chairs, laughing.

"And also that maybe every member of the band look at upgrading as well. I'm waiting on a quote before I put some options to Jeremy."

Roscoe gave a nod. "It certainly can't hurt."

"I agree," Ryan said. "Especially for Jeremy. Not just because of this latest shitshow, but because he's the only one of the guys who lives alone."

I hadn't really thought of that. I mean, I knew he lived alone. I knew the other guys in the band all lived with someone. Maddox had Roscoe, Wes lived with Amy, Luke and Blake shared two houses together . . . Jeremy was on his own.

I hated that. "Exactly."

Roscoe nodded. "Maddox is worried about him being by himself. He asked him last night if he wanted to stay at our place."

I ignored the stab of unease at the mention of that. I hated that idea too . . . Not because of safety concerns or anything. But because then I wouldn't have time with him . . .

That realization hit harder than the unease.

Was my judgment clouded when it came to Jeremy?

Yes.

Was I putting my own selfish needs before his?

"Not that it matters," Roscoe continued. "He said no. He wants to stay here."

Instant selfish relief flooded through me.

"And he's not alone," Ryan said with a grin. "He's got Steve."

I resisted growling. And blushing. "And Riko," I mumbled.

"All right," Jeremy said loudly. He was grinning at me, and Maddox was one step behind him. "This dickbag doesn't believe I'm gonna make lunch."

Roscoe and Ryan both turned to me, and I had to make myself not smile. "He is going to learn how to cook."

Maddox found that hilarious, apparently. I ignored the way Roscoe was watching me and focused on how Jeremy was smiling at me on his way to the kitchen.

"Hey, get this," Jeremy said, showing Maddox his coffee machine. "This can make iced coffee."

"No shit, dude. Really?"

"Shut the fuck up," he said. "How would I know that?"

"Because you have one every day."

"People bring them to me. Do you know the last time I actually went into a Starbucks?" He looked upward, as if he was trying to recall. "I cannot remember. I think we were in high school."

I checked the time and asked Jeremy, "Did you want to start making lunch now?"

He palmed his stomach. "Yeah, I'm hungry."

"Have you got some crackers or something?" Ryan asked. "Juice?"

Ryan knew that Jeremy needed to eat all the time. Of course he did. He was his manager . . . It still irked me that I didn't know until yesterday.

Jeremy went to his fridge and opened it, revealing that it was full. "Behold."

"Holy shit," Maddox said. "Are those . . . vegetables?"

Jeremy shoved him. "Fuck off."

Maddox laughed and pretended to wipe a fake tear. "Babe," he said to Roscoe. "Our boy is all growed up."

Jeremy ignored them, sighed, and looked at me. "This is your fault."

I laughed and turned to Ryan. "Sure you don't want to stay?"

He gave a nod. "I better go. I told Wes I'd stop by to see him. You're all in the offices tomorrow, right?"

Roscoe nodded. "Yep."

"See ya then."

After Ryan left, I went to the fridge and took out the chicken. "You ready?"

Jeremy looked at the raw chicken meat, then at me. He shook his head. "Uh, no."

Maddox laughed again. "Jer, I've never known you to cook. Ever. Maybe a frozen pizza. Not *actual* food."

He looked offended. "I cooked breakfast this morning."

I scoffed. "You did not. You watched."

"I took notes."

"It was bacon and eggs."

"And it was good too."

Maddox snorted out a laugh. "This is gonna be so much fun."

"You're not watching," Jeremy told him. "Go for a swim or something."

"Oh, hell no, I'm not missing this," he replied.

But Roscoe took him by the shoulders and led him out. "Leave them alone," he said. Then he gave me a smile over his shoulder as they disappeared out the door.

*What was that look for?*

"Do not have sex in my pool!" Jeremy yelled out.

We could hear Maddox laugh.

Jeremy rolled his eyes. "Can we undercook his chicken?"

I snorted. "No."

# CHAPTER FIVE

LUNCH WAS GRILLED chicken strips on flat bread with salad. It wasn't difficult but Jeremy still did a really good job, and helping him in the kitchen, standing next to him, teaching him, laughing with him was so effortless.

Sitting at the table on the back patio by the pool as we ate it—me and Jeremy, Maddox and Roscoe, and Robbie and Riko—it was so easy to pretend like some delusional fan that this was my real life. That I could sit at the table with them, as friends.

As a boyfriend.

Was I as bad as a deluded fan?

Christ. *Was I?*

"You good, Steve?" Maddox asked.

I realized they were all staring at me. The conversation had stopped. "Yeah, sure. I was just thinking about what you could have done better with the chicken."

They all laughed, thankfully. And Jeremy groaned. "Everyone's a freaking critic. And for that comment, Steve, you're cooking dinner, just so we all know."

I laughed. "I'm just kidding. It was actually pretty good."

"Nah, you can keep your compliments. You're still cooking dinner."

I rolled my eyes. "You can watch me cook. You might learn something."

Jeremy made a face, looking at Maddox. "He's awfully fucking judgy."

I snorted. "I'm not judging you."

"If it's any consolation," Roscoe offered, "Maddox can't cook either."

Maddox shot him a stunned look. "Hey."

Jeremy gave a nod to Maddox. "They forget we basically left home at sixteen. And then the five of us lived together and our parents took turns to bring us food, or we ate ramen. Or frozen pizza."

Maddox agreed. "We've spent half our adult lives in hotel rooms."

When they put it like that. "That's very true, sorry," I said.

Jeremy put his hand to his chest. "So you *were* judging me?"

"No."

He was indignant. "Anyway, I can cook on a grill. That counts as cooking. I mean, there's meat. And fire."

I laughed. "True."

"You're still cooking tonight," Jeremy said.

After this conversation, that wasn't unreasonable. "Fair enough."

I could feel Roscoe's gaze on me, as though he could see right through me. As though he might suggest I put someone else in charge of protecting Jeremy because I wasn't being professional.

He wouldn't be wrong. *Would he?*

"I'll clear these up," I said, quickly stacking plates. "And I should check on a few things." I gave Jeremy a nod as I walked away. "Compliments to the chef."

"I'll help," I heard Roscoe say, and I dreaded it. I knew he was following me in, vying for some privacy so he could perhaps ask me what the fuck I was doing.

Sure enough, he came in with his hands full.

"You can just leave those on the counter," I said, hoping he'd take the hint. "I'll take care of them."

"Nah, it's okay," he replied casually. "I think they're gonna swim anyway."

I glanced out to the patio and sure enough, Maddox was doing a bomb for the biggest splash into the pool, and Jeremy was taking his shirt off.

God.

"How's Jeremy been?" Roscoe asked.

"Yeah, fine. Like nothing's wrong at all." I shrugged. "Well, it's been one day and we haven't left the house. Having you guys here would be good for him, no doubt."

"And how are you with it all?" he hedged. He was going for casual but it really wasn't.

"I'm kinda pissed that we only found out about it yesterday," I admitted. That wasn't a lie, but it was a deflection from what he was really asking. "They've known this . . . person has been focused on him for six months and they're only just telling me now? We were on tour, for god's sake. At our most vulnerable, and they never said there was a possible threat."

"Yeah. I'm with you on that. I understand they have a lot of fans who say a lot of crazy stuff. But there's a difference between someone typing 'marry me, Jeremy' into

Twitter, and sending repeated, targeted mail and redirecting VPNs."

I nodded. "Yeah."

"Arlo's internet team will probably find this person before the FBI," he said. "They're pretty good at what they do. They can cut through social media crap like a hot knife through butter."

"Maybe they should give all the info to the fans," I suggested. "They'd have the person's name, address, place of employment, and social security number by dinner time."

Roscoe laughed. "Ain't that the truth. They don't miss a single thing."

I sighed and began rinsing a few plates. "You know, 99.9 percent of their fans are great."

"But that point-one percent, right?"

"Yeah. And the media. Some of those paparazzi assholes I'd like to meet in a dark alley with no cameras."

Roscoe laughed. "Same." He was quiet for a bit but I knew something was coming. It didn't take long. "Do you remember on the tour before last, you and I were in the van with Maddox and Jeremy and you said you thought Maddox and I had a thing? You said you could read people, and how he looks for me and waits for me, and you thought we were already together?"

Fuck. *Here we go.*

I continued rinsing the plates and gave a nod. "Sure."

"Well," he said, "I'm kinda picking up some vibes between you and Jeremy."

My gaze went to his. I knew it was coming but it still didn't prepare me for my reaction. "What?"

"He looks for you," Roscoe said. "He waits for you."

I shook my head, because that was ridiculous. I assumed he was going to talk about me. How *I* was around

Jeremy, not how Jeremy was around me. "That's ridiculous."

Roscoe raised an eyebrow and half-smiled. "Is it? Because I started to notice it on the *Code Red* tour. In London and Paris. Tokyo."

"He's on my detail," I tried. It was true though. Since Maddox took a step back, Jeremy took the lead, which meant as head of security, I took Jeremy. "He should look for me and know where I am. There were some pretty crazy crowds over there."

Roscoe nodded slowly. "True."

"And me being here is called *close protection* for a reason."

"I know. And I get that. It just feels different." He shrugged. "I dunno. Maybe I'm misreading it. I know he respects you, and after the week we spent in Vermont, just us four . . . you're closer to him than the others, and that's cool. It's no big deal."

I wasn't sure where this was going. "What's your point, Roscoe? If you're worried about me not being able to do my job . . ."

"No," he said with a laugh. "God no. I'm just . . . I don't even know. Maddox thinks I'm crazy. He said Jeremy's straighter than straight, but I'm not sure." He laughed and sighed. "Okay, look. I think he might have a bit of a crush, or a bro-crush on you? I don't know. And I have no idea which way your door swings, if you get what I mean."

Oh, fucking hell.

*Say nothing. Say nothing.*

"And we've all seen Jeremy with a lot of women," he continued.

Yes, we had. I didn't need the reminder.

"But I've never seen him with anyone like he is with

you. He laughs a lot with you, and he's a bit touchy-feely with you."

I remembered how he back-hugged me earlier. "He's always affectionate with the guys."

"Yeah. With the guys. Never with Ryan, never with Amber, not even with me. But he is with you."

"He trusts me," I said.

"He does. Steve, I'm just telling you what I see. And if he is truly straight, then maybe he's caught some feelings that might freak him out at some point? I don't know. I guess I'm just saying with everything that's going on, with the stalker and the FBI, and now maybe this? He's dealing with a lot. Just if you weren't aware, now you are."

I leaned against the kitchen counter and crossed my arms. Then, realizing how that made me look defensive or self-soothing, I shoved my hands in my pockets instead. "I know what he's dealing with." God, this was bad. I ran my hands through my hair. "Fucking hell."

"Look," he said gently, "I get it. Believe me . . ."

But then he stopped talking and did a whole lot of staring.

"Steve, do you . . . ? Are you . . . ?"

I shot him a death glare.

"Holy fuck." He shook his head, stunned. "I didn't know. It's not my business. I thought it was all him." He began to smile. "But if it's mutual . . . ?"

I sighed. "It's not. It can't be. He's . . ." I could barely form words. My mouth was dry. "He's, like you said, very straight. And I'd very much like to keep my job, so if you could not say anything to anyone, that'd be great."

Roscoe's eyebrows knitted as he tried to put my words together for a few seconds. I said Jeremy was straight, basically admitting that I wasn't. "Steve—"

"Not even Maddox." That wasn't fair and I knew it. "Sorry. I don't mean . . ." I let out a breath. "I can't have anyone finding out. I just can't. It's already cost me—"

"Steeeeeeeve," Jeremy called out from the pool.

I sighed.

"Steeeeeeeve," he called out again.

I bit back a groan and walked out toward the pool. Maddox was sitting on the step, his pale and lean body half hidden in the water. Jeremy was still in the water, but had his arms folded on the edge of the pool, his chin on his hands. His hair was wet, his skin glistening in the sun.

He grinned at me. "Maddox doesn't believe me."

"About what?"

"All the trophies in your apartment."

Jesus.

"Okay, one." Maddox laughed. "I can't believe you went inside Steve's apartment."

"I wasn't having him wait in the car alone. I'd hate to think of what trouble he'd get into."

Jeremy grinned, and Maddox laughed at him. "And two, what's this about an MMA national title?"

I looked at Jeremy and rolled my eyes. "There were no trophies for the nationals. Only regional and state."

*I never got to compete for the belt.*

Roscoe was now beside me but I refused to look at him. Yes, Jeremy had been to my place. But only because I wouldn't let him stay in the car without me.

"There's like twenty-something trophies," Jeremy said. "Regional, district, state. All champion too. No second place."

"Why was there no national trophy?" Maddox asked, still grinning.

I considered how to answer. "Injury."

They both made a pained face. They understood how injuries could derail a career.

"Hey," Jeremy said. "You never answered about the reminder."

"What?"

"You said you were going to pack the trophies away but they were a good reminder. You never told me of what."

I smiled at him and repeated back what he'd said to me. "That if someone broke into my place, they picked the wrong guy because I can kill people with my bare hands."

Jeremy laughed, then effortlessly lifted himself out of the pool. His muscular body dripping wet, his torso and arms rippling with muscles gleaming in the sun, his shorts low on his hips.

Christ.

I looked away and, of course, my eyes went straight to Roscoe's. And of course he was watching me. "I have some work to do," I mumbled as I went back inside.

Fucking hell.

In the space of twenty minutes, I'd managed to boot myself out of the closet to Roscoe and basically admitted that it wouldn't matter how much I liked Jeremy because he was straight.

Except Roscoe thought he might not be?

Had Jeremy been looking for me, waiting for me like Roscoe had said? In London and Paris and Tokyo. Those cities on tour were crazy-busy, and the boys were exhausted by then.

Had Jeremy fallen asleep on my shoulder in the van in London?

Yes.

He was tired. So what?

Had I relished every second of it?

Also yes.

Had he taken my arm when we'd left that restaurant in Paris because the paparazzi were there?

Sure he had. Because it was dangerous and the crowd closed in around us.

Did he ask me, and only me, to go with him to some Izakaya Alleys in Tokyo at one in the morning for the best street food in the world?

Yeah, but that was a safety thing.

And Singapore, when we left the press conference, he'd grabbed my arm again to walk through the lobby and climb into the van.

Weren't those all work-related? Where Jeremy needed my professional help, not my company.

Roscoe was imagining things.

Surely.

I was so sure Roscoe was going to call me out on *my* behavior, but no. He'd noticed Jeremy's behavior toward me.

*But I've never seen him with anyone like he is with you. He laughs a lot with you, and he's a bit touchy-feely with you.*

*He looks for you.*

*He waits for you.*

*I've never seen him with anyone like he is with you.*

And then this . . .

*If he is truly straight, then maybe he's caught some feelings that might freak him out at some point? I don't know. I guess I'm just saying with everything that's going on, with the stalker and the FBI, and now maybe this? He's dealing with a lot.*

He was dealing with a lot. Neverending pressure, and now threats against him.

He was dealing with a lot.

But the idea of leaving him, of someone else taking over his protection, of not seeing him every day, made me feel a bit ill.

I needed to get my shit together.

So I busied myself cleaning up the kitchen and then hiding with my laptop, writing reports and sifting through the newly adjusted schedule for next week. I messaged the transport team and drivers, and then I made the terrible mistake of searching up Jeremy on social media.

There were Facebook groups, fansites, Twitter, and TikTok accounts solely dedicated to him. Hundreds of them, if not thousands. I wasn't looking for any threats. That wasn't my job, and quite frankly, I wouldn't know where to start.

Most of the posts were pictures and photographs that weren't exactly difficult to look at. Jeremy on stage, sweaty, his shirt clinging to him. Or no shirt at all, drenched and ripped, microphone in hand, the veins in his neck straining as he sang.

The pictures were 'thirst traps' . . . whatever that meant.

Photos of him on the *Code Red* tour, laughing, smiling, with the guys, by himself.

With me.

It was strange to see myself in photos online. As if I was seeing photos of someone else.

Photos of me with him, escorting him to a van, out of a van, into a building, out of one. My hand on his back, him holding onto my arm.

London, Dublin, Paris, Munich, Prague, Rome, Singapore, Manila, Hong Kong, Tokyo . . .

Then, because I was a complete masochist, apparently, I clicked on my name.

There were a lot of photos of me. With all the guys from the band over the last seven or eight years. A lot of earlier pictures of me escorting Maddox, but lately more of me with Jeremy. And the comments . . . A lot of comments.

*Sexy Steve*

*Bodyguard babe*

*Steve 'Ice Man' Frost, the coldest bodyguard in Hollywood*

Christ. Who thought up that shit?

I wasn't cold, was I?

I mean, my work-face was usually stoic. I was watching every little thing, concentrating, focused. I wasn't there to smile at the cameras.

I remembered this shit from when it was all about Maddox and Roscoe. All that social media noise was utter garbage.

Except for the people who put the *fan* in fanatical, unable to separate reality from fiction. For them, we were a few select individuals. Five guys in a band and their security or managers. That was it. They knew every detail about us.

But what were they to us?

They were a few hundred thousand strong. All the faces in all the crowds, in all the concerts in all the countries just blurred together. Nameless.

Madness.

I understood a fan's excitement, and I would never belittle what a band like Atrous might mean to them. They wrote songs that fans connected with. They addressed issues that spoke directly to fans, that fans identified with. And that was a wonderful thing.

But to be fixated on them, to think they were entitled to

them, to threaten them? That was something I could never understand.

Riko stuck his head in. "Hey boss. I'm off the clock until 3:00 a.m. Gonna catch some sleep. Jeremy's in the front living room with Julio."

I checked my watch and stood. It was four o'clock. "Shit. I lost track of time. Are Maddox and Roscoe still here?"

"No, they left a few hours ago."

"God, I'm sorry." I hadn't even heard Julio arrive.

"It's all good," he said.

He went to his room and I walked out to the living room. Julio had brought his portable PT table. Jeremy was facedown on it with a towel across his ass, and Julio was standing on the far side, massaging the shoulder muscles. He lifted Jeremy's arm and rotated it, making all the muscles in his back bulge and slide. Then he dug his thumb along some muscle over his shoulder blade that made Jeremy groan.

Damn.

"Oh, hi," Julio said, seeing me. He thumbed another trench up Jeremy's trapezius "Steve's here."

Jeremy didn't lift his head but raised his arm a little. "Hmm."

"Just wanted to let you know that Riko's off and you got me," I said. "But I'll leave you two to it."

Jeremy moaned something close to assent just as Julio tapped his shoulder. "Turn over for me," he said.

And that was my cue to leave. Seeing Jeremy on the table with no more than a towel over his crotch was too much for me.

"How does your lower back feel now?" I heard Julio say as I went back to get my laptop.

I set up at the dining table instead of the couch tonight, thinking it might be more professional. I logged in to his security feed and quickly had the four security camera views on my screen. The front gates, the front door, the patio, and the back boundary fence.

I called Ivan, Jason, and Zoe, and they told me exactly what I wanted to hear. "Nothing to report, boss."

We all knew any protection detail was 99 percent boring. But it was that one percent we needed to be prepared for at any second.

Jeremy came in from the living room, wearing only his swim shorts, walked to the couch, and fell face-first onto it. "Ugh."

All I could see of Jeremy was one foot sticking out from the couch, and with a laugh, I met Julio as he got to the doorway. He had the table folded and his bag slung over his shoulder.

"Need a hand with anything?" I asked.

"No, I have it down to an art," he said. "But thanks."

"How's the patient?" I asked.

"Fucking tired," Jeremy mumbled into the couch cushion.

Julio smiled at me. "Which isn't surprising, considering what he put his body through these last two months. Four or five months, if you include the practice they did before the tour."

"Maybe spending the day in the pool with Maddox wasn't a great idea," I said.

"Hey, Steve," Jeremy said. He was still facedown on the couch but he extended his arm to produce a middle finger.

I chuckled, and Julio gave a nod. "Well, at least he's eating properly," Julio said. "He needs to eat more regularly."

God, did everyone know about that but me?

"So I found out."

"Aww," Jeremy whined. "My two dads are so cute."

"Hey, Jeremy," I said. He looked over his shoulder at me, so I gave him the middle finger right back.

He laughed and buried his face back into the cushion. "You're making dinner."

I rolled my eyes and Julio grinned. "Jeremy, I'll see you next week."

"Can't wait," he mumbled. "More relaxing massage, less torture next time."

I saw Julio out and locked the front door behind him. I walked past Jeremy who was still facedown on the couch and went back to my laptop. I watched Julio drive out, and as soon as the gate was closed behind him, I sighed.

Now it was just me and Jeremy again.

I went into the kitchen and cut up an apple and peeled an orange, threw a few crackers on the plate, grabbed a bottle of water, and took them to Jeremy. "Here you go," I said, sliding it all onto the coffee table in front of him.

Jeremy stared at it. "Is that for me?"

"Uh, yeah. Who else would it be for?"

He sat up and drew himself to the edge of the couch. "You didn't have to do that. But thank you. I am kinda hungry."

His blond curls were a bit of a mess after all the salt water and then a physical therapy session. He was still shirtless and he was a little sun-kissed.

I tried to remember a time when he was more beautiful than he was in that moment. Not even in designer suits and expensive jewelry.

Nope. A pair of old swim shorts and tousled hair was worth more than any label.

"You okay?" he asked, somehow managing to eat, smile, and talk at the same time. "You staring for any reason?"

Shit.

"No, sorry. Just thinking . . ."

"Oh good," he said, shoving in another piece of apple. "So was I." Then he shook his head. "This apple is so good. And the orange. That's so easy. Why haven't I been doing this for years?"

I shook my head. "I have no clue. Actually, I had no idea you didn't have food in your house."

He shrugged it off. "Been busy . . . for a decade."

I smiled at him. "Is that what you were thinking of?"

"Huh?"

"I said I was just thinking, and you said so were you."

"Oh, right. Yeah, I was thinking—" He took a sip of his water and smirked at me. "—that you could teach me some of your MMA moves."

I stared. "Uh . . . what?"

"Some self-defense, but also just so I can beat the shit out of the guys when they need it."

"I will not teach you anything so you can beat up your bandmates."

He laughed and threw a slice of apple into his mouth. "Then just teach me."

Before I could answer or before I could think of a dozen reasons why that was a terrible idea, my phone rang.

It was Neil Ambrose.

I clicked Answer. "Steve speaking."

"Yeah, Steve. I have some news," he said. "Just spoke to our guy at the feds. They have a person of interest in for questioning."

## CHAPTER SIX

JEREMY WAS EXPECTED at HQ at 9:00 a.m. to view the promotional footage of the *Code Red* tour, and we drove in relative silence. Actually, Jeremy had been quiet since my phone call with Ambrose. Hearing the news that a person of interest had been found had affected him. I thought he'd be happy with the development, but that didn't appear to be the case.

When I'd told him last night, he'd made a face and nodded slowly, making an excuse to go to bed early. And this morning, he'd only picked at his breakfast.

He'd barely said five words to me all morning. It put me on edge.

Riko was in the front seat and I was in the back next to Jeremy.

"ETA, five minutes, boss," Riko called out.

"Thanks." I turned to Jeremy and waited for him to look at me. When he didn't, I knocked his knee with mine. "Hey," I said.

He met my eyes and gave me a fake smile. "Hey."

"You okay?"

"Sure."

I smiled. "You know, after a decade of being in the spotlight and being asked all kinds of questions, I'd have thought you could lie better than that."

"I don't lie."

"You tell people what they want to hear. And I don't want that. I want you to tell me if something's wrong. I can react better if I know how you're feeling, okay?"

He grunted but stopped short of rolling his eyes.

So he was going with the silent treatment.

"I thought you'd be happy with the person of interest being brought in by the feds."

His gaze shot to mine before he went back to looking out the window. But he was holding his phone too tight, his knuckles white. "Yeah, I am. I guess."

"Jeremy," I whispered. There was no way Riko or the driver could hear me. Jeremy looked at me, his eyes guarded. "You'll be okay."

"Yeah, I know," he mumbled. "It just makes it real, I guess."

I wanted to say it was always real but figured he didn't want to hear that.

He rolled his eyes. "You can say it was always real. I know you want to."

I chuckled. "Am I that easy to read?"

He almost smiled but he settled on a sigh instead. "We deal with this shit all the time. Why is this one any different?"

I looked him right in the eye and told him the truth. "Because it's you. This person is fixated on you and we're not going to let them get anywhere near you. So you're stuck with me as a housemate until the threat is over, sorry."

His blue eyes met mine. "I actually don't mind having

you around. Apart from the whole cooking thing you're insisting I do. Do people really do that every day?"

I smiled at that. "If you think the cooking is bad, just wait until I show you what the cleaning up is like."

He chuckled and it made my heart happy to see him smile. "Oh, I think it's in one of my contracts that I can't do that. No cleanup of any kind. It's against company policy."

"Is that right?"

"Yep."

"Well, my contract clearly states that all parties must contribute equally. Cooking and cleaning up is compulsory, and it doesn't matter if you're one of the most famous singers in the world. You'll do your share."

He laughed quietly, and of course, he ignored the *famous* part. "Your contract?"

"Yep."

"I'd need to see that to verify, otherwise I'm calling bullshit."

"Oh, I have a copy right here," I said, reaching into my jeans pocket and pulling out my middle finger.

Jeremy laughed, his mood much better now.

"ETA, thirty seconds," Riko called out.

"Copy that," I replied.

Jeremy was watching me, a smile at his lips. "Did you seriously just say 'copy that' like a freaking marine?"

I didn't give him the snarky reply I wanted to. Given he was now joking with me, he was definitely feeling better about things after he'd admitted his stalker had started feeling a little too real.

The van slowed and went through the first set of gates and then a second set, where Sayed, our driver, had to show ID at a boom gate. This was part of the increased security Mr. Kim had installed at the Krüper building offices after the Roscoe and Maddox incident in New York. Platinum had its own level in the basement for parking with its own gates, and in the elevators, only approved keycards could access any of the floors Platinum owned.

As the van slowed down at the elevators, I reached over and patted Jeremy's knee. "Don't worry about the case or the feds. The authorities will handle it." Which was a lot easier said than done, I was well aware. "You just do what you normally do, and let us worry about the rest. Okay?"

Jeremy gave me that half-smirk that made my heart knock against my ribs. "Copy that."

Before I could snarl at him, Riko opened the van door. "All clear."

I exited the van and stood opposite Riko, waiting for Jeremy to get out. I walked with him to the elevator and pressed the button, ignoring the smirk he was wearing. The doors opened. The elevator was empty, so I held out my hand, gesturing for him to step in.

Jeremy looked at my hand. "Thought you wanted to hold hands there for a second."

I followed him in and Riko followed me. I stood at the back with Jeremy. Riko stood in front of us, facing the door.

"Holding hands is an extra charge," I said. "I'd need to run it past Ambrose."

Jeremy chuckled. "Copy that."

I sighed. "Sarcasm is also an extra charge."

He grinned. "It's not really sarcasm though, is it? What's the going rate for general smart assery? Double? Triple?"

"Zero. You just get Ivan instead of me."

Jeremy laughed. "Ouch."

The elevator stopped and the doors opened on our floor. We said hello to the reception staff as we walked in.

"Maddox and Wes got here a few minutes ago. Blake and Luke will be here in five," I explained.

"How do you know that?" Jeremy asked.

I held up my phone. "I know where everyone is."

We arrived at the lounge and Maddox and Wes were at the coffee machine. Ryan walked in, iPad in hand, at the same time we did. "Oh good, you're here," Ryan said to Jeremy. "We need to go through some concepts for the photoshoot . . ." Ryan stopped and frowned. "You look tired."

"Good morning to you too, Ryan," Jeremy said far too cheerfully. "Looking like something the cat dragged in yourself. Do you have a fixated stalker crazy person trying to kill you too, or is that just me?"

Ryan looked rightfully admonished. "Sorry. I just . . . I didn't think."

*No, you didn't think.*

I looked at Maddox and Wes. "He barely touched his breakfast. He'll need to eat something."

Jeremy sighed. "For fuck's sake, Steve."

Maddox laughed and wiped at a fake tear. "You two sound like my parents."

Jeremy shoved him. "Fuck off, dickbag."

"And he's not to leave this building without me," I added.

"Will you belt the piss out of him if he does?" Maddox asked with an excited smile.

"Out of Jeremy? No, of course not," I replied flatly. "But I absolutely would have a little chat with anyone who helps him escape."

Jeremy snorted. "I'm going to assume it wouldn't be a pleasant chat."

"Not for them, no." Then I turned to Ryan. "Is Ambrose in?"

"Haven't seen him, but I presume he's here somewhere."

I gave him a nod, then mine and Ryan's phones beeped at the same time. The text was from Ambrose.

*My office. Ten minutes.*

This could only be an update on the person the feds had brought in for questioning, surely.

My gaze cut to Jeremy and he was staring at me. He clearly could guess what the message was about. "Will let you know as soon as we know," I told him.

That worried look was back, but he gave a nod. "Copy that."

I couldn't even be mad.

"Is it news on the stalker?" Wes asked.

"The feds brought someone in for questioning last night," Maddox said. Obviously, Roscoe had told him.

Amber walked in, determined. Angry even.

"Meeting with Ambrose," Ryan said.

"Haven't you seen the shitshow circus breaking news flash?" she asked.

A cold hand of dread squeezed my belly.

Ryan shook his head. "No . . ."

She held out her phone. "Whoever they hauled in for questioning was just let go," she said, a look of disdain on her face. "And someone they knew posted all about it on fucking Twitter."

"What?" Jeremy asked quietly. "Posted about what?"

Maddox was already looking at his phone. He clearly found something in half a second because he looked at Jeremy, his face a little pale.

"Jeremy Dalton stalker." Maddox shook his head and

kept reading. "It's trending. FBI involved, crazy fans, Atrous stalker, save Jeremy." Then Maddox looked at Ryan and Amber. "How the fuck did this happen?"

Jeremy ran his hand through his hair. "Well, this is just great."

I wanted to go to him. I wanted to give his shoulder a squeeze, I wanted to reassure him, hold him.

Instead, Maddox put his arm around Jeremy and looked him right in the eye. "They'll get this figured out. In the meantime, we'll just do our thing, right?"

As much as I wished I could have done that, I was glad he had Maddox. If anyone would understand what Jeremy was going through, it was his best friend.

Jeremy's eyes met mine and I gave him a nod. I didn't have to tell Maddox not to leave his side—he wasn't leaving him alone for a second today.

"Give me a few minutes," I said, "and I'll tell you what we know."

Jeremy tried to smile, but it was brief. Though there was gratitude in his eyes.

Ryan, Amber and I took the elevator to the top floor. "This is exactly what we wanted to avoid," Amber said. She was pissed, and rightfully so.

"The freaking paparazzi are gonna be all over this," Ryan mumbled. "It's gonna be a circus."

What they said was true, yes. But all I could think about was Jeremy. He was in the eye of the shitstorm. Him. His life, his privacy, his safety.

I clenched my jaw so I didn't say any of this out loud. And when the elevator doors opened, I stepped out first and stalked down the corridor to Ambrose's office.

The door was slightly ajar, so I knocked and stuck my head in. Ambrose was on the phone but he nodded and waved me in. Roscoe was already there, sitting across the desk from Ambrose. "You heard?" Roscoe whispered.

"Just now."

"Where's Jeremy?"

"With Maddox in the lounge."

Roscoe sighed, relieved. "How is he?"

"I think he's more freaked out than he lets on."

My phone rang. It was Zoe.

"Zoe," I answered in a whisper. "What's up?"

"Media crowd gathering at the entrance gates."

Already? Fucking hell.

"Did you get in?"

"Yeah, boss. We're all good."

"I'm in a meeting. Stay with the guys in the lounge until I come back."

"Will do."

When I ended the call, Amber and Ryan had sat down and Ambrose put his phone on his desk. "That was Mr. Kim. He already has legal on it. The person who leaked the information is apparently a family member of the person of interest who first posted about the FBI taking their sister away *before* the sister was released. They're claiming they didn't know they were supposed to keep their mouth shut. Incidentally, the person who was interviewed was released without charge."

"Who was it?"

Ambrose sighed. "Just some overzealous fan who racked up a few email addresses with different VPNs to have sock puppet accounts on Atrous fandom chat rooms."

Jesus. I shook my head. "There's a big difference between chatroom shit-posting and actually threatening to kill someone," I said. "What the fuck were the feds thinking?"

Ambrose shrugged. "They have a few persons of interest on the list, apparently. That was the first."

"Oh good," I deadpanned. "The first one, and look at the mess."

Ambrose shot me a look, and I knew I was probably out of line but couldn't really bring myself to care. This was no joke.

"I'm not overreacting," I said. "This just made everyone's job ten times more difficult. Mine even more so." I held up my phone. "Zoe and Blake just arrived with Luke and Jason, and there's already a crowd of paparazzi and media downstairs at the gates."

Ambrose sighed. "We'll take care of that. At the moment," he went on, "it's an unfounded claim by some person on the internet who is not involved in the case. The *person of interest* in the case hasn't spoken about it, but the sister . . ." He scowled. "Well, the sister took a video of this person's bedroom, and it's wall-to-wall covered in pictures of Jeremy, cardboard cutouts, dolls, all that kind of thing. But it's not just the bedroom. It's the whole house, apparently. It's kinda creepy. Now it's all over the internet, and the media's latched on to that footage."

He turned his iPad around and tapped the screen, bringing a news site up. He hit Play, and sure enough, there was a bedroom completely plastered in pictures and posters of Jeremy. Even the comforter had his face on it, as did the pillows. A female voice could be heard saying, "The FBI came to question her about a celebrity fixation. No guesses as to who the celebrity is . . ."

Oh, just great.

"Where is this person now?" Maddox asked. "Not the sister, the one talking, but the person of interest who was questioned?"

"They lawyered up and were released about two hours ago," Ambrose replied.

Probably trying to figure out interviews and pay rates. None of us said that out loud but I knew we were all thinking it. So did Ambrose because he added, "They've been hit with a gag order."

"So *they* can't speak about it but that's too little too late for the sister who already blabbed," Ryan said. "Damage is done now."

Ambrose conceded a nod. "Mr. Kim has PR working on a formal statement."

I resisted sighing. Roscoe dug his thumb and finger into his eyes.

"The person who owns that bedroom . . ." I said. "What do we know about them? Male, female, age, location?"

Ambrose paused, and for a second, I thought he wasn't going to answer. Which was stupid because it was no doubt already all over the internet. "Female, nineteen years old. Address is here in LA. Her name is Lilian Sosa."

"And the other people of interest?" Roscoe asked. "You said there was a list. Have they been interviewed?"

"Just one, so far. A guy by the name of Adrian Thrift. FBI team in Ohio took him in for questioning early this morning regarding a mail redirection service. Apparently he has a whole redirection operation thing happening, but he has been cooperating."

The shady mail redirection was to provide random post marks to throw any suspicion off track. It was hard to connect dots when one letter came from LA, another from Ohio, and another from London.

For a fee, I could send several sealed and addressed letters in a package to Mr. Thrift. He would then distribute each letter to people in different locations who would then simply pop the letter in the mail. The letter would then have a postmark for a location it did not originate in.

It was shady as hell. And highly illegal. The only people who would have used such a service were either in hiding or cloaking their location. Liars, cheaters, tax evaders.

Stalkers.

Seemed like a lot of hassle to me. Same with the change of VPN. Not that I would even know how to do that, but it seemed backward to me.

"I don't get it," I admitted.

Ambrose tilted his head. "Don't get what?"

"If this fixated person is trying to get Jeremy's attention, if they want him to know who they are, why hide their identity?"

"They're hiding their identity from the cops and the feds," Ambrose said. "They want Jeremy's attention, not attention from the authorities." He answered as if it was a question, telling me this was, at best, just a guess.

I could see his point, but it just didn't ring true to me.

"You don't think so?" Roscoe asked.

They all stared at me, waiting for my answer. "No. I don't know. Admittedly, I'm not a psychologist and I can't begin to understand how detached and deluded this person must be, or what tracks as typical behavior. But," I added, "over the last decade, the one thing I do know is the type of fan who follows these guys. You know, who honestly think they're going to marry one of them. That kind of attachment and infatuation is something we've all seen a thousand times, right?"

They each nodded, more or less.

"I mean, it's probably not one hundred percent sane, but it's mostly harmless. They get excited and a little wild. They want the guys' undivided attention. They give out their names and phone numbers, addresses. What they *don't* do is hide."

Amber cocked her head. "What are you saying, Steve?"

"That the type of fan who has their room covered in posters and cardboard cutouts of Jeremy is going to want him to know who they are." I nodded to the iPad screen where we could still see the image of the bedroom. "We see those kinds of fans every day. Most of the time, they're great. They love the band, they support them, and they're protective of them. I bet you anything you like, the majority of the hashtags on social media are fans supporting to protect Jeremy."

Ambrose nodded. "There's a lot, yes."

I held up my finger. "But that one person, that 0.01 percent, who hates Jeremy—for whatever unjustified and stupid reason—they're who we should be looking for. Not someone who claims to love him. Look for those who hate him."

Ryan made a face. "I get what you're saying. But sometimes some folks can't tell the difference. What they think is adoration and love is some creepy obsession, and sometimes that obsession becomes something else entirely. And then they get that mindset that if they can't have them, no one else can. There are often some serious psychological issues at play."

"Yeah, I get that," I admitted. "But this doesn't feel like that. The hiding of their identity feels off." They all stared at me and I scrubbed my hand over my face. "I dunno," I said. I needed to shut up. "Sorry. I'm sure the FBI knows what they're doing."

I stayed quiet for the rest of the meeting. When it was done, they'd be relaying all the developments to Jeremy and the guys, so I pulled my team aside. I knew they'd be all waiting to hear.

"Hey, boss," Robbie said when I walked in. "What's going on?"

They all stopped and listened.

"Ultimately, there's no change yet to our set up, and things will stay as they currently are. I'll need to speak to transport because we can expect some media and crowd control, but that's up to ground security. We focus on our individuals, getting them to and from locations and ensuring personal safety and security."

I sighed. "I'm assuming you've all seen the footage of the house with the posters and pictures?"

They nodded. "The guys were watching it," Ivan said. "'S not good."

"No. Mr. Kim will be releasing a legal statement this morning, and hopefully that'll be the end of it."

"The fixated person who they brought in," Zoe said. "What happened to them?"

"Released without charge. But they're also talking to someone else in Ohio about the mail redistribution. And I believe they have a list of other persons of interest."

"So we stay as we are," Robbie said.

It wasn't really a question but I nodded anyway. "For as long as the current threat remains, we stay as allocated. The media finding out is not ideal, and yes, it makes our jobs more difficult. But it's nothing we can't handle. We'll rotate out in a few days so you can go home, see your families, get some decent sleep."

"What about you, boss?" Riko asked.

I probably should rotate out, let someone else cover my shift for a few days. But there just no way. "I'll be staying with Jeremy."

No one batted an eyelid. No one ever questioned me. And I wasn't sure if that was a good or bad thing, but I wasn't leaving Jeremy's side until this was all over.

Just . . . no.

When Jeremy and the guys came out of their meeting with the managers and Ambrose, I got to my feet, my heart thumping as Jeremy met my eyes.

"Hey," I said.

He shoved his hand into his back pocket and tried to smile. "Hey."

"You okay?"

He managed a nod, then let out a long sigh. "Yeah. It's all good. Just one more thing. All part of the job, right?"

"No," I replied flatly. "You didn't sign up for this."

"Kinda did, though. Fans and media hype." He shrugged. "The good, the bad, and the ugly."

Maddox clapped Jeremy on the shoulder. "Don't talk about Luke and Blake like that."

Jeremy smiled. Kind of. Then he pointed to one of the conference rooms. "We gotta view this tour footage."

"I'm getting the popcorn," Luke said as he went toward the lounge area.

"Grab some soda too," Wes called out after him, but then decided to follow Luke instead.

Maddox smiled after them before he slung his arm around Jeremy's shoulder as they walked off toward the conference room. "Come on, let's get the best seats. And I'll even let you cuddle me, but don't tell Roscoe."

Jeremy shoved him. "Fuck off."

I couldn't help but smile at them, but as they disappeared down the hall, something occurred to me.

The tour footage . . .

I needed to watch the tour footage.

I made a beeline for Ambrose's office and found him, again, with his phone pressed to his ear. He waved me in so I took a seat, and he wrapped up his call. "Thanks again for the update . . . okay, bye." He looked like he'd aged five years. "The police have been called to manage the crowd downstairs."

"Good." Then I added, "Might be worth asking them to take a drive to Jeremy's house. No doubt there'll be some leeches waiting at the gates."

Ambrose sighed as if he hadn't thought of that. "Might need an escort to get home at this fucking rate."

Ambrose didn't swear often, certainly not in my company. He'd clearly had a long morning.

"So," I hedged. "The tour footage the boys are watching. I was wondering if I could see it? More specifically, the raw crowd footage. I don't need any behind the scenes stuff of the band." That, I saw with my own eyes. I experienced it with them. I didn't say that out loud, though. "Any crowds gathering at the hotels, the airports, TV studios and interviews, anywhere the public was or had visual access to the band."

He stared at me. "You think this person was there?"

"I think we shouldn't rule it out."

"In Europe or Asia?"

"Yes. You said some letters came from overseas. And groupies following us on a world tour is nothing new."

Ambrose studied me, searching for something. I held his gaze with conviction. This was not out of my realm of responsibility. Could he have someone else scour the footage? Sure. Would they know what to look for?

*Would I?*

"I know how to read a crowd," I said. "I know how to

read an individual. I don't know what I'm looking for, *exactly*, but I think I'll know it when I see it."

He chewed on the inside of his lip for a second before he conceded a nod. "Okay. I'll see what I can do."

I tried not to smile. "Thank you."

His phone buzzed and he groaned. Given our meeting was over, I didn't want to waste any more of his time. I gave him a nod as I left, and he was already on his phone.

So, now the band would be busy for some time, I took Robbie and Riko down to the lobby. I wanted to see the crowd . . .

And that gave me another idea.

The crowd outside was big and mostly media types: TV, reporters, photographers. A lot of cameras, phones. But there were also a decent number of fans. The police were there now, controlling and dispersing, I guessed. The building security manned the front doors, checking IDs and clearances before letting anyone enter. Then there was secondary security at the reception desk and at the elevators.

Christ.

I saw a familiar face by the reception desk and made my way over. "It's a show, huh?"

Katarina was a security manager, in her security uniform with her hands behind her back, and she gave me a tight smile. "You could say that."

"Basement and parking lot the same, I assume?"

She nodded once. "Yep."

"Can I ask . . . CCTV scope? Do your cameras just cover the entrances and exits and internal floors? Or will there be footage of this crowd outside?"

Her sharp eyes cut to mine. "Limited footage outside, approximately fifteen feet. Any further than that and I don't know what kind of quality you'll get. Not if you're looking for facial details."

I nodded. "I'd like to see it. But I'll have the request come from the boss. Pretty sure I don't have the authority to just come and ask," I said with a bit of a laugh. "I just wanted to know if it was possible."

She smiled at that. "No problem." She scanned the crowd and pursed her lips. "FBI and cops, according to the news stations and entertainment sites. *Daily-E* is running an all-day story apparently."

I growled. "Figures."

She nodded to the glass wall and the crowd beyond. "You've got some fans too, it seems."

I followed her line of sight, and sure enough, reporters were trying to get my attention. Their muted cries were barely audible through the glass. "Steve! Steve!"

It was then I noticed Robbie and Riko had moved into position around me as if I needed their protection.

It'd probably be funny if a hundred people weren't yelling my name, waving their arms and cameras at me. There was over thirty yards and a glass wall between us, other security and police, and still . . . it was unnerving to have the attention directed at me.

I turned back to Katarina and gave her a nod. "Someone from upstairs will be in touch," I said. "About the footage."

"No problem," she replied. Her stoic gaze returned to the swelling and yelling crowd.

I went back to the elevators, and as soon as the doors closed, I sagged. "That was crazy. How do they know who I am? I mean, when I'm with the band, sure. But on my own?"

Robbie shook his head. "Boss, you need to look at the internet more often."

"I read the reports and briefings—"

"I mean social media. Not for the guys or the band. But to see what they're saying about you."

"Me?" But then I remembered the comments about me being cold and the Iceman. I rolled my eyes. "Don't believe everything you read online."

Riko sighed as the doors opened on our floor. "Leaving tonight's gonna be fun with that crowd."

"Pretty sure Mr. Kim will be releasing a statement," I said. "That usually gives the vultures something to eat for a while. Fingers crossed they leave us alone. But if you guys wanna catch up on some rest while the guys watch that tour footage, I'd suggest you do it now."

"Good idea," Robbie agreed as we walked past the lounge area. He threw his huge frame onto one of the couches. "No need to tell me twice."

I went back to Ambrose's office and requested the downstairs security footage as well, to which Ambrose readily agreed.

A man appeared at his door, holding a slip of paper. "Ah, Peter, perfect timing," Ambrose said. "This is the guy who needs the footage."

Peter handed the piece of paper over. "Your access code. Follow the link. It's single-user only, approved for *your* staff ID number."

"Thanks."

Peter left without another word and Ambrose sighed, scrubbing his hand over his face. "Sorry. Security measures around all unreleased footage. You know how that is."

I nodded. "Yeah. It's fine. Pretty sure my team is trying to catch up on some sleep in the lounge. I'll be in my office."

His phone rang again, though this time he answered immediately. "Arlo."

Ugh. *Good luck with that.* I waved him off and left him to it. I didn't envy his job. I liked Ambrose. He straddled that line of trying to keep everyone happy pretty damn well, though after the whole ordeal with Maddox a few years ago, he really made all the band members his first priority.

Where Arlo Kim was driven by numbers, Ambrose would put people over budgets. I respected him for that.

I went down to my office and flipped on the lights. It felt like an age since I'd been in here. I sat in my chair and fired up my computer. While I waited for it to boot up, I checked the news on my phone.

*Jeremy Dalton . . .*

*Atrous singer, composer, and producer, Jeremy Dalton . . .*

*Atrous stalker . . .*

*Atrous. FBI. Police.*

*Jeremy . . .*

*Jeremy . . .*

*Jeremy . . .*

I sighed and slid my phone onto my desk, having seen enough. I logged into my computer, followed the link Peter had given me, and entered the code.

Sure enough, it opened to a screen that showed . . . Christ. Fifteen hours of footage.

And this was *just* the footage I'd requested. Crowds at airports, interviews, in front of stadiums, outside TV studios, outside hotels.

I hit Play.

The footage naturally started with the beginning of the tour in LA. Interviews, a performance on *Late Nights*, photoshoots. The footage panned across the crowds, lines of people, hundreds, thousands of faces.

Clapping, cheering, screaming, excited fans who would

go ballistic at the mere sight of the band. Maddox and Jeremy, mostly, but Wes, Luke, and Blake too. Though they had made a deliberate effort to share the question seat in all the interviews, Jeremy and Maddox were still fan-favorites.

My stomach and its stupid butterflies would betray me every time Jeremy would appear or give that high-wattage grin as he waved. Which was stupid because in the footage, I was never far from him. Walking beside him, in front of him, behind him, a few feet at most.

It was disconcerting to see us interact like that.

Had he really smiled at me like that when he got out of the van at the TV studio?

I tried to think if we'd joked about something, but it was so many weeks ago. So many cities and tour-stops ago.

I couldn't think of anything in particular, but there he was, smiling at me, and there I was, smiling right back at him. Well, it was more of a smirk, but still . . .

Caught in 4K.

But then my smile faded as we made our way past the wall of screaming fans. Jeremy waved at them all and I kept myself in between him and the police, who were holding the line.

It wasn't until the footage cut to after the interview that I realized I hadn't even been watching the crowd. I'd been too busy watching Jeremy.

Christ.

So I hit Rewind and, this time, focused only on the crowds. The faces, the demeanor, the stances, the expressions.

Thirty-five minutes into the footage, I saw something that made me sit up and hit Pause.

Still in LA, the hotel we were all staying in at the beginning of the tour. We always stayed together on tour, even when in LA. Yes, we all lived here, but it was a security thing, a logistical thing.

There was a decent crowd on the street at the hotel. There always was. Mostly women, but not always, holding signs and banners, posters, pictures. Yelling, singing Atrous songs, laughing. Mostly overly excited at the possibility of seeing the band.

Except for one person.

A woman stood at the edge of the crowd. She had brown hair, a round, pale face. She wore a black long-sleeved shirt and jeans when everyone else wore T-shirts and shorts, like that didn't make her stand out enough.

But it was her demeanor that I noticed.

She stood still with her arms down. Where everyone else waved or danced, she never moved. There was no smile, no excitement. If anything, she looked mad. Confused, even.

I jotted down the timestamp and took a screenshot and kept watching.

Next stop was New York City. It was just a two-day stop on the way from LA to London. No concert, but there were interviews and publicity stints that were a necessary evil on a tour.

The guys were excited to be heading overseas again. It'd been a while between tours, and given their last tour was stateside, it was time to go back to Europe and Asia.

The tour was going to be another long one, but they'd prepared and trained well, and they had a whole new album of songs to sing live for the first time.

The American media was hyped, but nothing compared to the overseas markets, who had anticipated the tour and all the hype and profit that came with it.

I scanned every inch of the New York crowds at every event but found nothing that stood out.

The footage then skipped to London. We'd flown in privately, of course, and avoided the crazy mayhem of Heathrow. But the crowd at the hotel was scarily large. The fact the public had known which hotel we were staying at was a concern, but the local security and police had managed the whole thing very well.

Cameras panned across the screaming crowds, and though it was dark and wet, I could see faces clear enough.

None stood out.

But then the camera cast away from the crowd before they'd cut the footage, and the screen froze for half a second before it went to the boys leaving the hotel the next morning.

It was just a flash. A tiny moment. But I saw something . . .

I hit Pause and went back a few frames.

And there, at the edge of the crowd, was a brown-haired woman with a pale, round face. Not smiling. Even a bit angry.

I brought up the screenshot I'd taken and put the images side by side.

I couldn't be one hundred percent sure. And I wasn't a gambling man, but if I was . . .

I just think they might be the same person.

But two possible sightings were *maybe* a coincidence. And a maybe coincidence wasn't enough. I needed more. So I screenshot the footage and wrote down the timestamp.

*Fans can follow a band on tour. Groupies follow bands around the world all the time.*

I told myself it doesn't prove anything.

So I kept watching. The London schedule was full. I

remembered how hectic it was, how big the crowds were at every turn. Interviews, photoshoots, press conferences. Eating out at restaurants was out of the question, and sight-seeing was also a hard no.

But the London security crew that Platinum had hired was the best, and they stuck with us for most of the European tour. They were a capable unit, very professional, and took our lead without fault or question. They managed the crowds and even security for our stage crew and back-stage staff. I remember thinking in London how there was never a person out of place, despite the massive numbers we dealt with every day.

The interviews and publicity gigs were crazy enough, but the three concerts at the O2 were sold out. People lined up for hours. Merch stalls had nothing left.

I slowed the footage down of the crowds. Masses of people, thousands of faces.

No one caught my attention.

London.

Dublin.

Paris.

Berlin.

I was beginning to think I was imagining things.

A knock at my office door surprised me. I shut my laptop just as Jeremy poked his head in. "Here you are."

I got to my feet and checked my watch. "Shit. I'm sorry. Lost track of time."

"Relax. It's not that late." He pushed the door open wide and came in. "Whatcha doing in here anyway?"

"This is my office."

He looked around. "I've never been in here." Then he frowned. "It's kinda small."

"Has no one told you size doesn't matter?"

Christ. Why was I nervous about him being in my space?

Jeremy burst out laughing and put his hand to his chest. "No one has told *me* that, Steve. Anyone told *you* that?"

"Uh, no. Sorry, that just came out." I pretended I wasn't embarrassed. "And anyway, I don't need a big office, and I don't care about the view."

He peered out the blinds on the window. "Probably just as well. Because you didn't get one."

"I'm only in here to work on rosters and schedules," I said.

He gasped very loudly, startling me. But when I realized what he was looking at, I groaned.

"Is this Cyko?" He snatched the calendar off my desk and his blue eyes shot to mine, wide and disbelieving. "You have a Cyko calendar on your desk?"

Cyko was an all-girl band that Platinum had put together a few years ago. They'd had some success, but nothing compared to Atrous.

He was still holding the calendar, like it was evidence of a serious misdemeanor. He even looked offended.

"They were giving them out," I explained. "If Atrous gave me a calendar, I'd have yours here. But you didn't, so I don't."

His mouth fell open. He really was offended. "This won't do." He took his phone out and thumbed out a contact and pressed his phone to his ear. "Ryan, I need an Atrous calendar. Actually, all the Atrous merch we have. . . . Yes, I know that. This is very important. And have it delivered to Steve's office. . . . That is correct, yes. And while we're on the subject of Steve's office, we need to discuss why his office is so small and it doesn't have a view."

"No, we don't. I like my office just fine," I said, hoping Ryan would hear.

Jeremy just laughed. "Well, that's a shame. . . . Yes, thank you."

He ended the call, sighed, and pocketed his phone, then leaned his ass against my desk. He was still holding the damn calendar. "He said office allocation isn't really his call, but he'd see what he could do."

I rolled my eyes. "I'm not moving offices."

"It took me twenty minutes to find you. What if it was an emergency?"

"Then I would find you." I stood and walked around the desk to take the calendar from him, but he held it away from me.

"No, this is evidence," he said, grinning.

I considered making a reach for it but we were already close enough. Our feet and legs almost touching as it was. If I reached, I'd be between his legs, and that wouldn't be a good idea.

I crossed my arms and pretended that I hadn't just imagined being between his legs. "Evidence of what?"

"Your treachery."

"Treachery? Really?"

He held the calendar to his chest. "Exhibit A. Of you having the merch of another band on your desk." Then he paused and raised an eyebrow. "Oh. Do you like one of the girls? Which one? God, you like Jessie, don't you?"

Sure, she had blonde hair, blue eyes, and a killer smile. But I preferred Jeremy's blond hair, blue eyes, and killer smile. "God, no," I mumbled. "Are you done here?"

"Yes!" He shot off the desk. "It's home time. What are you cooking me for dinner?"

"I'm not cooking dinner," I replied. "You are."

"But Steeeeve," he whined.

I packed up my laptop and notepad and slid them into my backpack. "Quit your bitching."

"I'm going to undercook your chicken."

"You're going to do what to his chicken?" a familiar voice asked.

Jeremy and I both spun around to find Maddox watching us from the doorway. He wore an odd expression: half amused, half WTF.

"Uh," I began, not really sure how much he'd heard.

Jeremy pointed at me. "He is a bigger pain in my ass than you are. And that's saying a lot." Then he held up the calendar. "And he has a Cyko calendar on his desk."

Maddox's gaze went to me. "You a fan?"

I groaned and slipped the backpack over my shoulder. "Not really."

Jeremy walked behind my desk and held the calendar over the wastepaper. "I'm hurt. Wounded, even." Then he proceeded to look me right in the eye and drop it into the trash. "I'm not sure how you could ever make it up to me."

I sighed. "I'm guessing it has something to do with dinner."

Jeremy grinned. "And me not cooking it."

I walked to the door and hit the lights. "Is he always like this?" I asked Maddox.

"You gave in too easily," he deadpanned. "I thought you were stronger than that."

"Hey," Jeremy said, following us out. "I'm right the fuck here."

Maddox linked his arm with mine as we began to walk. "You need to be firm with him so he knows his boundaries. Kinda like a puppy. Oh, and if you're cooking, make it tofu."

Jeremy came up between us and shoved Maddox away.

"He's *my* Steve. You get your own Steve." He linked his arm with mine like Maddox had done. "And I fucking *hate* tofu."

*He's my Steve.*

His arm hooked with mine, his hand on my arm.

It all felt surreal. And far too good. Obviously it meant something different to Jeremy, but it made my heart skip a few beats and my stomach tied itself in knots.

"I think you hating tofu was the very reason he suggested it," I managed to say.

"What is for dinner anyway?" Jeremy asked.

"What about steak and salad?"

"You said burgers and fries wrong."

I couldn't help but laugh just as the elevator doors opened and Roscoe, Riko, and Robbie walked out. They stopped when they saw us approaching. I avoided Roscoe's gaze. I knew he'd read too much into the way Jeremy was touching me.

"Oh look, it's the three R's," Jeremy said, taking his arm back. "Reading, 'riting, and 'rithmatic. Hey Riko, want In-N-Out for dinner? Steve's buying."

"Steve's not buying," I said flatly. "Steve is begrudgingly cooking dinner."

Riko wasn't sure who to agree with. "Uh, I'm easy."

I looked at Roscoe then and to Robbie too. "Are you guy's done for the day?"

"Yep. Did you get far?" Roscoe asked. "Ambrose told us what you'd requested. It was a good idea."

"Requested?" Jeremy asked me. "What did you request? I asked you what you were doing in your office and you didn't answer me."

"Because you were too busy complaining about my calendar."

Jeremy turned to Roscoe. "What kind of calendar do you have?"

Roscoe looked a little concerned, but before he could answer, Maddox hit the elevator button. "Can we just go already?"

I looked to Robbie and Riko. "Has downstairs cleared?" I felt bad for being holed up in my office all day.

"Yeah, almost all. Majority left a few hours ago. Got sick of waiting, I guess. Cops are still there, though," Robbie said with a smile. The elevator chimed and the doors opened. Thankfully, it was empty.

"Uh, I use my phone calendar and the scheduling app," Roscoe answered as we all stepped into the elevator. "Oh, and we have that artsy one in the office at home. Maddox's Mom gave it to us. Ah, why?"

"Artsy one?" Maddox replied. "It's a calendar of naked male statues. Like *David* and shit."

Jeremy laughed.

"Never mind." I sighed. "Christ. I won't use the Cyko calendar anymore. Happy now?"

"Cyko?" Roscoe asked.

"You can't use it anymore," Jeremy said. "I threw it out."

The elevator doors opened to the parking garage and Riko stepped out first. Then as Robbie was stepping out, a loud bang echoed through the garage.

Robbie jumped back, blocking the elevator entrance. He slammed the Close Door button, and I grabbed Jeremy and threw him against the wall, pinning him into the corner with my body.

The doors finally shut, and my heart finally beat again.

"Fucking hell," Jeremy breathed.

I didn't dare move. I was pressing him against the wall, my body flush with his, every groove, every plane. Our chests rose and fell, our faces so, so close. His blue eyes searched mine.

"You okay?" I managed to ask.

He gave the slightest of nods, then he looked at my lips.

At my lips?

He gripped my waist.

"What the fuck was that?" Roscoe asked.

I spun then, remembering everyone else in the elevator with us. Robbie still stood in front of the now-closed door. Roscoe had Maddox in the opposite corner from us.

God, Riko was still out there.

My phone rang in my pocket. I snatched it out and saw Riko's name on-screen. "Report? Are you okay?"

"Yeah, boss. I'm fine," he replied. "It was a fucking table. Some *idiot*," he yelled, I could only assume so the idiot could hear. "Some idiot dropped a folding table."

"So we're all clear?"

"Yes, all clear."

I disconnected the call. "We're all clear." I forced myself to take a step back from Jeremy. Not far, but we were no longer pressed together. I put my hand on his face and lightly tapped his cheek. "You okay?"

He nodded woodenly.

"What was it?" Robbie asked.

"Some idiot dropped a folding table or something," I said. I pressed the button to our parking garage and gave Roscoe and Maddox a nod. "You guys okay?"

They both nodded. "Yeah," Roscoe replied, his breathing heavy.

The truth was, they weren't okay. And neither was Jeremy. We'd gone from joking to dead serious in a split second, and Jeremy was rattled. Justifiably so.

I'd gotten complacent. Distracted.

The elevator doors opened, and again, Robbie stood front and center. His huge frame took up most of the entrance. The only thing that greeted us was Riko. He was pissed off, a hard edge to his eyes. "It's all clear. Transport's ready to go."

Robbie took Maddox and Roscoe to their waiting van and I took Jeremy's arm. "Ready?"

He gave a nod and I ushered him to the van. Riko stood by us and I risked a glance toward the security booth. There was indeed a guard in uniform standing by the booth with a folded metal table leaning against the pylon. He gave an apologetic wave and I glared at him as I climbed in after Jeremy and sat beside him and put my backpack between my feet.

The door closed behind us and Riko was quick to get in the front passenger seat. "You okay, Riko?" I called out. He'd been out there on his own. It was harmless this time, but it might not have been. That loud bang could have been gunfire and he'd have been alone.

"Yeah, boss," he said over the seat. "Though that guard might wanna check his briefs. I might've scared the shit out of him."

The security guard had the good graces to lift the boom gate so we didn't have to slow down. I guessed because he didn't want another ass-chewing. He gave us another sorry wave as we drove through, making our way up to ground level.

Jeremy was quiet. I patted his leg. "You okay?"

He swallowed. "Hm, yeah."

He clearly wasn't. I slid my hand over his and squeezed. "Sorry."

"What are you sorry for?"

"That shouldn't have happened."

"Which part?"

I looked at him then. "All of it. I shouldn't have put you in a position that you were exposed like that."

He made a face as he thought about that. "You didn't put me in that position."

But I did.

"Actually, the only position you put me in was up against the wall."

My gaze went to his.

"One minute I was standing there. Then the next thing I knew you picked me up like a kid and pinned me to the opposite wall."

I still held his hand, and I thought to move it until I realized his fingers were gripping mine.

*He's holding my hand . . .*

*It doesn't mean anything. He's just had a bit of a scare, that's all.*

"Sorry about that," I said, my voice a little gruff. "Are you hurt?"

He gave a weak smile. "No. you're surprisingly gentle for a tough guy."

My cheeks grew warm. Jesus Christ.

I remembered how he'd looked at my mouth.

The van slowed again as we approached the ground level security. Not for ID checks or anything, but because of the crowd of papzz were blocking the exit. Even with the cops there. They yelled at the van, filmed, and clicked away.

Motherfuckers.

Jeremy squeezed my hand as we passed through them, and I did what felt natural. I threaded our fingers and held on tight.

He didn't speak for a few blocks, but he also didn't let go or make any attempt to move his hand.

I wanted to say something, anything, but knew if I did, he'd pull his hand away and this moment, whatever *this* was, would be over.

Then I realized I was using his vulnerability for my own stupid fantasy, and I pulled my hand back, tapping his hand as I did. "You're okay," I said. "We'll get you home and we can—"

"Get really fucking drunk."

"I was going to say cook an early dinner."

"I'm leaning toward the getting really fucking drunk mood."

I'd never really known Jeremy to drink much. Or any of the guys, for that matter. They certainly didn't drink on tour, and it was their rule not to drink alone.

"Well, you can drink," I said. "I'll supervise."

"Are you ever not on duty?"

His question threw me. "Uh, sure. When I'm not with you guys."

"So you're saying all I am is work?"

God, no. "Not at all."

"What do you do for fun, Steve?" He shot me a look. We were sitting so close, our shoulders and knees were touching. "Got a girlfriend we don't know about?"

I glanced at the back of Riko's head. He either couldn't hear us or was pretending he couldn't. I replied softly. "No."

Jeremy nodded slowly and was quiet for a bit. "Boyfriend?"

My heart skidded to a stop and my mouth went dry. I tried to keep my voice neutral. "No."

His gaze burned into the side of my face, but I didn't dare look at him. My heart was hammering now, my stomach in one giant, greasy knot.

He was going to say something else. I could feel it. He

raised his hand as if he was just about to speak . . . Then, like a freaking miracle, my phone buzzed.

I'd never answered a call so quick. I didn't even notice whose name it was on-screen, that's how off my game I was. "Frost."

"You guys okay?" It was Ambrose. "I just heard about the parking garage. Well, actually, I saw it on the news."

"The news?"

"Yeah, all those cameras heard the bang. The cops at the gate thought it was gunfire. Until the guard called it through. Said it was just a table."

"We're fine," I replied. "Sorry for not calling it in. I was going to call you when we got back to Jeremy's." That was a lie. I hadn't given Ambrose one thought, but I would have once I got Jeremy back to the safety of his house.

I don't know if Jeremy could hear Ambrose talking, but he had his phone out and was searching news sites.

"Did you find anything in the footage today?" Ambrose asked.

Jeremy shot me a look, so yes, he could hear.

"Maybe. I want to keep looking before I say anything for sure." But that made me think. "Can you get me the CCTV footage of the parking garage and elevator from this afternoon?"

There was a pause of silence from Ambrose. "Sure. Do you think there's more to it?"

"I don't know."

"I'll be in touch," Ambrose said, and the line went dead.

"It was just the guard with a foldaway table," Jeremy said. "Wasn't it? That's what Riko said."

"I'm not doubting what Riko said," I replied, knowing damn well Riko could hear. "Yes, it was a table that hit the concrete, and yes, the sound echoes in an underground parking garage. Maybe the guy was testing our reaction time."

Jeremy stared at me. "Do you . . . do you think that?"

"I don't know. That's why I want to see the footage."

He frowned. "How do you think like that? How do you *know* to think of that kind of shit?"

"Like what?"

"To anyone else, it was just a falling table. But to you it could be a test of some kind of your reaction time."

I met his gaze then, so impossibly blue. "I have to think like them. Like anyone who might want to hurt you. If I wanted to hurt someone famous, I'd need to know their weak spot. I'd want to see how their security reacted."

Jeremy shook his head. "That's fucked up."

Ouch.

I looked up front. "Yeah."

We sat in silence for a while and Jeremy went back to his phone. It didn't take long before he found the footage Ambrose had mentioned.

He held his phone so I could see it as well. Filmed by one of the smaller news stations, it showed the parking garage entrance, the security booth, and the police who were still managing the crowd. There was general chitchat among the film crews and the paps who remained when a loud bang sounded from inside the parking garage.

It was muted but somehow amplified through the concrete levels. People ducked and scattered. The cops ducked and yelled at everyone to get down and move, move! A security guard from the booth bolted into the darkness of the garage, yelling into the receiver at his shoulder.

The footage cut.

"Fuck," Jeremy breathed.

It looked like something out of a movie.

He scrolled to the next video. "Frightening footage from downtown LA today," the reporter said, "outside the Krüper building, home to Platinum Entertainment, of what was believed to be a gunshot. This development is just hours after the revelation that the FBI is investigating alleged serious stalker claims against Atrous singer Jeremy Dalton."

"Oh for fuck's sake," Jeremy said. He scrolled to the next article.

". . . singer Jeremy Dalton—"

The next one. "What was thought to be a gunshot in the Platinum Entertainment building—"

And the next. ". . . people scattering after what sounds like gunfire—"

Jeremy thumbed the screen and threw his phone at the door of the van. "Fuck."

The offending phone bounced back and landed somewhere near my feet. I understood his frustration, but I refused to pander to temper tantrums. I picked it up, not even looking to see if the screen was damaged. "Call your mom. She would've seen the news."

Jeremy growled and snatched the phone from me. "Fuuuck."

I wanted to save him from this. I wanted to protect him in ways beyond just doing my job. I wanted to console him, to hug him, to hold him.

I couldn't do any of that. So I did the next best thing I could think of. Or possibly the worst. I patted his thigh. "Did you still want me to teach you some self-defense?"

# CHAPTER SEVEN

"WILL this involve you throwing me against the wall again?"

We were on his back patio, both of us now wearing running shorts and T-shirts. Granted, his clothes probably cost ten times what mine did, but we were both barefoot.

"No. Unless you want me to?" I joked. I hadn't meant for it to sound like it did.

He didn't answer so I risked looking at him and he was fixing the tie at his waistband. "Well," he mumbled. "It was hotter than I expected. I didn't know I might have a thing for being manhandled by another guy." He looked at me then. "So it might be best if there's no wall throwing."

I stared at him.

Was he joking?

*I don't think he's joking.*

"Noted," I said. "Wall throwing to a minimum."

Jeremy just grinned. "So how do we do this?"

I couldn't believe this was happening. But it was a good distraction from the shitty day he'd had.

I just had to keep reminding my dick that this was not time for that.

Jeremy faced me, squatted, his hands up. "How's this?"

I grimaced. "If you need help with constipation, I can suggest some fiber rich food."

Riko laughed and coughed to cover it up. Jeremy glared at him, then stood up to his full height and put his hands down.

"Oh, here, I forgot this," he said, shoving his hand into his pocket and pulling out his middle finger.

I laughed and went to him. I tapped his foot with mine. "Bring your feet together. We're going to practice some breathing and movements."

Jeremy scowled at me. "If this is some Mr. Miyagi bullshit . . ."

I chuckled. "It's not."

"Tell me to say wax on, wax off and I'll have new security within the hour. Guys who let me eat burgers and don't make me cook."

I grinned at him. "Breathe in, nice and deep. I know you do all these kinds of breathing and diaphragm exercises for singing."

He rolled his eyes but he began to do some deep inhalations and slow, measured exhales. I needed him to clear his head and focus on his body, and breathing did that.

After a minute or so, I asked, "Did you do any wrestling in high school?"

He made a face. "Dude. I was on a freaking world tour when I was sixteen. Before that, I spent every high school minute in the music rooms."

"Okay, fair enough." I took his wrists and gave his arms a bit of a shake. "But you did dance."

He glared at me. "What the fuck is that supposed to mean?"

I laughed and shook his arms again. "It means you're light on your feet and you can go from bouncing on the balls of your feet to being grounded in a beat." I snapped my fingers. "You understand your center of gravity, and you have great spatial awareness. That's important for what I do."

"What is it you do? Apart from beating the shit out of people."

"I don't beat the shit out of people."

"But you could."

"Well, yeah. Sure. But that's only ever the very last resort."

"What're all the trophies for? MMA, right?"

"Yep."

"That's a bunch of different kinds, isn't it? What do you do? Like karate?"

"I never learned karate," I said. "But I always liked the discipline."

Jeremy's eyes met mine. "Discipline, huh?"

I nodded. "Yes. Karate is a great form of self-defense without a weapon." I shrugged. "Did you know karate means empty hand?"

He grinned. "Did you know karaoke means empty orchestra?"

I found myself smiling at him. And that I was still holding his wrist. I let go of him and cleared my throat. "I learned Brazilian jujitsu and Mauy Thai. I've also been teaching myself *Krav Maga*."

"Krav Maga? What is that?"

"It's a defense technique used by the Israeli Defense

Force. Also referred to as the Art of Staying Alive. It's close combat, dirty, but realistic."

"Jesus Christ. Who do you think you need to protect us from? Some foreign nationalist special forces unit?"

I laughed. "I hope not. The thing about most martial arts is that they are designed for self-protection. Which is great. But my job is not to protect myself. It's to protect other people."

"So you put yourself in between. And make yourself the target."

"Correct."

"As you did today. In the elevator. You put yourself between me and whatever was gonna come through the door."

I nodded. "Exactly. What I do with you is personal protection. I get you away from danger. All my years of MMA training taught me to attack, not retreat. So that takes some training to change that instinct."

"Defensive instead of offensive."

"Exactly. So if someone comes at you, while I might want to take them down, I have to think of getting you out of harm's way first."

"Or throwing me against the wall."

I smiled. "Yes. But you said you liked it."

He shoved me, just playfully, but I grabbed his wrist and manipulated it inward, upward. He immediately turned with it, bending down to relieve the pressure. "Ah!" he cried out.

It was an easy maneuver to incapacitate someone. If they didn't struggle, it didn't hurt.

I let him go. "See? No pressure, no strength. Just using your opponent's body and momentum against them."

"Yeah, but you're not supposed to use it on me." He

rubbed his wrist, then went to shove me again but stopped himself. "You have to teach me how to do that so I can do it to the guys."

"You're not to use these tactics on anyone. Least of all any of the guys. Okay?"

He grinned. "Sure."

"Jeremy."

He rolled his eyes. "Okay, okay. I promise."

I sighed. "Okay, so are you ready?"

He nodded, then shook his head. "You're not going to hurt me, are you? I'm too pretty to be hurt."

I laughed. "Pretty?"

"Shut up."

I was still smiling. "Okay, so if someone comes at you from the front, you need to assess a few things first. One, are they armed? Two, what kind of weapon is it? Three, check your surroundings. Four—"

His eyes narrowed. "How long do I have to do all that? Like a few minutes?"

"Well, if you're being attacked by a sloth, maybe."

Riko laughed. I ignored him. "You have half a second, maybe."

"Oh, okay, yeah no. I can't do that."

"You need to learn."

"No, that's what I have you for. I have my very own Steve for that exact reason."

I snorted. "Okay, let's assume the person coming for you is *not* armed."

"I would prefer that. I guess. If I got to choose."

"You won't get to choose, but for the sake of this exercise, okay." I stood back and raised my right arm as though I was about to swing for him.

Jeremy took a step back with his hands up. "Steve!"

Riko laughed again and I nodded to the door. "Can you go make a salad for dinner or something?"

Once Riko had finally laughed all the way inside, I turned back to Jeremy. "Okay, how about you come at me? Try a kick."

"Are you crazy?"

"You won't hurt me."

So Jeremy kicked me. Right in the fucking knee. "Ow! What the hell?"

"You said I couldn't hurt you!"

We could hear Riko laughing from in the house.

I stood up to my full height and sighed. "Okay, I should have specified."

"Are you okay?"

"I'm fine." I reset my feet. "Now, using your hands, come at me."

Jeremy made a pained face but he closed his fist and swung at me. It was a pretty good hit, but I blocked him easily, pushing his hand away and down, causing him to lose some balance. "See how I use your center of gravity against you?"

Jeremy nodded.

"Again."

So he did it again, and I blocked him again. And again, and a few more times, giving him an explanation of everything I did.

"Now you try," I said. "I'll just go slow. From the front." I pretended to aim the heel of my hand at his nose. He deflected okay, pushing my hand down across my body.

"Good. Now from the side," I said. "Turn your body this way, lower your center of gravity. You control the direction of your momentum, not your opponent."

We practiced some more, nothing serious, of course, just

some basics. I put my hands on his side, on his chest. I touched his arms, his wrists, his stomach, his hips.

God help me.

He was sweaty too, as the sun was getting low, casting an orange glow over the ocean in the distance, right up to his backyard. The light caressed his tan, giving him a glow that looked so good I wanted to taste the salt on his skin. His blond waves were damp with sweat, his cheeks were flushed.

He'd done well, but my mind was beginning to play tricks on me and I had to stop myself from doing something really stupid like sliding my hand along his neck and pulling him in for a kiss . . .

"Okay, I think we're done for today," I mumbled.

*Get a grip, Steve.*

"That was fun," Jeremy said, smiling.

We both turned at the same time to a delicious scent wafting from the house.

Steak.

"Damn, I'm hungry," he said.

"Riko must have got sick of waiting." I picked up my phone from a sun lounger. "Shit. It's late. I better get in there."

Jeremy gave me a lopsided grin. "Don't you want to cool off first?" He pulled his shirt over his head and I swallowed back a groan.

His lean torso, muscular and defined, glistened gold in the sunset. He looked kissed by sunlight, like a freaking vision.

"Just a quick dunk in the pool to cool off," he said, walking backward. "Shirt off, Steve."

Uh, no.

"You go right ahead," I said. "I need to check in. I'll freshen up inside."

He made a fake growly sound. "Such a party pooper." But he dove into the water and resurfaced a few seconds later, his hair slicked back. "Ugh that's so good."

I would have loved to be in that pool with him, swimming in the fading sunlight, like the outside world didn't exist. Like Riko wasn't inside and probably watching us. Where Jeremy would splash me and try to wrestle me under water, where I would push him against the edge, his legs wrapped around my waist. Where I would kiss him until he begged me to—

"You okay?" Jeremy asked. He splashed water in my direction but missed me.

Christ. Had I been staring?

"Yeah, I'm good. I just remembered something . . ." I turned and left, walking inside. Searing steak smelled so good. "Smells good, Riko."

He held up two fingers. "Two minutes."

I grabbed a quick and very cold shower, quickly rinsing off the sweat and dirty thoughts.

I needed to get my head in the game.

That wasn't exactly easy when Jeremy was in every corner of my mind.

I could remember how he felt pressed against me in the elevator . . .

Nope.

I shut the water off, dried myself off and changed, joining Riko in the kitchen just as he was plating up. "This looks great. Thank you."

"No problem. I'm gonna need to crash soon," he said.

"Yeah, I didn't realize the time." I looked out at the pool but clearly didn't need to ask.

Riko nodded toward the end of the kitchen. "Jeremy just went up to get changed."

"Okay, thanks." I took three water bottles from the fridge and carried them to the table, then took the plates and silverware.

"Something smells *so* good," Jeremy said as he appeared. He wore gray sweat shorts and a plain black T-shirt. His hair was still wet and he smelled like saltwater and sunshine. He had absolutely no business looking so damn good.

He sat beside me at the table and inspected his plate. "Riko, my man. What is this?"

Riko smiled at him. "Steak and salad."

Jeremy snorted. "Yeah, I can see that. I mean . . . what's in the salad?" He stabbed a forkful of salad and shoved it in his mouth.

Then he groaned, a low, guttural sound.

Christ.

Riko chuckled. "It's something my grandmother makes."

It was cabbage and carrot with some kind of crunchy noodle, slices of pear and spring onions and slivered almonds. The sauce was tangy, sweet and a little spicy.

It *was* good.

Jeremy nudged his knee against mine under the table. "Okay, so Riko's on dinner duty all the time because this is amazing."

"What's wrong with my food?"

"Well, nothing," Jeremy replied. "But is your grandmother Japanese and did she teach you how to make this?"

I snorted. "Well, no."

Jeremy devoured his entire meal and I had to wonder if he'd eaten enough during the day. Not that he'd spent hours doing choreo or long sessions in the gym, but still . . . I made a mental note to pack some kind of snack for him.

Was that weird?

Like a parent bringing snacks for their toddler?

Jeremy wasn't a kid. So why did I want to care for him? Protect him?

*Because you love him.*

That thought struck me like a blow to the gut. I put my fork down and took a sip of water.

Jeremy nudged my knee again, this time keeping his leg against mine. "You good?" he asked.

"Yeah, just didn't go down right."

Jeremy stared at me, his smile widening. "Hear that often?"

I had to think about what I'd said. Oh god. "Uh, no."

Jeremy laughed and clapped my back, and Riko, smiling, stood up and collected his plate.

"Leave it," I told him. "Jeremy's cleaning up tonight."

Jeremy's mouth opened, offended. "Jeremy is not."

I stared into his blue, blue eyes. "Jeremy is so."

He put his head on my shoulder and whined. "Steeeeve."

Riko laughed. "Good night," he said as he disappeared down the hall.

Jeremy kept his head on my shoulder, and his leg pressed to mine, and I was very aware of how he felt against me.

How alone we were.

*God, this is bad.*

"You're still washing up," I said, trying to keep my voice in check. "I don't care how cute and cuddly you are."

He chuckled, but he sat up with a sigh and started to collect plates. "You're helping."

He stacked the dishwasher, I cleaned the table and put everything else away, and when it was all done, I was very aware that it was barely eight. There were hours to fill, and it was just the two of us.

Jeremy must have been thinking the same. "So, what did you wanna do?"

If he only knew . . .

"I have emails to reply to and some things on my laptop that I need to catch up on. What about you?"

"Well, I was going to annoy you, but if you're busy . . ."

I remembered then what he'd said about being lonely. How coming back from a tour and being surrounded by thousands of people one minute to being all alone the next was hard for him. How being so isolated and not knowing who to trust was hard for him.

"How quiet can you be?"

Jeremy grinned. "Oh, like literally not at all. That's why I said 'annoy you' and not 'sit quietly with you.'"

I snorted. "Right."

I also got the feeling that he didn't want to be alone after the day he'd had.

"Fine, but I do have work I need to do."

He smiled at me in a way that made my insides melt. "Oh, I have work I could be doing too."

"Good."

Ten minutes later, I sat on one couch, he on the other. I had my laptop on my lap, checking emails, and Jeremy lay down with his long legs outstretched. Between answering and laughing at text messages to the guys, he was taking selfies.

"I should post this on my socials," he mused. "It's been a while." He turned his phone around to show me the screen. "This one or . . ." He swiped to another photo. "This one."

"I can't really see them. Not that it matters. I mean, can you ever take a bad photo? You have no bad angle."

He laughed but he rolled off the couch and came over, sitting right next to me, his legs all tucked up, his knees on my thigh. And he proceeded to show me the photos. The first one was kinda cute. Lying down, his head on a cushion, smiling and making a peace sign. The second one was a little more sexy, more of a smirk, a sultry gleam in his eye.

It was hot as hell.

"Depends," I replied, "if you're trying to make Ambrose happy, or your fans."

Jeremy laughed. "You're right. The second one it is."

"Wait," I said. "Were you told not to post anything on social media? Did Ambrose or the FBI tell you not to?"

Jeremy frowned. "No. They never mentioned it." Then he sighed. "You know, I should post something. Let the fans know I'm okay. No matter what they see on some stupid site or some made-up story on the news." He finally smiled. "And it'll piss Maddox off if I get more likes than him."

I chuckled at that. "God forbid."

"The man breathes and he trends on Twitter."

"I'd say the same about you."

He gave me a nudge. "Do you follow me on Twitter, Steve?"

I snorted at that. "Uh, no. Sorry. I really don't do social media."

"Probably smart." Then he glanced at my laptop screen. "Whatcha watching?"

"Neil sent me the link to the parking garage footage from this afternoon. Want to watch it with me?"

Jeremy glanced at me and nodded, but then he shuffled a little closer, his folded legs now fully resting on my thigh.

Trying to ignore him all but sitting in my lap, I hit the Play button.

The video began in the parking garage, this particular camera angled above the elevator doors, looking outward. It wasn't the best footage, to be honest, and the audio was even worse. But it was better than nothing.

We could see the two black vans parked at the front, and the two drivers stood by the second van, talking. Nothing unusual about that. I knew those two guys. Phil and Sayed had driven for us for years. Then we could see them talking to someone off-screen. The camera cut to show the security guard carrying a table from the booth to a utility room. "It's been broken for ages," we could hear him say.

Then he was carrying a different foldaway table back toward the booth.

"Elevator's on its way down," Sayed said, nodding toward the camera. He and Phil opened the van doors, as they always did, and got into their driver's seats.

The security guard tried to hurry, carrying the table, and we could see Riko step out and half of Robbie's foot before the security guard lost his grip and dropped the table. It hit the concrete, flat side down, which explained the bang.

But Robbie stepped backward and Riko stepped forward, pointing at the guard. The guard was apologizing and Riko hurled a string of curses at him before he pulled out his phone and pressed a button.

I hit Pause and checked the timestamp, then checked my call history. "He's calling me, see?"

Jeremy nodded.

Riko yelled at the guard some more, and the guard was

talking on his receiver at his shoulder. "Stand down, false alarm," he cried. "I dropped a table. I dropped a table."

Riko came to stand by the elevator doors again, his arms crossed, waiting. "Damn lucky it was me and not Steve," he grumbled. "He'd kick your fucking ass."

Jeremy laughed. "I've never heard Riko swear."

"He wasn't wrong, though. If it was me out there, I'd probably have kicked his ass first, asked questions later."

I clicked on the next link and this time it was the elevator footage. I was in the bottom corner by the door. Jeremy stood next to me, then Roscoe, Maddox, Robbie in the middle, and Riko by the door.

We were talking, laughing, smiling. I'd seen a whole lot of footage over the years of us in elevators, walking corridors, or exiting a building. And it took me a second to realize what was wrong with this.

I was smiling.

I even laughed.

But then the doors opened and Riko stepped out first. Robbie half disappeared from view, but then the familiar loud bang sounds. I pulled Jeremy by his arm into the corner by the door and I penned him in.

I could see now that Roscoe pushed Maddox into the corner opposite us. I didn't like that, because if a shooter had come to the door, they'd be an easy target. But Robbie stepped back in and hit the Close Door button.

I still had Jeremy pressed to the wall with my body.

I hit Pause and examined the scene on the video.

"It happened so fast," Jeremy whispered. "Like two and a half seconds, according to this footage. But it felt like forever when it happened."

I nodded. "It's funny how time does that."

He sighed. "You were pretty awesome though."

I made a face. "Mmm."

"What was bad about that?" he gestured to the screen.

"When it happened, all I could think about was protecting you, right? But seeing it now . . ." I pointed to the screen. "Robbie's completely exposed. Riko was on his own, under fire for all we knew. And Maddox and Roscoe are in full view of anyone coming through the door."

"Hey," he said gently. "You couldn't have helped that. You had no warning."

"I know, but seeing it now, all I can see are the mistakes we made."

Jeremy leaned in and studied the screen. "I dunno. All I'm seeing is you and me making out in the corner."

"Making out?"

He laughed. "It looks like you're kissing me."

I scoffed, more of a squeak, and tried to laugh it off.

"Oh my god, is that my hand on your waist?"

I didn't need to see it on-screen. I could feel the memory of it on my skin.

"Holy shit, we totally look hot." He mumbled something else under his breath that I didn't quite catch. "Jesus Christ. That shouldn't be hot, right?"

I wasn't sure what I could say . . . I actually wasn't even sure I could speak at that point.

"Hey," he asked, squinting at the screen. "Why are you facing me and not facing the door? Shouldn't you be facing the threat and not have your back to it?"

I cleared my throat. "Umm." *Fuck.* "You're right. I should have. I just didn't think. I just needed to get you out of view. So that's one more thing I did wrong."

"Hey." He sat up and frowned at me. "That's not what I meant. I didn't mean . . . you didn't do anything wrong. You went from laughing to being a human shield in a heartbeat.

It took me ten seconds to figure out what the fuck was happening, but you were already in 'assess the situation, remove the subject from harm' mode. I hadn't even had time to blink. If someone had've come through that door, you would've turned so fast the guy wouldn't have known what hit them."

I didn't agree.

He squeezed my arm. "I didn't mean anything by what I said. If you want to press me against the wall of the elevator face-first and get your grind on, that's fine."

I rolled my eyes. "I didn't get my grind on."

He just laughed and lay down, his head on the arm rest, his feet now on my lap. I had to move the laptop a bit, but he didn't seem to care. He just went back to looking at something on his phone.

I wasn't sure what the hell had just happened.

*Was it normal for someone to just put their feet in your lap? What the hell did it mean?*

I stared at the image on the screen, of me pushing him against the wall, his hand on my side, our faces so close. It did look like we were kissing. He wasn't wrong about that. I stared at it until my heart thumped like a reminder to not stare.

To not imprint that image into my memory forever . . .

I closed that screen and went back to the tour footage I'd been watching at the office. I'd only gotten ten minutes into the Berlin footage when Jeremy sighed.

"Steve," he said, ever so casually. "Why can't I find any footage of you online?"

I had to replay his question over in my head. "Of me? I'm on there plenty, apparently. The ice-cold bodyguard, or whatever they call me."

Jeremy laughed. "No, I mean, of your MMA fights. You

won state championships and whatever. I saw the trophies, and we've all seen that one fight you showed us the footage of years ago. Remember that? But now, no matter what I search, I find nothing under Steve Frost."

Fucking hell.

Fucking fuck.

"Why are you trying to search for me online?"

"I wanted to watch your fights. See how much of a badass you are and see how you really fight. Not how you pretended with me in the backyard."

"I wasn't pretending with you. I was teaching you."

He raised an eyebrow at me. "So, the videos . . . Is it because you're really old and it was all before the internet was invented?"

"Would you like another lesson without me pretending?"

"So you *were* pretending?"

"I was not."

"You're not that old."

I snarled at him.

He grinned. "You're not answering the question, Steve." He turned his phone around and there was a bunch of YouTube videos of what looked like competitive fights. "I can't find you. There's a Steven Hammond. He won some shit ages ago."

My eyes went to his, and my stomach sank to the floor.

Fuck.

Fuck.

He stared at me for a while, his smile fading. "What?"

"Steven Hammond . . ." I sighed, feeling a little ill. My mouth was dry, but god, I couldn't explain it . . . some part of me wanted him to know. "I, uh . . . I changed my name when I was nineteen."

He sat up. "What?"

"Frost is my mother's maiden name."

He blinked. "Steve . . ."

"Steve is my real name."

He shook his head and put his hand on my arm, moving closer. "No, Steve. I'm sorry. I didn't mean to pry. I was just . . . I just wanted to watch you fight . . . I didn't mean to bring up—" He stopped talking. "I'm sorry."

"It's okay," I replied. When really, it wasn't.

I wasn't.

"Jeremy," I murmured. "Do me a favor."

"Sure."

"Don't tell anyone. No one knows."

"Okay." He nodded, sad now. He chewed on his bottom lip for a second. "Can I ask why?"

I met his gaze. I saw concern in his eyes, but I couldn't give him the whole truth. Not yet. "It wasn't a good time in my life. I'd really prefer not to talk about it, if that's okay."

He nodded, but he scooted right over, hooked his arm through mine, and lay his head on my shoulder. And he stayed there, right there, cuddling me until he fell asleep.

## CHAPTER EIGHT

I'D BARELY SLEPT A WINK, and I'd barely said two words to Jeremy all morning. Not by choice. It was just the way it happened.

I didn't want things to be weird between us.

The truth was, we'd never been closer. He fell asleep on me last night on the couch until I woke him up and suggested he go to bed.

"Just wann-ed cuddle," he'd mumbled and stumbled out of the room.

It had taken a solid ten minutes before my heart rate returned to normal, and I damned near followed him up to his room . . .

If he wanted to cuddle, I'd happily lie beside him in his bed and let him cuddle me all he liked.

But I didn't.

He knew about my change of name.

He knew my old last name.

A quick Google search would tell him more about me than I'd told anyone in fifteen years. I'd left that part of my life behind for good reason.

I wanted to tell him to drop it, to never search for damn videos of my MMA days. But surely telling someone *not* to do something would make them do exactly that.

So I decided to never bring it up again. Don't mention it, just pretend it never happened, in hopes Jeremy wouldn't bring it up either.

Being busy with my phone stuck to my ear for most of the morning helped. We climbed into the van like always, I sat beside him like always, but I was on my fifth phone call of the morning before nine o'clock.

"Yeah, he'll be there at ten," I told Ambrose. "I need to speak to my team before he gets there. We're changing security detail tomorrow."

"Okay, I'll organize it. Good work, Steve."

The call ended, and I pocketed my phone.

"You're changing security detail?" Jeremy asked me. "You never mentioned that. What does that mean? And who are we all meeting with this morning?" His eyes narrowed. "Did something happen that I don't know about?"

"I might have found something in the footage," I said. "I don't know for sure, but I've asked the FBI guy to come and take a look. He's coming by at ten."

"What kind of something in the footage?"

"A person. Who doesn't seem to fit in. In the crowd."

"You picked out one weirdo in an audience?" He seemed to find that funny. "Steve, there are a lot of weirdos."

I shrugged. "Maybe."

"And what does changing security mean?"

"When it's full-time security, we should rotate out every four to five days," I explained. I nodded toward the front seat, to the back of Riko's head. "They need a break and some decent sleep. See their families. That kind of thing."

Jeremy shook his head. "I don't want anyone else."

"Riko has—"

"I'm not talking about Riko," Jeremy said. I had no doubt Riko could hear us, but Jeremy didn't seem to care. "I'm talking about you. I don't want to work with anyone but you."

Oh god.

"I'm not rotating out. I stay with you, that's the deal. For as long as it takes."

Jeremy seemed to relax then. He sat back and almost smiled. "Good."

*Christ, what does that mean?*

But then his eyebrows knitted. "How much sleep do you get a night?"

I almost laughed at the one-eighty in subject. "What?"

"You stay up till three, right? But then you're up at seven. That's not fair."

"I don't need much sleep. Never have."

"Four hours a night isn't sustainable," he declared. "You can't be at your best for any length of time when you don't sleep. Believe me, I know."

"I'll worry about sleep when this is over."

"No, tomorrow we don't have to be anywhere early," Jeremy said. "You can sleep in tomorrow. For as long as you need. Riko can babysit me."

"Riko is rotating out this afternoon. You'll have Carlos. You know him."

"Yeah . . ." He didn't seem pleased. He made a face and shook his head. "I don't know, Steve."

"About what?"

He turned in his seat and put his hand on my arm.

"Carlos is okay, but I know Riko better. And I'm used to living alone, so having people in my house is weird enough as it is without there being a revolving door. And is Carlos going to cook me his Japanese grandmother's epic salad for dinner?"

"Uh, no." Given Carlos was not Japanese . . .

"Exactly," he said with a sad pout. "I dunno. I was getting used to having you around."

Me around?

Just me?

Before I could think of something to say, Jeremy's phone chimed. It was a FaceTime from Maddox. Jeremy answered. "Hey, dickbag."

"Good morning to you too," Maddox replied. "You on your way in now too?"

"Yep. You?" The interior wall of the van behind him was clearly evident, but Jeremy asked anyway.

"Yep."

Maddox panned his phone to the left to reveal Roscoe. Roscoe was checking something on his phone but he looked up and smiled. "Morning."

"Morning," he replied, then turned his phone to show me. "Say good morning to Steve."

Maddox grinned. "Morning, Steve."

"Hey," I replied with an awkward wave.

Jeremy laughed. "What was that? Did you wave?"

"Shut up," I whispered.

Jeremy did a fake gasp, his hand to his heart. "Steeeeve."

Maddox rolled his eyes. "So anyway, I'm going to assume you haven't seen Twitter this morning."

"Nope, why? Oh shit. I posted a pic last night. I forgot." Jeremy laughed. "Freaking hell. What happened?"

"'What happened' he says," Maddox mocked. "Only

you could post a selfie, then forget it existed while the internet went into meltdown."

Jeremy snorted. "Meltdown?"

"Well, you're hotter than me now, apparently."

"Just now? I always have been, asshole."

"You're such a dick."

"That's why you love me. Because you love dick."

Maddox's middle finger filled the screen, then he disconnected the call. Jeremy chuckled and opened the Twitter app on his phone. "Oh man . . ." He grimaced. "Hashtag JeremyDalton is trending. And oh my god, so is hashtag FreeJeremy. What the hell does that mean? Free me? Like *Free Willy*? What are they freeing me from, exactly?"

"Maybe those fixated-folk who are caught up on the FBI details think they're freeing you from whatever they think the FBI is doing."

He exited out of the app and pocketed his phone, but then he sighed. He put his head on my shoulder. "I'm tired."

His hair smelled so good, and I had to stop myself from sniffing it like a creep. "You not sleeping? Or just still trying to catch up after the tour?"

"Bit of both, I think."

He sighed again and was quiet for a few blocks. He still had his head on my shoulder and I thought he'd fallen asleep, but then his phone rang. This time it was Ryan. He read the name. His thumb hovered over the Answer button, but with a groan, he let it ring out. "Fucking hell," he grumbled, still with his head on my shoulder. "I just can't deal with anything today." He switched his phone to silent and shoved his phone under his leg.

I patted his thigh and he slid his hand onto my forearm,

down to my wrist. He kept his hand there, so I kept mine on his leg.

I was surprised he couldn't hear my heart thundering.

Being with him like this, spending so much time with him, was starting to mess with my head.

My phone buzzed again, and sure enough, it was Ryan. "Thanks," I said, and Jeremy snorted.

I answered the call. "Ryan."

"Is Jer with you?"

"Yep. We're five minutes out."

"I just tried to call him. Twice."

"Yeah, look, Ryan, he's okay. He's just not up for talking right now."

There was a beat of silence. "What?"

"He said he doesn't want to deal with anything today. He has enough on his plate, don't you think?"

"Uh . . . We . . . I still have a job to do."

"Yes, you do. And so do I. We'll be there in five minutes."

I ended the call.

I had no clue if I'd just overstepped. I was leaning toward yes, but Jeremy slid his hand down my wrist to my palm and he linked our fingers.

"Thank you," he mumbled.

"You know," I suggested, "if you're not sleeping, Doctor Hardwick could probably get you something to help."

"I don't need any pills," he murmured.

"Okay."

"I just . . . I dunno. Everything's so fucked up right now."

"I know." I sighed. "Would it make you feel better if Riko and I both stayed on instead of rotating out?"

He nodded against my shoulder. "Yeah."

"Okay."

He squeezed my hand, and he didn't say anything else until we arrived. If Jeremy dozed off in those few minutes, I wasn't sure. He didn't seem too happy to have to go inside. In the elevator, he hid behind me with his forehead pressed to my shoulder blade.

He was so close, I could feel his body heat against my back.

"We'll leave early today, okay?" I said.

He nodded, and when the elevator dinged at our floor, he sighed. But as soon as we were out of the doors, Luke grabbed him and dragged him to the other guys. Maddox all but tackled him in a hug while cursing him for being more popular on Twitter.

I felt a pair of eyes cutting into me, and sure enough, I found Ryan giving me daggers. "A word?" he said.

"Sure." I didn't move. If he had anything to say to me, he could damn well say it right where we were.

I liked Ryan. I really did. The three managers did a great job. But I stood by what I said to him.

"Look," he said. "I'm sure you can appreciate my concern—"

"Of course," I replied. "And I'm sure you can appreciate mine." I glanced over to where the guys were still talking, not paying us any attention and not within earshot. "He is one hundred percent my only concern right now. When I'm with him, I do what's in his best interest. And if he doesn't want to speak to anyone, then I respect that. You should too."

"Steve—"

I kept my voice down, almost a whisper, and locked my gaze onto his. He took a small step back and I didn't care. "Ryan, I have spent every minute of the last few days with him, and I'm telling you, he's not handling this well. So cut him a fucking break."

I noticed then that Robbie was standing, watching. So was Zoe. Both ready. For what, I wasn't sure. I didn't want to cause a scene or have some kind of stand-off. But I was protective of Jeremy, right or fucking wrong.

Ryan swallowed hard, and by now, Jeremy and the guys were watching too.

"Everything cool here?" Ambrose asked from the door, clearly reading the room.

I dragged my eyes from Ryan's to Ambrose's. "Sure."

"Steve, Agent Zielinksi is here. You have something to show him?"

"Yes, I do." I turned and left, sparing a quick glance at Jeremy on my way out.

He was smiling at me.

If I got reprimanded, so be fucking it. That smile made it all worth it.

"Wanna tell me what that was about?" Ambrose asked as we walked down the corridor.

"I told Ryan to give Jeremy a break. He's not handling this whole ordeal like he's letting on."

Ambrose stopped walking. "Is he okay?"

I wasn't sure what to divulge here. There was a fine line between being honest with Ambrose for Jeremy's sake but also not abusing Jeremy's trust. "Have you ever known Jeremy to not want to deal with anything, not want to come to work, or not take phone calls from Ryan?"

"Never."

"Then you have your answer. He needs this whole ordeal to be over. And he needs a break. He needs time away from the madness."

Ambrose studied my eyes for a long second before he

conceded a nod. "Okay. We'll work that out. First, we shouldn't keep the FBI waiting."

"Hey, Steve, wait up," Jeremy called out as he walked toward us. "I want to see what you found."

If Ambrose thought that was a bad idea, he never said anything.

But then Maddox, Wes, Luke, and Blake followed. Where there was one, the other four were never far behind.

"Sure," I replied. "I don't have a problem with that."

---

ALL THE GUYS, Agent Zielinski, and Ambrose watched the footage I'd timestamped. This same woman was in the crowd watching the band get out of cars, entering hotels, waving at their fans, but she was not cheering, not yelling, not even smiling in three different countries. In LA, in London, and I found her again in Tokyo footage this morning.

And that was just the footage I had access to. I had no idea if she was in any other location, or any concert crowds.

"I know it's not unusual for fans to travel to see the band. Some fans do the entire tour, every country," I explained. "But they're typically excited and they want the band to know who they are, right? They don't stand there like that." I gestured to the screen, where this particular woman was now frozen. "That is a look of disdain. Now, maybe that's just her face. I don't know. But three countries. The US, England, and Japan. That's a very big and very expensive effort to go to just to stand in the front line with that kind of contempt."

Jeremy snorted. "Just her face. Nice, Steve."

I shrugged, but his smile made me happy.

Zielinski chewed on the inside of his lip for a moment, but then he nodded. He was studying the screen for a beat too long. "I agree. It's worth looking into. Can I get a copy of this?" he asked. He smiled at me. "Good work."

"This is just crowd footage," I added. "It was all I asked to see. And I didn't even get all the way through it. I noticed her in LA, thought it was weird. Noticed her in London. Twice is a coincidence, but a third time is a pattern. As soon as I saw her in Tokyo, I'd seen enough. There are still a few hours left to watch. I can get through them tonight if you want. I just wanted to let you know what I found before I wasted another day."

Zielinski gave a nod and turned to Ambrose. "I'll need to double check ticket sales information, such as names and credit card info to identify the repeats. I'm assuming a ticketing agency was used for that. Can you get me that?"

Ambrose nodded. "Of course."

"I'm going to need a copy of all this footage, including the timestamps Steve marked. I'll have our team go over it. Steve, you're more than welcome to keep watching." Zielinski smiled at me. "More eyes looking the better."

"Sure." I'd have about five hours to kill tonight after Jeremy went to bed.

"Don't we have plans tonight?" Jeremy asked.

I turned to him. What the hell? "Uh, do we?"

He aimed a cheeky smirk right at me. "Yeah, we have another martial arts lesson, and then you get to cook me dinner."

I stared at him. Because what the fuck was he playing at?

"No, it's your turn to cook dinner," I mumbled, trying not to be embarrassed.

"The fuck?" Luke asked Jeremy, stunned and a little

offended. "He cooks for you?" Then he stared at Blake. "How come Jason and Zoe don't cook for us?"

Blake shrugged. "Because you guys know Jeremy can't cook for shit."

Luke considered this, then nodded. "True."

"Though I have to say, Robbie's never cooked for us either," Maddox added. "I might have to suggest a roster or something."

Jeremy shook his head slowly. "Guys, I gotta tell ya, Riko made a salad that I'm never gonna stop talking about."

"Riko cooks too?" Blake cried.

"Ah, guys," Ambrose said. "Can we focus here? I don't think Agent Zielinski needs to be here for this conversation."

The guys all shut up, but Jeremy met my eyes and his smile was smug, as if he'd accomplished whatever it was he'd set out to do.

I would have to ask him about it later.

"Now," Zielinski said, clapping his hands so the attention drew back to him. "The incident I saw on the news last night? An issue in the parking garage?"

"It wasn't gunfire," Ambrose was quick to say.

I nodded. "I requested the footage of that as well, and the crowd that had gathered earlier in the day at the front of the building," I admitted.

"You should see the footage of inside the elevator, when Steve goes into Steve-mode," Jeremy added. "Not gonna lie, it was kinda hot."

Oh my god.

Jeremy?

Maddox whacked him with the back of his hand and laughed. "Dude, what the fuck?"

Grinning, Jeremy shrugged, but he looked directly at

Zielinski, which was odd. Something was definitely going on inside that pretty head of his, but now was not the time to unpack any of that.

I did my best to ignore the guys and focused on Zielinski. "I couldn't find anything out of the ordinary in the garage footage. It did appear to just be a guard who dropped a table, which sounded like gunfire, yes. I wanted to make sure there was no one around who shouldn't have been there, checking for reaction times, that kind of thing. I couldn't find anything or anyone in the crowd footage either. But I'm not an expert."

"You found that woman just fine," Zielinski said wryly.

"I know crowds and how to read people. But I can't tell you if footage has been doctored or altered."

Zielinski's eyes narrowed. "Do you think the footage has been altered?"

I put my hand up. "No. God, not at all. I'm just saying I wouldn't know if it was. I'm not a digital forensic person. People, crowds, individuals, I can read. But all that tech stuff is out of my realm of expertise. Don't take my word on anything. Have your experts look at it."

"I will, thanks," Zielinski replied.

He and Ambrose began discussing the transfer of files and information and I turned back to the screen, which still had the woman's face on it. "Uh, Agent Zielinski, can I ask you something?"

He smiled and came to stand by me. "It's, uh, Special Agent. But sure, ask away."

I pointed to the screen but kept my eyes on *Special* Agent Zielinski. "This woman, do you recognize her?"

His eyes darted to mine. "Why do you ask?"

"Because when you first saw this footage, you did a

double take. Super quick and you hid it kind of well, but I'm guessing this woman is already on your watch list?"

He held my gaze but raised his chin, just slightly. So that was a yes.

Jeremy was suddenly standing beside me. "Is this her? The one that was questioned and released?"

Zielinski looked at Jeremy, then back at me. His expression was stoic while he clearly weighed what to say. Then he relaxed, decision made. "It's not the woman we questioned," he said quietly.

Hmm. "It's not?"

He shook his head and glanced at the screen like he needed to confirm something in his mind. When he turned to us, he looked right at Jeremy. "It's the sister."

The sister . . .

A shiver ran down my spine. "The sister of the woman you questioned? That spilled all the details about the superfan with the crazy wallpaper of Jeremy?"

Zielinski gave a hard nod. "I'll be asking surveillance for a formal identification, but I'm sure it's her."

# CHAPTER NINE

I'D RECEIVED a phone call from Gerald Dubrowski to let me know the security cameras he'd ordered had arrived. It was a good excuse to leave early, and when I told Jeremy, he stood up and said his goodbyes.

The meeting with Zielinski seemed to put Jeremy in a weird mood. Well, he was weird during the meeting with Zielinski. And afterwards, after the revelation that the face I'd spotted in the crowd was known to the FBI, he was quiet. Pissed off, even.

He was quiet in the van, choosing to scroll on his phone for a while, and when that pissed him off too, he huffed.

"You okay?" I asked, knowing he wasn't, but giving him an opening.

"Agent fuckwit," he said. "Sorry, Special Agent fuckwit. He corrected you. I thought you might've at least given him the death stare."

"I misaddressed him. If he's earned that rank, then—"

"He's fucking useless."

Okay, wow. He was pissed off.

"He would've had no idea that woman followed us

around the fucking world if you hadn't pointed it out. You found her. Not him. Not the FBI."

"It was luck on my part," I said, trying to play it down. "They would have found it. I just helped."

He glared at me and clenched his jaw shut. He was clearly really pissed about something.

"Jeremy, what's wrong?"

"Nothing."

"Okay."

He huffed. "What do you mean, *okay*?"

"You clearly don't want to talk about it and I'm not going to push. You want to talk about it, I'll listen. If you don't want to tell me, in particular, then maybe I'm better off not hearing it."

He glared. "The fuck, Steve?"

I took a deep breath and tried for some patience. "I know everything is stressful right now, but I think your anger directed at the FBI agent trying to help—"

"Special agent," Jeremy snapped. "Don't forget the special. Apparently it's important. More like nothing-special agent."

Okay, so Jeremy was in a mood. And maybe he was entitled to be. His entire life was under a microscope and someone was fixated on him, and not in a good way.

I could give him a little grace. I was happy to let this go and give him some time to cool down.

"Have you eaten?" I asked, changing the topic. "I packed some trail mix for you as a snack, in case your blood sugar got low."

He rolled his eyes and sighed. "I feel fine."

Okay then.

"Riko will be back around six," I said. "He said he's happy to stay on instead of rotating out, but he wanted to surprise his girlfriend at work, take her some flowers or something, then grab some clean clothes on his way to your place."

Jeremy mumbled something under his breath, then he growled, "Fucking hell."

"Jeremy," I tried.

"I don't need a babysitter. And can you stop doing thoughtful shit when I'm trying to be mad at you?"

"Mad at me? What did I do?"

"Nothing-special agent Zielinski was checking you out. That's what you did."

I had to replay that over a few times in my head to try and make sense of it.

What the actual fuck?

"Okay, one—no, he wasn't. Two—even if he was, what someone else may or may not have done has nothing to do with me. I'm not responsible for that. And three—I'm not interested in him. And four." I held up four fingers. "And this is the really important one. What the actual fuck, Jeremy?"

"I don't know!" he yelled.

"I don't know either! What the hell am I in trouble for?"

"Because I . . ." He groaned and ran his hands through his hair. "I don't fucking know. I don't . . . Gawd!"

Okay, so this was new.

Was he jealous?

Roscoe's words came back to me . . .

*"I've never seen him with anyone like he is with you. He laughs a lot with you, and he's a bit touchy-feely with you . . .*

*"I'm just telling you what I see. And if he is truly straight, then maybe he's caught some feelings that might freak him out at some point? I don't know. I guess I'm just saying with everything that's going on, with the stalker and*

*the FBI, and now maybe this? He's dealing with a lot. Just if you weren't aware, now you are."*

Maybe he'd caught some feelings . . .

Christ.

It was the worst possible time for this. Then again, if there was no stalker and I wasn't spending every second of every day with him, he wouldn't be *catching feelings* and quite possibly questioning his sexuality.

Fucking hell.

"Jeremy," I murmured.

"Forget about it. I don't know what's fucking wrong with me."

"Nothing's wrong with you," I said. "Nothing at all."

He dug the heels of his hands into his eyes and scrubbed over his face, clearly agitated. So I took his hand and gave it a squeeze.

"You're allowed to be stressed and all out of sorts, Jeremy. We'll get this stalker shit all squared away and life'll return to normal."

He played with my fingers. "I don't even know what normal is anymore."

"Making music and writing songs, hanging out with the guys, that kind of thing."

"Hmm."

I knew the changing dynamics of the band bothered him. Maddox had Roscoe, Wes had Amy, and Luke and Blake were still the partying, sex-crazed guys they were eight years ago. They had so many women they could honestly install a deli ticket dispenser at their front door.

But not Jeremy. It used to be him and Maddox. And they still were best friends, but that dynamic had changed too.

Everything was changing for Jeremy, and that had to be rough.

"You know, you should invite Maddox over. Or all the guys," I said.

"Hmm."

"For dinner. Have a few beers, grill some steaks." I shrugged, not sure what else to suggest. "Or order the entire menu from that Korean BBQ place you like."

He almost smiled. "Maybe. I miss the studio days. Sitting around, writing songs, lyrics, melodies."

"When this stalker shit is over, you should go up to the ranch for a bit. All of you. Get out of this city, away from it all. Sit around the campfire with your guitars and do what you love."

He let his head fall back with a groan. "Can we go now?"

I rubbed my thumb over the back of his hand. "Not sure. We should ask. Your schedule next week is pretty tight. The week after that is prep for the award show next month, is it not?"

He mumbled something under his breath that ended with a resigned, "Don't fucking know."

"Maybe after the award show, you could all take a week."

"They're probably busy," he murmured.

"They will cancel anything for you." I threaded our fingers. "They would do anything you ask, anything you need."

He sighed and put his head on my shoulder, like he had this morning. "I'm not mad at you anymore."

I snorted. "Glad to hear that. Considering I did nothing wrong."

"But that nothing-special agent can go fuck himself. He

can find himself his own Steve. This one's busy."

Warmth bloomed from my heart, in my blood, along my veins.

He *was* jealous.

I liked that way, way more than I should have.

"I am busy," I murmured.

And in relation to Agent Zielinski, by *busy*, I meant *not interested*. I certainly didn't notice him eyeing me, not that I was looking. I was more caught off guard by Jeremy's weird reaction to him. Which even Maddox thought was odd.

Jeremy was freaking jealous.

I was trying to figure out what to say next, without making it weird, without scaring him even more, when his hand relaxed in mine and his head felt a little heavier.

He'd fallen asleep on me again, still holding my hand. It made me stupidly happy and it did crazy things to my heart, not to mention my head.

I committed every second of it to memory—the feel of his fingers, the weight of him leaning against me, knowing he was doing this because I made him feel safe.

When this was all over, I'd have moments like this to look back on. I was half tempted to tell Sayed to keep driving, take the scenic route, just to keep the van moving so Jeremy could get some sleep, but we had to get back to his house for the security upgrade.

When we finally pulled up at his house, I squeezed his hand and nudged the top of his head with my chin. "Jeremy," I murmured. "You're home."

He stirred awake and looked around, confused. "Shit. Did I fall asleep?"

"Go get some rest," I suggested, "while I meet with the security camera guy."

"Hmm."

I led the way inside his house and he headed straight toward his room. He was out of my sight for all of five seconds when he let out a yelp, followed by, "Argh, fuck!"

I dropped my backpack and raced up the stairs to his room, bursting in, ready for anything. Jeremy was standing by the wall, leaning against it but bent over.

There was no obvious threat. Certainly no one else in his room—the glass doors were still locked.

"What's wrong?" I asked, possibly too close, crowding him against the wall. "Jeremy, are you hurt?"

"Yes!" he cried. "I kicked my fucking toe." He was trying to stand up, trying to hold his foot. "Ow."

I almost laughed but managed not to. "Come here," I said, putting my arm around his shoulder and helping him to his bed. He sat down and lifted his left foot, and honestly, if it had been anyone else, I'd have probably called them an idiot and left them to it. But this wasn't anyone else. So I kneeled down and examined his foot.

His two smallest toes looked a little red and even a bit scratched. "How'd you do it?"

"Door."

"Can you move your toes?" He wiggled all his toes. "You're fine."

He pouted. "It hurt like a bitch."

"Did you want me to get you an ice pack?"

He shook his head. And it was not lost on me, the position we were in right now. He was sitting on the edge of his bed and I was on my knees at his feet. Between his legs . . .

I stood up and was half tempted to assist him in lying down, but that *would* have been weird. It was already weird that I was in his room with him.

"Have a nap," I said instead.

"A nap? Am I five?"

"Do you know how many adults would kill to be able to take a nap during the day?"

He smiled and fell back on the bed, his arms wide, his feet still on the floor. "I am fucking tired, though."

God, his thighs, his slim waist, his arms out in a 'have me however you want' kind of way.

Fucking hell. I needed to not be here.

"Rest, nap, sleep, whatever," I said, walking toward the door. "But you're still making dinner tonight."

As I went down the stairs from his room, I heard his whiny, "But Steeeeve." It made me smile but I didn't go back.

I met with Gerald Dubrowski and his team that were doing the install of the upgraded security cameras, and by the time that was done and he'd shown me the computer software and we'd sorted out access codes to the footage, it was getting late.

I hadn't seen Jeremy in a few hours and I assumed he'd taken that nap, but then I heard music drifting from the living room. Or, more specifically, coming from the grand piano.

I left the laptop and followed the sound, and sure enough, Jeremy was sitting at the piano. He was skimming his fingers across the keys so effortlessly, the music complex and soulful.

I stood, leaning against the doorway, and watched him play. His profile, the afternoon sunlight, the music. It was something I hadn't heard before, certainly nothing of theirs. Something he was working on?

"Is that new?" I asked quietly.

His fingers stilled, the music jarred to a stop. "Sorry. I forgot—"

"Don't apologize. It was beautiful."

He looked at me then, with an odd expression. Something a mix of awkward and painful. "It's new. Something I've had in my head for a while. Decided to try it today."

"Then I'm honored to be the first to hear it."

He put his hands back on the keys but was reluctant to keep playing.

"Did you want me to go?" I asked. "Sorry. I didn't mean to interrupt."

He shook his head. "Come and sit here." He scooted to one side and patted the seat next to him.

I did as he asked, though I was so nervous, I was surprised my feet carried me. I sat beside him, our sides touching. He put his hands back on the keys, took a deep breath, and began to play.

It was soulful, yes. But there was a torment to it, a sadness. Uncertainty, even.

The way he moved his body when he played, I could tell he felt every note. It came from inside him, from his bones and his heart, somewhere deep. From something he'd experienced, something that left a scar.

Every note rang in the quiet of the house, reverberating and echoing, like a private concert just for me.

His long, elegant fingers caressed the piano like a well-practiced lover, and his body moved as he played. He was lost in this song.

Sitting right there beside him in the fading sunlight, being witness to such a personal thing, I fell in love with him a little more.

It struck something in me I couldn't explain.

When the final note rang out, he lowered his hands to his lap and waited for me to speak.

I had to swallow the lump in my throat. "You know

when you miss something you never had? When you feel like you've lost something you can't explain?"

Jeremy's eyes met mine.

"That's what that music feels like."

He gasped out a breath. His eyes were glassy. *Christ, was he about to cry?* "Steve." Then he shook his head and laughed at himself. "That's exactly what it is. How did you know to say that? I thought you were going to say it was nice or lovely."

"Jeremy, I've been with you guys now for a lot of years. I know when you like the songs you sing. Some songs, some music you sing, you perform, and you do it perfectly. But then there are some songs that you love, that you feel, and it shows."

He stared at me, his eyes darting between mine, like he was trying to tell if I was serious or not.

"And you feel this song."

He quickly turned back to the keys, as if looking at me was too much. "I do."

"What's it called?"

"It doesn't have a name," he whispered. "I don't know what to call it."

"Well, thank you for playing it for me."

And then, whether it was because of how close we were sitting or everything that'd happened these last few days—the hand-holding, his head on my shoulder, his jealousy—or how personal this moment was, I murmured, "I don't know who you wrote it for, but you should tell them."

His gaze shot to mine, blue eyes piercing, searching. He opened his mouth . . .

And my phone rang.

Fucking hell.

Fuck!

Jeremy startled and put his hands back to the keys, but then shoved them in his lap, clearly nervous. The connection, the moment we'd just had was lost, so I pulled out my phone.

It was Riko, needing to be let in. I didn't want to walk away from Jeremy right that second but had little choice. After I'd let Riko in, I went back to the piano room to find Jeremy gone.

I didn't want things to be awkward between us, and I certainly didn't want him to feel he had to hide from me in his own house. So I had a choice—I could let him hide, I could hide from him, or I could make it not awkward. I opted for the last one.

I knocked on his door. "Jeremy?"

It took a second for his door to open. He chewed on the inside of his lip. "Yeah? Wassup?"

"Dinner, and you're cooking."

He stared, and I grinned and eventually he smiled back. "You are a pain in the ass," he said flatly. "Can I swap security with Robbie or Zoe? They don't make anyone cook."

"Nope. You're stuck with me. Ever made tacos before?"

He made a face. "Not very well. And at the risk of sounding very privileged, why would I try something that I will undoubtedly fuck up when the very good folks at any Mexican place do it all so exceptionally well?"

I nodded toward the stairs. "Come on, it's dinnertime."

He whined but he followed me down to the kitchen where, for the next hour, we made tacos. And a huge mess. But being with him in the kitchen was fun. It was so easy to be with him like that. We stood close, touching some of the time, almost touching most of the time, and we laughed a lot.

He asked how to slice most things and I had to help him

with the fish because he flat-out refused, but as we got it done, all awkwardness between us was gone.

And the tacos were good!

"You know, these aren't bad," Riko said after he'd eaten his fourth one.

"He can actually cook," I added, giving Jeremy a smile. "He's good at it too."

Jeremy glowered at me. "I'm actually disappointed in myself for enjoying cooking. And if you tell anyone that I just said I enjoy cooking, I'll deny everything and request you do security detail with Luke and Blake."

I snorted at that. "Your secret is safe with me."

He did the glowering thing again. "You're washing up."

I laughed. "That's fine."

Riko chuckled but he took his plate to the kitchen. "Hate to eat and run, but I gotta catch some Z's."

His smile told me he wasn't sorry at all. "No worries. And thank you for staying on."

"No problem at all."

"Yeah, thanks," Jeremy said quietly.

Riko gave a nod and disappeared down the hall, and Jeremy's mood took an obvious nosedive, and he collected his plate and took it into the kitchen.

I began stacking the empty trays and plates when a loud smash rang out. "Agh! Fuck!"

I ran to the kitchen. "Jeremy."

"Everything okay?" Riko called out, clearly hearing the noise.

"I'm okay," Jeremy called out. "Just a plate. And a glass. Fucking hell."

"I got it," I said. Jeremy stood in his kitchen, barefoot, with shards of shattered crockery and glass everywhere.

"Stay there. Don't move," I said, stepping into the mess. I stood in front of him. "Hold on."

"Uh . . ."

I lifted his hands to my shoulders, then with my hands under his ass, I hoisted him up onto my hips, then transferred him to the kitchen counter and stood right between his thighs. He was lighter than I imagined. Closer, too.

"Oh," he breathed.

"This is . . ." *So wrong? So right? Everything I ever wanted?* "Uh, this is why I wear shoes," I said, taking a step back. "Let me get this cleaned up."

I swept up what I could, then I saw Jeremy was picking at the sole of his foot.

"Did you get some glass stuck in there?"

"I think so. It's on the side."

I took his foot and I could see the tiny shard of glass. "Hold still," I murmured and I tried to pull it out.

"Ow!" he pulled his foot back, pouting. "Steve. Ouchies."

Christ.

I grumbled at him. "I don't have nails."

"We need tweezers."

"Do you have a first aid kit?"

"I have no idea."

"Scissors?"

His eyes widened. "For *what*?"

"To pull it out?"

"We're not in a war zone, Steve. We don't need to improvise. I have eyebrow tweezers in my bathroom because I'm not a heathen. And Didi will not allow a unibrow."

Didi was the make-up team leader. Very short, very feisty. Everyone adored her.

Jeremy touched his eyebrow. "And honestly, I'm gentler than she is so I just do it myself."

I laughed and turned around, taking his legs in a piggy-back-style.

"What are you doing?"

"I'm going to carry you to your bathroom. Unless you'd like to walk through the really fine glass dust the dustpan missed?"

He put his arms around my neck and chest and I lifted him easily.

"Are you going to lecture me about not wearing shoes in the house?"

I snorted. "No."

"But this is why you wear them?"

"Yep. If I have to carry you through broken glass or twisted metal, we're not going to get far if I'm barefoot."

"Ooh, like *Die Hard*." Then he did a terrible German accent. "'Shoot the glass!'"

It made me laugh. "Exactly."

I went up the stairs to his room. "Christ, Steve. How much can you bench press? You just carried me up those steps as if I weighed nothing." Then, holding on with just one arm, he gave my biceps a squeeze. "Okay, Mr. Muscle."

"Ah." I jerked my arm away. "If you could not tickle me while I'm carrying you, that'd be great."

He laughed. "You're ticklish? Oh my god, that's awesome."

"I am ticklish, but just so you know, if you tickle me, I am not responsible for your injuries."

He laughed again, this time warm and breathy against my ear.

I went into his room and nudged the bathroom door

open with my foot. Then I went to his toilet and knocked the seat down, also with my foot.

"Holy shit, you have Mr. Miagi balance," he said, as I turned and lowered him to the seat. "Have you considered doing one of those reality TV shows for combat training? I bet you'd kick ass."

I ignored that. "Tweezers?"

He pointed to the cabinet, top drawer on the left. "In the bag."

I opened the drawer, and sure enough, there was a travel toiletry bag.

"I don't bother unpacking it," he said.

I handed it to him. I didn't want to go through his toiletries.

God, what if there were condoms in there?

He handed the tweezers to me. "You're not going to do it?" I asked.

He shook his head. "Nope. Can't reach it."

He freaking could so.

I kneeled down in front of him and put his foot on my thigh and plucked the tiny piece of glass out, dropping it into the wastepaper basket. A small dot of blood pooled at the puncture, so I took a few squares of toilet paper and dabbed it. "All done."

He plonked his other foot onto my thigh. "Can you check my other one?"

Smiling, I shook my head at him. "You're enjoying this a little too much."

He smirked. "I could say you might have a thing for feet, given this is the second time today."

"Or you could stop hurting yourself." I ran my hand over his foot, top and bottom, and he didn't recoil, which meant no splinters. "You're fine. Now I'll need the vacuum cleaner so I can finish the kitchen floor."

He made a face. "Uh, try the utility room?"

"How do you not know where your vacuum cleaner is?"

He made another face.

I sighed. "How do you not even know if you have a vacuum cleaner?"

"Because I don't use it." He scowled at me. "You're awfully judgmental."

I stood up and held my hand out, which he took, and I pulled him to his feet. "How does that feel?"

"Fine. Thank you. I don't know how I dropped the plate. I went to put it down and kinda missed the counter, tried to catch it with the drinking glass."

"It's no worries. I'm just glad you weren't hurt."

"Can you give me a piggyback ride back down the stairs?"

"Absolutely not."

He laughed. "It was worth a try."

"And I wasn't being judgmental," I said. "I was—"

"You were being judgmental."

"Okay, maybe a little bit."

He sighed. "Steve, I don't know half the shit that goes on in my life. I have people that do everything. Not that I want them to. It's just the way it is. People who organize schedules, who tell me what to wear, how to pose, what to say. Hell, someone has brought me coffee every day for the last however many years. I only learned the other day that I can actually make the iced coffee I drink."

"You can make it," I said. "And you can cook. And clean up a kitchen, and you're about to learn how to vacuum."

His mouth fell open. "My foot is really sore." He faked a limp. "Ouch."

I lightly shoved his shoulder. "You're so full of shit."

He laughed and went down the stairs ahead of me. "Let's go look in the utility room. I *do* know where that is."

We did find a vacuum cleaner, and I quickly ran it over the kitchen floor because Jeremy argued he wasn't wearing shoes. So he sat on the counter and kept me company, and when I was done, I made him help load the dishwasher.

He complained the whole time but he was also kind of smiling, and to be honest, I loved that he was hanging out with me. "What are you doing now?" he asked. "We could practice more self-defense?"

"We could," I allowed, and to be honest, the idea of doing some kind of physical contact with him was very appealing to me. But that voice in the back of my mind told me it was a bad idea. "I told Agent Zielinski I'd watch the rest of the footage."

"You mean Special Agent. Nothing-Special Agent."

I smiled. "Yes, him."

He narrowed his eyes at me and hummed. "Then I'm watching it with you."

His jealousy at the mere mention of Zielinski's name made me happy. It was ridiculous and unfounded, but I liked it nonetheless.

"Fine."

We parked up on his couch and I put my laptop on the coffee table. Within five minutes, he put a throw cushion on my thigh and lay down, his head in my lap.

That wasn't normal *friend* behavior, was it?

That wasn't typically what a straight guy did with another guy, was it?

Did I like that he was comfortable with me? Of course. Did I like that he felt free enough to put his head on my lap? Hell yes, I did.

I tried not to wonder why he was being clingy with me. I tried not to read too much into it. He'd admitted to feeling alone and being lonely, and the whole stalker thing would be enough to send any person a little crazy.

He obviously needed some human contact, so I rested my arm on his shoulder and he never said a word.

In fact, I think he smiled.

We watched some footage, starting back in Japan. Next was South Korea, and Jeremy was sound asleep by the time we got to the Singapore footage.

I rubbed his arm and I wanted to run my fingers through his hair so badly. But I didn't.

I probably should have woken him up and told him to go to bed. I didn't do that either.

I wanted to savor this moment forever. That was creepy of me, I realized, because he was asleep. But god, I'd loved this man for years and he fell asleep with his head in my lap. I wasn't cutting that short for anyone.

His blond hair, his stubble, his pink lips.

He looked like a sleeping angel.

I somehow managed to concentrate on the footage some more and found one screen of a possible sighting of the stalker. The image was grainy so I couldn't be sure, but I sent off another email to Agent Zielinski with the time-stamp and screenshot of the image. He could verify and investigate.

My job was to look after Jeremy. The close contact kind.

God, I was letting my mind wander to dangerous ground. It wasn't exactly wandering alone, given Jeremy had planted himself on my lap and fallen asleep.

We were up to day five, and I was losing focus. I needed to fine-tune and concentrate and stop allowing my heart to overrule my head.

What I needed was a workout session, like a good ten miles on a treadmill and a sparring session with one of the MMA instructors. I needed to expend some constructive energy and get my mind off Jeremy, which wasn't easy, considering he was asleep in my lap.

It wasn't as if I could go for a run outside. I couldn't leave the grounds. And the treadmill would be loud as hell at—I checked my watch—two o'clock in the morning.

But maybe I could do a few laps of the pool.

It might also help me sleep.

I did a check on the new security screens, and seeing absolutely nothing out of the ordinary, I carefully lifted Jeremy's head and propped a comfortable cushion under his head. His soft snore told me he was still fast asleep. So I changed into some gym shorts, grabbed my towel and went to the backyard.

The days were still warm, given it was November, but the nights were a little chilly.

I edged into the cool water and began swimming a few laps. The burn in my lungs felt good, the stretch of my muscles felt amazing, and I settled into a rhythm. Even strokes, measured breaths, lap after lap, until I felt someone watching me.

I stopped at the deep end of the pool to find a tired and confused Jeremy walking out the back door and coming toward the pool.

"Hey," I said, keeping my voice kinda low.

"Steve, the fuck are you doing? It's two thirty in the damn morning."

"I needed to do some exercise. Sorry. I should have asked if I could use your pool."

"I would be offended if you asked. You can use anything here. You don't need to ask."

"Did I wake you?"

"No. I woke up on the couch and the back door was open. Figured you were out here. Maybe scoping out a bad guy or something."

Jesus. "How about next time you think there could be a bad guy out here that you don't come looking?"

He grinned. "Then who'd save you?"

I smiled back at him. "Riko."

He gasped, offended. "Rude. Possibly true, but still rude. I would come save you."

I clung to the edge, not really wanting to get out in front of him.

"Is the water cold? I'm just not convinced I should get in." He came to the edge and dipped is toe in. "It's not too bad."

Then, to my absolute horror and delight, he pulled his shirt over his head and dove in. He surfaced, his hair slicked back, his smile wide, and he treaded water. The moonlight glimmered off the water, off his skin, and my god, I'd never seen anything so perfect.

"How many laps you do already?" he asked.

I kept my back to the side wall of the pool, keeping my chest underwater. "I wasn't counting."

"Do you swim often?"

"Not as often as I'd like. I forgot how nice it is. Beats a treadmill."

"If you wanna do more, I'll keep count."

"Nah, I think I'm done. I probably should've waited until Riko was up and on duty. I mean, there are sensor alarms on the new security system, so I'd hear if someone tried to break in."

He swam over to me and hung onto the edge of the

pool. "How can something happen to me when I'm here with you?"

We were probably too close. And too alone. My blood buzzed with anticipation.

Why was he looking at me like that?

Was he closer?

This wasn't good. Was I imagining this? Was I seeing something that wasn't there? Something that could never happen?

I wasn't blind, and I wasn't stupid. I could read people and see the intent in their eyes.

He was definitely looking at me some kind of way.

It wasn't wishful thinking.

But confusion also flickered in his eyes. Trepidation, maybe even a little fear.

This wasn't good.

Tension bloomed between us, the distance between us seemed to narrow, and his gaze went to my lips.

Fucking hell.

"I should get out," I whispered. "Before Riko gets up."

I planted my hands on the edge of the pool and lifted myself out, hoping to god he didn't watch. Or maybe there was enough shadow to hide in.

But of course he lifted himself out of the pool easier than what I'd done.

I went for the towel I'd brought out, realizing there was only one at the same time Jeremy seemed to realize that as well.

He made a dash for it but I was quicker, pulling the towel to cover myself. "Gotta be faster than that," I joked, holding the towel to my chest.

But he wasn't smiling.

He was staring at my abdomen. At my torso. At my disfigured skin.

I hadn't been quick enough.

"Jesus Christ," he breathed. He gently moved the towel, then took it from me. I let the towel go, every bit as scrutinized as I felt. He ran his fingers along my side, over my ribs, and along the three deep and jagged scars, his touch warm on my cold skin. His gaze cut to mine, eyes wide and concerned. "Steve, what the hell happened to you?"

# CHAPTER TEN

"IT'S, uh . . . It was a long time ago . . ." I took a step back from him. I wanted his touch, craved it, even. The way his thumb sent a wake of goosebumps across my skin was something I would never forget. But I couldn't tell him.

I didn't want that secret, that life, to upend this life I'd made for myself.

"Steve?" Riko's voice drifted from inside.

"Ah, yeah. Coming in now," I called out.

He appeared at the door, squinting into the darkness, confused at seeing Jeremy with me. "Oh. Everything okay?"

"Yeah. I just wanted to get in a few laps before bed," I replied.

Now, I had a choice. I could wrap the towel around me so Riko didn't see my scars, but that would leave Jeremy out here with no towel at all. And his comfort would win every time.

I handed the towel to him and walked back inside, knowing damn well Jeremy could now see the scars on my back as well. And Riko could see the scars on my front, and when I walked past him, he no doubt saw my back.

I didn't care.

I just needed to leave.

I made it to my room, showered under water as hot as I could stand it, trying not to panic, not to let it all unravel, and finally crawled into bed.

Tomorrow, things would be different.

In the last week, Roscoe figured out I was gay, Jeremy knew my old name, and now Jeremy and Riko had seen my scars. There was no undoing this.

I'd spent a decade keeping a lid on all this for a very good reason. It had ended my last career and it had almost ended me.

I didn't want to relive that, and I didn't want it to become public knowledge. It was potentially another scandal that Platinum didn't need right now.

Not to mention that Jeremy had enough on his plate without me adding to it. I shuddered to think how Jeremy would react.

What he would think of me . . .

As I tried to sleep, all I could see was him, dripping wet, body glistening by the soft house lights, the concern clear on his face as he touched my scars.

I never let anyone touch my scars.

Tomorrow, everything would be different.

Needless to say, I didn't sleep much.

---

I DRAGGED my tired ass out to the kitchen by seven, after maybe two hours' sleep. Riko was at the dining table, and he stood up when he saw me. "I just made fresh coffee."

"Thanks," I mumbled. "So I'm going to need to go past my place this morning. Probably best to do it before Jeremy even gets up. He won't surface for a while yet. You all right to stay here with him? I won't be long."

"Yeah, sure," he replied. "Everything okay?"

"Yeah, I just need to pick up a change of clothes, that kind of thing."

"Oh, sure."

I thumbed out a message to the transport team, and Sayed had arrived before I finished my second coffee. I avoided eye contact with Riko, and to be honest, I was aiming to avoid any contact with Jeremy.

I just wasn't ready for it.

"Just you today," Sayed said as he opened my door.

"Yep, just me. Any papzz at the gates this morning?"

He shook his head. "None this morning. Maybe they got sick of waiting."

"Let's hope so."

But he was right. The gate entering into the estate was clear. Maybe other celebs in Jeremy's community got sick of the harassment and had the cops move them along. I didn't know. I was just glad they were gone.

I checked my email and messages on the way to my place, and I even scrolled through the usual social media sites for anything related to Jeremy.

His usual fans and Atrous fans were still commenting and posting photos and memes, but he wasn't trending this morning.

His schedule was clear today. A rare day off. I hoped he'd sleep through most of it.

I ducked into my place, grabbed everything I'd need for a few more days at least. The FBI had a new lead with the sister, so in all likelihood this full-time security gig would be over.

When I got back to Jeremy's, the house was silent and

Riko was on the couch in front of the CCTV split screen. "Hey," I said, dropping my bag near the hall. "Jeremy been up?"

He shook his head. "Nope. All quiet here." Then he nodded to the screen where Sayed and the van were still parked out front. "Is the van staying?"

"Nope. I thought you might want to play runner today. We're gonna need more groceries, that kind of thing. I made a list."

He got to his feet. "No worries. Sayed's good to go?"

I nodded. "Yeah. And thanks."

I sent the list I'd made to Riko's phone and watched him leave on the screen. I tried not to think about how it was just Jeremy and me in the house. I certainly wasn't going up to his room to check on him. I would let him sleep and pretend he wasn't going to come downstairs and ask me a bunch of questions about my scars.

I was one hundred percent sure it was coming.

It was like waiting for the ax to fall.

Jeremy came downstairs just before lunch and headed straight for the kitchen. "Good afternoon," I said.

His reply was rough and croaky. "Morning."

"Want an iced Americano?"

"I can make it," he replied. Then he messed around with the coffee machine a bit while frowning at it, finally got it to work, poured it over ice, and added cold water. He closed his eyes as he took the first sip.

"Sleep okay?"

Great, Steve. Just lead him straight into the conversation you wanted to avoid.

Jeremy shook his head. "Went to sleep when the sun came up."

Jesus.

"You hungry? Did you want me to make you something to eat?"

He shrugged and drank more of his coffee.

"Riko should be back soon with groceries," I explained. "I sent him on a bit of an errand run today because we didn't have to be anywhere. Figured you could use the sleep."

He drank more of his coffee, but he was avoiding eye contact. He was nervous and standoffish, which . . . well, I wondered briefly if I'd have preferred him to just come right out and ask.

He nodded toward my laptop. "You watch more of the crowd footage?"

"Yeah."

"Find anything?"

"Not since the one possible visual in Tokyo."

"Well, that's good." He shrugged again. "I guess."

God, I hated this.

We'd had so many small steps forward, and this felt like one giant leap backward.

"Look," I began.

He spoke at the same time. "I searched for you online."

I stared at him, the blood draining from my face. "You what?"

"I knew you wouldn't tell me if I asked."

"Jeremy," I whispered, trying to regulate my breath, slow and measured.

*Stay calm, Steve.*

"Will you tell me what happened to you if I ask?"

My mouth was dry, and I could barely shake my head. "I'd rather not."

"See? I knew you wouldn't tell me."

"It was a long time ago," I mumbled. Blood pounded in

my ears and I took a step back. "And it was not a good time in my life."

"But you can tell me, Steve."

I shook my head. "Not you."

"Why not? Why not me?" He glared at me. "I knew you'd do this. Last night you walked away, outside by the pool, when I asked you not to walk away, but you did."

I met his eyes. "I . . . I didn't hear that."

He raised an eyebrow, clearly not believing me.

"Sorry," I said quietly. "I didn't hear you say that."

"So tell me now."

"I can't."

"Why not?" He whacked his cup down on the counter and raised his voice. "You're supposed to tell me these things. We're friends, right? Well, I don't know what the fuck we are. It's confusing as hell. But you know every single thing about me, and I don't know shit about you."

*I don't know what the fuck we are. It's confusing as hell.*

God, was that . . . was he saying what I thought he was saying?

Roscoe was right. Jeremy was confused about what he felt for me.

I met his eyes. "What's confusing, Jeremy?"

His jaw clenched. "Don't try and turn this on me."

I couldn't remember ever seeing him this mad.

He ran both hands through his hair and fisted his curls. "You told me your old name, so I looked that up. Wanna know what I found, Steve?"

My heart beat cold and my nostrils flared. "If you already know, why ask me?"

"Because I want you to tell me! I want to hear it from you!"

"I can't!" I yelled back at him.

He shouted right back. "Why not?"

"Because it ruined me!" I roared. He recoiled a little, and I lost all fight in me. "And I can't have you looking at me like they did. The way you are now . . ." I shook my head. "I already lost enough. I can't lose you too."

Jeremy stared at me. He opened his mouth and shut it again and was just about to speak—

"Uh, is everything okay here?" Riko asked from the hall.

I hadn't even heard him come in. He was carrying brown grocery bags and now looking between me and Jeremy like a tennis match.

"Everything's fine," I replied, despite knowing he'd probably heard every word we'd just screamed at each other. "Are there more bags?"

"Uh, yeah," he answered. I brushed past Jeremy and ignored Riko's gaze as I walked through the too-big fucking house to the front where Sayed would be parked.

This was all a huge fucking mess.

I brought more bags in while Riko unpacked the first load. Jeremy stood leaning against the kitchen counter, staring at me. He was chewing on the inside of his lip as though he was trying to understand something in his head.

I took a packet of crackers from the top of the closest bag and put them on the counter near Jeremy. "You need to eat something."

He stared some more, his brows furrowed, and he shook his head. He walked out. "Not hungry."

I took a deep breath and exhaled slowly. Riko was holding a carton of eggs and frowning. "You sure everything's cool?"

Then, with impeccable timing, my phone rang. Ambrose's name flashed on the screen. I hit Answer. "Got news for us?" I asked. "You're gonna tell us they've got that woman in custody?"

Ambrose sighed. "Ah, yeah. About that . . ."

I groaned. "Fuck. What now?"

Riko let his head fall back, but he went back to putting the groceries away and I left him to it, walking out by the pool for some privacy.

"Long story short," Ambrose said. "The woman in the footage. The sister who followed the band around the world then tried to set the sister up?"

I didn't need the recap, but whatever. "Yeah?"

"Well, they can't find her."

What?

"What do you mean?"

"She's disappeared, gone off-grid. The sister said she hasn't seen her or spoken to her in two days."

Fucking great.

"Do they have any idea of her possible location?"

"No. But Zielinski believes she's here in LA. Figures she wouldn't go far from wherever Jeremy is now that they're onto her, and he's advised us to be cautious."

I scrubbed my hand over my face. "They think she's dangerous," I concluded.

"She's made purchases recently," Ambrose said. "That the FBI are concerned—"

"What kind of purchases?"

"A Springfield handgun, 9mm. And ammunition."

What the fuck?

"Did you not think you should probably have led with that little piece of information? Jesus fucking Christ, Neil."

Silence.

"What else?"

"She's made several purchases of hardware items and camping gear."

Hmm. "Camping or climbing?"

"Zielinski said camping. I didn't ask for specifics. I just assumed it was because she was going off-grid."

For fuck's sake.

"What else?"

"Uh . . ."

"Neil, I'm all outta patience."

"There's been more mail received by the head office. Not just online, but actual letters. Threatening, unhinged shit. We've handed it all over."

"Jesus. From her?"

"I don't know. It was handed right over to the FBI. I didn't see it myself."

My chest felt a little too tight. "Threatening Jeremy?"

"Actually, no. This is threatening Platinum and Arlo Kim. For hiding Jeremy, for not letting him be free. Threatening to destroy the company."

Christ.

"Jacqueline Sosa is now an official person of interest and is wanted for questioning by the FBI."

"So they're pretty sure it's her?"

"I think she's the best lead they've got. That's all we know so far. I just got off the phone with Zielinski."

"Well, tell him he can come here and tell us every sliver of information he has." God, I wanted to kick the shit out of something. "Actually, I have his number. I'll tell him."

A quiet sigh followed by more silence. "How's Jeremy coping?"

"How do you think? He's not."

*He's pissed off and frustrated, probably scared out of his mind. But he's also mad at me, directly, for some stupid reason.*

I groaned. "I'll talk to him," I mumbled. "Though that's not likely to go down well."

"That good, huh?"

"Hmm." Fucking hell. "We just need this to be over. Whatever it takes."

"Agreed." There was another beat of silence. "Look, we have the interviews next week and the *Late Nights in LA* appearance. How about I ask Jeremy if he wants to skip them? We can say he's ill or resting a sore throat."

"I think that's a good idea. Nothing would make *me* happier, but that'll go down like the Titanic with him."

"Hmm." Ambrose grumbled something to himself. "Let me see what I can work out. I'll call him and let Ryan know. I'll be in touch."

I ended the call and let my head fall back with a groan. I hadn't had enough sleep to deal with this.

"Everything okay?" Riko asked behind me.

I shook my head. "Suspect is missing. FBI can't find her, but they believe she's now armed." I walked past him and back into the house and made my way up to Jeremy's room.

I knocked and waited, and there was no answer. "Jeremy?"

Still no answer.

I cracked the door and peered inside. I couldn't see him. The room was empty, his bed rumpled. "Jeremy?" I called out, a little louder this time.

His bathroom door swung open, steam billowed out, and Jeremy stood there with nothing but a towel around his waist. His wet curls, perfect face, lean body, abs, happy trail.

Oh, sweet Jesus.

I'd seen him wearing just shorts yesterday in the pool. Why was this a thousand times hotter?

"S-sorry . . ." I had to make myself look away, so I stared at the wall while the outline of him seared into my memory.

"What's the emergency?" he asked.

I steeled myself and met his gaze, very deliberately not looking anywhere but in his eyes.

"I just spoke to Ambrose. The FBI have news on the suspect. I need to talk to you about a few things." I swallowed hard. "If you could get dressed and come downstairs . . ."

Jeremy stood-stock still for a long few seconds. "I take it it's not good news," he said flatly.

I shook my head and looked away again. "I'll wait for you downstairs."

"Or you could wait for me here."

I shot him a look, but he was walking into his walk-in closet, his back to me. Christ, his back was just as sexy as his front. I let out a long, quiet breath and tried to get that image out of my mind.

He didn't close the door, so I moved out of any possible line of sight. I decided sitting on the bed was a bad idea and went to the huge glass doors instead.

"So they ID'd the person?" he asked.

"They have a suspect, yes."

"Is it the sister?"

"Yeah. Her name is Jacqueline Sosa," I replied. "But they can't find her."

There was silence, so I turned and he was standing in the doorway wearing shorts, his T-shirt still in his hand. "What do you mean?"

"She's disappeared. Sister hasn't seen her, hasn't gone to work." I held his gaze. "Jeremy, she bought a gun recently."

He recoiled a little. "Well, fuck."

"I want to speak to Zielinski," I said. "I want him to come here, but I wanted to check with you first, considering you don't like him . . ."

Jeremy's gaze narrowed. "Oh, here, I have something for you." He put his hand in his shorts pocket and pulled out his middle finger.

But then he smiled.

"I have no issue with Nothing-Special Agent Whatever. So go right ahead and invite him over. I'm sure he'll be stoked to hear from you."

I looked at the shirt he was still holding. "You should swap that shirt for a green one. Green really is your color."

He laughed. "Fuck off. I'm not jealous."

"You're totally jealous. And that's fine. Understandable, even. And for a special treat, I'm gonna let you beat the shit out of me."

He did a double take. "What?"

"Fight practice. I brought over pads and gloves from my house this morning."

He pulled his shirt on. "When did you go to your house?"

"About seven o'clock."

He squinted at me. "Did you sleep at all?"

I shook my head. "Maybe an hour or two."

"Steve—"

"I'm fine."

"You're not fine. That's not enough sleep." He frowned, as if he was about to bring up last night, my scars, our fight this morning.

And god, I just couldn't go through all that again.

"Come down when you're ready," I said softly and tried to leave.

He grabbed my arm, our bodies close, his eyes locked on mine. "Are you okay?"

"Yes, of course. Why wouldn't I be?"

"You're distracted."

I wanted to look away so badly, but I made myself stare at him. "I'm fine," I repeated. "I'm just worried and exercising caution. There's a fixated person out there who wants to hurt you—"

"I'm not talking about that psycho or even about me," he murmured. "I'm talking about you, Steve."

Dammit.

He still had a hold of my arm, we were still far too close, and he smelled too damn good.

"I'm fine," I breathed.

"Will you ever tell me?"

I knew what he was asking but played dumb. "About what?"

"Who hurt you?"

My eyes cut to his. He didn't call them my scars. He didn't ask what happened. He wanted to know who hurt me. He'd found me online, or so he'd said this morning. The old me, my old life. He would have read the stories, seen news articles, maybe.

But I just couldn't.

I never talked about it. Right or wrong, I just couldn't.

I shook my head. "If you know already, you don't need to hear it from me."

His hold on my arm tightened and he pulled me closer. "Goddammit, Steve."

And something inside me just snapped.

I twisted my arm out of his hold, grabbed his wrist instead, and bent his arm behind his back, locking it in place, pulling him against me. It was painless for him but he was immobilized, pressed to me from chest to thigh. My face was half an inch from his.

I hadn't even realized what I'd done until he grunted in surprise. His eyes went wide, then he looked at my mouth.

Like he wanted to kiss me.

I could just lean in a fraction and press my lips to his. God knew I wanted to . . . I wanted to claim his mouth, push him against the wall, and taste that beautiful tongue . . .

His chest rose and fell. He licked his lips. "Hmm," he breathed. Then he blinked. "Whoa."

I snapped out of whatever mindfuck I had going on, let go of his arm, and took a step back. "Sorry. I'm sorry."

Jeremy shook his wrist and scowled at me, angry now. "What the fuck was that?"

"Sorry. Jeremy, I'm sorry. Fuck." I could barely catch my breath. "I should have been more careful. Are you . . . okay? Did I hurt you?"

He took a few deep breaths and eventually shook his head, still holding his wrist. "No. I'm . . . I'm fine."

I took another step away, not able to look him in the eye. "I'm really sorry."

I turned and walked out, my heart hammering, hands trembling.

Fuck, fuck, fuck!

I took my phone out to call Zielinski. Not that I really wanted to speak to him, but at least this way Riko couldn't ask me what the fuck was going on.

My head was a mess.

I picked up my gym bag and took it out to the patio while I called Agent Zielinski. It took a minute to get through to his extension, but he eventually took my call. "Mr. Frost, what can I do for you?"

"I've just spoken to Neil Ambrose," I explained, unzipping the bag. "He told me about the developments with Jacqueline Sosa."

"Yes?"

"You mentioned she bought camping gear. Can I ask if it included any climbing gear?"

"Uh . . . Mr. Frost—"

I threw a knee pad onto the lawn. "Did she buy any kind of bolts or anchors? Any equipment that she could use to—"

"I'm not comfortable discussing this over the phone, Mr. Frost."

I took a pair of sparring mitts from my bag and tossed them next to the knee pad. "Good. Can you come to Mr. Dalton's home address? I'm assuming you have it. Then you can see why I'm asking about the climbing gear."

He agreed and the call ended. I threw my phone by my bag and pulled on some gloves. Riko came out. "Need a spotter?"

I nodded. "Yeah. That'd be great. Agent Zielinski will be here in about thirty minutes."

Riko strapped on the knee and thigh pad, then picked up the mitts, and as I bounced on my toes for a bit and shook out my hands, Riko grimaced at me. "Take it easy on me," he said.

I rolled my shoulders and stretched my neck, letting some of the tension go. "Yeah, of course."

He stood in the brace position, grounded his feet into the grass, lowered his center of gravity, and raised the mitt.

Riko was good, and out of all my team, probably the only one I could spar with. He knew how to get hit, how to spar, and how to lean in and away as needed.

I began slow and easy. Just a few taps and kicks to get

the heart rate up, and the more I did, the better I felt. The faster I hit, the harder I hit, the better I felt.

It was good to focus, to expel some energy and let go of the frustrations and anger.

So I hit and jab, jab, jabbed. Tapped, punched, kicked until the sweat was dripping off me.

Riko eventually put his hand up and disengaged. "Time out," he said, puffing almost as much as me. His short black hair glistened in the sun. "Christ."

"You good?" I asked.

He almost laughed. "Sure. Are you?"

"Feel better now."

"Good," he replied. "You've got an audience," he murmured quietly. "He's been watching from inside."

I kept my back to the house, and I ignored Jeremy. I took the punch mitt from Riko. "Your turn."

So Riko ran through some moves and a few strikes and kicks. Pretty sure he appreciated the energy-burn as much as I did. Jeremy stayed inside . . .

Until I began giving Riko some instructions. I tapped his leg. "Keep this knee bent." I patted his sternum. "Power from here." I moved Riko's hip. "Square your pelvis."

That was when Jeremy came out, as if he didn't like me being one-on-one with Riko. God, was he really jealous? He cleared his throat. "Yeah, Riko. Keep your pelvis square."

I spared a glance at Jeremy but held the mitt against my outer forearm and readied my stance. "Come on, Riko. Give me a right kick. Hard as you can."

Riko kinda smiled and gave me a few test kicks first, but they got harder and harder, and I had to brace and grunt against the impact.

It felt great.

I changed arms and Riko gave his left leg a bit of a work out, but apparently Jeremy didn't like that either.

"Now it's Steve's turn to kick as hard as he can while Riko holds the pad."

Riko stopped to catch his breath, clutching his side. He made a face at Jeremy. "Are you crazy? You come and hold the pad and let him kick you as hard as he can."

Jeremy grinned as he came over and motioned for me to give him the mitt pads.

"No," I said. "I'm not kicking you. Practice or not."

"Oh, come on," he said, trying to mimic the stance he'd obviously seen Riko and me do. "Just a small one, then."

So while he stood there, holding the pad and smiling, I gave him a gentle one-two-three kick. And proceeded to knock him off balance. He didn't fall, but he looked kinda horrified. "Jesus."

"I barely touched you," I said.

"That was twenty-five percent," Riko agreed. "At most. And you wanted him to put a full hundred percent on me."

Jeremy huffed but he looked at me. "How come your little pretend lesson with me the other day didn't look like you and Riko just now?"

"Because Riko and I have done this for years," I said. "And you've done two minutes."

"I want to be as good as you," Jeremy said.

For fuck's sake.

I took the pad from him. "Okay then. Your turn."

So, then he tried to hit the pad.

"Stop!" I said, throwing the pad toward my bag. "Jesus, you're gonna break something." I took his fists in each hand. "Wrists have to be straight. You break your wrist or your hand or your fingers and there's no piano or guitar for weeks. Ambrose will kick my ass."

He stared at his wrists as if they belonged to someone else.

Christ.

I chuckled. He did countless hours of choreography in front of a mirror, so I used that technique. "Okay, you're overthinking this. Think of it as if I'm going to teach you a new dance routine. Mirror my stance." Learning dance steps, he could do. I got in the ready position and he mirrored me. His feet were good, his knees bent properly, but his arms . . . I put my hands on his elbows. "Keep these in close to your body at all times." I took hold of his fists. "Keep this one up to protect your snooze button."

"My what?"

I tapped his chin. "Your snooze button. Your chin."

He smiled but then looked down. "How can I keep my elbows in and my hand up here at the same time?"

"Like this." I stood beside him and showed him. "Lead with your front foot. You're right handed, right footed. Elbows in, hands up."

He copied me and I threw some slow, deliberate punches, defensive steps, taking him through every move as if it was the choreo team in the dance studio. "One, two, three. One, two, three."

And he got it.

I picked up the punch mitt and stood in front of him. "Keep going, one, two, three."

"I'm having flashbacks of learning to waltz." He smiled but kept practicing. "You knew to treat it like a dance if I wanted to learn, right?"

I smiled. "Sure. A good teacher should understand how the student learns. And you learn to a beat."

Jeremy stopped punching. His gaze met mine. "That's really true."

God, when he looked at me like that, when there was no bullshit between us and we were just us, my heart ached for him. It physically ached. I ached to touch him, to tell him . . .

And my phone buzzed on the ground.

I startled and picked my phone up. "It's Agent Zielinski," I mumbled.

Jeremy raised an eyebrow. "Does he call you often?"

I ignored that and answered my phone. It was a five second phone call to say he was at the gate, and I told him we'd let him in.

Riko, who was taking a long drink of water, gave a nod. "I'll go."

I took the punch mitt and held it up for Jeremy again. "No, he doesn't call me. I called him."

Jeremy's eyes cut to mine. "Oh, really."

"Keep practicing." I shoved the mitt toward him, jostling him a little. "Count the rhythm in your head, one, two, three." He snarled and jabbed at the mitt. But he was holding back. "Harder."

So he did. He jabbed with a bit more force and stepped forward, leading on his front foot. "Good." Jab, jab, jab. "And he's coming here to help us, so maybe try being nice to him."

His eyes narrowed at me as he jabbed twice. "I'll be as nice to him as he deserves."

I smiled as he hit with a little more force.

"Stop fucking smiling," he grunted as he hit harder still.

I stepped back and lowered the mitt to waist height, and he frowned at me. "What the hell. I was just getting the rhythm."

"You're going to hurt your hands. Now do this," I said,

showing him. "Keep your elbows in, hands up, but you're going to drive your knee into this pad. Like this."

I did a few quick knees to show him.

Jeremy tried a few gentle knee-raises and I tapped his knee with the mitt. "Good. Put your hands on my shoulders until you get your balance." Not that he would probably need to, because he had such good balance . . .

He slid his hands onto my shoulders and lifted his knee again. "It's not like I'm going to rest my hands on some guy who's trying to attack me," he said, bringing his knee up into the pad.

"Yes you will," I replied. "Use his body, his head. Grab hold of him and drive your fucking knee into his face until something breaks."

Jeremy stopped his knee and his eyes went wide. "Jesus Christ, Steve."

I shrugged. "What do you think I'm teaching you here?"

He frowned. "I guess . . . I just didn't think of it like that."

His hands were still on my shoulders and he began to pull them away. I put them back on my shoulders, holding them there. "Let's focus on what you should do if someone tries to grab you and how you can get out of it."

We were standing close. Too close. Realizing I needed to make this stance look deliberate, I said, "Grab my shirt like you want to hurt me."

He fisted my collar.

"You always draw his center of gravity away from your body," I said, pushing his arm out and down. "Now you try it."

I grabbed his shirt and his eyes flashed with something that wasn't fear. He tried to push my hand away and down, but he stepped in too close and I instinctively palmed his chest to stop him from falling into me.

And that was when Riko and Agent Zielinski came out through the door.

Jeremy gripped my waist and leaned into me, very deliberately, while looking at Zielinski.

Jesus Christ.

That was a blatant territorial move.

He *was* jealous. Jeremy Dalton just marked me in front of another guy.

What. The. Actual. Fuck?

# CHAPTER ELEVEN

ZIELINSKI STAYED for maybe thirty minutes. He gave us the same rundown that Ambrose had, and once I explained my concerns about the camping or climbing gear, I showed him the edge of Jeremy's property.

"I'd already made a comment that the only boundary concern he really has here is if someone knows how to climb," I said. We were standing on the edge of the sheer drop, maybe thirty feet down, to the canyon below.

Zielinski nodded. "It's a valid concern. The camping gear was a gas cooker, tent, sleeping bag, water cannisters. A hunting knife. But no climbing gear. No hooks, no rappelling gear."

"A hunting knife? Christ."

"And the gun and ammunition."

"Is she an experienced camper? Does she do this often?"

Zielinski shook his head. "No. According to the sister, not at all. Her spending history indicates no similar purchases either."

"And you have no idea where she's gone?"

Zielinski's gaze met mine. "We have some leads we're following."

"Is that Fed-speak for 'we got nothing' or Fed-speak for 'I'm not saying'?"

Before he could reply, I added, "We have a booked schedule next week. We've put off all we can this week, and he's barely left the house. But next week he has contractually obligated appointments, and everything he does is scrutinized by the media. We can't have this turning to shit in public. Not just for his safety, but the hundreds of fans that line the streets just to see him everywhere he goes."

Zielinski studied me for a long few seconds, and I stared right back at him. "When I say we're following some leads, I would ask that you trust us. I understand you have a personal relationship with Mr. Dalton and I can appreciate—"

"A what?" I stared. "I have a what with Jeremy?"

He glanced back to where Riko and Jeremy stood near the pool, watching us. "I just assumed you and he—"

"Well, that was your first mistake."

"When I walked in, I interrupted an embrace, and he hasn't taken his eyes off you since I got here."

"No. He hasn't taken his eyes off you," I corrected. "He doesn't trust strangers."

Zielinski tilted his head just so, and he kind of smiled. "I'm sorry if my insinuation that you are involved with Mr. Dalton offended you."

I wanted to bristle, but instead, I smiled right back. If he thought he could rattle me, he was wrong. I was the king of keeping my cool. "Oh, I'm not offended. In fact, I'm flattered." I smiled a little sweeter. "Though I'd hate to question what other assumptions you've made about this case."

And that was basically the end of his meeting with me.

He spoke to Jeremy for a bit while I tried to simmer down. Jeremy was right. The guy was a fucking jerk.

"So I take it that went well," Riko said. We both stood watching Jeremy and Zielinski talking. We couldn't hear what was said but I wasn't letting Jeremy out of my sight.

I crossed my arms. "Hm."

"Yeah, Jeremy likes him about that much too."

"He has *leads*, apparently," I mumbled. "Which means a whole lotta fuck all."

Riko sighed. "I thought he was nice."

I whipped my head around to glare at him, only to find him smiling. "He's a pretentious brat," he said. "Expensive suit, expensive watch, expensive haircut. Type of guy that might appeal—"

"Shut the fuck up."

Riko laughed. "Yeah, that's about what Jeremy said too."

I growled at him, because from that comment, I could guess he was totally aware of whatever tension Jeremy and I had going on between us.

We used to laugh and joke and talk and talk . . . Now we snapped and goaded each other. There are glimpses of how we used to be, but now there was tension and . . . and I didn't know what to call it.

Goddammit.

Zielinski gave us a nod goodbye, and as Jeremy walked him out, Riko said, "Oh. Before I forget. While you were talking to your favorite agent, Jeremy asked the guys to come over for beef and beers."

He had my attention now. "Who? The guys?"

He nodded. "Yep. All of them."

"When?"

Riko shrugged. "Lunch, so . . ." He glanced at his watch. "Uh, now?"

MADDOX AND ROSCOE ARRIVED FIRST, with Robbie, and I met them at the front door. "Hey. Jeremy's out back trying to figure out the grill."

"Oh, god help us," Maddox mumbled as he walked through.

"Hey," Roscoe said, looking awfully relaxed and casual in his shorts and T-shirt. It wasn't often I saw him in civvies. He looked good.

He looked happy.

"Boss," Robbie said, giving me his usual grin as he followed Maddox.

As Roscoe and I stood there, we heard Jeremy's loud, "Hey, dickbag!"

Roscoe chuckled and it made me smile. "So, how's he been?" Roscoe asked.

I made a noise that was half grunt, half sigh.

"That good, huh?"

I looked up at him. "I don't know. I think he needs today with the guys, you know? Just to hang out and be themselves."

Roscoe nodded. "Yep. Totally get it. Maddox is the same." He nodded toward the back of the house. "How . . . how are things between you two?"

I groaned and shook my head.

"Also that good, huh?"

"Not good at all."

Another van arrived and I opened the door to see Zoe let Luke and Blake out of the back. "Oh good," Luke said to us with a grin as he stepped out of the van. "The muscle is here to help us." He slid the door back fully to show three cartons of beer and a cooler. Blake took one carton, Luke took another, and they grinned as they came into the foyer. "Out back?"

I nodded. "Yep."

Roscoe grabbed the remaining carton of beer and I took the cooler, which was the heaviest by far. "Jesus."

Jason joined us at the side of the van. "It weighs that much because it has half a cow in it," he said. "They ordered enough food to feed an army."

Jason took the other end of the handle for me and we carried it into the house.

Was this an ideal way to spend the day?

Probably not.

Did I want all five guys of the world's biggest band under one roof when a fixated person was on the loose with a gun?

No, I did not.

But did Jeremy need this?

Absolutely.

They'd cracked their first beers by the time Wes and Amy arrived, and they hung out by the pool while Maddox and Jeremy tried to figure out the grill. They shoved a beer in Wes's hand and welcomed Amy. I admired her, to be honest.

Roscoe had talked about how hard it had been sometimes to be an addition to such a close group of guys. He had the advantage of knowing them all for years and already having that established base with them, and he slipped into being one of the guys so effortlessly. Amy didn't have that luxury.

And she was the only woman. There were no other girlfriends, no other dates. Apart from Roscoe, but he had now taken over trying to get the BBQ going, which was probably a good thing.

I stayed inside, mostly, keeping an eye on the security cameras, particularly the front gates. Zoe and Jason checked the back boundary. Robbie and Ivan looked after the sides of the property.

The thing was, we weren't here to drink and laugh with the band. It'd be all too easy to sit around with them, crack a few beers, and listen to the funny stories.

But we weren't part of that inner circle.

We were employed by the company to look after them.

And that was a very timely reminder for me. Had I really thought Jeremy would ever be interested in me? I was not in their inner circle. I was now questioning whether Jeremy and I were ever even friends.

I would have thought yes. Despite who he was—a world-famous household name—and the fact I was just the hired muscle.

It wasn't even that I was not part of the Atrous inner circle. I certainly wasn't. The truth was, he was so far out of my league, I wasn't even in the same game.

I wasn't saying Jeremy treated me differently because of status or wealth. He didn't. None of them did.

But while I wished I could be out there with him, with the band—and while I could only ever dream of being with Jeremy the way Roscoe was with Maddox—I was kidding myself.

"Hey, Steeeve," Jeremy called out.

I stood up from watching the CCTV cameras. "What's up?"

He had a full beer in his hand. "Why don't you come out with us?"

Uhhh. God, when he said stuff like that, I didn't know what to think.

I gestured to the screen. "I'm kinda working."

He frowned. "Oh. Fair enough." He clearly wanted to say something else but chose not to. "Anyway, the steaks are done. If you want. And all the others. There's even a salad." He shrugged. "But Luke made it, so it's probably questionable. I'd stick to the meat. Just to be safe."

I smiled at him. Was he nervous? Disappointed? "Thank you. I'll let the others know."

He took a few steps away, then stopped. He made a face and shook his head. "You can take an afternoon off. You said before this place was as safe as it got. If you can relax anywhere, it's here. Especially when there are five other security here."

I couldn't expect my team to work when I wasn't. That wouldn't be fair. But I wasn't having that conversation with Jeremy today.

"Maybe later," I replied. It was an easy out, but better than lying outright to his face.

He saw through it anyway. He held my gaze, clenched his jaw, rolled his eyes, and walked out.

He was *so* angry with me. Angry *at* me.

Justified or misdirected, I didn't even know anymore.

I did let the others know that food had been offered, but I gave Jeremy some space. He needed some time with the boys, a sense of normalcy, and to forget about all the stalker crap.

I saw him eat a bit, something, at least, but he was knocking the beers back pretty easy. They never drank much, which was rare considering their lifestyle.

The absolute horror stories I'd heard and read over the years of bands and various musicians and their nosedive into drink and drugs. But these boys weren't like that, and if Jeremy wanted to get absolutely shitfaced, considering everything he'd been through in the last week, I wasn't opposed to that at all.

He needed this.

He had a few days before the responsibility of interviews and photoshoots beckoned, and it was actually kinda nice to hear him laugh and being his usual loud self.

His old self.

"Everything okay?" Roscoe asked. I hadn't heard him walk in. "You were a million miles away."

I hated being caught unaware. "Oh, yeah. Fine. Just thinking..."

He sat on the sofa across from me. I'd only seen him drink maybe one beer the whole afternoon. It was now going on three o'clock. "I love that they're having some fun out there, but oh my god, they're talking some shit."

I smiled at him. "Loud, too." It was true. They were talking louder, laughing louder. Not that I minded.

Roscoe eyed my laptop. "So, you watching those screens for anything in particular or just avoiding Jeremy?"

My gaze went to his and I sighed.

"You don't have to say anything. He's the same out there. He's laughing, sure. But he's in a pissy mood, and he keeps watching the back door like he's looking for someone." He shrugged. "You. He's watching for you, Steve."

I gave a quick shake of my head. "We've had a few disagreements. He's hot and cold with me—laughing and touchy one minute, pissed at me the next. He's stressed, for obvious reasons, and he's probably sick of having me here."

"He likes having you here."

"What?"

"He told Maddox. Maddox asked if Jeremy wanted us to come over the other day, or if he wanted to come to our place, but Jeremy said no. I mean, he said you were a pain in his ass, who made him cook and clean up, but that you weren't actually too bad to have around."

I almost smiled.

"Has, uh . . . has anything happened between you two?" Roscoe asked quietly. "I'm picking up on some tension or something."

My eyes darted to his before looking over my shoulder toward the patio door. They were still being loud and drunk.

"Something has?" Roscoe's eyes widened.

"No," I said quickly. *Jesus.* "No. Not like that." Did I tell him there'd been a few moments where Jeremy had been close enough to kiss, where he'd looked at my mouth, licked his lips . . . "There's been—"

"Hey, m' favorite cat herder," Jeremy said to Roscoe as he came in, his words slurred. He ignored me.

"Jeremy, have you had enough to eat?" I asked.

He spun, surprised. "Oh, you wanna talk t' me now?" He was clearly drunk, staggering a little as he walked through. "Need m' guitar."

His words stung.

Roscoe and I watched him disappear down the hall and Roscoe's gaze landed back on me. "What was that about?"

I sighed, not sure what I could say.

He was about to say something else but then Maddox appeared. "Here he is!" He made a beeline for Roscoe and all but fell onto him, sitting on his lap, his arms around him, and he kissed him.

Right in front of me.

Had I seen them be affectionate? Yes. Touching, a quick peck, hugging, holding hands? Of course.

But this was a full-on kiss, with tongue.

Roscoe was obviously surprised, but he enjoyed it for a

few seconds before pulling back. Maddox jumped off and pulled Roscoe to his feet. "Jam session time. Come on."

Roscoe went willingly, smiling as Maddox dragged him out the door. "We'll talk after?"

I gave a nod. Not that it would make much difference. I didn't know what to say now. I doubted I'd know any time soon.

Jeremy appeared with his acoustic guitar. I got to my feet. "Jeremy," I tried.

He ignored me again, walking past me as if I didn't even exist.

It hurt more than if he'd struck me.

He held the guitar up like a trophy as he went back to everyone. They were all sitting around now, a circle of sorts. Jeremy stood with his foot up on his chair and began to strum his guitar. Luke tapped two beer bottles together. Wes used the beer cooler like a bongo drum. Blake did some kind of beatbox noise, and Maddox did the main vocals, though they all harmonized.

I leaned against the doorframe and watched them.

First song they sang was "Fly." It was Jeremy's favorite, so I wasn't surprised he played it first. Then "Oceans," followed by "Reflection." It was how all their concerts started. Then "Puzzle" and "Jisei."

It was magical. So much fun, so much talent.

But when he played "Code Red," Maddox sang it to Roscoe. It was hard not to watch and smile.

The others harmonized, but Jeremy never sang a word.

He looked at me, though, as he strummed.

And that perhaps said more than the lyrics.

Amy took Wes's phone and recorded them singing in the sunny shade, all drunk and smiling. She circled them, mostly doing close-ups of Wes but the others, too.

When that song ended, Jeremy strummed right into "Come Together" by The Beatles. And then they sang "House of the Rising Sun" by The Animals.

"Okay, requests," Jeremy called out.

"'Can't Help Falling in Love' by Elvis," Roscoe said first.

Jeremy strummed a chord or two. He looked up from his guitar and frowned. "Don't know it. Pick something else."

"It's C G A—" Robbie said, holding an imaginary guitar. He stopped talking when everyone spun to look at him.

"You know how to play?" Blake asked.

Robbie grinned. "Sure I do. All my family does. Uncles, aunties, cousins."

"The fuck, man," Jeremy said, handing his guitar to Robbie. "Play, play."

Robbie took the guitar and everyone waited...

And he played.

He strummed the intro and everyone cheered, but then he sang the first line and everyone went dead quiet . . . until they erupted in cheers and began to sing with him.

I had no idea Robbie could sing.

He was a big guy, easily two hundred and fifty pounds, but he had a sweet voice. He played the guitar like it was a ukulele and he totally had the Polynesian vibe, but holy shit. He was good. And I was stone-cold sober. The guys who were all drunk must have thought he was the best thing they'd ever heard.

They were quick to their feet, sang every word, very loud. Jeremy had one hand in the air as he danced, his eyes closed, singing at the top of his lungs. Maddox had his arm around Jeremy's shoulder, Luke and Blake and Wes all danced, and Amy filmed it all.

Then he played "The Chain" by Fleetwood Mac. It was crazy to me how the band could completely ad-lib but know how to harmonize a song they'd probably never sung together before. Robbie did that strum/thump thing with the guitar, and the five singers fucking nailed it.

It was incredible.

When the song was over, Robbie handed the guitar back, but Maddox took it instead of Jeremy.

"You wanna be careful, Steve," Luke called out. "Platinum might wanna sign him."

Robbie shook his head and waved him off. "No thanks."

Wes watched the footage that Amy had filmed and the others took a quick look too. It would no doubt end up on their Twitter or TikTok.

"Here, let me see it before you post it anywhere," Roscoe said.

Thank god.

Maddox played some Kings of Leon and the mood simmered down a bit. They still sang, but they drank more beer.

Until Jeremy decided it was time for tequila.

Not long after that, Wes and Amy called it a day. They said their rounds of goodbyes, and Ivan herded them into their van and they drove off.

"Yeah, we might go too," Luke said.

"Nah, let's go out," Jeremy said.

I whipped my head around so fast, I'm surprised my neck didn't crack. Jeremy seemed pleased by my reaction. "Let's hit the club. Wanna dance, find some girls."

His words churned like grease in my belly.

Luke turned to me. I could tell by his face he didn't want to go. "I'm sure Steve doesn't think that's a good idea."

It was the worst idea. And having a stalker aside, him

going out when he was already drunk was *not* a good idea. But that was a PR issue, an image issue. My concern was security.

I shrugged. "No, I don't think that's a good idea. But if he wants to go, then we go."

Luke grimaced and turned back to Jeremy. "Next time, brother. I might have plans tonight?" He cringed. "Which I'm trying to keep on the DL."

Jeremy stared at him. "A date? Who the hell with? One of your repeats?"

Ouch.

Luke stared at him, then spoke to Blake. "And that's why I didn't want to say anything."

"Jer, that's not fair," Blake said.

"No, she's not a *repeat*," Luke said sharply. "If you really have to know, it's Vana. I'm kinda seeing her."

Jeremy stared at him and it took a second for the penny to drop. He swayed, the bottle of tequila heavy in his hand. "Vana, from Cyko? Blonde hair?"

Luke didn't answer for a second and I wondered if he would at all. "Yeah."

Jeremy nodded slowly, then took another swig of tequila. "She's cute." Then he pointed the tequila at me. "Steve loves Cyko. Had a calendar 'n' everything till I threw it out. Who's yer favorite, Steve? Which girl?"

I gave Luke an apologetic smile. "Sorry, I'm not overly familiar with them."

"Nah, Steve won't answer," Jeremy went on. "Likes secrets 'parently."

I ignored that, and I smiled at Luke and Blake instead. "The calendar was just a promotional thing."

"I threw it in th' trash," Jeremy slurred. "If he's gonna have a fucking calendar, it's gonna be of me."

"Yeah, okay, Captain Jose Cuervo," Blake said. "We'll see you tomorrow."

Jeremy mumbled something drunk and unintelligible, took another swig of the tequila, and went in search of Maddox.

"Sorry about that," I said. No, it probably wasn't my place to apologize on his behalf. "He's been really stressed with the stalker . . ."

Luke nodded but kind of rolled his eyes too. "Yeah, among other things."

*What was that supposed to mean?*

Blake clapped my shoulder. "Bet he's been a real joy to be around."

"And he's gonna be hungover as fuck tomorrow, so good luck with that," Luke added, and along with Zoe and Jason, they left. I watched their van drive out the gates on the CCTV screen, and when I couldn't put it off any longer, I went out to the patio.

It was late afternoon now, almost evening. Maddox sat in a chair beside Roscoe. Maddox was still nursing a beer, but I think he'd stopped drinking it a while ago.

Jeremy sat next to Maddox. He was now holding his guitar, the tequila beside his chair. He strummed a few chords, then sang, "Steve, Steeeve, Steee-eeeeve," to the tune of Dolly Parton's "Jolene."

Then he strummed a different tune. An angry tune. Harsh, violent strums.

"You okay there, Jer?" Maddox asked.

He didn't reply, just strummed harder.

*So that's a no.*

Riko and Robbie came over from the rear boundary. "The back's all clear. Gonna head to bed for a bit," Riko said. He checked his watch and grimaced.

"Make it five," I said. "I'm guessing he won't be up early tomorrow."

The strumming stopped, and Riko and I both turned. Jeremy was staring at me.

God, he was staring like he hated me.

"Maybe I should check the CCTV screens," I said, deciding to give Jeremy some space. I gave Roscoe a nod and turned to leave.

"You know, maybe you should," Jeremy yelled. "Fuck off inside. Don't wanna see you no more."

It wasn't even his words that hurt me. It was the look on his face. Yes, he was drunk, but still . . .

Everyone stared at him. "Jeremy," Maddox whispered. "What the fuck, dude?"

Jeremy stood up and stumbled a little, pointing at me. "No, fuck him. Liar."

That word hit me like a bucket of ice water.

"Liar?" I asked quietly. "I have never lied to you, Jeremy."

"You didn't tell me the truth, either."

"I'm not doing this now."

"You know what?" He could barely stand still, he was so drunk. But my god, he was *so* angry.

"Jeremy," Maddox said, standing beside him now. "Just chill."

Then he turned to face him. "You know, I think I want new security."

*What?*

"What?" Maddox and I asked at the same time.

"Want new security. Then I won't be . . ." He ran his hand through his hair. "Such a fucking mess."

He wanted new security.

Was he firing me?

Holy shit. He was firing me.

Well, that changed everything.

"We can talk about this tomorrow," Maddox said. "You're drunk as fuck right now."

"No. Now. I'm done. I'm done with this . . ." He motioned between us. "Whatever th' fuck this is. Call Ryan, Ambrose." He patted down his pockets, obviously looking for his phone.

But I couldn't move.

Was he firing me from his detail? Or was my job working with Atrous over?

Jeremy sneered at me, swaying. "Can't do this anymore. You can leave, Steve."

"Jeremy, no," Maddox said.

"Stay out of it, Madz," Jeremy snapped.

My heart felt like stone, cold and heavy. I felt sick to my stomach, but I managed to nod.

"Of course," I heard myself say, the sound distant and subdued as if it came from underwater. Riko and Robbie stood there, speechless. I'm guessing their faces matched mine. "Riko, you've got lead."

I somehow managed to get my feet to move, the urge to run, run away bubbling just under the surface. I made it inside before I could breathe, and every step I took felt as if I was walking in glue. My vision was off-kilter, my blood pounded in my ears.

"Steve, wait," Roscoe called out.

I didn't realize he was so close, so when he grabbed my shoulder, I spun around, my fists up. Defense mode, strike first.

"Whoa," Roscoe said. He took a step back, his hands up. Fuck.

I showed him my palms instead. "Sorry, sorry."

"He's drunk. Don't listen to him right now. He doesn't mean any—"

"Jeremy," Maddox said outside. There seemed to be some kind of scuffle in the darkness and Jeremy all but fell inside the doorway.

His eyes were trained on me. Wild, angry. Drunk. "You."

I wasn't doing this now. Not when he was so drunk.

Roscoe faced him. "Jeremy, leave it alone."

Jeremy ignored him. He was still staring at me, as though Roscoe hadn't spoken at all. "You can just walk away."

My heart hurt so bad.

I shook my head.

"You can just fucking walk away so easy." Jeremy swayed a little. "Like nothing matters."

"Jeremy," I breathed.

He pointed at me. "Fuck you. Who th' fuck do you think you are? You don't walk away from me."

"You told me to go," I shot back at him. "The hell do you want me to do, Jeremy?"

"Act like you give a shit."

*What?*

"You have no idea," I said. I was angry and hurt. I didn't give a shit who knew. "Don't tell me I don't give a shit, Jeremy. When every fucking thing I do is for you."

Riko was inside now, standing back but close enough. Maddox and Roscoe too, both wide-eyed and wondering what the hell was going on.

"For me?" Jeremy shook his head and stepped closer. "You were supposed to be someone, Steve, but you can just walk away like it all means nothing."

"For fuck's sake, Jeremy," I yelled, pointing outside. "You just told me to leave. I'm doing what you want."

"You don't know what I want?" he screamed back, rushing forward like he wanted to hit me, but before he could get a hold of me, Roscoe was between us.

I never moved a muscle.

Jeremy tried to shove Roscoe. Roscoe held him easily, but Maddox grabbed Jeremy. "Get your fucking hands off him," Maddox said, shoving Jeremy off Roscoe. Jeremy stumbled back and Riko caught him, but Jeremy fought against him.

And I just saw red.

I saw nothing but Jeremy struggling.

My body was in motion before my brain could catch up. I pulled Jeremy from Riko and wrapped my arms around him and spun us both out of harm's way, keeping my back to everyone.

Jeremy struggled a little but I held him tighter. "I got you," I whispered. He sagged, giving up, his face in my neck. And we just breathed, the room dead silent.

"You," Jeremy mumbled, his voice cracking. He slid his arms around my back, holding onto me so perfectly, and he sighed, a painful sound. He shook his head and his body tensed up, his arms letting go, and I knew it was over. "Shouldn't feel so right."

He pushed away and I let him go.

*You shouldn't feel so right.*

Jeremy took a step back, unable to meet my eyes. He looked around, seeing Riko, Roscoe and Maddox, Robbie. He shook his head again and stumbled out the door.

Maddox followed him. "Jer."

Fucking hell.

I wanted to go after him but knew it would do no good.

He needed Maddox right now. Not me. I ran my hand through my hair. "Fuck!"

Roscoe shook his head. "Steve, he's drunk—"

A loud splash cut the air. Then Maddox screamed. "Jeremy!"

# CHAPTER TWELVE

I BOLTED out the door in time to see Maddox diving into the pool, and I didn't even take one second to assess the situation. I just ran for the pool and dove in.

Underwater, in slow motion, I saw Maddox with his arm around Jeremy, trying to pull him to the surface. Jeremy had his eyes closed, his mouth open, and a cloud of red billowed out from a split on the side of his forehead.

No, no, no.

I grabbed Jeremy's other arm and we broke the surface. Maddox gasped for air and I heaved Jeremy to the edge of the pool. Roscoe hauled him out, and I climbed out. Riko helped Maddox, and by the time I got to Jeremy, Roscoe had him on his side and was patting his back.

Jeremy coughed and then vomited, but I could see the gash on his forehead was deep and wide. If his vomiting was from being drunk, from the knock to his head, or from swallowing pool water, it didn't matter.

"Riko, call an ambulance," I yelled.

Jeremy heaved again and I put my hand on his forehead.

"He fell," Maddox said, kneeling down next to us. "He stumbled toward the pool and fell. He hit his head on the edge."

Jeremy groaned and rolled from his side to his back. "Jeremy," I said. Blood ran in red rivulets down his face and into his hair.

Fuck.

I pulled my wet shirt off over my head and balled it up, holding it to the cut. "Jeremy, can you hear me?"

He groaned again and opened his eyes slowly. "Hm."

I leaned over so he could see my face. "Jeremy?"

His eyes took a second to focus on me. "Oh, hey," he mumbled.

I wanted to throttle him and kiss him, hug him and kill him. "You're a fucking idiot," I said.

Maddox laughed and Jeremy tried to sit up, but Roscoe and I kept him still. "Just stay there," Roscoe said.

Riko was talking on the phone. "Yes, he hit his head and fell in the pool. He's conscious but he's vomiting . . ."

God. What a mess.

Jeremy groaned. He let out a shuddery breath, heaved before he rolled onto his side, and vomited again.

"Ambulance's on its way," Riko said, his phone to his ear. "I'll have to meet them at the gate . . ."

I nodded but my focus was on Jeremy. I took my shirt from his wound, and seeing it was soaked through, I re-balled it and put the pressure back on the cut.

"Jesus," Maddox said.

"All cranial contusions will open up like that," I said. "But he's gonna need stitches or glue."

Jeremy slumped onto his back again and tried to push my hand away. "Just stay still," I said. "The paramedics are on their way."

He mumbled something and his eyes closed.

"Hey," Roscoe said loudly, giving Jeremy a bit of a shake. "Keep your eyes open."

He turned his head and heaved again, so I rolled him onto his side and kept pressure on his wound and just murmured that he'd be okay.

He had to be okay.

It felt like an eternity, but soon enough, Riko brought the paramedics through. They ushered us out of the way, quickly taking over and assessing him and asking us questions.

Maddox was soaking wet, and both he and Roscoe were trying hard not to look at me. It was then I realized why. I was shirtless, my jeans and shoes dripping wet.

But my torso . . . my stomach.

My scars.

"Jesus, Steve," Maddox murmured. "The fuck happened to you?"

"I should get changed," I said, turning back to the house, but I was out of time.

The paramedics lifted Jeremy onto the gurney and strapped him in. "Who's coming with him?" one of them asked.

"I am," I replied.

"We'll follow," Maddox said with a nod.

"Here, boss," Riko said. He took his own T-shirt off and handed it to me.

"Thanks," I said quietly, pulling the shirt on. The rest of me was still dripping wet: jeans, socks, and shoes. But it would all just have to wait.

When we walked back through the house, I spotted my phone by the laptop. *Thank god I didn't have it in my pocket.* I grabbed it and followed the paramedics out to where they loaded Jeremy into the ambulance.

I told Roscoe I'd call him when I knew where they were taking him. "And Ryan," I added. "He'll have all Jeremy's insurance details."

Roscoe gave a hard nod. "On it."

The paramedics closed the doors and I was surrounded by those familiar and awful fluorescent lights, the clinical smell, the noises: beeps, the radio, and eventually the siren.

I hated ambulances.

Jeremy groaned and lifted his hand. I took it quickly. "Hey, you're okay, Jeremy. I'm here. We're just gonna get the doctors to look at the gash on your head."

"Mm" was all he said.

The paramedic began the usual questions. He kind of spoke to Jeremy but also to me. *How many drinks did he have? Did he have a history of alcohol abuse? Had he taken any drugs? How long was he underwater? Did he lose consciousness?*

Same questions they'd asked back at the house. Maybe they were just checking to see if the story remained the same. I didn't know.

Jeremy didn't answer much. Just a few short words, mostly grunts. His blinks were slow but his grip on my hand never loosened.

"He rarely drinks," I said. "He's been under a lot of stress lately and he thought a cookout with his friends a few beers was a good idea." I squeezed Jeremy's hand. "Do you know where we're taking him? I'm going to need to call people and it'll likely be a security issue. If people or the press find out, if they haven't heard on any emergency scanner already, we're going to need to call the police."

As soon as they were cleared to take him to Cedars-

Sinai Emergency, I texted Roscoe. Then I went right back to holding Jeremy's hand.

They wheeled him into the hospital, taking him straight through to the back, citing things like head trauma and alcohol and possible secondary drowning.

Christ.

A doctor assessed him, asking all the same damn questions, looking in his eyes with a penlight and she asked Jeremy a bunch of concussion test questions.

I got shoved in to some small exam room while they took him for scans, and I waited . . . and waited. I was still soaked through and now getting cold. My feet squelched and my jeans were sticking to me in all the wrong places.

Maddox and Roscoe arrived with Robbie. Maddox had a cap pulled down low, though he still had all his earrings in. Anyone with eyes could see who it was. Roscoe and Robbie also stood out in a crowd. We were going to get noticed at some point.

I gave them a brief rundown of what I knew. Which wasn't much at all.

When Maddox handed me a bag of clothes, I noticed he was now dry and wearing Jeremy's track pants and a long-sleeve shirt—at least his famous tattoos were covered. "These are also Jeremy's," he said, nodding to the bag. "He won't mind."

"Thanks."

I found a bathroom and changed as quick as I could. Maddox had chosen some of Jeremy's track pants for me too, a T-shirt I'd seen on Jeremy at least a dozen times, some socks, and a pair of tennis shoes that probably cost what I earned in a week.

I made my way back to the waiting room just as Ryan came running in. He looked like he might have run the whole way. "What happened? How is he? Where is he? Is he okay?"

Roscoe answered. "He was drinking. Fell in the pool and cracked his head on the way down. Maddox and Steve pulled him out. They've taken him for scans."

"Scariest fucking thing," Maddox whispered.

Roscoe rubbed his back. "He'll be okay. You always said he had a hard head."

Maddox managed half a smile and a bit of a nod. He looked at me. "Did he say anything in the ambulance?"

I shook my head. "Not really."

Ryan paled and ran his hand through his hair. "Jesus. How bad is it?"

I met his wide eyes. "We don't know. Probably a concussion. He'll definitely need stitches or glue."

Just then, a woman in scrubs came in, asking about insurance and all that crap. Ryan switched into gear. "I can help you with that."

"Did you call the others?" I asked Maddox.

He gave a quick shake of his head. "Not yet. Didn't know what to tell them and didn't want them—" He sucked back a too-short breath. "—to worry." He took some measured breaths, the kind he took to stave off panicking.

Roscoe took his hand and led him to the chairs, kneeling in front of him. "It's okay, baby," he said calmly. "I can call them. Just breathe."

Maddox inhaled deeply and nodded, exhaling slowly. He did that a few times with Roscoe holding his hands, and they never broke eye contact.

I hated seeing him struggle like that. It was hard to watch, but honestly, I thanked god Maddox had Roscoe.

I noticed belatedly that Robbie stood in front of the door, his back to us, guarding perfectly, should someone try to come in. At least he had the presence of mind to actually do his job.

I, on the other hand, felt as if I was outside my own body.

Roscoe called Wes first, on Maddox's phone, and on speaker. Wes answered with a laugh. "Did you see the video? Two million likes in forty minutes—"

"Wes, it's Roscoe."

There was a beat of silence. "What's wrong?"

Roscoe gave him a very brief rundown. "There's no point in you coming here," he said. "They won't let you in, anyway. We'll call you as soon as we know anything."

Next was a very similar call to Luke and Blake, and they took the news as well as Wes had. "No, they won't let you in, and the last thing we need here is a full security operation to come rescue you. No doubt the media will be on this," Roscoe tried.

When the call ended, Roscoe looked up at me and grimaced. "I told them not to come . . ."

Maddox let his head fall back against the wall. "Thank you for talking to them."

Roscoe said nothing but took Maddox's hand instead.

I checked my watch to find it had stopped. I tapped it and sighed. It was supposed to be completely waterproof. So I checked the time on my phone instead and saw two missed calls and three messages from Ambrose.

"Fuck."

I hit Call. I didn't need to put the call on speaker because he yelled loud enough for everyone to hear. "I've been trying to get a hold of you. What the hell happened?"

I told him what we knew, and by then, Ambrose had calmed down a bit. "Can I ask how you knew?" I asked.

And he was back to yelling. "Well, first there was the

social media meltdown over the video of the little impromptu concert you guys had with Robbie singing and playing the guitar."

Robbie glanced at me and cringed.

"Nothing like having a video of the entire band drunk-dancing going live without any warning. So that was nice, thank you. PR team sends their regards." Ambrose was clearly pissed. Probably out of concern. I wasn't sure. I didn't care. "And then," he barked. "Then there are the reports of paramedics being dispatched to Jeremy's home address for head trauma. On top of this week's FBI and stalking rumors, can I even begin to tell you how this looks?"

"Looks for who?" I shot back. "For you having to put out internet spot fires? Or for me and Maddox who had to drag an unconscious Jeremy out of the fucking pool with blood pouring out of his head? Wanna know how *that* looks?" I wanted to punch the shit out of something but swallowed it down. "Maddox is fine, by the way."

I disconnected the call and threw my phone onto the seat beside me.

Maddox and Roscoe both stared at me.

"So that was probably my job," I mumbled. "Fuck."

Maddox smiled, then snorted. "No it's not." He was still holding Roscoe's hand, but he had his head leaning back against the wall, looking at me. "No one's getting fired. Jeremy wouldn't let you get fired anyway. Neither would I."

Jeremy wouldn't *let* me get fired?

"Jeremy *did* fire me, remember? He fired me tonight."

Maddox shook his head. "No he didn't. He was drunk and in a bad mood. He's been in a weird mood for weeks, before this stalker bullshit. And, for some reason, he wants to take it out on you."

My gaze shot to his.

"Last person in our whole company whom I'd pick to misdirect some anger at," Maddox said with a smirk. "But Jeremy never was the brightest."

I narrowed my stare.

Maddox just smiled wider. "That's the same reaction Jeremy gets when we mention you." He sighed and shook his head slowly. "Never thought for a million years I'd see the day Jeremy—"

Roscoe tapped Maddox's leg. "Maybe this conversation can wait," he murmured, nodding to Robbie's back.

The conversation ended anyway when Ryan returned. "Have we heard anything?"

We all shook our heads.

Did I tell him that Jeremy had fired me? Because after tonight, if Jeremy didn't, maybe Ambrose would? God, they'd had enough to deal with tonight without me adding to it.

"You okay?" Ryan asked me.

I shrugged. "Yeah, I'm fine. I'll be better when we hear he's okay."

"Steve did a forty-yard dash faster than Usain Bolt," Robbie said proudly. "Then dove to the bottom of the pool. Didn't even stop."

He was trying to lighten the moment with his big grin and gentle tone. Before I could tell them that Maddox was in the water before me, a medical team came in, pushing a bed.

Jeremy.

But as they wheeled him in, the doctor called us out of the room so he could speak to us. My heart damn near stopped. "Mr. Dalton's team, I assume?" he asked.

"Yes," I replied, but gestured toward Ryan.

He raised his hand. "Well, me. I'm his manager, but honestly, these guys—"

Maddox stepped forward. "I'm one of his brothers. Doc, is he okay?"

My stomach was so knotted, I felt queasy.

The doctor looked at each of us. "He's got himself a decent knock to the head. There're no fractures, swelling, or internal bleeds, so he's very lucky in that regard, but we're monitoring him for concussion."

I almost sagged with relief. Pretty sure Maddox was the same. Roscoe put his hand on Maddox's shoulder.

"His high blood alcohol doesn't help," the doctor added. "We're waiting on tox results. That's standard. He's having his wound seen to right now and he'll need to stay until he clears the concussion test."

"Can we see him?" Ryan asked.

The doctor held up two fingers. "Two minutes. Then I'm going to have to get you all to clear out. Figure out between you who's staying. One person only. This isn't a hotel."

Maddox went in first. Ryan no sooner had his phone back to his ear, talking to who I could only assume was Ambrose.

Speaking of phones . . . I found mine and shot Riko a quick message.

*Scans all clear. Be a few hours yet.*

His reply of *good news* was almost instant, and I felt bad that he'd had to wait.

Roscoe was a wall of patience and calm next to me. "Good news so far."

I nodded. "Yeah."

He studied me for a second. "When did you sleep last?"

Before I could answer, he added, "More than three or four hours?"

I rolled my eyes. "I'm fine."

He gave me a look that called bullshit.

Then Ryan waved to get my attention, making a face, but he spoke into the phone. "Yeah, Steve's here. . . . Yeah, sure." He put the phone to his chest. "I'm on hold for a second. What the hell did you say to him?" he hissed. "Fucking hell." Then he put the phone back to his ear. "Yep, sure. Got it. Okay, thanks." He disconnected the call and gave me another wild look. "Well, you're not his favorite person right now."

No surprises there. I glanced at Roscoe and he smiled at me. It was probably wrong to laugh, but fucking hell. I chuckled and Roscoe did too. It was either laugh or cry. Then I scrubbed my hand over my face.

What a freaking day.

"Crowd's gathering downstairs," Ryan announced. "Media, papzz, fans. It's all over social mdia."

Aaaaand this day just got impossibly worse.

Ryan gave me another look. "Ambrose is trying to fix it."

I almost felt bad for yelling at him.

"You guys will have to leave via one of the service entries," I said. I sounded tired, even to my own ears. "Kitchen, laundry, utilities. Hospitals have several. We just need to speak to hospital security and call our drivers, or even a cab." I looked up at Ryan. "Just ask for the hospital's head of security to come see us. I'll speak to them. No big deal."

Ryan nodded, his phone already to his ear as he walked out.

"We should let the FBI know too," Roscoe said quietly. "Agent Zielinski or whatever his name was."

I made a face. "Well . . . I'm probably not his favorite person either. He came by this morning . . ."

Christ. *Was that today?*

Roscoe stared, then he laughed. "Oh, Steve."

I growled. "He assumed me and Jeremy . . . You know, that's not even the point. The point was that he assumed something. What kinda cop assumes anything in the middle of an investigation? So I told him what I thought about that."

Now it was Roscoe who made a face. "He assumed you and Jeremy, huh?"

"Please don't start." I shook my head. "Because *that* is the reason for this whole mess."

He was absolutely going to say something but Maddox appeared at the door. "Babe?"

Roscoe went in, and a few very long moments later, Ryan returned with the head of security.

With Robbie and Ryan, we discussed an escape plan, and I called the drivers to let them know where we needed them to be.

Ryan went in to see Jeremy for a few moments before he left, and then it was just me and Robbie. "Just us, huh?"

He smiled. "Jeremy'll be fine, boss. And I'm sorry about the singing thing. I didn't think you'd get into trouble because of me."

"It wasn't because of you."

It was because of me.

It was all because of me.

I sighed. "What a fucking mess."

Roscoe appeared and gave me a kind smile. "He wants to see you."

Oh.

Was I ready to see him?

No, and yes.

I stood on unsure legs and went in. Maddox sat beside the bed. Roscoe went and stood by him. Jeremy looked . . . well, he looked awful. Still beautiful, and he still took my breath away. But now for another reason.

I wasn't prepared to see him so vulnerable.

He had a patch of hair shaved above his temple and an angry purplish line through it. It was about two inches long and had been fixed with surgical glue, and I couldn't tell if it was bruised or just the terrible lighting.

He was pale and looked tired as hell.

"Hey," I murmured.

"Ryan gone?" Roscoe asked.

"Yeah."

"Can we stay?" Maddox asked.

I shrugged, because I'd assumed he'd be the one person staying. But Roscoe answered. "We should go," he said, giving Maddox's shoulders a squeeze. "The doc said only one person can stay, and given the FBI case and the need for security, it has to be Steve."

I could see Maddox considered arguing, but after turning back to Jeremy, and a silent exchange between them, he nodded. "Yeah, okay."

God, he was leaving me with Jeremy . . .

Maddox gave Jeremy a soft kiss on the forehead before they walked out. "Text me when you know you're allowed to leave."

"Will do."

"Robbie knows how to get you out. The driver's been notified," I said.

Roscoe gave me a nod.

And then it was just Jeremy and me.

My insides were heavy and I was afraid of what he

might say. I wasn't even sure if he wanted me to sit with him.

"Hey," I said, not sure how close I should go.

He lifted his hand off the bed and it took me a second to realize it was an offering. I somehow got my legs to work and took his hand. He squeezed my fingers and I could have cried.

"Hey," he whispered.

"Can I get you anything?"

He swallowed but gave a gentle shake of his head. "Just stay with me."

"Okay."

He slow blinked and let out a heavy breath. "Feel bad."

Oh shit. "Can I get the doctor for you? Want me to press the button?"

"No. Feel bad for what I said. Did."

Oh.

"How about you don't worry about that right now. You just rest."

"Wanna go home."

"I know. I'll take you as soon as they let me."

He was quiet for a few long seconds. "I'm sorry. About before."

"You mean I'm not fired?"

His hold on my hand tightened. "No. Well, if you let me drink tequila again, probably, yeah."

I chuckled, so relieved. "Noted."

"Maddox said you yelled at Ambrose."

I groaned. "I'll have to apologize. I was out of line."

"Madz said what you said was right."

"Ambrose is a good guy. He deals with a lot. He caught me at a bad time. Which is not an excuse. I'll call him later."

Jeremy sighed again, slow blinked a few times, but kept

a hold of my hand. "Thank you. For pulling me out of the water."

"Maddox got to you first."

"You helped. Or so he said."

"You don't remember?"

He shook his head a little. "No. I remember puking on the ground and being in wet clothes." He made a face. "Feel like I wanna puke but can't. They gave me something. I dunno. I'm never drinking again."

"What did the doctor say?"

"That I'm an idiot."

I smiled at him. "Pretty sure she didn't say that."

"Yep. It's in my file and everything."

"I see they gave you a bit of a haircut."

He frowned. "Maddox took a photo and showed me." He let his head roll to the side so he could see me better. "Am I still pretty?"

I looked him right in the eye, and even though my stomach swooped and my heart squeezed, I told him the honest truth. "Jeremy, you're so much more than pretty. You're so much more."

His eyes met mine and he nodded as if he finally understood something. His chin wobbled a little and he got teary, then let out a shaky breath.

What was that reaction?

"You okay?"

He nodded again but then shook his head. "I don't know."

"Jeremy?" I whispered.

His grip on my hand was tight, like he was afraid. I wanted to say so much more. I wanted to stupidly tell him everything. I wanted to lay it all on the line. I wanted to ask what he was so afraid of. Was it me? Was it this?

But a nurse bustled in, startling us both. I wasn't sure if I was disappointed or thankful.

"How's the patient?" she asked as she checked his IV and the monitor he was hooked up to.

I went to let go of Jeremy's hand but he kept ahold of mine. "I want to go home," he said.

"We need to go through the concussion test," she said. "Do you remember the four pictures we showed you?"

"Beach ball, house, cat . . . keys."

The nurse smiled. "Good."

"Can I go home now?"

"One more test. I'll be back in a bit."

"Oh," I said, stopping her. "Can he sleep? I should've asked before. He's tired. It's been a big week."

She smiled. "Sure he can."

When we were alone again, I put my other hand over our joined ones. "Want me to turn the lights out? Need a drink or some ice?"

He smiled sweetly. "Just stay with me."

My heart knocked against my ribs. "Okay."

He slow blinked once, then again, but this time his eyes stayed shut. I studied his handsome face and the awful wound on the side of his head and the shaved strip of hair. It was bruised. I could see that now.

Was it normal for a personal security guard to sit and hold their charge's hand?

No, it wasn't.

Was our relationship normal?

Not anymore.

What were we, exactly? Friends? Close-professional? Just professional? More than that?

I had no idea.

There was something between us, and it scared him.

Hell, it scared me, and I was gay. He had, up until whatever this was, considered himself straight. And now he was having confusing feelings for a guy.

For me.

He was clearly unsure and had some issues to work through, and we'd probably need to have some kind of conversation about it.

Not to mention all the other stress he was under with the fixated person and the media circus.

Right now he needed to not be alone, and he needed someone to hold his hand. And that someone just happened to be me.

Needing a distraction while he dozed, I scrolled through the internet to see what the media was saying about him.

I shouldn't have looked.

Atrous was trending. That was no surprise. They usually were.

But the footage of Robbie singing and playing the guitar had gone viral. And it wasn't just him. It was the band singing and dancing, clearly drunk.

And me, in the background, leaning against the door, looking on, laughing and smiling at all of them.

Smiling at Jeremy.

Of course, the Atrous fans had examined every millisecond of the footage. Every frame in detail, every movement, every single thing. Not just the clothes everyone wore, but jewelry, hair-styles, shoes. The back of Jeremy's house, Amy in the reflection of the windows recording the whole thing, and me, of course.

The headings and grab lines were terrible.

*The Iceman smiles!*

*Steve 'the Iceman' Frost thaws out.*

*Normally stoic and serious, but smiling as the band sing in the backyard, head of security, Steve Frost . . .*

*Footage of Atrous enjoying some downtime even has Steve the Iceman smiling . . .*

*Atrous security manager smiles only for Jeremy while Maddox and Roscoe get cute . . .*

For fuck's sake.

Admittedly, most of the accolades were for Robbie and his ability to play the guitar and sing. Robbie was also trending on all major social media sites.

They were all trending to some degree.

Clearly posting a video of the band drunk-dancing and singing hadn't been a great idea.

No wonder Ambrose was pissed.

There was also mention of paramedics being called to Jeremy's home address, but it hadn't really picked up momentum yet. The drunk-dancing video had the spotlight for now.

More sites were reporting it as a rumor, and 'our sources say' kind of bullshit. Given he was obviously drunk in the dancing and singing video, most reports were connecting the dots. One person had even claimed to see Maddox and Roscoe entering the hospital.

I mean, they weren't wrong. But they had nothing confirmed.

Jeremy groaned and I almost dropped my phone. I retook his hand and looked him over. He was still asleep, from what I could tell. So I forgot about my phone, about the internet, about the world outside, and just watched Jeremy instead.

THE DOCTOR ALLOWED him to leave after the next concussion test. He remembered the images correctly, four consecutive times in separate intervals. With promises to return if he experienced any dizziness or blurred vision, vomiting, or onset headaches, we were allowed to get him home.

I'd called in a company driver and he picked us up from the service dock and drove us back to Jeremy's home. He was so tired, he'd almost fallen asleep on me in the backseat of the car. Not that I minded, but I had to rouse him to get him inside.

The house was mostly dark, but a sleep-rumpled Riko met us in the hall. "Sorry, I fell asleep."

I wasn't surprised, since he'd been up since 3:00 a.m. and it was now going on . . . I checked my still-not-working watch. I had no idea what time it was.

"No worries," I said as Jeremy went on ahead. "I better get him to bed. And Riko, sleep in tomorrow. I don't think any of us will be up too early."

"Okay, boss."

"Night."

I caught up to Jeremy as he was taking the stairs to his room. "Hey," I said, resting a hand on the small of his back. "Not so fast."

"Hm" was all he said.

I managed to get him into his room and I pulled the covers back from his bed. "You sure you're okay?"

"Hm. Shower or bed?"

I wasn't expecting that. "Uh . . ."

"Bed," he said, answering his own question. "Should change."

The hospital had given him a change of clothes, donated from local churches, or so the nurse had said. It was a pair of brown pants and an old blue button-down. He looked bohemian chic.

If I wore that, I'd look homeless.

Regardless, it was better than the wet clothes he'd arrived in, and I was very grateful they'd given him anything.

Jeremy unbuttoned his shirt and let it drop to the floor, then he undid his pants and stepped out of them. Completely freaking naked. When he said he was going to change, I hadn't realized he meant right where he stood.

Christ.

But he got into bed, pulled the covers up to his waist.

*Say something, Steve.*

"Can I get you anything?" I asked.

"Hm," he said as he lay down, very careful of the right side of his head. Then he reached out and patted the other side of the bed. "Will you stay?"

Uh, what?

Had I heard him correctly?

"Please," he mumbled. "Stay."

Holy hell.

"Um, okay," I whispered.

I walked around his giant bed, and even in the dark, I could see his eyes on me. I lay down on top of the covers, facing him, pulling a pillow under my head. He didn't smile at me. In fact, I think he looked scared.

But he reached his hand out and I took it. My heart was thundering, banging against my ribs.

This was absurd.

He closed his eyes, and in just a few seconds, his grip on my hand loosened when he fell asleep.

*Wow.*

*What a day.*

I tried not to overthink the fact I was in Jeremy's bed, holding his hand while he slept. And I tried not to think about the fight we'd had earlier, all because he'd seen my scars and I wouldn't tell him what'd happened.

That was what the whole fight had been about. He thought I didn't trust him, but that wasn't the case.

Lying there, watching him sleep, I knew come morning I'd tell him the whole story. It would mean outing myself to him, it would open a box I could never close.

I didn't know what it would mean or how it would end. But after the day we'd had, it was the right thing to do.

But that was tomorrow.

Right now, I had every intention of staying with Jeremy for a few minutes, until he was sound asleep. Then I'd go back to my room and leave him be.

But I was so tired. So, so tired. I just had to close my eyes for a second . . .

---

I JOLTED awake to a light-filled room, startled, heart racing. I didn't know where I was, what time it was.

Until I noticed Jeremy, lying there facing me, smiling despite the fresh wound on his head.

I scrubbed my hand over my face. "Fuck. Sorry. I fell asleep. How's your head? Need me to get you anything?"

The corner of Jeremy's lips curled upward in a half smile. "You're wearing my clothes."

# CHAPTER THIRTEEN

HE WAS CLEARLY FEELING OKAY.

"Yeah, I took a dive in the pool yesterday fully dressed. Maddox brought these clothes to the hospital. He wore something of yours too."

His eyes softened and he blinked, still kinda smiling. "It looks good on you. Bit tight."

"What time is it?" I asked.

"I have no idea." He reached over and took my wrist, looking at my watch.

"It died yesterday."

Jeremy frowned. "From going in the water?"

"Yeah."

He lifted my wrist closer. "At five thirteen. Is that the time I went into the pool?"

I nodded. "Sounds about right."

He sighed. "I dunno where my phone is. At the bottom of the pool, probably."

I tried to think. "I don't remember seeing it."

He stared at me for a long moment. "I don't think I want to find it. I want to lie low for a few days."

I remembered the social media hype about their drunk video from yesterday and the rumors about his trip to the hospital. And I thought about the people we would have to call this morning. Maddox, Luke, Wes, Blake, Ryan, Ambrose . . . God, I had to apologize to Ambrose. I had the sudden urge to throw my phone in the pool too. "You should call your mom."

He smiled again. "I'll need to borrow your phone."

I studied his wound, his scar, for a bit. There was some bruising, but it looked otherwise healthy. "How's your head?"

"Sore."

"You have pain pills and antibiotics. We brought them home from the hospital. But you should eat first. You hungry?"

"Mm."

I sat up and swung my feet to the floor. "I'll make you some breakfast."

Jeremy sat up and pushed at the covers, quickly pulling them back up. "Uh, Steve? I'm not wearing any clothes."

I shook my head. "Because you stripped last night. Don't you remember?"

He squinted. "I remember getting undressed. I didn't realize I was naked."

I laughed as I spotted my phone on the bedside. I picked it up, and ignoring all the missed messages and phone calls, I saw the time was 9:20 a.m. "Holy shit. We must have slept for ten hours. I have so many missed calls." I was in so much trouble. I made my way to the door. "Eggs and bacon in ten minutes."

I dashed down the stairs, rounded the corner, and almost tripped over myself when I saw Riko, Maddox, and

Roscoe sitting at the dining table. "Morning," Maddox said brightly.

He knew I'd spent the night in Jeremy's bed. Not that anything had happened, but still . . .

"I just woke up, sorry."

"Yes, I stuck my head into Jer's room."

I sighed. "He asked me to stay. I fell asleep."

"I know," Maddox said, his smile far too smug. "I saw. You were a good boy on top of the blankets and everything."

I growled at him, which just made him smile even wider. "Where is he?"

"Coming down now. He needs to eat before he can take his meds."

Maddox lost his smile at that. He got up from the table and dashed up to Jeremy's room.

Roscoe reached for a bag on the table. "We bought some egg and bacon sandwiches from Starbucks. Nothing crazy, but we figured, apart from the really sore head he'd have, that he'd need hangover food. And coffee."

I was suddenly starving and *so* grateful. "You're a lifesaver."

I patted Riko's shoulder. "Everything okay? Sorry I overslept."

"It's all good. I spent two hours watching the gardeners on the CCTV. I'm going to give my dad lawn care pointers."

I chuckled at that. I could see on the security screens that the gardening team was in the front yard, and Robbie was in the back. "Is the big guy okay?"

"Yeah," Roscoe said. "I think he's a bit worried that the hype over yesterday's video might be an issue for the boys. Jeremy, in particular, with everything going on."

I sighed. "I'll talk to him again. It wasn't his fault." My phone buzzed again and I groaned when I saw another message. This time it was Ryan. "I need to make a dozen phone calls too, apparently."

Roscoe grimaced. "I've spoken to Ambrose this morning, if that's what you mean."

"He called me too," Riko said. "When you didn't take his call. I told him your phone was on silent. That you got home late, that Jeremy was home. He wants you to call him."

I bit back the mother of all sighs. "Yeah. Thanks. I will."

Riko stood up. "Oh." He went into the kitchen and took a container from the side of the sink and placed it on the counter. "Jeremy's phone. It was at the bottom of the pool. Rice is supposed to help, but I don't know how much good it'll do."

"He wondered where it went."

Roscoe physically put a takeout coffee in my hand. "Drink."

I took a large swallow and it was heavenly. "Thanks."

But I couldn't put off the inevitable. I shot a quick message to Ambrose.

*Jeremy's okay this morning. His phone is currently in a box of rice. Will call shortly.*

Then Roscoe shoved a breakfast sandwich in my hand. "Eat."

"I feel so out of the loop," I mumbled, more to myself than to them. "I'm normally up for hours by now and have everything organized and under control. I haven't even had a shower."

"It's been a bit crazy, huh?" Roscoe said.

I bit into the sandwich and nodded. "Jeremy wants to lie low for a couple days, and I think that's a really good idea."

Roscoe nodded just as Jeremy and Maddox came in. He

shoved an iced coffee in Jeremy's hand and a sandwich in the other while he inspected the doctor's handiwork. "Looks pretty good this morning. I mean, it looks sore as hell, but it looks okay."

"Hmm," Jeremy said, with a mouthful of food. "This is so good. Thank you. And I just want to say sorry for yesterday."

Roscoe rubbed Jeremy's arm. "Apology accepted. I'm just glad you're okay. Maddox was worried sick. All the guys were."

"I don't know where my phone is. I can't call anyone," Jeremy said around a mouthful of food.

"Your phone's in the container of rice," I said. "Riko fished it out of the pool."

Jeremy sipped his coffee. "Thanks, Riko. But I wouldn't have cared if it stayed in the pool."

"It's probably just as well if you don't go on the internet anyway," Maddox said. "It's a shitshow today."

Jeremy sighed long and loud, and Maddox gave him a hug and didn't let go. "I'll post in the group chat that you're all right," Maddox said. "We'll speak to Ryan and tell him you're okay but that you want some downtime, okay? He'll make it happen." Jeremy nodded and Maddox finally pulled back but kept him at arm's length, his hand on Jeremy's face. "Take as much time as you need."

Jeremy sighed. "We've got a busy week coming up."

"First interview is two days away," Maddox said. "If you don't want to do it, then you don't have to do it. It's that simple."

"How can I do anything looking like this?" He waved at his injury. "I've got a fucking headache and I just wanna lie in a dark room for a day. Or two."

Maddox kissed his cheek. "Then that's exactly what

you'll do. We'll leave you alone now. I just wanted to see that you were okay. I'll text Steve later to see how you're doing. Oh, but you'll need to call your mom. She'll be worried."

Roscoe seemed a little surprised that Maddox was leaving so soon, but he certainly didn't argue. I walked with Robbie out to the van and made sure he was okay. "Is Ambrose still mad at me?" Robbie asked. "Is he mad at you because of me?"

"No. He's certainly not mad at you. He's mad at me because of how I spoke to him. I'll go in and call him now and figure it all out. He'll want to know that Jeremy's okay."

"*Is* Jeremy okay?"

I nodded, smiling up at him. "Yeah. He just needs some time to rest. We'll have a quiet few days, I think."

Maddox came and put his arm around my shoulder, which was a little odd. "You look after my boy."

The way he said it was odd.

"Of course."

"Small, gentle steps."

"Uh, pardon?"

He just laughed and climbed into the van. Robbie followed him in and closed the door behind them. I watched them drive out and made sure the gate locked.

*Small, gentle steps.*

What the hell?

Trying not to think about what he meant by that, I went back in to find Jeremy in the kitchen. He'd found his pills and washed his antibiotics down with a grimace.

"You feeling okay?"

"Headache. Tired. Feel kinda shitty about bailing on everyone, especially because this whole mess is my fault for being a drunken dick yesterday, but I just can't deal with anything today."

I put my hand on his arm but when that didn't feel like enough, I trailed my fingers up to his shoulder, then to his neck. It was an intimate touch, and we were probably standing far too close. "You're okay, Jeremy."

His blue eyes cut to mine and he whispered, "I don't know what I'm doing."

"About what?"

He made a pained face. "Can you give Riko the day off? I don't mean to sound ungrateful, but Steve, I don't want anyone here right now."

Oh.

I dropped my hand from his neck. "Well, Riko, sure. But I'm not leaving. I'll . . . I'll just stay out of your way."

He fisted my shirt. "Not you. I didn't mean you. I meant everyone else."

"You want me to stay?"

He nodded, but god, he looked so confused. Tormented, even. He let go of my shirt and took a step back. "I need to go take a shower," he said. "Brush my teeth. I feel gross."

"Okay." I didn't tell him that I would go do the same because that sounded like an invitation. Or a suggestion? So instead, I went with, "I need to call Ambrose."

He nodded again and backed away until he turned and disappeared. I let out a slow and steady breath. Things were weird. A good weird, as if something was about to happen between us, maybe? It was a thrill of anticipation and dread.

Somewhere in my head, a voice was saying not to let it happen. It could jeopardize everything. It would change everything.

But my heart . . .

"Boss?" Riko's voice startled me. He eyed me cautiously. "Everything okay?"

Clearly fucking not.

"Yeah, I was just thinking. Jeremy asked for some space today. I told him I'm not leaving, but I'll just stay out of his way." This was not a lie. "I was thinking you could go into the office, today and maybe tomorrow. You could get some stuff done for me."

He almost smiled. "And also be your ears and eyes."

I smirked. "Yeah. I don't think Ambrose wants to see me right now." I shrugged. "And it might not hurt if you hear any office rumors or rumblings."

"Sure thing."

By the time a car came to pick Riko up, I'd had a shower and was feeling decidedly more awake. Riko said he'd call me when he got into my office, and as I watched him leave on the security cameras, I knew I couldn't put off the call to Ambrose I'd been dreading.

It was tense, to say the least.

The thing was, what I'd said to him was right, which he said he understood. But what he'd said to me was right too. He was under a lot of stress and pressure, and honestly, I didn't envy his job at all. But we'd had a close call with Jeremy yesterday, and I wouldn't apologize for prioritizing his life over what strangers said on the internet.

Except, those 'internet spot fires,' as I'd called them last night, were now raging wildfires.

"Maddox said it was bad. He told Jeremy not to look."

"Smart."

"He's, uh, his phone went in the pool so it's dead," I explained. "He said he's not interested in having it fixed, and he wants to lie low for a few days. He knows about the busy week ahead, but to be honest, I don't know if you should include him in anything next week. You'd have to explain the whopping gash in the side of his head. I guess the photoshoot they can just catch his good side? I don't know."

"Hm," Ambrose grunted.

"I'll ask him to call you tomorrow. Hopefully he'll be feeling better—"

Just then, Jeremy came down from his room, and my words died. He was holding a pair of hair clippers, and his hair was gone.

He'd given himself a buzzcut all over.

"Uh, Ambrose. I have to go."

"Is everything okay?"

I was so stunned I could barely speak. "Um, sure. Nothing urgent. Uh, I'll call you later."

I disconnected the call and was still staring at Jeremy. He grinned and held the clippers out to me. "Can you see if I missed any in the back?"

All I could do was laugh. "Joining the army?"

He snorted. "I couldn't very well have a strip shaved into my hair. It looked stupid."

I took the clippers. He'd shaved it down to a number two. "Come out onto the patio."

I led the way but he squinted at the sun and used his hand as a visor, so I pulled him into the shade. "Better?"

He nodded, still squinting.

He had a few strips where he'd missed on the back of his head, and it just took a second to tidy up. When it was done, I took his hand and brought him back inside. "You need to stay indoors with the blinds down," I said, leading him to the couch. "Here, take a seat. I'll get you a pill for the headache." I opened the blister pack and gave it to him with a glass of water.

He downed it without any argument, then closed his eyes. I closed all the blinds before I sat beside him and took his hand. "Is that better?"

He nodded and smiled. "Yeah." He had his eyes open now, so that was an improvement. He took a couch cushion, put it in my lap, and lay down, using me as a pillow.

*All right then.*

I gently rubbed his newly shaven hair, careful of his scar. It was soft and lovely. Maybe not as nice as his curls—and the guys and Ambrose were probably going to freak the fuck out—but it kinda suited him.

He closed his eyes and dozed off, smiling as my fingers teased his scalp.

The line of purplish surgical glue that ran through the scar almost matched the faint color of his closed eyelids. His long lashes fanned out perfectly, his pretty nose, his pink, kissable lips . . .

My god, he was so good looking.

He slept for a little while and I scrolled through emails and messages on my phone. And then I made the mistake of checking Twitter and TikTok. Every entertainment news site was reporting on that damned drunk-singing video and the reported rumors of Jeremy being taken to the hospital. On top of the rumored FBI investigation. Platinum Entertainment had declined to comment. There was footage of Jeremy's front gates, footage of the media scattering at the sound they assumed was a gunshot, footage of Jeremy on stage.

*Jeremy Dalton, Jeremy Dalton, Jeremy Dalton.*

*Atrous, Atrous, Atrous.*

Every damn site.

I shouldn't have looked.

I wanted to protect him. Not just from a security standpoint. I wanted to take him away from it all. Where none of that mattered, where he could just be himself.

I wanted to shield him from the world.

I wanted to be honest with him.

I ran through the conversation I needed to have with him a hundred different ways. While he was asleep in my lap, I stroked his scalp, tracing my fingers through his shaved hair, coming to the realization that I was going to tell him everything.

He needed to be able to trust me and I needed to be honest with him.

When his eyelashes fluttered open, it was now or never.

"You feel okay? Headache gone?" I assumed the pain meds had kicked in.

"Yeah." He sat up. "Fell asleep, sorry."

"It's fine."

"You did the drawing finger pattern thing on my head. It's lights out, every time."

That made me chuckle. "Good to know."

"It's nice and dark in here, like a movie theater. We should do a movie marathon. Or an entire TV show on Netflix, every season, every episode. Something funny, preferably."

"Sounds good." Actually, it sounded amazing.

"What's wrong? Did something happen?"

"No, no," I said, suddenly very nervous. *Here goes nothing.* "Can I tell you something?"

Jeremy nodded, frowning, expecting bad news.

"You, uh, you wanted to know about my scars . . ."

He stared at me, stunned. Maybe a bit panicked. "Only if you want to tell me. You don't have to. I know I asked, but I was being a dick, sorry."

"I've not told anyone," I admitted. "This isn't easy

for me."

He took my hand. "You don't have to tell me. If it's too much."

"I want you to know. I know you read the articles when you searched my old name but I want you to hear it from me."

He met my gaze, intense and honest. He tucked one leg up underneath his ass, held my hand in his, giving me his undivided attention. "Okay."

"I was nineteen," I began. "I'd qualified for the national MMA title in Vegas. There was a group of us that did the circuit together. We did all the same tournaments, competitions. We even trained together sometimes. Kinda friends, kinda not."

Jeremy nodded.

"Anyway, there was one guy I was closest to. We started to spend a bit of time together . . ." I let out a breath and steeled myself for the next part.

"We began hooking up. It was—"

"Hooking up? With women?"

Fuck.

"Uh, no. With each other."

He blinked, twice. But then he smiled and squeezed my hand. "Steve, I had no idea. Well, what I read online about you said you were, but I don't believe most of what I read online."

"No one knows. I never told anyone at the company. Well, Roscoe knows."

His eyes widened. "Roscoe? Oh my god, did you two—"

"Absolutely not. He guessed, very recently, that I'm . . ." *God, this never got any easier for me.* "That I'm gay."

*God, I said it out loud.*

"Hey," he murmured, now holding my hand with both

of his. "It's cool."

I shook my head. "I've had to hide it all my life."

Jeremy's concern turned to realization. "Oh Steve. Your scars . . ."

I swallowed thickly, my mouth dry. I managed a nod. "Trey, that was his name. The guy I was hooking up with. We'd known each other for years, just through the tournament circuit. I caught him looking one time, or maybe I checked him out. I can't even remember. But we started hooking up, and that went on for a few months. We got to the nationals, sharing a room in Vegas to cut costs, right? A few other guys did that, no big deal. Not that they knew we were hooking up with each other. Believe me, being gay in that crowd was a death sentence."

"Oh, Jesus," he breathed.

"We were careful. We weren't stupid. But a guy with a ski mask busted in while we were . . . you know. In bed." I shook my head at the flashback memories, like a freaking strobe light. "He had a knife. Got me three times in the back before I could turn around, and then he got me three times in the front. We struggled and he ripped the knife upward and slashed outward, trying to do as much damage as possible." I shuddered. "He was crazy, real frenzied. I think that's what scared me the most. I thought I was going to die."

Jeremy looked like he might cry. "I'm so sorry."

"Thanks."

"What happened to Trey?"

"Scared the shit out of him. He didn't compete again. Left town the next day. Last I heard, he was working for a construction company in Ohio."

Jeremy's face was pure concern. "You knew the guy? That stabbed you?"

I nodded. "We got the tournament draw and I had a few easy first rounds. Guys I knew I could beat. But the quarter finals would be a guy by the name of Chase Hystek. He was good. A bit wild and had a temper problem, which made him easy to beat. I'd beaten him before, in the regionals. He didn't like that much." I inhaled as much calm as I could.

Jeremy squeezed my hand and scooted closer, our bodies touching.

"The motel we were staying at was kinda sketchy. Certainly no cameras back then. Hystek probably would have gotten away with it, but I got his knife from him and stabbed his arm. He took off . . ."

"Oh my god," Jeremy breathed. "Steve, I'm so sorry."

I smiled at him. "The cops got his fingerprints from the knife, picked him up with a stab wound to his forearm. He didn't just admit to doing it. He gloated to them." I shook my head. "I spent six hours in surgery and woke up to find myself fully outed as being gay. The cops had told my parents that I'd been in bed with a man, that they'd charged Hystek with a string of offenses, including a hate crime against me because I was gay."

He paled. "They didn't know before?"

I shook my head. "No. They didn't take it well."

"Fuck." He got a little teary and all but climbed into my lap, half hugging me, holding my arm. "Steve."

"I lost everything that day."

"You said you didn't compete for the national title because of an injury. I thought you meant a hamstring injury. Steve, I had no idea. And you changed your name? Because of your parents?"

I nodded. "Partly. My fighting days were over, and the court case . . . My name would be forever associated with that. I moved into security and started over. I took my mother's maiden name, trying to keep some part of me. I dunno. I didn't want that shit following me. I still don't, Jeremy. I don't want that to reflect on you guys in any way."

"I won't tell anyone." He swallowed and shook his head. "I shouldn't have asked. I had no right to make you relive that. I'm sorry."

I studied his blue eyes. "I wanted you to know."

He was so close, touching me, holding my hands, half sitting on my lap.

His gaze went from my eyes to my lips. His lips parted and he leaned in as if he was going to kiss me . . . then shook his head and shot up off the couch. "God, sorry. I'm . . . I'm not . . ." He bolted for the kitchen.

Shit.

I went after him. "Jeremy," I called out.

He was in the kitchen, standing at the far end. He ran his hand over his newly shaved head and winced when he bumped his scar. "Fuck."

I went right up to him. "Hey. It's okay."

"I'm not gay," he whispered. "I'm not bi. I'm not." He shook his head. "But you . . ." He sucked back a ragged breath. "Fuck. I don't know."

*But you . . .*

Me.

"It's okay, Jeremy."

He was about to freak out. Or bolt.

He'd had such a shit twenty-four hours. And I'd just dumped my past on him, and now I wanted to make him feel better.

I put my hand on the left side of his head, down to his jaw, and he seemed to take this as some kind of invitation.

He leaned into me, his face in my neck, and he slid his arms around me.

Holy fuck, he was hugging me.

I wound my arms around him and he sighed, relaxing into my arms. He gripped my shirt at the back but he was heavy against me. But then I could feel his hand tremble.

Oh, Jeremy.

"You okay?" I murmured.

He shook his head against my throat.

"Did you want to talk about it?"

"I . . . I don't know." He pulled back and his hands ran up my chest, balled into fists. His eyes were full of fear. "This is . . . I don't know what this is."

And Maddox's words came back to me. Small, gentle steps.

"It's okay," I whispered.

I had no intention of doing anything. He was very clearly warring with himself. But then his eyes went to my mouth. He licked his lips and leaned in.

Holy shit. He was going to kiss me.

I stopped breathing. Every cell in my body was electric.

His lips parted and he was so close . . .

But then he shook his head. "I don't . . . I'm not . . . this isn't . . ."

My heart felt as though it was on fire, scorching and consuming. My stomach was knotted to the point of pain. I closed my eyes and took a step back. "Sorry."

Jeremy snatched a fistful of my shirt. He was looking down . . . at his hand? At the floor? Anywhere but at me. "Don't go," he breathed. "I don't know what this is. But you leaving right now feels wrong."

"Jeremy," I whispered.

He looked up, his blue eyes full of fire, fear, and uncertainty. His grip tightened on my shirt and he pulled me closer. "You shouldn't say my name like that."

He was killing me.

I wanted this. For years, I'd wanted this.

Him.

We were so close. His body heat, his breath. His scent. His beautiful face. Those blue eyes and his mouth.

God, his mouth.

My eyes went to his lips—parted, pink.

I wanted to kiss him. To hell with the consequences. I drove my hand up his chest, up his neck to hold his face. I tried to be gentle, but desperation won.

He grunted, and it almost did me in.

"Jeremy."

His hand on my shirt pulled me closer. Our bodies collided and he kissed me, mouth open, tongue deep and desperate.

Wonderful.

Everything.

I pushed him against the counter, well aware that the feel of a man against him might be too much for him but unable to stop myself.

But he didn't freeze. He didn't stop.

He groaned and melted into me, his mouth open for the taking. I wanted to hitch his leg up. I wanted to do things to him.

But for now, this kiss would be enough.

It would be enough forever.

So I kissed him deeper, harder. And he let me.

He surrendered, and that was the moment I slowed down. I didn't want to scare him. Reality was going to crash down around us as it was.

I pulled his bottom lip between my teeth. Then, keeping my forehead to his, I gave us time to breathe.

I gave him time to realize he'd just kissed a man.

That he'd just kissed me.

He shook his head, his brow furrowed. "Fuck."

And here was reality.

Cold and dreadful, but not unexpected.

I put my hand on his chest, our breathing rough. I didn't want to make eye contact, afraid of what I'd see there. Afraid that I'd find regret looking back at me.

But he cupped my face and lifted my chin, and he crushed his mouth to mine and turned us around, pushing me against the kitchen counter. His whole body pressed perfectly against mine. Surprised but eager, I opened my mouth and let him kiss me this time, let him do whatever he wanted.

He kissed me hard, his lips, teeth, tongue. His hands dug into my back, fingers raking as he clawed, desperate.

I ran my hands down his back and over his ass, pulling me closer still. I could feel his arousal, hard against my own.

He had to feel that.

And if I'd have thought it might scare him, it just seemed to spur him on. He wasn't gentle. He wasn't tentative or unsure.

He was frantic and eager, taking what he needed, all hands, mouth, body.

He kissed with his whole body.

He was about to undo me.

I broke the kiss and pushed him off me, but not too far. I just needed to breathe and to get my body in check. "Gimme a second," I murmured.

I still expected him to freak out. I expected him to be mad that I ended the kiss, pushed him away. God, I could barely catch my breath. I waited for him to back away farther, to turn and run. But he didn't.

He pressed his fingers to his lips and laughed.

# CHAPTER FOURTEEN

JEREMY and I stood in the kitchen, staring at each other.
He laughed first, then I laughed.

Relief? Amazement? Shock?

Yes.

"Well," I said. "That was . . ."

He nodded. "Yeah. It was."

I laughed again, then licked the corner of my mouth.

Of course, he looked at it and took my chin in between
his thumb and forefinger. "First man I ever kissed."

Oh wow.

I felt giddy, my knees were weak. "And? How was it?"

His grin was wicked. "Fun." He pushed me against the
counter again, his grip on my jaw a little tight. A lot hot.

And he kissed me again.

Rough, hard, deep tongue and sure hands. I let him do
what he wanted until my body was fast approaching that
point of no return. I broke the kiss, and this time he bit
down on my jaw to my neck. Hot jolts of pleasure shot
through me and I pushed him back with a laugh. "I don't

think you're ready for what'll happen if you keep doing that." I had to readjust myself. "Christ."

He grinned, smug. Wet lips, desire in his eyes. "You're probably right." But then he searched my eyes as if he was trying to find the answer to something in his head. "I don't know why . . ."

Oh boy. "Why, what?"

"Why you? Why a guy? It's absurd. But you . . ."

"But me?"

"Yeah, but you. I just kissed you! And I'd like to do it again. It doesn't make sense. I am not gay. I'm not even bi. I like women. Always have." He shook his head. "But you . . . You're different."

"Uh, thanks."

"And you just unloaded a lot of baggage from your past, so my timing is probably way off."

"And you almost died yesterday. You've got a crazy stalker, and we had a pretty big fight where you fired me, and you shaved your head this morning."

"I didn't fire you. Well, I did, but I didn't mean it. I don't even think I have the capacity to fire you. I was mad. I thought you didn't trust me to tell me about what happened to you. I thought we had something, something deeper, where you should trust me like I trust you."

"I do trust you."

"I know." He frowned. "And to be honest, I was mostly pissed at you because I kept thinking about you and how I wanted to kiss you and how that was so fucking bizarre. It was kinda making me crazy. It's confusing as hell. And even now, I don't really want to think about what it means."

Fair enough. I knew the mental ping pong I played when I'd first realized I was attracted to guys. I didn't want to think about what it meant or what labels were what.

"You don't have to think about it," I offered. "You don't have to put a name to anything, Jer."

He ran his thumb along my jaw. His eyes watched on in wonder. "Stubble, rough skin. I'm used to soft and gentle. I don't know why it's different with you. This shouldn't feel so good."

I leaned into his touch. It had been so long since anyone had touched me like that. It actually made me a little light-headed. "Wow."

He lifted my face and pressed his body to mine. "Why is this so hot?"

I barked out a laugh, and in one quick movement, I turned us around and backed him against the kitchen counter as he'd done to me—not too forceful, but not exactly gentle. My hips against his, hard and fast.

"Holy fuck," he gasped.

God, I wanted him.

I wanted him in every way imaginable. But he wasn't ready for that.

I let out a shaky breath and tried to channel some self-control. "We should slow down."

He grunted. "Should we?"

"Jeremy," I breathed. "My self-control is barely holding on. It's been a very long time for me, and this is all a bit too much, too fast. I'm going to embarrass myself."

It took him a second to catch on, and of course he laughed. He pulled me even closer by my hips, his fingers digging into me, and I had to take a step back.

I put my hand to my forehead. My body was strung tight, my dick was hard, and my balls were well past blue. "Yeah, okay, I wasn't kidding. I need a minute."

He laughed and thankfully gave me some space, but

then he reached up to his newly acquired scar, and he grimaced.

That was a hard-on killer. I inspected it, looking for any sign of redness. "Is it sore? How's your headache?"

"It's okay. I kinda forgot about it. You distracted me."

I smiled at that. "Did you wanna lay on the couch and just watch TV? Or have a nap? Are you hungry?"

"We could watch TV." He rocked back and forth, then chewed on his bottom lip. "Will there be making out on the couch?"

I chuckled, my heart thrilling at his words. "If you want."

"I want."

So he led me to the couch and proceeded to push me onto it and pat the cushion. "Your head here. Lie down."

"Okay, bossy. Do you always get what you want?"

He smirked as I did what I was told. "Come on, Steve. You know I do." Then he lay down next to me, facing me. My arm was his pillow, and he snuggled into me.

Okay then.

I let my arm slide around him and I carefully kissed his forehead near his scar. "Uh, Jeremy? You're not facing the TV."

"Hm." He sighed. "This is better."

This was sooooo much better. And very surreal.

How was this even happening?

"Hugs are good," he mumbled.

"They are." Hugs were the best. I'd missed this kind of contact. Being intimate with someone, affectionate.

And here I was, being intimate, affectionate . . . with Jeremy.

*It has to be a dream.*

"Feels like a dream," I murmured. "To be here with you like this."

He ran his nose along my throat. "Not a dream. It is weird, though."

"Weird?"

"Yeah. How do you smell good? I'm used to floral scents and girly body mists. You're the opposite of that. You smell like . . . well, I don't know. A guy."

"Funny, huh?" I really shouldn't have joked about it when it was all so new and strange to him. "Sorry. I know it's gotta be strange for you."

"It is." He ghosted his lips along my neck and I shivered, making him smile. "You're all muscles and hard angles, stubble and hard hands. I wanted to kiss you for weeks. God, holding hands with you was a rush." He pulled back to meet my eyes. "It is strange, and it's confusing. I'm trying not to think about it too much."

I thumbed his cheek. "Just do what feels right."

"Well, I was trying to in the kitchen but you needed a minute."

I chuckled. "Lying here with you like this isn't doing me any favors either, just so you know."

"When you said it'd been a while for you, how long are you talking?"

Oh god. "It's, uh, it's been years."

Jeremy stared. "Years? Christ. I thought my six months was a lifetime."

"Six months, huh? I wondered why you weren't hooking up with anyone on the tour."

His eyes flickered between mine. "Because . . . because of a dozen reasons. Mostly because I was starting to take notice of someone that scared me."

"Scared you? Who? Which country were we in?"

He laughed. "Not a stalker or anyone *scary* scary . . . well, he can be. When he's mad. I'm talking about you."

Wait.

What?

"You've been thinking of me like that for six months?"

He scowled at me. "Don't let it go to your head. It really pissed me off to be honest. Because, what the fuck? A guy? And you? Mr. Steve the Iceman Frost, can kill anyone with a well-aimed glare, snaps at everyone. Wants everyone to think he's a hard-ass when really he's sweet and funny. I mean, he still is a badass, but he's *also* sweet and funny. Looks a bit like Jason Bourne. Acts a bit like him too. Is very protective, which is hot. Not gonna lie. Yeah, *him*, that guy. Like I said. What the fuck? I tried to talk myself out of it. Which went really well, as you can see."

Wow.

I chuckled. I couldn't help it. "Sorry to disappoint you."

He sighed with a smile and slow blinked, seemingly content to just lay in my arms on the couch. "When you said it'd been years . . ."

I snorted. "I mean years. It's not easy for me to relax enough when I'm with someone. Considering the last time I got into bed with a guy, I got stabbed six times."

His gaze cut to mine and he caressed my neck. "Thank you for telling me," he whispered. "About your scars and the asshole who did that to you. For trusting me."

"I do trust you."

"You're relaxed now," he said. His tone made it a question.

"I am. I feel safe here."

He studied me for a moment. "I hope he got what he deserved. The guy that did it."

"He got two years."

"Two years? Is that all?"

I shook my head. "Initially. But he found himself some more trouble in prison. There was a fight and some other inmate died, and a guard was injured. Hystek got another fifteen years added on to his sentence."

"Good," he growled. "Well, not good for the guy who died, obviously. But good that he's still locked up."

My phone buzzed. I had to maneuver my thigh in between his so I could retrieve my phone from my pocket. Jeremy groaned and I bit back a laugh as I answered. "Riko."

"Yeah, boss. Can you talk?"

I knew Jeremy could hear every word but I had nothing to hide from him. "Sure."

"I'm in your office. There's a . . . there's a lot of merch in here. Like boxes and bags of it."

"Merch?"

"Yep, shirts, hoodies, pencils, diaries, posters, that kind of thing. There are four different calendars on your desk."

Jeremy laughed. "I asked Ryan to get you one of everything."

Riko would have heard how close Jeremy's voice was to mine.

"And, uh, boss," he added, "there's a life-size cardboard cutout of Jeremy."

Jeremy laughed. "Ryan should get a raise."

There was a second of silence. "Am I on speaker?" Riko asked.

I rolled away from Jeremy the best I could, half on my back, and tried to keep the phone away from Jeremy. "No, sorry. Jeremy's just being annoying."

Jeremy sat up and gave his best offended frown-pout, but then his eyes went to my chest, and lower, lower,

lower . . . It was hard to feel scrutinized when he was watching with part fascination, desire, and confusion.

Riko was in my ear, telling me about Ambrose meeting with the feds and the LAPD, and heated meetings with the PR team, all while Jeremy was eyeing my crotch.

I didn't need to be a mind reader to see he was trying to figure out just how far this attraction went. Physically, that was. It was one thing for a maybe-bi guy to hold hands with a man, to kiss him. But when dicks got involved, it could go downhill pretty quick.

I gripped his chin, bringing his eyes up to meet mine. "Thanks, Riko. Keep me posted." I disconnected the call, not breaking eye contact, and slid my phone onto the coffee table.

Was he about to freak out?

Jeremy pulled at the hem of my shirt and lifted it, then ran his hand over my abs and the waistband of my jeans.

Okay then. No freak out.

"You okay there?" I asked, my voice rough.

He smirked, his eyes full of mischief and heat. And then he pounced on me. He crushed his mouth to mine and pressed his weight on me, his hand slipping under my ass and he hitched my leg up.

Fuck.

He delved his tongue into my mouth, his hips rolled, and he grunted.

I broke the kiss with a gasp. I'd gone from zero to a hundred in an instant. I was too close. "Jeremy, god . . ."

It had been too long for me. He was as hard as me. I could feel him, and he was everything I wanted.

If he didn't stop now, he was going to make me come.

His eyes were full of fire. "I want this. Tell me you want this too?"

Oh sweet heavens.

All I could do was nod.

He kissed me again, hard and deep, fit one leg between mine, and he ground against me. We moved, rocking back and forth, still fully clothed. I gripped his ass and drove my hips up, rubbing my hard-on against him, desperate for more. When he groaned into my mouth, I knew there was no going back.

He was as aroused as I was.

His erection pressed into my hip, his thigh between my legs rubbed my balls. I dragged my hands down his back, over his ass, feeling every inch of him I could reach, while grinding against him.

I still couldn't believe I was doing this with Jeremy.

*The* Jeremy Dalton.

That he wanted to do this with me.

He had to break the kiss to breathe. Ragged and hitched, he drove his body against mine perfectly, his back arched as his fingers dug into me. He closed his eyes, groaned, and shuddered.

Holy shit, he was coming.

I gripped his ass and thrust, chasing the friction, hurtling toward my own orgasm. Then Jeremy grunted and bucked, his whole body jerking.

And that coil low in my belly, that pull in my balls, came undone and I shot my load. I held onto him, my body tight, as pulse after pulse of pleasure washed over me.

Jeremy collapsed on top of me, his face in my neck, his weight sending a ripple of shudders through me. After a few long moments, he laughed. "What the fuck was that?"

I chuckled, barely catching my breath. "That was . . . that sure was something."

Untouched, still dressed, like horny teenagers. I came in

my jeans, Jeremy in his track pants, and the smell of sex was heavy in the air.

He propped his head up on his hand, heavy-lidded. I wondered for a second if things would be awkward . . . but then he smiled and kissed me again.

And he kept kissing me, deep and languid, with a slow tongue and tender lips. It was a serious kiss that had my heart knocking against my ribs.

Was this just physical exploration for him?

Or did it mean something more?

I wasn't game enough to ask in case it burst whatever surreal bubble I was currently in.

He slowed the kiss, ending it by pulling my bottom lip in between his. "I could kiss you all day," he said dreamily. But then he peeled himself off me and stood up. He extended his hand. "Come with me." Then he stopped. "Oh. You already did."

I burst out laughing. *Gawd.*

"I meant come this way . . . or let's go this way." He laughed. "Though I'm down for more coming. It's the best hangover cure."

He pulled me to my feet and I let him lead me, as it turned out, to his room. Well, his bathroom. Where he walked in and took his shirt off like it was no big deal. "Shower time," he declared. "I haven't jizzed in my pants since I was like sixteen."

He was so open about everything, as he was with all subjects. I don't know why it surprised me that he'd be the same with this.

He walked into the shower and turned the water on, then came back out and slid his hands under the waistband of his track pants. "You can't have a shower with your clothes on, Steve," he said.

Hmm. Getting naked was never easy for me. They'd see my scars and were either repulsed or weirdly curious. But this was Jeremy . . . He was different, wasn't he?

I didn't have much time to contemplate, because he slid his pants down and stepped out of them.

Jeremy was naked in front of me. His lithe and fit body, trim and muscular, bare chest, defined abs, and a gorgeous cock that hung half-hard. His foreskin intact. Sweet mother of god.

I was standing in his bathroom with him when he was completely naked. And we'd just made out until we both reached orgasm.

I was beginning to wonder if maybe I'd hit my head in the pool and that this was all some kind of cruel dream.

"I'm not supposed to get this stupid surgical glue wet for another day." Then he glanced in the mirror and did a double take. "Shit. My hair."

I gestured to the trash. "If you're looking for it." There were clumps of his hair in it. And in the sink. "And in there. You did a shit job at cleaning up."

Jeremy snorted. "Shut up and get into the shower. You're wasting water."

Ugh.

Right, then.

I pulled my shoes and socks off, shirt and jeans. I'd never actually showered with anyone before. What did I do? Just walk in?

"Here," Jeremy said, handing me a soapy loofah. "Helps if you're actually wet though."

I was sure he was just doing that to make me feel more at ease. It worked. It gave me something to focus on, at least.

His shower was huge, ridiculously so. There were several jets of water and enough room for six people, let alone two. I washed the jizz off first before soaping up my chest and under my arms. Jeremy watched me, smiling.

"I've gotta keep my head dry, otherwise we could have awesome shower sex."

I coughed on the steam. "Ahhh."

Jeremy laughed. "Just kidding."

"I've, uh, I've never even showered with anyone before, let alone had sex in a shower."

"Never?"

"Never." I shrugged. "Plus, water-resistant lube is a bitch to clean up."

His smile died as realization hit him. "Oh."

It was my turn to laugh. "Just kidding."

He shut the water off and I handed him a towel. "I'll need to go grab some clothes," I said.

"Just wear something of mine. I have an entire wardrobe of shit I never wear." He dried his body, then dabbed the towel at his sore head. He had zero modesty, no shame whatsoever. All those years of getting changed in a dressing room full of people would probably do that. He noticed me staring. "What?"

I shook my head, smiling, embarrassed. "Just you. You're fucking beautiful." I gestured to his body. "And I'm here with you, like this. After what we just did on your couch . . . feels like I'm dreaming."

His smile quirked at one corner. "It's crazy, huh? This is weird, you and me. Don't get me wrong, I've wanted this for weeks, months, even. And I told myself to get over it, lusting after a guy was weird." His smile softened. "But now that we're here, it's not as weird as I thought it'd be."

I tied the towel at my waist, and not once did Jeremy look at my scars. "I'm glad it's not weird. But you know if it does start to feel weird or get a bit overwhelming, you can tell me. Just call a timeout."

He met my gaze and gave me a small nod, but then he winced.

"Headache?"

"Hm. A little. Could stand a nap." He walked into his walk-in closet stark-ass naked and came out wearing boxers. He threw me a pair of gym shorts and held up a shirt. "This be tight enough? I mean, big enough?"

I chuckled. "This outfit, although I'm sure was painfully expensive, is hardly work appropriate."

He stopped. "Work? Are you working right now, Steve?"

"Well, no . . ."

"Were you working on the couch with me?"

"No."

"In the shower? Was that work?"

I sighed. "No, of course not. Sorry. That's not what I meant."

"Then get dressed. Unless you want to stay in the towel all day." He sat on the bed, picked up some kind of remote, and the blinds began to close. Clearly bright daylight wasn't doing his head any favors.

I pulled the shorts up. They were kinda tight. "Sorry, I should have thought to close the blinds in here."

He sat on the bed. "'S okay."

I pulled the shirt on, and yes, it was tight, but I automatically felt less insecure now that I was covered. I lifted my arms to try to stretch the fabric. "Is this a small?"

Jeremy smiled at me. "I think it's just right."

I scowled at him. "I need to get my phone," I said. After the whole 'am I just a job to you' comments, I added, "Not for work. Just in case there's some kind of emergency. My phone is the only way anyone can reach us."

He gently touched around the scar on his head. "Yeah, okay."

"Lie down and I'll bring you some of your pills."

"And maybe something to eat? Or juice?"

Shit.

"Of course."

He nodded and lay on his side, so I ducked out and went downstairs. I found my phone on the coffee table, smiled as I straightened up the cushions on the couch, remembering what we'd done there.

So surreal.

I grabbed his meds, poured some juice and a glass of water, then added some fruit and crackers. Jeremy laughed when I carried a tray into his room. "I've never had this kind of room service before."

"I should hope not."

He took his pills with the juice and ate some crackers. "Thank you," he said quietly. "You don't have to do this for me."

"I don't mind."

I pinched some of the fruit, eating some, feeding some to him, making sure he ate enough.

"You feeling better?"

"Yeah." He lay back down and patted the other side of the bed. "Stay with me."

I put the tray on the floor and climbed over him, settling in beside him with my head on the pillow, facing him. He smiled at me, sweet as could be. "Can I ask you a question?"

Oh boy. "Sure."

"You're a top, right?"

# CHAPTER FIFTEEN

"WHAT THE . . . ? JEREMY—"

"It's just that I know Maddox isn't. He talks about getting dick, taking dick, he's all about the dick. Well, he doesn't talk about it so much anymore. Now that he has Roscoe's constant big dick, apparently. But from the ages of eighteen to twenty-five, do you know how many times we heard about it?"

I couldn't help but laugh. "I sat in a car with you guys for years. I heard enough."

His eyes went wide. "Oh my god, you heard all those conversations?"

"Most of them."

He laughed. "Well, shit."

"Honestly, I stopped listening a long time ago. Too many things I didn't want to hear."

"About?"

"About conquests, and taking you guys to bars, and hearing managers talk about NDAs, that kind of thing."

His nose scrunched up. "Gross, huh?" Then it seemed to dawn on him. "Oh . . . because of me?"

I laughed and hated that I could feel myself blush. "Well, yeah."

He studied my face. "How long . . . how long have you . . . you know?"

Oh god, here we go . . .

I didn't want to have this conversation so early in whatever this was. Or at all, but here we were. Despite being nervous, despite feeling foolish, I decided to go with honesty.

"I always noticed you, Jeremy. Always. I never once thought of you in that kind of way . . . until Vermont. When we spent a week there with Maddox and Roscoe."

"That was over two years ago," he whispered.

"I know."

"Why didn't you say something?"

I rolled onto my back—it was easier not to look at him when I spoke about this. "I never would have dreamed something with you was ever possible. You were straight, for a start. But also the professional slash personal thing isn't easy. I still don't know what any of this means." I sighed. "And putting that shit out there isn't really my thing. It's not easy for me to put myself in a vulnerable place. Even now. Telling you this, even, is hard. I don't want you to think just because I've noticed you for a long time that I'm emotionally invested while you're just here for some fun and trying new things. This is very new to me too." I palmed my face. "Fuck."

Jeremy scooted closer, snuggling in and resting his head in my armpit. "I don't know what this means either, Steve. But I'm not just trying new things for fun. This whole being-attracted-to-Steve thing scared the shit out of me. For what it's worth, I've been trying to convince myself not to lust after you for months. Clearly that's working out really well, considering you're in my bed right now."

I let my arm fall around his shoulder. "We don't have to let it mean anything," I said. "Or it can mean whatever we want. It can be as much or as little as you need."

I felt him tense a little and he was quiet for a few long seconds. "What do you want?"

God.

"I want you to be happy. That's all."

He leaned up and scowled at me. "That's a bullshit answer."

I snorted. "What do you want me to say?"

"The truth."

"I do want you to be happy. That's not bullshit."

He patted my chest. "No, what does Steve Frost want? Not for me. What does he want for himself?"

Christ, he was going to make me say it.

"I want to take this one day at a time. Considering it's barely hours old, anything else would be foolish. I want you to be comfortable in exploring this, to see if being with a guy is right for you. I want this, yes. But not at the expense of anything else. Not my job, not your safety, not any*one* else. That's what I want. Just one day at a time, with you."

I didn't even want to think about work. Ambrose would pitch a fucking fit if he found out, especially after what I said to him on the phone last night.

Jeremy sighed, kinda smiling, kinda not. "That's a very . . . sensible answer."

I manhandled him so I could pin his hands to the bed, lying between his legs. I was gentle but his eyes went wide with shock and desire, his mouth a stunned smile.

I kissed him. "I'm a sensible guy, Jeremy. It's what I do. I want you to be happy. Isn't that enough?"

He nodded and licked his lips. "Fuck."

I rocked my hips into his and gave him a filthy kiss until he melted underneath me. His legs fell open, he arched his back.

Surrender.

I drove my tongue into his mouth and he took it, groaning when I rolled my hips. He was getting hard again.

My smile broke the kiss. "And what do you want, Jeremy?"

It took him a second to focus. "I want you to finish what you started."

Laughing, I kissed down his neck, nipping at his jaw, sucking on his skin below his ear.

He shivered. "Steve?"

I pulled back. "Yeah?"

"About what I asked before . . . about you being a top . . ."

Ah, jeez.

"Okay, first up, Jeremy, slow down. Yes, I am. But there's no rush for that."

"I don't know if I can do it," he said quickly. "I know what Maddox says and I know where the male g-spot is, thanks again to Maddox, who explained in vivid detail—"

I couldn't help but laugh. Not that I meant to. But god . . . I kissed him with smiling lips. "Jeremy, slow down. You don't ever have to do that. I wouldn't care if you never wanted to do that. It's not a deal breaker. There's a hundred other things you can do that don't involve anal sex."

He sighed. "Being with you like this is great. You dragging me across the bed just now was fucking hot. I've never been . . . uh . . ."

"Manhandled?"

He laughed. "Yes, manhandled. And honestly, when

you did that thing, pinning me to the bed, I'm pretty sure I'd agree to anything you wanted to do to me if you did that again. And you're a totally in-charge kinda guy. It's what I like about you. It's what I find so appealing, if I'm being honest. But . . . god, this is so embarrassing."

"Don't be embarrassed," I said, kissing him softly. "I'm glad that you want to talk about it. But as I said, it's not something you ever *have* to do. A lot of gay guys don't do that."

"Maddox said—"

"Maddox said his truth. You're not him. You're not going to like everything he likes. And Jeremy," I said, pecking his lips again. "You've been experimenting with a guy for a about one hour. Real life is not a porno."

He groaned a painful sound this time and covered his eyes. "I watched a lot of gay porn. Trying to see if it was hot or if it was just you that interested me. I have so many questions."

I burst out laughing and took his hand away, making him look at me. "Anything you want to ask me?"

His cheeks were pink. "Maybe another time?" I laughed again and started to pull back, but he slung his leg around mine. "Or you could stay right where you are," he mumbled. Then he rolled his eyes. "See? This is hot. You feel so good on top of me. I can feel your dick. It turns me on." His gaze went to my mouth. "I can kiss you harder than I ever could kiss a girl. I can grab you harder, hold you harder, push, pull, touch . . . it's like you're unbreakable. That's hot."

I snorted. "Well, I *am* breakable." But then I lightly ran my fingers down the side of his face, along his jaw, and ran my thumb across his lip, light as a feather. I sucked his earlobe into my mouth and whispered, gruff in his ear. "I can be gentle too."

His eyes rolled and his dick twitched.

Then I took his hands and held them above his head, widening his thighs with my knees. "Or I can be rough."

He arched his back. "Fuck, Steve."

It sounded like a plea.

"Want me to suck your cock?"

His eyes opened, dark and feral, and his dick twitched again. He was harder now, rolling his hips in search of friction.

"I'm going to need you to answer me," I breathed, kissing down his neck.

He gasped out a groan. "God yes, fuck please. Yes."

I smiled as I kissed down his chest, his stomach, until I found his cock straining in his shorts.

Jesus, yes.

I peeled back the elastic and revealed his erection. Sure, I'd seen him in the shower, I'd seen him stark naked, but not this close, and not this erect.

Pink, veiny, intact.

He was glorious.

His foreskin was begging to be played with, tongued, slid back and forth, and sucked, so I did that first.

Jeremy gripped the comforter at his sides before his head shot up to look at what I was doing. "Fuck," he breathed. "Jesus what the . . . ?"

I smirked while I tongued his foreskin, his slit, and he fell back on the bed with a groan.

I settled in then, intent on enjoying it, working him over, sucking him hard and slow and all the way down into my throat.

His thighs trembled, his hands found my hair, and his abs flexed as he gasped in each short breath. "Gonna . . . gonna . . . fuck, I'm gonna . . ."

*Hell yes, give it to me.*

I cupped and massaged his balls and he cried out as he came, a low and guttural groan. His whole body tensed and trembled as he pulsed into my throat.

I hummed as I took it, and he twitched and jerked as I sucked him clean. He collapsed, utterly spent and heavy-lidded, a bewildered smile on his face.

I couldn't help but feel a little proud. I crawled up his body and fell next to him. Jeremy turned his head and slow blinked. "What the fuck was that?"

"A blowjob?"

"No, what kind of wizardry was that?"

I chuckled. "Glad you liked it."

He rolled to face me, snuggled into my chest, using my arm as a pillow, and after a few deep breaths, he was asleep. I kissed the top of his head, careful of his injury.

This man, this beautiful man, was heaven in my arms.

It still felt like a dream, even though I was certain when reality came crashing down—yes, *when*, not *if*—this thing between us would be over. I didn't know what that meant for my job, or how awkward it would be between us.

But I was determined to enjoy every minute while I could. Even though it was easy to forget about the stalker, and about all responsibilities outside his bedroom door.

He snoozed on my arm and, knowing I couldn't put off the inevitable, I thumbed out quick replies to messages and emails with my free hand.

After all, I was technically still supposed to be doing my job.

There was a message from Riko.

*Change of plans. Meeting now scheduled for tomorrow 9 am. Expect Ambrose to contact you.*

I replied. *Thanks for the heads-up.*

Then there were messages from Luke and Wes and Blake, all for Jeremy to call them.

And Maddox had sent about ten. I could only assume it was the longest they'd gone without being able to contact him at all. It was sweet of them, though I understood Jeremy needing a few hours' break from the world.

I didn't dare look at the internet or any social media sites again. I didn't search Jeremy's name or look for any drama. If there'd been any urgent updates, Ambrose would have called.

Besides, this bubble I was in with Jeremy was every dream come true. I didn't want to be the one to burst it.

I didn't have to. Consecutive messages from Ryan and Ambrose burst it for me.

Ambrose: *Mr. Kim has requested a meeting 9am tomorrow in the conference room. Jeremy and yourself are expected to attend.*

Short and not-so-sweet but to the point. I didn't expect anything different.

Ryan: *I've organized Sayed for a pick up at 0820 tomorrow. If Jeremy needs anything just let me know. New phone perhaps?*

Jeremy sighed against my chest. "Is it anything important?"

I rubbed his back. "Meeting tomorrow at nine with Arlo Kim. Car will be here at eight twenty. If you need anything, let Ryan know. You need to call all the boys, they miss you. And Maddox is having withdrawals." He snorted and I handed him my phone. "You can read all the messages."

I had nothing to hide from him. Certainly no dating apps or booty calls or anything like that.

My entire life was work. The only emails and messages I got were from Ambrose, Roscoe, Ryan and Amber, or any of my team. There was nothing in my phone I wouldn't want him to see.

He wriggled down the bed a bit, and using my stomach as a pillow, he took a selfie.

"What are you doing?"

He chuckled. "Madz hasn't seen my new haircut." He showed me the photo. You couldn't tell he was lying on me. The shirt I was wearing just looked like a cushion of some kind. And then, scrolling through the contacts, he sent it to Maddox's number.

"You called Maddox's number often?" he asked.

"It's saved in the contacts, but I don't think I've ever called him. Roscoe, yes." I chuckled. "Jealous?"

"You've never called me before."

"And you've never called me."

He turned his head, eyes narrowed, and he looked about ready to say something snarky but my phone rang with a FaceTime. It was Maddox.

Jeremy held the phone up so only his face was on the screen, much like the selfie he took, and he answered. "Hey, Dickbag."

"The fuck did you do to your hair?"

He snorted. "I shaved it."

"Well, I can see that. Do you need to talk about why? Are you okay, dude?"

"I'm fine. Much better this afternoon. Do you think Ambrose will like it?"

Maddox laughed. "I think he'll shit a brick when he sees you."

"I had a strip shaved into the side of my head," he added. "I was just finishing the job."

"How's your head, anyway? The scar looks good, from what I can see."

Jeremy brought the phone in close so Maddox could get a better look before he zoomed back out. "It's not so bad."

"Jeez, Jer, you could at least put a shirt on. Are you lying on your bed in your underwear? Christ, poor Steve. What would he say if he walked in on you right now?"

Oh hell . . .

Jeremy laughed and aimed the camera at me. "Dunno. Ask him."

Maddox dropped his phone.

# CHAPTER SIXTEEN

MADDOX WALKED into Jeremy's living room, his eyes as wide as his smile. "Nice of you to get dressed and out of bed. Got the blinds drawn for a reason? Keeping it cozy?"

Jeremy rolled his eyes. "We'd still be in bed if you didn't insist on storming the fort."

I half raised my hand. "For the record, I was dressed."

Maddox, still grinning, pointed at me. "You're next. First, you," he said, grabbing Jeremy by the arm, "are coming with me. We need to talk."

He dragged Jeremy down the hall, leaving me alone with Roscoe, who looked the same mix of stunned and amused as Maddox. "So . . ."

I let out a slow sigh, trying not to smile. "So . . ."

"Things are going well."

I laughed. "I don't even know, to be honest. It's great but will probably be all over by tomorrow."

"Why tomorrow?"

"Well, the meeting at nine with Ambrose and Mr. Kim. Because I've had a few run-ins with Ambrose and Ryan in the last few days, so I'm guessing the meeting might be about that and possibly me being taken off detail. Or whenever Jeremy realizes his temporary insanity has passed. Whichever comes first."

"I don't know what the meeting tomorrow is about. Ambrose said it was just another update, but you know how that goes." Roscoe stared at me, smiling. "And I don't think Jeremy will plead insanity. I think he's finally figured something out, made his peace with it, or just said to hell with it. He likes you, that much is clear."

I couldn't dare believe that.

I didn't know what was going on between Jeremy and me, but I was absolutely certain I was way more invested than him.

I let out a long sigh and ran my hand through my hair. "I dunno, Roscoe."

"Has he . . . ? Have you—" He made a face. "—done anything?"

I wasn't going to answer that, but in the end, I conceded a nod. "He's still not sure about what any of it means," I said quietly. "Neither am I. He wants to do stuff, and he's certainly not shy. But I'm waiting for him to say that being with a guy is not for him. That all this stress he's been under and being held hostage by me in his house made him do stuff he wouldn't normally be comfortable doing."

"Like Stockholm Syndrome?"

"I guess. I dunno."

"No. You're not holding him hostage. Steve, I'm telling you, he's liked you for a while. He just didn't know what to do with it or how to move forward. Being confined with you helped him with that. Maddox said Jeremy requested you stay with him when there was talk of rotating shifts or something."

"He likes routine and his privacy. He was used to me and Riko."

"But then he asked Riko to leave."

"Yeah. He said he couldn't deal with anyone being around today."

"Except you."

I sighed and nodded. "Yeah."

"Steve. He wants this."

"But he's . . ."

"What? A world-famous star that could have anyone in the world and for some stupid reason they want you?" Roscoe pointed to his chest. "You don't have to tell me about that. I thought Maddox had lost his damned mind when he showed interest in me. But you see, what's different with these guys is trust. Oh, they could have anyone in the world, for sure, but who can they *really* trust? A handful of people, and that's it. Maddox trusted me for years first. We had that foundation of absolute trust, and that's a rock-solid base. And I'd bet you anything you like that Jeremy's the same with you. He *trusts* you. And for these guys, that's the most precious thing they can have."

It made so much sense when he put it like that. "I guess."

"So if he's unsure about being with a guy, he can trust you not to pressure him. He trusts you to walk him through it."

"I don't know what I'm doing either. I have no experience with this. I haven't had any kind of relationship since . . . a long time ago."

Shit.

"But you know him."

I sighed again. "I'd like to think I do."

"So maybe you need to trust him, Steve. Trust him like he trusts you."

My gaze shot to his, and my mouth was suddenly dry. "Trust is . . . not something . . . trust is . . ." I swallowed dryly and regrouped. "I trust my team. I trust the five guys in the band to keep me on my toes. I trust Ambrose to piss me off at times. Professionally, I trust procedure and protocol. Personally, trust isn't something . . . it's hard for me."

"Trust him. Will it be perfect? Will it be forever? No one knows. But trust him when he says he wants to try."

His words hit me so damn hard it felt like a physical blow.

"Right, now where is Steve?" Maddox said, walking out of the hallway. He was smiling. "It's Steve's turn."

Jeremy was one step behind him, looking embarrassed and apologetic. He also looked tired, and seeing the scar on his head reminded me that he needed to be taking it easy.

I stood up, ignoring Maddox, my focus only on Jeremy. "You okay? Headache?"

"Hm," he replied.

Which meant yes.

Maddox turned to him. "Why didn't you say something?"

"You were busy dissecting my life. I didn't want to interrupt."

Checking my phone for the time, I grabbed his pills with some juice and made him a very quick sandwich. "You're due to take two. Plus, you should eat something." I added some grapes and strawberries. "Here, please eat."

Jeremy gave me a small smile and took his pills gratefully. I wanted to caress his face, ease that line of worry on his brow so badly, but it wasn't appropriate in front of company.

"Jer, I'm sorry," Maddox said quietly.

He ate some fruit. "It's okay, I get it. You're crazy jealous that I never looked at you."

Maddox laughed. "Piss off." Then he shrugged. "Not jealous. More curious. I mean . . . You never even considered it? We had a lot of opportunities over the years. Shared beds, shared bathrooms, shared cars. And you never once—"

Jeremy looked at Roscoe. "How do you deal with the ego?"

It was Maddox who answered. "Do you wanna know what he does to me?"

"No," Jeremy and Roscoe answered at the same time.

I laughed, which of course made Maddox look at me. "You," he said. "I haven't begun your inquisition yet. First question, was that shirt sprayed on?"

Jeremy chuckled. "Leave him alone. I made him wear it."

"Because it was tight?"

"It was a contributing factor."

Maddox laughed. "God, you sure you're not gay?"

Jeremy shot him a look.

Maddox put his hand up. "Sorry. He's not gay or homosexual. He's not bisexual. He's Steve-sexual."

"Fuck off." Jeremy threw a strawberry stem at him.

"Leave him alone," I said, repeating Jeremy's line. I knew Maddox was joking—they joked shit like this all the time. But Jeremy hadn't got his head around labels yet. He didn't know what applied and what didn't.

But Steve-sexual?

"Yeah, leave me alone," Jeremy said. Then, to my surprise, he grabbed the front of my shirt and pulled me close and laid his head on my collarbone.

I put one arm around him, not sure just how much I should hold him. He clearly needed the contact.

"Say something smart now, dickbag," Jeremy mumbled. "I fucking dare ya." He lifted his head and smirked at his best friend. "I have a Steve. He knows six kinds of martial arts, so please, go right ahead and piss him off."

Maddox replied with a laugh and a slap on my shoulder. "You're so cute together. Love to see it. But," he added, "I do have questions that are non-shirt related."

Roscoe came into the kitchen and took Maddox's arm. "We're leaving."

"But—"

"But it can wait. You've seen all you needed to see."

I smiled at Roscoe and he smirked as he all but dragged Maddox out of the house. Jeremy stayed right where he was. If anything, he held me a little tighter.

I kissed the side of his head. "You okay?"

"Tired."

"Did he say anything to upset you?"

He snorted. "Nah. Just a hundred questions that I couldn't really answer."

I rubbed his back before I pulled away and lifted his chin. "You don't need to have all the answers, Jer. Just be you."

"I don't know who that is anymore," he whispered. His eyes searched mine. "I don't know what I want. I don't know where I want to be. And not just with me and *this*. Because that's confusing enough. But everything else . . . I don't know what Atrous is anymore or what we are as a band. I don't know. I'm just so tired."

Holy shit.

I cupped his face and pressed my lips to his. "You need a break. Time to rest and think."

"You know what I really want?" he asked, his voice soft.

"What's that?"

"A real life. A normal life. I don't know what that's like. I'm a grown ass adult who can't cook, who rarely drives. I own two cars—never drive them. I have nothing in my life that's normal. I have the guys, who all live a crazy life just like me. It's all we know. I just want simple things. I want to do something normal."

"Like what? Let's go do it."

He smiled sadly. "There's papzz at the gates, or so Maddox said. Apparently the hospital story has gained some credibility. There're photos of Maddox and Roscoe leaving the hospital. I think Ambrose is gonna do some press release. I don't fucking know. I don't care anymore." He sighed. "I'm so tired."

I kissed his forehead and pulled him back in for a hug. I hated that every single aspect of his life was so heavily scrutinized. "Wanna go lie on the couch again? Take an actual nap this time?"

"Hm."

Taking his hand, I led the way to the couch and propped up some cushions. We ended up with me on my back and him on his side between my legs, his head on my chest, my arms around him.

It was better for his scar that way, and I could kiss the top of his head while he snoozed.

Reaching out to the coffee table, I pulled the laptop closer and viewed the CCTV screens. Yes, there were still papzz at the estate gates, some cars pulled off the sides of the road. It was stupid because they weren't getting in the first set of gates, let alone Jeremy's front gate, and all it did was piss off the neighbors.

And yep, not a few minutes later, a cop car pulled up and dispersed the crowd.

They'd be back though, no doubt.

They always came back.

While Jeremy slept, I thumbed out messages to my team, checked emails, and replied to Ryan's inquiry if Jeremy needed anything before tomorrow morning. I put in a request for his iced Americano, knowing he'd appreciate that tomorrow when we got to the office. I even said please and thank you.

Then, because Jeremy was still asleep, I brought up the footage from where he went into the pool and cracked his head.

I had a rough idea of what time it happened, because that was the time my watch stopped.

5:13 p.m.

The footage was in black and white but it was crystal clear. I guess that hefty price for the new HD state of the art cameras was worth it.

Thankfully there were no cameras in the family room. There'd never be footage of what we'd done on the couch earlier today, but there was also footage of our fight before Jeremy hit his head.

But the outside camera picked up the second Jeremy all but fell out the patio doors, drink in hand, staggering out. He was clearly angry, his expression hiding very little. Maddox followed him out, hand outstretched, and he said something. Jeremy spun around near the pool, stumbled, and went backward. He couldn't get his footing, arms out. He tried to turn, went into the pool, and hit his head on the edge as he went in.

It made me feel sick to see it.

Maddox ran and dove in after him. I appeared on the

screen one second later and dove headfirst into the pool. Maddox and I brought him up, Roscoe pulled him out of the water, and I lifted myself straight out after him.

I remembered it, of course. But to see it happen was something else.

We crowded around him, rolled him onto his side, and he vomited. The resolution was so clear, I could even see the blood pouring out of his head. I pulled my shirt off and pressed it to his head to stop the bleeding. Riko was soon there, his phone to his ear.

"Looks bad," Jeremy mumbled.

Shit.

I hit Pause.

"Sorry. I hadn't seen it and I . . . I thought you were asleep. Sorry. I should have asked you first."

"Nah, it's okay. Probably good for me to see it, to be honest. I missed the first part."

"Want me to rewind it?"

"Hm."

So I rewound it to right before the fight. "This is the part where we argued in this very room. You walked out, and that's when you come into view outside."

We watched it unfold again and it gave me a chance to look at the background, at the surroundings, to see if I might have missed something. Everything looked as it should.

"Can you stop it?" I did as he asked, and he was quiet for a long few seconds. "You and Maddox saved my life."

"Maddox got to you first."

"But you ran right in. Didn't hesitate. Just dove right in. And you put your shirt to my head."

"Maddox and Roscoe saw my scars."

"I know. Maddox told me."

Fuck.

"Riko gave me his shirt."

He shuffled around so he was facing me and propped his head up on his hand. "I owe you a new watch."

"No you don't."

"We should totally go buy one." He frowned. "What time is it? I have no idea. I don't even know what day it is."

"You don't owe me anything. The watch wasn't even that expensive." Well, it was expensive to me, but surely not to Jeremy.

"It's not the point. It was my fault."

"No it wasn't. You tripped and fell. Rather spectacularly, I might add."

"Shut up." He put his head on my chest. "I was drunk. No excuse, but I don't usually drink much. Alcohol isn't good for me."

I rubbed his back. "You don't owe me anything, Jer," I repeated. "I'm glad you were okay."

He was quiet again, staring at the screen. "What's that?"

"What's what?"

He pointed to the screen. "That. Is that a bird?"

In the right corner of the screen, above the trees, was a small flat dot. No, not a dot. A rectangle . . .

What the hell.

A drone.

"Fuck." I tried to sit up. "Hop up for me."

We untangled ourselves and I sat up, pulling the laptop closer. I slowed each frame down, zoomed in, and sure enough, a freaking drone was flying over Jeremy's house.

I pulled out my phone, scrolled for the number I was after, and hit Call. Of course it went straight to Message. "Gerald Dubrowski, this is Steve Frost. You did a new camera install for Jeremy Dalton. I need you to call me ASAP."

How could I have missed that in the footage?

*Because you're too focused on watching Jeremy, that's why.*

God damn it.

Next number I hit was Ambrose's. He answered on the second ring. "Steve."

"We might have had a security breach at Jeremy's house," I said.

"What kind of security breach?"

"A drone."

He was quiet for a second. "Goddammit."

"Neil, it was when Jeremy hit his head and went in the pool. We were looking at the footage and Jeremy spotted something on the screen. It's possible that this footage is out there."

"Jesus."

"I'm waiting for the security company to call me," I said. "These new cameras are supposed to detect that kind of thing. He told me it can recognize drone registration numbers or something. I'll forward anything I get on to Zielinski."

"Good idea."

"It could be nothing," I added, giving Jeremy's leg a squeeze. "But I'm not taking any chances."

"How's Jeremy?"

I met Jeremy's gaze, knowing he could hear Ambrose, and gave him a small smile. "He's okay. Still tired, and he's sick of dealing with this kind of shit. And I'll be honest with you, Neil, it'll depend on what we find out about this drone before we decide if we'll be in tomorrow at nine."

Would he argue about that? He probably wanted to, but

in the end, all he conceded was a sigh. "Okay. Keep me informed."

I ended the call and Jeremy ran his hand over his shaved head. "Fuck this. Why me? What the hell did I ever do to anyone?"

"You didn't do anything. We don't even know if that is a drone or if it's even related to your case."

"You think it is."

"I'm not taking any chances. Not when it comes to you."

He sagged back on the couch and let out a frustrated sigh. "How come people can fly drones over my house, spying on me, but I can't shoot them down? How is that fair?"

"You can't shoot at anything in Californian airspace."

"That's fucked up. What about my rights?"

"You can't shoot a drone. But they also can't be flown over people's houses trying to spy on them. That's against the law. If we can find the serial number of the drone and hand the footage and details over to the cops, they can press some pretty serious charges."

"If they can find the person," he replied. "Or maybe she's gone off-grid and not even the FBI can find her."

"They will find her." I gave his hand a squeeze. "I'm sorry if I'm overreacting or freaking you out. I don't mean to. I just need to be thorough."

He stared at me for a long moment. "Because you're not taking chances. Not when it comes to me."

He hadn't missed me saying that just now.

"Absolutely not. I won't let anything happen to you."

Jeremy almost smiled. "I can't decide if that's sweet, hot, or a little bit creepy."

I laughed, incredulous. "Since when is taking a bullet for someone creepy?"

"A bullet? Jesus." Now he really stared at me. "Would you take a bullet for me, Steve?"

I looked him right in the eye. "Yes. If it was life or death, yes I would."

"You answered that so easily."

"If I hesitate, you could die."

"Christ." His gaze fixed on mine. "Would you kill someone to protect me?"

"If it was life or death. If someone tried to hurt you and it was either them or you, I'd take them down. Of course I would. But would I kill someone just because you asked me to, without a justifiable cause? No. Absolutely not."

"Not even if I asked super nicely?" he joked. "Batted my eyelashes and used my very best manners?"

I gave him a nudge for being a dick. "No."

"Not even when Maddox won't share his M&M's with me?"

I snorted. "I'm not killing Maddox for not sharing his candy with you."

His smile faded slowly. "I want to go to the meeting tomorrow. I need to do my job. I need to get out of the house." He studied my face, my eyes, my lips. "Can you let them deal with it? Please? I know you want to save me and protect me, and that's great. I appreciate that, I really do. If someone comes bursting through the window, you can go all Jet Li on them. But I can't deal with this shit anymore. I just want to shut it all out and pretend the outside world doesn't even exist. Can you do that?"

He was asking me to stop being his security detail and to just be with him?

Like a tug-of-war between my head and heart, between what I should do and what I wanted to do.

It was never a contest. Not with Jeremy. My heart would always win.

"Yeah, of course," I said quietly, trying to ignore the swarm of butterflies in my belly. "Anything you want."

He grinned, the corners of his eyes creasing. "Anything?"

"Are you kidding me? Hell yes, anything."

Now he laughed as he got to his feet. "Good." He held out his hand. "Come with me."

# CHAPTER SEVENTEEN

"THIS IS NOT what I had in mind," I said.

Jeremy laughed. "I know what you had in mind. But I want you to show me how you do it."

I put the chopping board on the kitchen counter and handed him the onion. "Dice."

We had all the ingredients for his mother's spaghetti lined up. He'd called her and written down the recipe while I emailed everything to Zielinski—the footage, the contact details for the security company, Gerard Dubrowski's personal cell number, with requests for the FBI to follow up on the drone serial number.

If Jeremy wanted to block it all out and let *them* deal with all the details, then I was happy to hand it over. Not that it was my job. I knew that. But I had the footage. It was my job to hand it over and let the authorities deal with it.

My job was to keep Jeremy safe. And that meant in the kitchen too . . .

"Not like that," I said. "Hold the onion like this." I stood behind him, holding his hand over the onion, his other hand gripping the knife. "So you can't cut your fingers."

He hummed. "You just wanted an excuse to get all close."

"True." I kissed his neck and scraped my teeth along his skin. "But you want to cook, so . . ."

He put the knife down. "Fuck."

I was about to step back but he grabbed my hand and pulled me against him and pressed my dick against his ass.

He held me there. I didn't dare move, but I used my free hand to grip his hip. Hold him still.

Was he testing himself? To see if he liked it? Wanted it?

Was he testing me?

"You haven't finished chopping the—"

He spun around and pulled me closer by the waistband of my jeans, and yeah, he was hard.

"How hungry are you?" I asked, my voice rough.

His eyes almost set me on fire. "Starving."

He wasn't talking about food.

"Your head? Is it sore?"

"Orgasms make it better."

I chuckled. "Good." I kissed him, and when I pulled back, he chased my mouth. I lifted his chin and sucked on his Adam's apple. "First course first."

He groaned. His knees knocked against mine. "God, Steve. What the . . ."

I smiled as I kissed up to his stubbled jaw and palmed his dick between us. "Bedroom."

He nodded woodenly, and it was such a thrill to know I could turn him on like that.

I snatched up his hand and led him out of the kitchen, up the stairs to his room, and pushed the doors open. The blinds were still pulled down, the bed rumpled. I would have pushed him onto it if he didn't have a wound on his head.

I had to be more gentle . . .

So I turned him around, the backs of his legs hitting the bed, and forced him backward. He went willingly, smiling, licking his lips, watching me crawl up his body.

I crushed my lips to his, driving my tongue into his mouth and rubbing his erection. I wanted to do everything to him, with him, but I had to tread carefully, take it slow . . .

I slipped my hand under his waistband and wrapped my hand around him. He shuddered, moaning into my mouth. But then he fumbled with the button on my jeans and my fly.

I wasn't sure who was more stunned, me or him. He seemed to realize and stumbled a little. He took a second to catch his breath, searching my eyes before he continued. He undid the fly and palmed me through my briefs.

He wanted this. He wanted something . . .

I took his hand out of my jeans and pinned it above his head. He liked that. His whole body reacted, searching for friction, searching for more.

I stroked him a few times, kissing him deep. Then I freed my dick. Aligning our erections, I slid them both in my fist.

Jeremy gasped and closed his eyes, his head pushed back. I could've sucked on his neck, kissed him, bitten his ear, but so help me god, I couldn't take my eyes from his face.

We were slick with precome. Mine, his, I wasn't sure. It made the slide easier, wetter, hotter.

And when he came, the swell, the pulse, the sounds he made pulled me over the edge with him.

I imagined being buried inside him. I imagined him taking me in, taking what I gave him, every inch, every drop.

I came so fucking hard.

My senses came back to me with gentle scratches on my back and a warm chuckle in my ear. "You in there? Earth to Steve."

"Fucking hell," I tried to say. It was barely a mumble.

He laughed underneath me and rolled us onto our sides. He kept me close though, dusting soft kisses along my cheek, my nose, my lips. "I've never done anything like that before," he said. "And I've done a lot of shit."

I chuckled, trying to open my eyes. "Because you've never done it with a guy."

He smirked. "Maddox always said it was hotter with a guy. Never believed him. And whatever you do, don't tell him he was right. I'll never hear the end of it."

That made me laugh.

"He was already trying to give me sex advice today," Jeremy added. "All kinds of advice, actually. Kinda horrifying. Not gonna lie." He kept drawing circles on my back. "What did Roscoe say to you? When it was just you two. Did you talk about us?"

"Yep. He's actually kinda knowledgeable when it comes to secretly fooling around with a world-famous person. He imparted some pretty good wisdom."

He snorted. "Unlike Maddox's nuggets of wisdom, which I'll spare you from."

I chuckled again and kissed Jeremy's neck, his jaw. At least I had full use of my faculties back. That orgasm had wiped me.

*Speaking of wipe . . .*

"I should get you cleaned up," I said, trying to get my leg out from between his.

"Or we could just do this," he said, half sitting up and pulling his shirt off. Then he pulled at my shirt. "And yours."

I didn't like being shirtless, not around anyone. But Roscoe's words came back to me. *Trust him like he trusts you.*

So I pulled it off by the hem and tossed it onto the floor. We fell back into each other's arms, Jeremy's head on my chest and shoulder. I rubbed his back and he worked gentle patterns on my side.

His fingers skimmed my scars, but they never lingered. He never made them a point of focus or attention.

I gave him a squeeze. "Feeling okay?"

"Hm, yeah. Bit dizzy. Three times in one day will do that. You?"

So much better than okay. "Yeah."

"Still want to cook dinner with you."

"Sure," I said, then tried to get up.

He held me close. "Not yet."

I settled back in, smiling as I kissed the side of his head. He sighed and we stayed like that for a while, just peaceful and quiet. He seemed so content to just lie there, and while I didn't want to ruin the mood, we needed to start talking about whatever this was.

"Whatcha thinking about?"

He sighed. "Everything and nothing. I'm in that in between space."

I rubbed his back and gave him another squeeze.

He was quiet again for a few minutes, his fingers skimming my side absentmindedly. "Can I be completely honest with you?"

Oh god. "Yeah, of course."

He pulled back so I could see his face. "I still don't know what this is," he said, his eyes honest and searching. "But it's the realest thing I've felt in a long time."

Oh.

My heart knocked so hard against my ribs I couldn't speak.

"I often think about what Maddox went through," he continued. "That separation of reality, the struggle. I get it. I understand completely. This life doesn't feel real. We can stand in front of a hundred thousand screaming fans at a concert, then go back to locked hotel rooms or our empty houses. It's so freaking lonely. It makes it all feel so detached, and it's easy to lose who you are." He sighed. "For years I chased that buzz, ya know? The fame and the sex. And then I chased it just to feel something. In the end, it just made me feel . . . empty. I dunno. Used."

"I noticed you stopped going to the clubs with Luke and Blake a long time ago. Not just on the last tour but before."

"You did?"

I smiled. "Of course I noticed."

"God, did you hate it when you'd have to take us to nightclubs to hook up with someone?"

"It wasn't my favorite thing, but I understood."

"I'm sorry."

I cupped his face. "Don't apologize."

He slow blinked, his long lashes framing his eyes. "None of them were real. None of them meant anything. They used me like I used them." He made a face. "Sounds terrible but it's the truth. Until I just couldn't do it anymore. I needed something more. Something real."

I thumbed his cheek, too scared to speak.

"Something like you," he whispered.

I swallowed hard.

"I don't know what this is," he said again. He shook his head and got a little teary. "And forgive me for saying this, but I don't want to be gay. I'm not. I'm not sexually attracted to men—"

"Hey," I said, gently stroking his face again. "You don't need to wear any label you don't want."

His chin wobbled. "I know that sounds so bad. But I'm trying to get my head around this. I can admit when a guy is hot. I mean, who can't? But I've never wanted to . . ." He cringed. "Well, there was that one guy in Helsinki whom I looked twice at. But I just figured I'd been on the road too long."

I couldn't help it. I smiled. "Jeremy, you don't need to explain anything. You can just explore this and see where you land—"

"I'm attracted to you," he blurted out. "I have no idea why . . . Not that you're not attractive, because you are. That's not what I meant. I just meant that I see you and I want to do things I've never done, and that scares me because you're a man. And I guess that makes me bi? Maybe? I don't know."

What Maddox had said now made sense. "Steve-sexual."

"Exactly." He groaned. "Sorry."

I laughed and kissed him. "Don't apologize. You're working your way through a lot. Plus, with everything else going on, it's no wonder you're confused."

He shook his head. "I'm not confused about you. You're the realest thing in my life. And you understand the craziness and schedules, and you don't treat me any different. You never have. You don't want anything from me."

"Just honesty. That's it. Even if it's not what I want to hear."

"Maddox used to say that about Roscoe, and I never really understood. Now I get it." His face softened and he frowned. "I have no experience with relationships or anything like that. I don't know what you expect. I don't even know what I expect. But this is the most time I've ever spent with anyone, in that kind of way. I don't know what I'm doing."

"I don't know either," I admitted. "I've never been in any kind of relationship. Not since . . ."

"Since you lost everything."

I smiled sadly. "Yeah. I've, uh . . ." I rolled onto my back so I didn't have to look at his face when I said this. I wanted to be honest but it was still hard to say. I felt down his arm until I found his hand, and I threaded our fingers. "The only love I've known has been conditional. There were limits, boundaries, and that's not what love should be. I was outed and my parents disowned me, my friends turned their backs, the sport I gave my life to turned its back on me. I've never let myself be vulnerable like that ever again. It's not easy, even now." I looked at him then. "You're different. You're worth it. No matter how long it lasts. No limits, just us being what we are. No pressure. Whatever we become, I will have no regrets."

He let go of my hand and covered his eyes. "God. I haven't even thought about anyone finding out. I mean, Maddox knows. But he's different. The media? The fucking paparazzi."

"They never have to know."

"My mother."

And what could I say to that?

Nothing. Not a freaking thing. I turned back to the ceiling, a sinking feeling in my stomach.

*What did you just say, Steve? Ten seconds ago? No regrets?*

Yeah, well . . . regret lodged itself right under my ribs, like a barb.

"Hey," Jeremy said. He pulled on my hand. "What did

you just say? Like half a minute ago? And you're already zoning out on me because I mentioned my mother?"

I shook my head. "No. I mean, kinda. I'll be whatever you need me to be. That's the truth. But if you think your mom will disown you, I can't be the reason—"

"Hold the fuck up," he said with a laugh. He rolled a little closer, and taking hold of my chin, he made me look at him. "My mom won't disown me. She likes you, anyhow. So just chill. I'm just trying to get my head around having to tell people. It's not as though I've ever had to tell anyone anything before, not even that I'm dating a woman. My mother will be more shocked that I've seen the same person more than once *more* than she'd be shocked that it's a guy. She'll probably think it's the best news she's ever heard, and she'll want to come for dinner so we can watch gay theater together."

I snorted. "Oh."

"You bailed on me pretty quick there."

"No. I just . . . when you mentioned telling your mom, my mind went straight to somewhere bad. That's on me. I'm sorry." I let out a shaky breath. "And, if I'm being completely honest, when I said I'd be in this for as long as it lasts, I was kinda hoping it would be longer than this conversation."

Jeremy laughed. "I hope so too. Because I just told you that you were the only good thing in my life, and ten minutes later you were mentally out the door."

I shook my head again. "I'm not bailing on you. You're the only good thing in my life too. If we're admitting shit like that. Out loud. For the first time ever in my life."

Grinning, he climbed over me, kissed me soundly, then got off the bed. "Come on, I'm hungry for real now. And no more kitchen shenanigans until I'm fed."

He didn't even give me time to grab a shirt. So we made spaghetti in his kitchen with no shirts on, and not once did he look at my scars.

Not once.

He did try to twist my nipple when I told him he should have added salt to the pot of water. But we ate from bowls as we stood in the kitchen, laughing and slurping, and it was possibly the best dinner of my life.

The spaghetti was pretty good too.

Jeremy put his bowl on the counter. "I'm so full. Where's your phone? I need to tell Mom that mine was better than hers."

I laughed. "I'm sure she'd love to hear that."

"It will come from your phone so she'll think you said it."

I gave him a shove with my elbow. "Hell no. For that, you can clean up."

He gripped his forehead. "Ow, my head just started to really hurt. I should go lie down."

"It would probably help if you weren't smiling when you said that."

He stopped pretending. "You know, it was kinda cute when you first made me clean up, but it's not so much fun anymore."

"It'll take us two minutes," I said, already busy loading stuff into the dishwasher.

He, apparently, was busy checking me out. "How do you stay so fit? Even after months of traveling on tour. I mean, you're kinda jacked. For an old guy of thirty-five."

"I'm going to pretend you didn't say that." I gave him a playful nudge. "Hotel rooms are good for sit-ups, push-ups, burpees. Most hotels have a gym or a pool, and I spend a lot of time alone in my hotel room."

He lifted my arm. "Damn. You've even got defined obliques. You know how hard they are to maintain?"

I chuckled, seeing right through his ploy. "You still need to help clean up."

He rolled his eyes and finished clearing away. "I was being serious about your physique. I can acknowledge when a guy's got a hot body, when he works out. I spend a lot of time dancing and doing cardio and shit. I know what kind of dedication a body like that takes."

He was now looking at my abs, my chest, my shoulders and biceps. And he was looking. Not at my scars, no. At my body. A male body, and he was appreciating it in ways I doubted he had before.

"You can acknowledge my body any time you like," I said quietly. "You can touch it too. Anywhere you want."

His eyes cut to mine and he put his palm flat on my abs and up to my chest. "I like how it feels. It's hard, not soft." He skimmed his hand up my throat to my jaw. "And this . . . the stubble, the hard jaw. Fucking hell. That shouldn't turn me on, but it does."

"You probably shouldn't say stuff like that to me," I warned. I sucked his finger into my mouth. His pupils dilated as he watched his finger slide between my lips, licking it as I drew it out. "Or we'll be back in your bed."

"Ugh, god, how much sex between guys is normal?" He brought our hips together. "Because a few days ago, I wasn't even sure if I'd be able to kiss you and now . . . now I've come three times already today, and that's with a head injury. Probably not a good idea. But I could probably go again. A few more times. That's not normal, right?"

I held his hip. "There is no normal. Just whatever feels right. But you're probably right. Three times with a head injury isn't a good idea. When you put it like that . . ."

"I didn't mean it like that. I mean, sure, it sounds bad, but I'm all for going another round. Honestly haven't been this horny since I was eighteen." His eyes went wide and he gently touched the scar. "Maybe it's the knock to the head. Maybe I'll wake up tomorrow with you in my bed and be like 'Well, that's weird.'"

I knew he was joking. His stupid gorgeous smile gave him away.

"What makes you think I'll be sleeping in your bed?"

"Because . . ." He pouted. "Because I like it? Please?"

"And if you *do* wake up straight-and-horrified that I'm in your bed, what then?"

"You mean if I wake up tomorrow and I'm no longer a Steve-sexual?"

I chuckled. "Yeah. What then?"

He took my hand and rubbed his dick with it. He was semihard. "I'm pretty sure that's not gonna happen. This has been an issue whenever I'm around you for weeks now, not just since I hit my head."

"I really should take care of that for you," I murmured.

He pushed against my hand, seeking friction. "Can you do what you did last time? With both of us . . . I want to watch this time."

Frotting. He liked it.

"Then you should get naked and get on your bed," I said, rubbing his cock and giving it a pull through his pants. His pupils dilated. He licked his lips and nodded.

We hadn't been naked in bed together. In the shower, yes. But we'd always had the safety of some kind of clothing in bed. That was about to change.

He was getting bolder, more comfortable. He certainly wasn't afraid of seeing a dick that wasn't his. Considering I was his first male experience, he was definitely okay with it.

When I had him on the bed, both of us naked, he lay back, resting on his elbows so he could see everything. He watched as our cocks slid together, the heads nudging through my fist, sliding, slicked.

So fucking hot.

"Holy shit," he breathed, driving his hips upward, meeting my fist.

He wrapped his hand around mine and I let him take over. He gasped and his erection grew harder, his body taut.

I tried to stave off my orgasm, but it hit too hard, too fast. I fucked his fist, shooting come over his hand and belly. Pleasure exploded from my bones, deep inside me, seeping and blinding.

He came a few seconds later, his whole body jerking, a rough groan escaping his throat.

When I let my weight fall on him, he let his legs rest open, even hitching one leg over mine. He held me tight until his grip loosened and I knew he was asleep.

Whether it was the exertion, the amount of times he'd come today, or the carbs he'd eaten, he was utterly spent. I found the shirt he'd worn earlier that day and wiped us over, and he almost woke up, but he quickly pulled me into his arms again.

I let him sleep, kissing his temple every so often, rubbing circles on his back. His gentle snores made me smile. His lips parted the sweetest way, he looked so utterly peaceful.

The room was dark with the blinds pulled, hiding the fading sunset, hiding the world outside. But there, in his bed, in his arms, my heart wasn't hiding at all.

Every wall I'd put up was in ruins. Every safeguard was down.

For the first time in my life, I'd allowed myself to fall in love.

I'd known for years that Jeremy had an emotional hold on me. But I'd kept a lid on it, a professional and personal boundary.

But not anymore.

I was in love with Jeremy Dalton.

As if the thump of my heart lured him closer, he snuggled in, his head on my chest. I wrapped him up as tight as I could, never wanting to let him go.

Never wanting to let this moment go.

This perfect moment.

This perfect man.

Then my phone buzzed in my jeans pocket on the floor. Reality didn't care about life-changing realizations and falling in love for the first time.

Reality would never wait.

---

I WOKE UP ALONE, a foreign sound rattling me from sleep. I hadn't gone to bed alone. Jeremy had still been sound asleep when I finally climbed in beside him.

Now his side of the bed was empty.

And the noise . . .

The sound . . .

Deep, resounding, soulful.

His piano.

And his voice. Oh my god.

I checked my phone. It was 3:42 a.m.

I went downstairs and stood by the wall. He was cast in faded light from the hall, sitting at his grand piano, coaxing notes out of it like a god.

It wasn't a song I'd heard before. Strong, sweet, absolutely beautiful.

He saw me and his hands stilled.

"Keep playing," I whispered. "I could listen to you forever."

He smiled, kept his eyes on me, and began to play a different song. Seemingly random notes that morphed into a song I knew.

"Wicked Game" by Chris Isaac.

He sang the lyrics, still looking at me.

He sang them *to* me.

Slowed down, soulful, almost tortured. Maybe it was the things he couldn't say. Maybe he could sing them instead.

Every word burned into me.

The way he sang. I'd never heard him sing like that.

I wanted to go to him but wanted to let him sing. He got lost on the last verse, his vocals giving way to the piano. His emotions on display with every chord.

I went to him then and put my hands on his shoulders. "That was beautiful."

"I couldn't sleep. Watched you for a while . . . until that felt creepy. Wrote a song instead."

I massaged his shoulders, not realizing how tense he was. He groaned and let me do it.

"So I was thinking," he said casually. "About tomorrow. About this whole stalker bullshit."

Oh no. This never ended well. "What's that?"

"I'm done with it. I'm done with hiding away, or lying low or whatever."

"Okay . . ." I wasn't sure what he meant. "I understand your frustrations. I hate that you're subjected to this. But, Jer, pretending it's not happening won't make it go away."

"Oh, I know," he said. "That's why I'm going to end it."

My hands stilled. "You're what?"

"I'm going to end it. Whoever this fixated person is thinks they have the advantage, but I'm gonna take back control."

Freaking hell.

I tried to keep my voice calm. "And how are you going to do that?"

"How anyone traps a rat." He played a dun-dun-dun-dah sequence on the piano. "I'm going to make myself the bait."

Then he keyed the piano rather abruptly and began to sing "Trapped" by Bruce Springsteen.

# CHAPTER EIGHTEEN

"I WOULD JUST LIKE to say for the record—"

"That this is a terrible idea and you're against it," Jeremy said. "Just like you've been saying all morning. A hundred times."

"The company sends drivers. We have special vans for transport, for safety reasons, Jer. This is—"

"Pick a hand?" He held up both hands.

"Absolutely not."

"If you're driving, then you choose."

Christ.

Me driving was the one argument I'd won over breakfast, at least.

When I didn't answer, he pouted. "We already canceled the driver to come pick us up. Poor Sayed. I'm sure he misses me. So you either drive, or I do."

"You're not driving."

He threw one set of keys to me. I saw the logo. "Absolutely fucking not driving that." I threw it back to him. "Give me the keys to the Jeep."

He grinned, and I was certain this had been his ploy all along. "Do you have something against Lamborghinis?"

"Yes. The price tag, the insurance, the damages, the repair bill, the everything I cannot afford."

He laughed and climbed into the passenger side of the Jeep. I probably couldn't even afford that, but it was a helluva lot cheaper than the sports car. The Jeep itself was one of those off-road, custom modified things, black with tinted windows, and to be honest, I liked it. It wasn't as big or as pretentious as a Hummer but it was sporty and surely didn't cost over $200,000 like the car it was parked next to.

I climbed in behind the wheel and Jeremy grinned at me. "This is fun. We need to do more fun stuff."

Despite the warmer day, he was wearing sweats and a long-sleeve shirt. And a beanie to hide the wound on the side of his head and his very new lack of hair. He was sporting a bit of scruff now, which, in my opinion, looked hot as hell. Felt good too . . .

And we were, much to my dismay, driving ourselves to the office.

I'd told him what I'd found out last night while he slept. That the security company had passed on all the information and all the footage of what we'd thought was a drone. Special Agent Zielinski would be at the meeting at nine.

Jeremy was hopeful they'd found the person of interest and that it was all over.

I wasn't so optimistic. But his smile was contagious. He wasn't kidding when he said he needed this all to be over. I hadn't seen him smile like that in a long time.

The garage door went up and I started the engine.

His grin got wider. "Hope you can drive a stick."

With my eyes on his, I put my foot on the clutch and

slid the gearstick into first, and we rolled out of the garage. "Put your seatbelt on."

"Hm, should that be sexy?"

I laughed. "Probably not."

"Leaving the house today means I won't get to break my record of most ever orgasms in one day. That's disappointing. But you'll have some making up to do when we get home."

I couldn't help but smile.

The garage door went down. "Where's your phone?" he asked.

I fished it out of my pocket and handed it to him. "You said all of ten minutes ago you didn't want to bring your phone."

"I don't want mine. I'm very happy without it. I want yours." He scrolled through something before pressing buttons on the car stereo and he cranked up the volume.

"Drive My Car" by The Beatles almost blew out my eardrums.

Jeremy laughed. "I was gonna play 'Shut Up and Drive' by Rihanna."

Smiling, I shook my head at him, and had to yell over the music. "Is there a song called Turn It Down?"

He grinned. "Imma write you one."

"Does that not hurt your head?"

He rolled his eyes and pressed a button that made his front gates open, we drove through them and the gates closed behind us. We drove down to the estate gates, which rolled open for us, and the few remaining photographers didn't pay us any attention at all.

They were waiting for the company van to come collect him first.

"See? It worked," he yelled over the music.

I held up one finger. "It'll only work once."

He laughed. "Now for my favorite song ever. Are you ready for it?"

"No."

His grin widened. "Behold the best song ever written!" "Eleanor Rigby" by the Beatles began to play, and he turned it up and sang every word at the top of his lungs.

It was hard not to smile.

He just kept grinning and singing, music blaring, all the way downtown.

---

"*HEY*, HERE HE IS!" Wes cried, and Blake and Luke were quick to their feet when Jeremy and I walked in.

"What's with the beard?" Luke asked.

"Three-day growth is hardly a beard," Jeremy said before they all hugged him, like they always did.

He could tell me he'd needed time away from the world, but anyone could see how much he'd missed them.

Even if it had just been a few days. Two, at the most.

He needed these boys in his life. They were a part of him.

I went to my team who were all off to one side. "Hey, boss," Robbie said.

"Hey guys," I said. I felt bad for not being a good boss these last few days. Aside from a few texts, I'd been largely absent. "How are we all?"

"All good," Riko replied.

"Any clue what this is all about?" Zoe asked.

I shook my head. "None. First, we didn't have to be

here, then we *had* to be here." I shrugged. "Your guess is as good as mine."

A very loud "Hey" made us all turn in time to see Maddox walk in. He took one look at Jeremy, grinned, and said, "Well, well, well, don't you look relaxed?"

And then he looked at me.

For fuck's sake.

But before Jeremy could reply, Maddox engulfed him in a crushing hug, almost taking him off his feet. And then he pulled Jeremy's beanie off.

"Holy fucking shit!" Blake cried. "What did you do to your hair?"

Roscoe was trying not to smile as he walked over to me while Wes and Luke were inspecting the surgical glue in Jeremy's head.

"I told him not to say anything," Roscoe mumbled.

Just then, Ryan and Amber came in with a full tray of various coffees. Of course they were surprised to see Jeremy without hair, but his scar was a blunt reminder. "Just glad you're okay," Ryan said, handing him an iced coffee.

"And a heads-up," Amber said. "Neil and two FBI guys are incoming in three, two . . ."

And two seconds later, Ambrose and Agent Zielinski and another guy in a suit walked in. Neil scanned the room and zeroed in on Jeremy. He was obviously shocked at the shaved head and scruff, but the fresh wound . . . it stopped criticism in its tracks.

"You okay, Jeremy?" he asked.

Jeremy sipped his coffee and smiled. "Never better."

Clearly a lie, or sarcasm, but Ambrose wasn't about to question him in front of the suits.

"We have some new information," Neil said instead. Then he looked at me. "Steve, a word?" Then he held his hand up to everyone else. "Give us five minutes, then meet us in conference room two."

Jeremy's eyes were on me and he looked about to object to me leaving, but Maddox put his arm around him and drew his focus back to the group.

Roscoe gave me a nod. "I got them."

Begrudgingly, I followed Ambrose and the two feds into the conference room with no idea what I was about to walk into.

Zielinski was about to talk first, but Ambrose put his hand up. "Just a second, please. Steve . . . Jeremy, is he okay?"

"He's, uh . . ."

"He has a beard and shaved his head. I almost didn't recognize him. God, he has photoshoots and interviews and pressers this week."

Was he kidding me?

"He also has a two-inch cut in his head," I snapped. "Which I'm sure you noticed. The doctors had to shave a strip into his head in the hospital. He shaved his own head. Said he just finished the job."

I was trying really hard not to lose my cool, but by god, he wasn't making it easy.

"I'd like Jeremy to see Dr. Hardwick," Ambrose added.

"That's something you need to run by Jeremy."

"He's . . . he seems to be comfortable around you. Not Ryan, not even Maddox. From what I heard, he didn't even want Maddox around—"

"I don't know where you're getting your information from, but it's wrong. And in light of all that's going on—" I gestured to the two FBI agents watching our exchange. "—I would think the importance of accuracy should be a little higher on your list of priorities. He and Maddox are as tight as ever. In the last three days, Maddox has been at Jeremy's house every day, twice yesterday, plus phone calls, text messages, FaceTime. Not sure what else you want them to do."

Ambrose looked as if he wanted to murder me.

"He drove himself this morning," he added sourly. "It's not really up to him to decide if he can cancel a driver."

"He didn't drive. I did." That was a petty technicality, but I didn't care. "Canceling the driver was a courtesy. Otherwise Sayed would still be waiting out in front of the house."

"It's not the point. He's going against the grain on everything."

Christ. Did he invite me in here just so he could complain? "Why are you telling me this? Is there a point that involves me?"

"He doesn't want anyone else around *but* you."

We were getting into some murky waters . . .

"He trusts me. And right now, *clearly*, that's all he's got."

Zielinski cleared his throat, obviously wanting to redirect the conversation. "Uh, Mr. Frost," he said. "Do you trust everyone on your team? Riko Murata—"

It took my brain a second to change gears. "Um, yes. Of course. Why?" I shot Ambrose a glare. "What the fuck?"

He winced. "I told them you'd say that. They asked me about all the staff."

I turned my gaze back to Zielinski. "I trust my team. With my life. With Jeremy's life, with Maddox's life, with Luke's life—"

He put up a hand. "Yeah, okay. I had to ask."

Like hell he did.

He just went on as if asking stupid questions was what

he did for a living. "Do you know if Jeremy has his phone on him?"

"No. He doesn't. It's still in a container of rice from when he went in the pool and Riko fished it out hours later. I asked him this morning if he wanted to see if it would work, but he said no. He hasn't had a phone for days."

"You said he's spoken to Maddox on the phone, texted, and FaceTimed," the other agent said. It wasn't a question but it really was. He was maybe thirty, dark hair, broad shouldered, cool demeanor. He looked sharp as a tack. Offered no introduction, no apology. I certainly couldn't be mad at his question because at least *someone* here was paying attention.

"Mr. Frost," Zielinski said. "This is Special Agent Richardson. He's part of the cyber team."

I looked at Richardson. "Jeremy used my phone. Called his mom a few times, called all the guys, texted them."

Richardson gave a nod. "We're going to need to take a look at your phone."

"What for?"

"We believe there may have been a data breach," Zielinski said.

I handed my phone over. I had absolutely nothing to hide. "What kind of data breach?"

Richardson answered. "The serious kind."

I was still trying to decide if I liked him or not when the doors opened and Jeremy walked in. The others were right behind him, of course, followed by Roscoe, Amber, and Ryan, and then my security team filed in.

Jeremy took one look at me and saw Richardson had my phone. Maybe he could feel the unease in the room. "What's going on?"

"Everyone, please take a seat," Ambrose said. "This is

Special Agent Richardson, and you're familiar with Special Agent Zielinski."

We moved around the large conference table, Jeremy ushering me to sit beside him, Maddox on his other side.

Zielinski spoke first. "We've had some developments."

"Have you found that woman?" Luke asked.

"No. There's been two credit card transactions in Nevada, but we have reason to believe her card may have been stolen. The store footage shows an unknown person using the card." Zielinski sighed and looked directly at Jeremy. "But something else has come up. The footage from your house, Jeremy, sent to us by Mr. Frost—"

"Of the drone," Jeremy finished.

"Jeremy spotted it in the footage," I added so the others were up to date. "Not me. I just sent it. I take it the security company could identify the owner of the drone?"

Richardson took over. "Yes and no. Great technology, by the way. The drone captured in the footage was not recording visual or audio. Smaller by design, harder to detect. And illegal in the US."

*What?*

"Not registered, of course," Richardson continued. "No identifying serial numbers. Remote Wi-Fi control, scrambled VPN."

Jesus Christ.

A cold shiver ran down my spine. "If it wasn't recording footage or audio, what was it doing?"

Apparently that was the right question because Richardson gave me a nod. "This software latches onto the Bluetooth network and gains access to all devices. Phones, computers, internet, home security. Contact lists, internet banking, calls, texts, photos, videos, passwords, social media accounts."

I felt a little sick.

"We're going to need your phones," Zielinski said.

Everyone stared, stunned.

"For how long?" Maddox asked.

"Undetermined at this stage," Richardson replied. "Depends on what we find. I'd like to say just a few hours, but I can't promise."

I had to push the heel of my hand to my stomach to stop the roll of nausea. I'd been so focused on a physical breach, I hadn't considered a virtual one.

"All of us?" Luke asked.

"Everyone who was at Mr. Dalton's or who has been at his house in the last four days." Richardson looked around at everyone's stunned faces. "We believe there've been several sweeps."

"The new security cameras were supposed to detect this," Jeremy said.

"They can detect registered drones," Richardson explained. "That should've been enough. This kind of technology is believed to be out of the Japanese black market. As I said, it's illegal here."

"But it's still here," Jeremy shot back. "Legal or not."

My head spun. Fucking hell. "This is . . ." I had to exhale slowly. I turned to Jeremy. "I'm sorry. I was focused on a physical attack. I didn't even think—"

"Hey, this isn't your fault," Jeremy said. He gave my hand a squeeze. "This is some Matrix shit. This goes way beyond your responsibility." He turned to the feds. "What information did they get? What can they do with it?"

"We've shut down all company servers. Even our website shows a maintenance screen," Ambrose said. "Arlo Kim isn't taking chances. He has the IT people working overtime. It's precautionary at this stage, but the truth is, we don't know if they gained access to the Platinum system."

"This particular software acts like a spiderweb. It branches out to any other network it connects with," Richardson said. "We've seen it before. So if you're infected at ground zero, then take that infected device to your house or place of work, use the Wi-Fi, Bluetooth, they can then gain access to that location." He looked around the table. "If you were infected at Jeremy's house and then used that device at home on Wi-Fi, we would have to assume your house has been breached as well."

Christ almighty.

"What are they after?" Jeremy asked, not for the first time.

"We don't know," Zielinski answered. "At first we thought they wanted information on you. But now we think it might be bigger than that, and maybe they're targeting Platinum Entertainment."

There was that nauseous feeling again.

"Who's behind this?" Wes asked. "Is this the same crazy bitch who's after Jeremy?"

Zielinski pursed his thin lips. "We use the term fixated person."

"I don't give a fuck what term you use," Wes shot back.

"Wes," Ryan murmured.

"No. This is fucked up. Amy was there . . . Oh Christ. I need to call her." Wes reached for his phone.

"You can't use that," Richardson said. Wes stared at him. We all did. "We're going to need all your phones. We'll be sending a team to your houses to retrieve any infected devices and to check over your security systems."

Christ.

"I suggested the new security systems," I said. "It was supposed to protect them, not be a portal into their homes."

"This is not your fault," Jeremy said. This time he massaged the back of my neck.

"I tend to agree with Mr. Dalton," Richardson said. "It wouldn't have made any difference. In fact, if the new system hadn't been in place, we'd *never* have known about the drone. And Mr. Dubrowski, the owner of the security company, has been more than accommodating. He's horrified."

"And to answer your question," Zielinski said, "we don't know who is behind this. My team is still focused on finding Ms. Sosa. We believe she can help us with our investigation."

"The last lot of crazy mail received were direct threats against Arlo and Platinum," I volunteered, considering neither Ambrose nor Zielinski did.

Ambrose's eyes hardened in my direction and I didn't give one single fuck.

Discussions ended with everyone's phones on the table and plans to meet with the specialist tech teams at every-one's homes.

Ambrose had produced eight cheap burner phones, brand new, in sealed boxes, each with twenty bucks call and text credit. One for each of the guys and the three managers. No Wi-Fi connectivity, and eight random, brand-new disposable numbers.

"Where'd you get these from?" Luke asked with a laugh. "1997?"

"It's a Nokia knock off," Blake said.

"My grandmother has one like this," Wes grumbled.

Ambrose ignored the complaints. "You can contact each other, and more importantly, we can contact you. But they're not connectable to the internet or Bluetooth. They can't be hacked by this person."

Maddox stared at it, held it closer to his face. "Can I text? How do I text?"

Roscoe pointed to the keyboard. "You need to press the seven button three times to get an R, then the six button three times to get an O. Then seven again four times to get an S . . ."

The five of them stared at him, horrified.

"The fuck I will," Maddox said.

Jeremy laughed and slid his phone across the table to me. "You can have it."

I ignored the fact Ryan and Luke were watching us, and I ignored them when I slid it back to him. "Have it yourself."

"Security have their own," Ambrose said, putting another bag on the table. The phones were the same as the others, brand new in sealed boxes. They couldn't be tampered with, could they?

Why did I feel as if we were being handed tracking devices?

But we exchanged numbers and Jeremy and the others left the room, laughing about their phones. I talked with my team. It was a good time to catch up, not that I could tell them much. They'd been in the meeting, heard all I'd heard, knew all I knew. I couldn't make any plans moving forward until I knew what the band was doing.

But I couldn't get Zielinski's question out of my head.

*Do you trust your team? Do you trust Riko?*

Of course I did.

If anyone on my team had done any damage, it was me. If that hacking software had the capabilities to access my phone camera or the laptop camera to see inside Jeremy's house, to spy on him, they'd have close-up footage of us making out on the couch.

God. I'd given him a hand job on the couch. In front of the laptop.

How could I be so stupid?

We'd shut the world out, yes. But did they have eyes inside the house?

"It's scary," Robbie said. "People having remote access to our phones and stuff."

Ivan nodded. "We can't protect them from someone we can't see."

"I agree," I said. "All this time, I was so worried about a physical attack. I didn't imagine the threat would be virtual."

"What do you think they're after?" Zoe asked.

"Dunno," Riko replied. "My question would be why they haven't used it yet?"

We all stared at him.

He shrugged. "If they've had access for four days, they've seen footage of Jeremy's dive into the pool, the paramedics coming. They've got photos and phone calls, even bank account information, and whatever else they said. Why hasn't any of that been posted online or sold to a news channel?"

I nodded. "Maybe that's what Zielinski meant when he said they're now thinking they want Platinum and not Jeremy."

The conference room door swung in. It was Ambrose. "Steve, we got a problem."

"What's up?"

"It's Jeremy."

Adrenaline jolted through me, followed by a drenching of dread. My blood ran cold. "What?"

"He's downstairs. Just walked out the front of the building to the paparazzi."

Fuck, fuck, fuck.

I sprinted for the elevators and smashed the down button. It took a hot second for the elevator to even think about it, and I considered running down the stairwell, trying to calculate how long that many floors would take me when the elevator dinged and the doors opened.

I thumped the button for the lobby and before the doors could close, Riko and Ivan slipped through to join me.

"What the hell is he doing?" Riko asked.

I spoke through gritted teeth. "I'm gonna fucking kill him, that's what he's doing."

I tried inhaling slow and counting in my head.

*One Mississippi. Two Mississippi. Three . . .*

The doors opened at the lobby, and I could immediately see the gathering swarm of cameras, flashes, and fans outside the glass wall.

And Jeremy.

Talking to them as if it was a fan meet and greet.

"Ivan, man the door," I murmured. "Riko, you're on his left."

I crossed the lobby and pushed through the revolving doors. Camera clicks announced my arrival and Jeremy glanced behind him. He saw me and grinned.

He fucking grinned.

And, I realized far too late, he wasn't wearing his beanie. His shaved head and new scar were on full display.

Jeremy gestured to me. "Here he is, the man who saved me. Well, one of them anyway."

Jesus.

H.

Christ.

"Steve, can you tell us what was going through your mind when you pulled Jeremy out of the pool?"

"Steve, was Jeremy breathing when you got him out of the pool?"

"Steve, is Jeremy . . ."

"Steve, is . . ."

"Steve . . ."

I leaned toward Jeremy. "Are you done?"

He leaned toward me. "Are you going to answer them?"

"No."

I resumed my position, hands behind my back, feet apart, facing the crowd, ready.

And the media waited for me to answer.

They could fucking wait until they died of old age for all I cared.

"As I was saying," Jeremy continued, "I wanted to thank our fans for their concern. But as you can see, I'm fine. Back at work and feeling great."

"Can you tell us about the internet blackout going on in Platinum Entertainment right now?" one reporter asked.

Jeremy smiled. "I don't know anything about that."

"Can you give any details on the FBI investigation?" another reporter asked.

"What's going on with Platinum? Is the blackout related to the FBI investigation?"

Jeremy sighed. "Does anyone have any questions about music, new songs? A new tour? Plans for Atrous next year?"

"Are you seeing anyone?" someone yelled.

"For fuck's sake." Jeremy sighed and waved. "Okay, thanks guys. Now you can leave. Stop hanging out here all day." He pretended to shoo them. "Go report on things that actually matter. Atrous fans know if we want to share anything, it'll be directly from us via our social media channels or an official statement from Platinum. So, unless you hear it directly from us, it's safe to assume it's bullshit."

He stepped back and I cleared a space for him to get through the doors. People yelled questions, they yelled his name, they yelled my name. Cameras pushed forward but we got him through the doors, and the noise was muted.

I kept my hand on his back and ushered him toward the elevator.

Ivan stood in the elevator entrance, holding it open. Riko covered Jeremy's other side. "How pissed is Ambrose?" Jeremy asked.

"Not as pissed as me," I growled at him.

"Steven Hammond!" A man screamed behind us.

I spun around, more at the aggressive tone rather than what he actually screamed. I stepped in front of Jeremy, putting myself between him and the threat.

The threat . . .

Was a man, possibly thirties, wearing brown pants, stained. A yellowed shirt, dirty. His brown hair, short, his pale face, dirty.

And he was coming at me.

But he was running, scrambling even, through the doors, through the building security. He held no obvious weapon, and he was going to tackle me?

I drove the heel of my palm up into his sternum, grabbing his throat while taking his legs out from under him. I followed him to the ground, pinning him by his throat.

He couldn't fight back. He could barely breathe.

The building security had their guns out, pointing at him. People were yelling, screaming. The cops who had been doing crowd control outside burst in, their guns drawn.

I looked back to see Riko and Ivan both in front of

Jeremy, and Jeremy's wide eyes on me from behind their shoulders.

"Get him upstairs," I yelled.

"No, Steve," Jeremy tried. "Wait. Steve!"

But they had him in the elevator and the doors closed.

I released the guy's throat and stood over him, my hands up. And then the cops moved in.

# CHAPTER NINETEEN

I SAT in my office and waited. Not by choice.

I hadn't seen Jeremy, though Ambrose told me he was fine. Ambrose was *pissed* off. Actually, he was a whole new level of angry. At me, at Jeremy, at the whole situation.

But mostly at me.

The entire debacle was news on every station, on every social media site, on every radio station.

I didn't blame Ambrose for being mad. The band, the company, Jeremy in particular, already had the spotlight on them, and now this . . .

Was it my fault the man charged at me?

No.

Had I used excessive force in front of twenty cameras?

Hm.

In front of the cameras, yes. Excessive force? Not in my opinion, but it wasn't my opinion that they cared about, apparently.

I heard someone coming toward my office door.

"They can suck a bag of unwashed dicks for all I care," a familiar voice said, just as the door swung inwards. Jeremy stopped when he saw me. He smiled, but when he saw my expression, it became a frown. "Hey. I've been looking for you. I tried calling you on those stupid phones."

Maddox was behind him.

I'd thrown that stupid phone into my top drawer, still switched off. "I'm supposed to wait here," I said, my voice flat.

"What for?" he came in and around to my side of the desk, leaning against it, his feet next to mine. "Steve, what's wrong?"

I felt sick to have to say this out loud. "To be honest, I think they're going to fire me."

He stared at me, then he laughed incredulously. "Like fucking hell."

I looked up at him and smiled, a lot calmer than I probably should have been. Maybe resigned was the better word.

He held out his hand and I took it, then he laced our fingers. "There's no way. No they won't. That piece of shit came running in like he was out of his mind."

I didn't reply to that. Honestly, I wasn't up for conversation . . .

Maddox lifted one of the flaps to the many boxes lined against the wall and peered inside. "What is all this?" Then he gestured to the cardboard cutout. "Uh . . ."

Jeremy grinned. "I asked Ryan to have one of every bit of merch with my face on it delivered to his office. He needed the Jeremy desk calendar."

"Four of them, apparently." Maddox picked up the closest one, laughed at the front photo, and threw it to Jeremy. "Why the hell anyone'd want to look at your face three hundred and sixty-five days in a row is beyond me."

Jeremy just grinned. He flipped through till the right

month and placed it carefully on my desk, pretty much in the exact spot he'd taken the old one from. "Much better."

Then he got to his feet and tried to pull me up. "Come on. We're all watching replays of you Hulk Smash that piece of shit into the floor, like a hundred times."

"Jeremy," I tried.

He stopped and cupped my jaw, and right in front of Maddox, Jeremy kissed me. His blue eyes bore into mine. "It'll be okay. I promise."

God, I could almost believe him.

A knock on the door startled all three of us. The door opened and Ambrose appeared. He certainly wasn't expecting to find Jeremy and Maddox with me, and he most definitely wasn't expecting to see Jeremy all but pressed against me.

"Ah, Steve?" And with a nod to the corridor, I was assumed to follow.

Yeah. This really wasn't good.

The knot in my gut churned, but I pulled my hand from Jeremy's and followed Ambrose. I only got four steps away before Jeremy fell into step beside me. "You're not going in there alone."

I thought we might've been going to another conference room, but no. I couldn't be so lucky.

Mr. Arlo Kim's office was huge. Sparse but expensive furniture, original artwork, and rows of gold albums framed along one wall. All of them for Atrous. Every single one.

I'd been in this office three times in all my years working for Platinum. Mr. Kim sat behind his huge desk. His digital forensic security specialist, Hetty Reyes, sat on one of the sofas, tapping away on her laptop. She didn't even look up.

And Zielinski and Richardson sat off to the side of Mr. Kim's desk.

Oh goodie.

"Jeremy," Ambrose said quietly. "I would ask you to please wait outside."

"Neil," Jeremy said brightly. "And I would ask you to pick any fucking day but this one."

Right, then.

And then, without saying a word, Maddox followed Jeremy in.

There was only one seat across from Mr. Kim, so yeah, this was definitely a termination-of-employment chat.

Having Jeremy and Maddox with me changed the odds a little. I certainly didn't ask them to come with me, but I was glad they were. Even if just to witness it.

Mr. Kim looked about to oppose Jeremy and Maddox being there but decided just to pretend they weren't there at all instead. Sooo, Jeremy and Maddox took either end of one of the couches and carried it over, moving my single seat out of the way. Arlo Kim ignored them, as did the others, much like a school teacher would when teenagers messed up the seating arrangements.

They sat down, Jeremy in the middle, and he patted the vacant spot next to him. So I sat and waited . . .

"Steve," Mr. Kim said. "We have another problem. I'm hoping you can shed some light on this for us."

He pointed a remote control to the wall, and what I thought was paneling turned out to be a screen. The talk show *LA Today* appeared on-screen—two hosts and one guest.

"And in breaking news," one host said, "we can reveal the real identity of Atrous' head of security Steve Frost."

My stomach dropped.

"His real name is Steven Hammond."

It felt as if the floor gave way underneath me or my spine turned to jelly. I was grateful to be sitting down.

Jeremy's hand gripped mine.

"Steven Hammond trained for years as a mixed martial artist fighter, undefeated in regional and state titles. He was set to compete in the national titles when tragedy struck."

The screen cut to actual footage of me fighting in tournaments. Of course they only showed the full contact shots, me taking opponents down to the mat, me knocking them out, me ending every fight I was in.

Then the story cut to old news footage in Las Vegas, all those years ago. Police lights flashing, a cheap motel, paramedics, and a new reporter with a microphone. "Hammond, an MMA national title contender, was stabbed up to six times, taken to the hospital where he remains in a critical condition. Police have arrested the alleged suspect, a Mr. Chase Hystek, an opponent Hammond was pegged to meet in the grand final of the national titles. Hammond was the odds-on favorite to win what was expected to be a killer match."

They cut back to the studio. "In an interesting twist, the violent attack was reported as a gay hate crime. Mr. Hammond was with a male lover at the time . . ."

*An interesting twist.*

"Jesus Christ," Maddox murmured. "Steve . . ."

I couldn't speak.

"Did that bitch say it was an interesting twist?" Jeremy asked. "I'll give her an interesting twist."

The host kept smiling as she continued. "It's believed Mr. Hammond changed his name to distance himself from the incident. He never fought competitively again, instead taking his talents to a new field of personal protection."

Their "expert" as it turned out, was some MMA sports

strategist who, upon seeing my Hulk Smash, as Jeremy had called it, thought I looked vaguely familiar. "He was called Steve 'The Hammer' Hammond for a reason. You can see from this footage here, his trademark maneuver was the hammer," he said, showing footage from years ago when the boys did a concert in Chicago and some rabid fans cleared a barrier in the airport and tried to swarm Maddox. I put them on their asses. "He uses their own momentum, expending very little energy himself. It's the same tactic as he used today."

The footage cut to today where the man had run at me. And yeah, I used this guy's own momentum, his own energy mass against him.

"It's a very effective method," the expert went on. "And it looks brutal, but there is very little damage. It's a classic move to incapacitate and remove any incoming threat. Believe me, if he wanted to impose serious harm, he could. But he didn't. The man on the ground should maybe consider himself lucky it wasn't someone with half the training Steve Hammond has."

"In your opinion, if he'd wanted to, could Steve Frost have killed that man?"

The expert didn't even hesitate. "Absolutely. No doubt in my mind at all. He is, without a doubt, a lethal weapon."

Arlo Kim pointed the remote and paused the TV. The screen stopped on the crowd outside the building, on all the cameras and fans who'd seen the whole thing play out in real time earlier today. Dozens of faces. I studied them for a second until Arlo Kim cleared his throat to get my attention.

He was staring at me like he was waiting . . . I wasn't going to speak first. No way.

"This network broke the story half an hour ago," Mr. Kim said. "It's already global. We can't contain it."

I shook my head, my mouth dry. I didn't know what to say . . .

Jeremy did. "It's none of anyone's freaking business. Platinum needs to release a statement reminding how seriously we take our staff's privacy. And that fucking talk show host needs a real expensive lesson on what is deemed 'an interesting twist' because violent hate-crimes ain't it. And neither is splaying out someone's private life for television rating points."

Arlo Kim gave him a placating smile. "You knew about Steve's other name?"

"Of course I did."

It wasn't the point. What Jeremey had said about the press release was the point. There wouldn't be one. Only damage control.

*Holy shit.*

He really was going to fire me.

Zielinski spoke next. "You changed your name," he said, reading something in his little notebook. "Mr. Hammond."

Jeremy bristled. "Look, asshole, his name is Steve Frost."

"Jeremy," Ambrose rebuked gently.

Jeremy glared at Zielinski, jaw bulging. "Oh, I'm sorry. It's really rude when people deliberately use the wrong name, isn't it, Agent Zero? Or was it Agent Zilch?"

I put my hand on Jeremy's thigh to calm him and let out a breath. "I changed my name legally when I was twenty years old," I said, my voice flat. "Social security, passport, driver's license all say Steve Frost. It'd been my name years before I started working here. Steve Hammond no longer exists. He hasn't for a long time."

Zielinski didn't even bat an eyelid. "Did you not think it pertinent to divulge this information?"

"No," I replied. "My employer has the correct name and tax information. Check with the IRS."

"I'm not talking about your tax information," he said coolly. "Chase Hystek has been incarcerated at the Berchman Prison in Nevada for fourteen years. Two year original sentence, another fifteen added for a subsequent crime inside."

I shrugged. "So?"

He read off his notepad. "Chase Hystek has been visited eleven times in the last year by a Miss Jacqueline Sosa."

My blood ran cold.

"They've exchanged letters for a year before that."

I couldn't believe what I was hearing.

"I didn't know that," I whispered.

Jeremy snatched up my hand. "You couldn't have known that." Then he looked at them. "How was he supposed to know that? You can't seriously blame Steve for that?"

"If we'd have been informed—"

"Then you should have thought to ask," Jeremy shot back. "Where is *your* due diligence?"

"Jer," I whispered, squeezing his hand. I looked at the two FBI agents. "So am I the target? Is he using her to get to me? Or using me to get to Jeremy?"

Zielinski stared at me for a long moment. "We don't know. He's being interviewed as we speak."

I felt sick.

I had to breathe through the nausea. The idea that I could be the reason . . .

"Steve, look at me," Jeremy said. "Look at me."

I met his eyes. He looked a little pale but his eyes were such a clear and honest blue.

"This is not your fault."

I wasn't convinced.

I thought I might actually be sick. Suddenly, being fired wasn't the worst thing they could have said.

This was so much worse.

"Steve," Mr. Kim said. "I think it'd be best if you weren't working with Jeremy right now. For everyone's safety. Until we learn what the real motives are."

"No way," Jeremy said. "No fucking way."

"I can understand your hesitance," Mr. Kim continued, ignoring Jeremy. "However, the long hours, lack of sleep, and stress you've been under this last week could lead to poor judgment calls."

"Poor judgment calls?" Jeremy said. He was sweating now. "He did what he had to do. What he's supposed to do. You think it's fine for him to protect us as long as some expert fucking hack on a tabloid talk show doesn't get his fifteen minutes of fame using trigger words like *lethal weapon*."

I know I probably should have told Jeremy to chill for a second, but honestly, I liked that he was defending me.

I liked that Arlo Kim was hearing it from him.

"Jeremy's right," Maddox said calmly. "What Steve did was right. You might not like it, Arlo, and from the view in your office, I can see why this might look bad. But down there, the only thing between us and a thousand crazy fans is Steve and his team. I don't care what the press says or what they think will sell a story. I care about the safety of the band, and that's what Steve does. The only reason one of us hasn't been seriously hurt is because of him."

There was a long beat of silence.

"It's interesting to me," Jeremy said, squinting, "why this needs to be said. Why you haven't released a press statement yet, and why you're not defending the team. Steve's part of the Atrous team, and that piece-of-shit man who tried to attack him is not the victim here."

"He had to be taken to the hospital," Arlo replied. "We can expect his lawyers to be in touch."

"Let them try," Jeremy shot back. "There are a dozen different video angles of him attacking first. He started it. Just because he got his ass handed to him does not make him the victim." Jeremy blinked twice and swallowed. He shook his head. "Christ, Arlo. You got two feds on your side of the desk and us sitting over here like it's a trial. It's obvious which side you're on, and to think you wanted Steve in here on his own. Fuck that, and fuck all of this."

He blinked again and then squinted. He pressed his palms to his thighs and his fingers began to tremble. He made fists, but then his hands began to shake. The color drained from his face.

Jesus.

I quickly knelt between his legs and held his hands. "Maddox, get him something."

Maddox leaped off the couch and raced out of the office, almost pulling the door off its hinges. I held Jeremy's hands. "You're okay, Jer."

"S-s-sorry," he breathed, then tried to swallow. He was so pale and sweating, clammy.

"What's wrong with him?" Arlo said, standing up. "He needs a doctor!"

"No, he needs some juice and something to eat," I said. "And for people to stop stressing him out." I put my hand to Jeremy's cheek, making him look at me. "Jeremy, focus on me. Does your head hurt?"

Maddox raced back into the office and cracked the lid on a bottle of juice. He put the bottle to Jeremy's mouth.

Jeremy's hands were shaking bad but he managed to hold the bottle with Maddox.

And he sucked in that bottle of juice as if it was nothing.

Then Roscoe was beside us, handing over a packet of crackers and a second bottle of juice. "Here, have this." Wes, Luke, and Blake were now at the door.

When Jeremy had caught his breath and had some color, I ripped into the crackers and put it in Jeremy's hand. "Eat this, please."

He nodded and took a small bite, shrinking in on himself as he chewed. Embarrassed, no doubt. His hands still trembled as he drank more juice.

"That was a bad one," Maddox mumbled, his hand to his own heart.

I nodded. It sure as hell was. "Did he not eat all day?" I looked up at Ambrose. "Did he not eat? Who was looking after him?"

Ambrose floundered. "Uh, um . . ." He had no idea.

"Hey," I said, tracing Jeremy's scar. It didn't feel hot. It wasn't red or inflamed. "Do you have a headache?"

"Should he go to the hospital?" Ambrose asked.

Jeremy shook his head and chewed. "No. No hospital. Wanna go home. Lie down."

"Okay," I said. "Let's get you home." I helped him to his feet and handed him to Maddox. Wes came in and took the other side of him and they walked him to the door.

Mr. Kim was still standing up. "I'll arrange for Doctor Hardwick to do a housecall."

Oh, he was concerned now?

"You know what, Arlo," I spat, "he's not a cog in your fucking money machine. He's a human being. I will defend him, even against you."

I was so fucking mad, and all of a sudden, I didn't give one fuck what he did to me.

"I'll be at Jeremy's house. If you want to fire me, you know where to find me. You do whatever you need to do." I walked over to the TV screen on the wall. "If you want this whole mess to end and to find this Sosa woman, my advice, Mr. Kim, is to hire a private investigator. Hell, enlist some fans from social media. They can see one photo from today and within two minutes have three different photos spanning eight years with details of when they wore that exact shirt, with the date and the location, which they can tell because of the stitching in the goddamn fabric. Nothing gets by them." I gestured to Zielinski and Richardson. "These two feds, whom you're so keen on taking advice from, can't even see one of the FBI's most wanted when her face is on every news channel in the country." I tapped a familiar face on the screen. "Jacqueline Sosa was here today."

The three of them all spun to stare at the screen. It was so synchronized, it was almost comical.

I wanted to punch the TV into the wall, but instead, I walked out, trying to stay calm, past Blake and Luke who were obviously wondering what the hell was going on. Amber and Ryan were near the elevators with Jeremy, Maddox, and Wes, who were concerned about Jeremy. He looked better but still not great.

"You ready?" I asked. Jeremy nodded, so I hit the elevator button.

"Oh," Ryan said. "Did you get your phone? They cleared everyone's, apparently. Found nothing."

"I don't want it," I replied as the elevator doors opened. I took Jeremy's arm and walked him inside.

"Jer, be good," Maddox said. Then he looked at me. "Take care of him. We'll be around later."

I gave a nod as the doors closed. Jeremy leaned heavily against me, his forehead pressed to my shoulder. "I'm so sorry."

"It's okay," I said, kissing the side of his head. "The meeting was done anyway." I rubbed his back. "You feeling okay?"

He nodded. "Tired. And embarrassed."

"Baby, you gotta eat."

He froze before he pressed his forehead into my neck, sinking into my embrace a little more. "Did you just call me baby?"

"I think I did. Sorry."

He pulled back and was smiling, but by god, he looked tired. The elevator doors opened, and seeing the parking lot was clear, I led him to his Jeep. I opened his door for him and helped him up before getting in behind the wheel.

Man, I wished we'd not driven today. *A van with a driver would be ideal right now.*

I slipped the Jeep into gear and drove up to the ground level. There were so many people waiting around the exit, the cops were doing crowd control. Thankfully, they cleared the driveway, but it was still scary as hell.

I wasn't trained for driving in crowded situations like this, with papzz shoving their cameras at the Jeep windows and windshield.

"Christ, do these people ever quit?" Jeremy mumbled.

"Apparently not."

We got through without hitting anyone, and I kept a constant eye on my rearview mirror to make sure we weren't being followed. Not that I'd know what to look for . . . it wasn't like the movies.

The car was quiet. No phones meant no music, and

Jeremy had switched the radio off, which was probably a good thing. He was bound to be newsworthy.

He just sat there holding his second bottle of juice, turning it like it gave him something to do with his hands. Traffic was shit, like it always was. At least my heart rate was somewhat back to normal.

"I really appreciate you doing this," he said after a while.

"Driving you home?"

"And taking care of me back there."

"You're welcome."

"And how you're gonna lie on the couch with me."

I looked over at him. "Is that right?"

He nodded. "And take a nap with me. And rub circles on my back. Maybe kiss my head a time or two."

I chuckled. "Pretty sure I can do that."

He was quiet again for a while, but then he turned in his seat to look at me, his head on the headrest. He looked tired, yes, but also peaceful. "Today was the first day I think I seriously considered leaving."

I shot a look between him and the slow-moving traffic and back to him. "Leaving what?"

"Atrous. Platinum." He frowned. "I mean, I've considered leaving before. For a while, actually. But today . . . for real. I thought I could really call it quits."

I reached over and took his hand. "Jeremy, not because of me? If Arlo Kim is going to fire me, that's not a reason to disband. What I did today was . . ."

"Was what? The perfect response? Fuck that guy for charging at you. And for yelling out your old name. Fuck him."

"I probably could have handled it better. I was pissed at you for thinking you could just walk out there into the press without me. Or without any security, for that matter. I was already on edge, and that wasn't good. I just saw that guy coming at us, and I needed to keep you safe."

"I told you I was going to make myself a target."

"Yeah, well, you did that."

"I'm sorry it became a whole scene and your secret is all over the news. That's on me. I'm really sorry, Steve. If I hadn't gone out there, none of it would have happened. It was supposed to make me the target, not you."

I gave his hand a squeeze and sighed. "If you hadn't gone out there and created this whole chain of events, we may never have found the correlation between Jacqueline Sosa and Chase Hystek."

"God, your face when they told you that . . ."

"I thought I was gonna puke. The idea that anyone would try and hurt you because of me makes me feel ill."

"It's not your fault. If she's mentally unstable or if he's somehow manipulating her to target us, then that's on them. Not you." He sipped the juice. "And no, I didn't consider leaving Platinum because Arlo was about to fire you. Well, partly. It's because he's not listening. He's not . . . I don't know. Things are different now. The band is different. We're not those young kids who needed guidance. He's got younger bands coming up now that he can manipulate and control. He can't control us like he used to. Maddox is getting married, if they ever pick a date. Wes and Amy'll probably be next. And now Luke is dating that Cyko chick. Can't remember her name."

"Vana."

He gasped. "You know their names? And you had their calendar on your desk. Steve, is there something I should know? Are you a secret Cyko groupie?"

I rolled my eyes. "No. I just remember what Luke said."

He smiled but then he studied our joined hands for a bit. "We're not the same. Atrous is not the same. We're getting lives outside of the band for the first time ever. And I was pissed about that. In the beginning. I didn't want things to change. But now, I think they have to."

Okay, wow.

"Sometimes change is necessary for growth," I offered.

"True. And sometimes it's the domino that brings it all undone." He smiled sadly this time. "There was a real disconnect with Arlo Kim today. For me at least. I didn't like what I saw. I didn't like the man I saw today. That side of him is not who I want to work with. And I've been thinking a lot about where things are with the band and what I want in the future. We all have. We've talked about it, but we were always so unsure. And for the first time ever, I just don't know . . . I'm not so unsure anymore."

Ho. Lee. Shit.

He was really considering pulling the pin.

"You'd think I'd be sad," he added quietly, "when I think that the road Atrous is on might be ending. And it is sad. But honestly, I'm more relieved."

He rubbed his thumb over the triangle tattoo on his wrist. They each had one triangle tattoo, separate parts making up the pentagon that was the Atrous logo. "I just don't know," he whispered.

I drove the car along the winding, quiet street through the community gates and the second gates to his house, thinking about what he'd just said. The weight of it, the seriousness of it. "Have you mentioned this to Maddox?"

He shook his head. "Not yet. I need to get it right in my head before I tell him. Who knows? I might feel better about everything when all this shit is over. I dunno."

I parked the Jeep and shut the engine off. "You need to

rest. Pretty sure there's a couch in there with cuddles and forehead kisses just waiting for you."

He smiled. "And a nap."

I was going to add, *and healthy food, and a visit by the FBI tech team, and Maddox and Roscoe, and a house call by Dr. Hardwick,* but I figured that could wait for just a bit.

"Let's get you inside."

Jeremy went straight to the couch and fell onto it like a marionette with cut strings. He groaned and patted the cushion. "Steeeeve."

Smiling, I sat next to him, and he pulled me down to lie with him. I all but picked him up and maneuvered him so he was safely tucked into my side.

"That better?"

He chuckled and slung his leg over my hip. "Much."

I pulled back enough so I could see his face. His eyes were closed, a smile on his lips. But there were dark circles under his eyes and it was easy to get lost in how gorgeous he was, but he'd had a pretty decent health scare today.

He needed to rest, and he needed me to let him sleep. Not to ogle him. No matter how good it felt to have him against me, my arms around him, his leg over my hip.

It felt even better to keep him safe.

I drew circles on his back and I kissed the side of his head, just like he wanted, and he slept. For maybe an hour. I even managed to doze off a little . . .

Until I heard a noise toward the front of the house at the door. "Steve? It's just us. Don't come in swinging."

Maddox.

Ideally, I'd have liked to peel myself away as fast as possible to not be caught in any compromising position. It rankled against my instinct, especially because I had my back to the room.

But this was Maddox and Roscoe.

And Jeremy was sound asleep.

"Hey," I said, stroking the side of Jeremy's head. "Wake up."

He grumbled something and sighed, just as Maddox and Roscoe came in. "You do realize neither of you have a phone—" Maddox stopped when he saw us.

I put my finger to my lips in a *shh* sign.

"Aww, is he sleeping?" Maddox came over and he cooed. "You're both so cute."

Jeremy, still with his eyes closed, produced a middle finger. Maddox laughed.

Okay, so Jeremy was awake. I tried to pull my arm free, but he grumbled some more. "Just wanna sleep." He reluctantly sat up and I did too. He glared at Maddox. "The fuck you want?"

Maddox snorted. "We had no way to contact you. You both ditched your phones."

"For good reason," Jeremy said.

"Hardwick's gonna be here in ten minutes," Maddox said. "Thought we'd come to warn you in case you were getting your freak on."

Jeremy almost smiled. "He should be so lucky."

"Robbie's out front," Roscoe added. "I asked him to wait for Hardwick and to let him in."

"Arlo Kim's been trying to call you," Maddox said. "The no-phone thing has him worried, I think. They can't contact you and they're not used to that."

Jeremy shrugged.

"The tech people will be here soon too," Roscoe said.

Jeremy sighed, and I patted his leg. "How about I make you something decent to eat?"

Roscoe followed me into the kitchen, giving Maddox and Jeremy some privacy.

"How is he?" Roscoe asked quietly.

"Tired."

"Maddox is worried."

"So am I."

"He was acting oddly all day." Then I sighed. "But then again, the last week's been . . . weird. His blood sugar dropped too low today."

I made some sandwiches and cut up an apple. Roscoe watched me. "For what it's worth," he said. "You pointing to the TV screen, to that woman's face? When you left, Arlo Kim lost his shit at Zielinski. Ripped him a new asshole in front of everyone. Said you made them all look like idiots."

I snorted. "They made themselves look like idiots."

"Maddox is really pissed at Arlo Kim," he murmured.

"He's not the only one." I grabbed a bottle of water from the fridge. "Want one?"

Roscoe shook his head. "No, thanks. How are you, Steve? Maddox told me the meeting today was intense."

That made me smile. "You could say that. They were absolutely going to fire me today. I'm . . . I'm okay. I'm just . . ." Fuck. Waiting for the wheels to fall off. "I'll be better when I know he's okay."

"Ah, knock, knock?" Robbie called out. "Boss?"

"Hey, doc," we heard Maddox say.

I carried the plate and bottle out. Robbie smiled when he saw me. Truth was, I missed the big guy. Doctor Hardwick had zeroed in on Jeremy and was inspecting the glued up head-wound.

"Jeremy," I said gently. "Here's something to eat." Then I gave a nod to Robbie. "I'll come find you in a few minutes."

"Sure thing," he said and went back the way he'd come.

"I'll go with him," Roscoe said, following Robbie out.

"Before you eat that," Hardwick said. "We'll do a prick test."

"I've been tested by enough pricks today," he joked.

"Where's your glucose meter?"

Jeremy shrugged. "No idea."

"When was the last time you used it?" Jeremy made a face and Hardwick sighed. "Jeremy."

"Sorry." He didn't look particularly sorry, but he gave Hardwick his hand. He had a small black device I recognized as a blood glucose meter.

"Is he supposed to be using one of those?" I asked.

Hardwick gave me a stern glare. "Yes. He knows this."

I stared at Jeremy. "You never told me that."

Jeremy sighed but said nothing, and as soon as Hardwick pricked his finger and got his blood sample, Jeremy bit into the sandwich.

"How long were you feeling off before you crashed?" Hardwick asked.

"Midmorning," he replied. "I kinda felt off all day. Light-headed, a bit nauseous. Can't focus too well. I'm really tired, doc."

The device beeped and Hardwick frowned. "I'm not surprised, Jeremy. This is too low."

"It shouldn't be. I had a bottle of juice. I don't know, an hour ago, maybe?"

I nodded. "You never told me you weren't feeling well."

He chewed his mouthful and swallowed it down with a sip of water. "Don't want anyone to worry."

I wanted to pull my hair out.

Maddox squeezed Jeremy's leg. "Dude. You need to tell us."

"What did you do yesterday? Delayed reactions are not uncommon. Training, choreo, anything vigorous?"

Oh no.

Jeremy glanced at me before he smiled at Hardwick. "Uh. I had a lot of physical gratification yesterday . . ."

I wanted to die.

Maddox snorted. Hardwick sighed. "How much?"

"Four times."

"Four times?" Maddox cried. He stared at me, his mouth open. "I said *small steps*."

Hardwick ignored us and took Jeremy's blood pressure, then listened to his heart. He shined a penlight into his eyes and did all those usual tests. Fifteen minutes after the first blood sample test, he did a second.

"Your reading isn't coming up as it should."

"It will."

Hardwick shook his head. "Not this time."

"I can manage it with food, like I usually do. I just didn't eat. It's no big deal. And a good meal and some sleep'll fix me."

"You *used* to be able to manage it with food," Hardwick said. "But it's becoming more frequent. Is that two or three times this week? A day of alcohol certainly wouldn't have helped. When you fell into the pool, did you pass out from booze, or was it blood sugar?"

He frowned. "I tripped."

"Hm." Hardwick shook his head. "Regardless, the hypos used to be once every other month. This increase is cause for concern."

"It's been a really shitty week."

"And how long have you felt off? How long have you *really* noticed you needed to eat more, got light-headed, dizzy? No bullshit. Tell me the truth."

Jeremy didn't answer.

"Weeks? Months?"

He rolled his eyes but gave the slightest of nods.

Jesus fucking Christ.

"Jeremy, I'm making an appointment for you to see the diabetes specialist," Hardwick said. "It's a private clinic. The best endocrinologist in LA."

"I don't need—"

"Jeremy," he snapped like a pissed-off parent. "I'm not kidding. This is serious." He counted on his fingers. "Heart failure, stroke, kidney failure, coma, death. Pick one. Or would you prefer erectile disfunction?"

Jeremy rubbed his eyes. "Fuck's sake. When am I supposed to do that? How long does it take? We're back on schedule this week."

Hardwick was duly unimpressed. "You're not. No schedule, no exercise, no alcohol. Effective immediately, Jeremy, you're on medical leave."

# CHAPTER TWENTY

THE FBI TECH team arrived while Hardwick was arranging Jeremy's appointment with the specialist. We changed all the passwords again, and they ran all kinds of tests to see if anyone was piggybacking or mirroring firewalls and a whole bunch of other tech-speak I didn't pretend to follow. They gave the camera security system the all clear and that should have been a relief, but I still wasn't feeling any better about it.

Then Ryan turned up and the house, even as big as it was, was getting kinda full.

Jeremy sat on the sofa, looking overwhelmed and exhausted. Maddox was by his side, of course. "Hey, Jer. God, it's a circus out the front gates," Ryan said, sitting on the sofa opposite. He produced a brand-new phone, still in its sealed box. "Ambrose wanted—"

"I don't give a fuck what he wants," Jeremy mumbled. "Give it to me and I'll throw it in the pool with the other one."

Ryan put his hands up in surrender. "I just had to give it to you. What you do with it is up to you."

Hardwick clicked off his phone call and sat on the coffee table in front of Jeremy. "Okay, it's all set. And I just told Ambrose, which went as well as you could imagine." He sighed. "You'll be admitted tomorrow at 10:00 a.m. Overnight stay, at the very minimum, so pack a bag. I'll be here at nine to pick you up and take you in."

"Wait," Ryan said. "Where is he going?"

Hardwick gave him a hard, well-aimed glare. "He's on medical leave."

"Until when?" Ryan asked.

Hardwick's reply was short and very sharp. "Until I say, that's when. Ryan, if you have no official reason to be here, you can leave. Sorry, but I'm pulling rank." Then he shot the two tech guys a glare. "Anyone who doesn't need to be here can leave. He's supposed to be resting."

Ryan and the two techs all blinked, stunned.

I smiled.

I really liked Hardwick.

The tech guys were done anyway, but they packed up and left. Roscoe walked Ryan out.

The doctor took Jeremy's hand and did another prick test. "God, it pisses me off how everyone thinks they're entitled to a piece of you boys," he mumbled to both Jeremy and Maddox. He sighed again, though it sounded more like a growl. "Sorry."

"'S okay, doc," Jeremy said. "Pisses me off too."

Maddox snorted. "Fucking saaaaaaaaame."

"What did Ambrose say?" Jeremy asked.

Hardwick rolled his eyes but the device beeped. He read the screen. "Okay, that's better. Who's staying with you tonight?" He looked expectantly at Maddox.

Maddox nodded to me. "Steve."

Hardwick turned to me. "Blood sample every hour.

Write down everything he eats and drinks, and exact times. He's to eat every two hours."

"Okay."

Jeremy sighed and sagged down on the sofa. "I hate this."

Hardwick patted Jeremy's knee before he began packing up his bag. "You'll be okay. I'll see you tomorrow at nine o'clock."

"Come on," Maddox said, standing up. He pulled Jeremy to his feet. "I'm taking you to bed. Not the man you want, but too bad." He stopped and looked directly at me. "And just so you both know, when the doc says no exercise, he also means no sex. Four times? Fucking hell."

Jeremy shoved his shoulder. "Fuck off."

I tried not to die and I pretended Hardwick wasn't putting pieces together. "I'll walk you out," I said.

He didn't say anything until he got to his car. "What Maddox said is correct. No sex," he started.

"Yep. Got it. Thanks. All good." I waved him off. "Jesus."

Roscoe caught it all, of course. "Everything okay?"

"Yeah. Just . . . embarrassing."

He laughed. "Oh. *That* conversation. Been there, done that."

"You okay, boss?" Robbie asked.

I gave him a smile. "Yeah. How about we go inside?"

We sat at the dining table. The house was still kinda dark, but at least it was quiet. "The boys are in Jeremy's room," I said, keeping my voice down. "How was Ryan when he left?"

"Uh, kinda pissed," Roscoe replied.

"I don't know what Ambrose said to Hardwick on the

phone, but it pissed him off." I sighed. "Been a day for it, apparently."

Robbie smiled at me. "I dunno what went on in that meeting, boss. But that guy you took down in the lobby deserved it. He was lucky that was all you did to him, and I heard Luke and Blake tell Ambrose that too."

"They defended me?"

A flash of confusion crossed his face. "Of course they did. They told him they didn't want anyone else in charge of security."

"Maddox did too," Roscoe said. "Don't be so surprised, Steve."

I sighed. "They were going to fire me today. For real. And then to have my past blasted all over the news . . . I bet the news and online trolls are just having a field day."

Roscoe grimaced. "Well, yeah, it's big. But Steve, there are a lot of positive voices out there. More than the negative. Fans are defending you and thanking you for keeping Jeremy safe. They know it's your job and you'd do anything to protect him. They're singing your praises right now."

"That guy wasn't after Jeremy. He was after me." I murmured. "Well, I bet he was paid to come for me. He was no match for me, and Jacqueline Sosa was watching the whole thing unfold. I'd bet anything she paid some random guy to do it."

"Why?" Robbie said. "Just to see what you'd do?"

"He yelled my name. My old name. She was exposing me."

"But what for?" he asked.

"To create a media circus," Roscoe said with a shrug. "To keep us juggling as many balls as we can. We're bound to drop one at some point."

I met his eyes. "Maybe."

"Divide and conquer," Robbie said.

I nodded. "Feels like it." I sighed again. "I've not been the best boss or security manager this last week. I don't even have a phone. I hope everyone knows I haven't abandoned them. I've just been . . . focused on Jeremy right now."

Robbie shook his head. "We're all good, boss. We know what we have to do. And honestly, we go from their house to the office and home again. There've been no events or traveling. It's been easy."

"I don't know if the schedule will change again this week," I admitted. "Supposed to be having that interview tomorrow. Jeremy's definitely out. But they still might want the other four to go ahead with it. I doubt they'd let me know anyway . . . even if I had a phone. I'll probably find myself having some recommended vacation time if they don't fire me." I sighed again. "Either way, Ambrose or Arlo is gonna have to come here to tell me personally. Not having a phone right now is not ideal, I know. Sorry."

"The phone thing was weird today," Roscoe said. "How the FBI took them."

I wanted to rant about the damn phone exchange but didn't want them to think I was paranoid. *Maybe I was being paranoid but . . .* "I don't know who to trust," I admitted. "None of what's gone on lately sits with me. It felt as if I was being handed a tracking device today. And Jeremy has enough to worry about at the moment without the shit Arlo Kim pulled today. I don't know what he was thinking . . ."

"Like he knows more than he's letting on?" Robbie asked.

Roscoe and I both stared at him.

"There've been whispers." Robbie shrugged. "Nothing direct, just everything today seemed so hush hush, you know, the secretive glances. It's not normally like that. Just feels . . . different."

I nodded. "Thought it was just me."

"Definitely not just you," Roscoe said, then he groaned and pulled his phone from his pocket. There were a few message notifications on his screen. "Has not stopped." He read through the messages. "Interview tomorrow is off, in light of Jeremy's medical appointment. Four other guys are expected at the offices for concept photos and design trials, starting at nine."

Both things Jeremy could miss without too much hassle.

"Well, it's smart to drop anything press-related," I said. "An interview with *any* press right now wouldn't be good. Especially after Jeremy's impromptu address today. And then my Hulk impersonation. I bet the news and social media sites are just loving it. God. It's really no wonder Arlo wanted to fire me today." I rubbed my temple. "I would probably fire me."

Roscoe laughed, but then Maddox appeared in the hall leading to Jeremy's room. "Steve?"

I shot to my feet and went to him. "What's wrong?"

Maddox shook his head. "Nothing. He's almost asleep but he wants to see you."

"Oh. Sure."

Maddox handed me his phone. "I know you don't want this, and Jeremy certainly doesn't, but I need you to take it."

"Maddox—"

"What if you need to call an ambulance? What if there's some kind of emergency? Please. Not for any other reason but him." He swallowed hard. "I would feel better."

Fuck. When he put it like that.

I took the phone.

"There's nothing on there, really," he said. "Nothing I

wouldn't let Jeremy see, anyway. And this is *my* phone, so if anyone's listening or whatever, they'll think it's me. Not you or him."

I nodded. "Thank you."

He met my eyes and there was something profoundly sad in his. I had to wonder what they'd talked about for him to look like that. Maybe he was just worried . . .

"I'm gonna get going," he said. "Leave him to get some sleep."

"Okay. We're not going anywhere. Until tomorrow, that is."

Maddox nodded. "Look after him."

The way he said that sounded as if he was handing his best friend over. It took me a second to find my voice. "Of course."

I wasn't imagining Maddox's change in demeanor because from how concerned he was, Roscoe clearly noticed it as well. But I saw them out, locked up behind them, reset the security codes, and raced up to Jeremy's room.

He was lying atop the covers, and his eyes opened slowly when I walked in. "Hey, you," he said, his voice soft. He frowned and his chin wobbled. "Could kinda use a hug right now, if that's okay? Can I ask you for a hug? I don't even know . . ."

I slid onto the bed and scooped him up in a fierce embrace. He hugged me just as tight. "Of course you can ask," I murmured, kissing the side of his head. "Just say the word and I'm here."

He nodded into my neck. "Thank you." He sighed and tightened his hold on me. "What are we, Steve? What is this?"

I froze and my heart skidded in my chest. "I don't

know," I answered honestly. I pulled back and cupped his cheek, our noses almost touching. "I don't know what to call it. I don't know what you want from me, but whatever you want, whatever you need, I'm here."

His eyes were glassy. "Steve . . ."

"What is it, baby?"

He laughed but got a little teary. "I've never had anyone . . . No one's ever called me baby before. I used to tease the shit out of Maddox when Roscoe called him baby, but I get it now. It's kinda great."

I swept his cheek with my thumb and kissed him softly. "Baby."

He closed his eyes. "I don't know what to call this either. But I know I need you, and I want you around. All the time. I feel safe with you." He opened those blue eyes and stared right into the depth of me. "Everything is shit right now. Everything but you. I don't get it, and I've stopped trying to understand. You make me feel things . . . I don't even know how to make sense of it. I just want to be with you."

Oh my god.

"I just want to be with you too. You make me feel things too. Things I haven't felt in a long time. Things I never thought I'd feel again."

He nodded but his face crumpled and a tear escaped.

"Jer," I whispered. "You okay?"

He shook his head and more tears fell. "I told Maddox I want out. Of the band. I'm done."

# CHAPTER TWENTY-ONE

"I DON'T WANT them to hate me," he said, fresh tears falling. "They're my brothers, my family."

I stroked his jaw. "They could never hate you. They love you."

He showed his wrist, the Atrous tattoo. He ran his thumb over it. "We always said it would be the five of us or none of us. That was the rule. If someone wanted out, that was it. Atrous would be over. It was always supposed to end that way. I just didn't think it would be me." He shook his head. "I *never* thought it would be me."

I pulled him in close and held him tight. "It's okay, baby. You're allowed to do what's right for you."

"But it's not just us," he mumbled into my shirt. "What about everyone else? Didi and Amy and all the make-up girls, wardrobe, the roadies. God, Roscoe, Ryan, and Amber. What about you and your team?" He looked up at me. "What about you?"

"You can't be worrying about anyone else," I whispered. "Everyone else is employed by Platinum. They'll start working with another band."

"Do you really think Roscoe would manage anyone else but Maddox? Spend sixteen hours a day with someone else? Do you think Maddox will let that happen? Christ, no wonder he was pissed at me."

"He's not pissed at you. He's worried. He loves you. So there'll be changes. Big deal. Maddox and Roscoe are rock-solid. They'll work it out." I kissed the tip of his nose and stroked the side of his face. "Do you feel a bit better now that you've told him?"

Jeremy sighed. "We've always talked about when or if it would happen. But when I first started to think about it, for real, it was awful. It felt inevitable and I kept ignoring it, hoping it would go away. But when I started to seriously think about it, and with everything else going on, it was a relief. Like a burden had been lifted. And I wasn't going to tell him yet. I wanted to maybe think it over some more, but we were talking and he asked me . . . about what I wanted with you, and about Arlo, and I told him. I've wanted to tell him for a while." He sighed deeply. "I think I feel better. Until I start thinking about the ripple effects. God."

"You can't be stressing over the what-ifs and the maybes. You need to do what's right for you."

"What about what's right for you? What will you do?" Jeremy's eyes were wide and imploring. Even a little scared. "Will you spend sixteen hours a day with someone new? Go off on world tours for months at a time with someone new?" He got teary again. "Fucking hell, you will. Steve, I don't know . . . I don't know how I feel about that. I don't want you spending all your time with someone new. We just got together. Fuck, I wasted so much time."

I pulled him in for a kiss. "You didn't waste anything. Jeremy, you can't be stressing over anyone else. It's not your fault. If Atrous is no more and people find their employment situation has to change, then so be it. That's not on you." I ran my hand along his shaved head. "And you seem to be forgetting that my employment with Platinum was almost over today anyway. Probably already is, and they're just waiting to tell me."

His eyebrows knitted together. "If Arlo Kim fires you, he'll be in for a spectacularly bad day."

I smiled and kissed him again. "Baby, please don't worry about anyone else right now. You just worry about you. Oh, that reminds me . . . I need to grab your glucose meter."

He groaned his disapproval when I unwrapped myself from his hold, and he grumbled as I ran out of the room. He was staring at the ceiling, arms out wide, when I came back. He held his finger out to me. "Vampire me."

Smiling, I sat on the edge of the bed. I wasn't sure how to use it. I'd seen it done but had never done it myself. "Now's a good time to learn," he'd said, then walked me through the process. It was simple and fast. His reading was okay, thankfully.

"How are you feeling?"

"I feel . . . tired. I'm just wiped." He opened his arms out again. "Would feel a lot better if you were in here."

I crawled over and lay back down beside him. He put his head on my chest and I began drawing patterns on his back. "Maddox suggested we go up to the cabins—all of us—when I get out of this stupid medical jail. Guess we need to talk about everything."

Over the last two years, when they spent time at the cabins around the firepit and in the recording studio they built, they'd always come back recharged and with their friendships renewed. "That sounds like a good idea."

"Will you come?"

"Well, yeah. If this woman is still on the loose—"

"No, I don't mean as Steve the security boss. I mean as Steve . . . with me. My Steve."

My hand stilled on his back.

*My Steve.*

He lifted his head to look at me. "Is that okay? Too much? I don't know—"

I pulled him in for a kiss, tilting his head and opening his mouth with mine. He moaned into the kiss and dragged his body up so he could kiss me deeper. His fingers found my hair and I raked my hands down his back, gripping his ass.

The sound he made was obscene.

I wanted more, I wanted it all . . . until I remembered what Hardwick had said.

Goddammit.

I broke the kiss. "The doctor said no sex."

He licked his lips, eyes heavy-lidded. "Bold of you to assume that's where this was going."

I chuckled. "You're supposed to be resting."

"I'm lying down." He ground his semi against mine. I hissed and rolled us onto our sides. He slung his leg over my hip, which didn't help at all. But every inch of us, from hips to chest, was pressed together. He wriggled until he was comfortable, his arms tight around me. He sighed heavily and relaxed.

"Steve?"

"Yeah."

"Kiss me until I fall asleep."

I groaned, my heart lurching in my chest. But I did as he asked. Languid and lovely, slow and sleepy. A little deep, a little sweet. He smiled as he fell asleep on my arm.

I traced gentle patterns along his scalp, along his cheek, my heart thumping louder the more I watched him.

I was *so* in love with him.

There was no going back for me. When I told him 'whatever he wanted, whatever he needed from me,' I wasn't kidding. I'd do, be, whatever he needed.

I didn't know what to call what this was. I wasn't a fan of labels. But he said he was feeling things for me, and I admitted the same to him. It was a declaration in itself.

So was the way he held me.

So was the way I kissed him, and so was the way he surrendered to each of my kisses.

I let him sleep until it was time for another glucose reading. I kissed his forehead, his eyelids, his nose. "Jeremy," I murmured.

Nothing.

"Hey, baby."

He barely stirred.

"Hey, beautiful."

His eyebrow twitched.

"Hey, sexy. I want to do things to your body. I want to make you come all night long. I want to wring pleasure out of you until your body can't take anymore."

His eyes opened.

I smiled. "Just kidding. I mean, I'd love to do those things to you, but really, I need to do another glucose reading."

His eyes narrowed, his sleepy gaze transforming into a glare. "The fuck?"

"We can't. We're not allowed." I chuckled. "Doctor's orders."

He rolled away from me. "I'm gonna hold you to that. All those things you said. I heard them."

I grabbed the reader and a test strip. Then I climbed

over and straddled him. I took his finger, ignoring how he was looking at me. "You all right there?"

I shoved his finger in the device and pressed it. "Yep."

I took the strip and let it seep into the tiny pool of his blood, then shoved it into the reader. I put it beside us on the bed, then leaned down and kissed him. "I fully expect you to hold me to those promises. When you're up for it, I will do those things to you all night long."

He gripped my hips and thrust against me. "I am up for it."

It just about set my blood on fire. I was about to claim his mouth with mine when the reader beeped.

Fuck.

We both groaned in frustration, but he snatched up the machine and read the numbers. He frowned and showed them to me. They were lower than before. Not dangerously low, but there was a drop.

"Come on," I said, rolling off him. I held my hand out, which he took. "Let's have a snack. Then we can cook an early dinner. Maybe watch a movie or something easy."

He hauled himself up and off the bed with some effort. "Can it be X-rated?"

I snorted. "Probably not a good idea. I'm not opposed. Actually, I would normally be all for that, but Doctor Hardwick said no." I led the way to the kitchen and pulled out a container of berries and some crackers.

Jeremy took a berry first. "Technically, Maddox said that. Not the doc."

"Hardwick told me when I walked him out. In front of Roscoe. It was horrifying."

Jeremy chuckled. "Nothing is private in this band. So Hardwick knows . . . about us?"

"He connected the dots, yes. Is that okay?"

He nodded. "I mean, Maddox knows. I'll tell the others. If you're gonna come up to the cabins with me, then they'll know for sure, I guess."

"Are you sure you're ready for that? Telling them?"

The corner of his mouth curled up. "They'll be as surprised as me when I realized why I was so mad at you."

"Mad at me?"

"Yes. You had no right to make me want you. Honestly, what the fuck?"

I chuckled. "Should I be sorry? Because I'm not."

He bit another strawberry and I couldn't resist. I leaned in and kissed him, tasting the fruit on his lips.

He groaned. "Doing shit like that doesn't help."

I licked my lips. "But you taste so good."

He fisted my shirt and spun me around so I was against the kitchen counter. He pressed himself right up against me and bit into another strawberry. He let his lips trail over the shape, the juice pooling on his lips before his tongue swept them clean. I leaned in for a taste but he pulled back. "Oh. Should I be sorry? Because I'm not."

I groaned and pulled his hips back to mine, letting him feel what he was doing to me. "Doctor Hardwick is about to be really disappointed in us."

Jeremy smirked. "Never figured you for a rule breaker, Steve."

I fake-snarled at him. "You're supposed to be on bed rest."

"So take me back to bed." He took hold of my chin and brought me in for a hard, dirty kiss. Then he whispered, "I know you want to."

I groaned. "Jeremy."

He took a small step back, undid his pants, and slid his

hand into his briefs. "I'm gonna get myself off. You can help if you want."

*Fuck.*

I snatched his hand away and dragged him back to his room. He almost tripped up the stairs, and he laughed when I pushed him back on the bed.

His laughter, his smile, soon died when I took him into my throat. His back came off the bed, his hips flexed, and he groaned as he fisted my hair.

He lasted about a minute.

Then spent a few minutes twitching and groaning, smiling and chuckling.

"Fucking hell."

I fell onto the bed beside him. "Who's laughing now?"

He snorted, and after a few seconds, he rolled onto his side to face me. "Your turn."

Oh god.

"Jeremy, you don't have to do that." He'd never done this before . . .

He climbed on top of me, resting between my legs, his face near my belly. "I want to try."

The idea of him sucking my cock made my head spin. My already aching dick throbbed. "I want to say no, but . . ."

He undid the button of my jeans. "But?"

"But you've never . . ."

He undid the zipper. "I've never done any of what we've done. Not with a guy."

"Jeremy."

He pulled my briefs down and my cock slapped my belly. "You smell good."

His words sent a wave of heat through me. "Oh fuck."

He chuckled, his warm breath washing over me. And then he took me in his hand, pumped me a few times, then licked a stripe up my shaft. Then he did it again, his tongue flat this time.

And again, flicking the frenulum with his tongue.

Christ.

He leaned up and sank his lips over the head. I tried to watch. I wanted it burned into my brain. But it felt too good. He was too gorgeous . . . Jeremy. Jeremy was giving me head.

Holy fuck.

He pulled off and licked his lips, getting used to the taste. Then he did it again and I tapped his shoulder. "I'm close. God, so close."

He pulled off again and I wrapped my hand around his. A few pumps had me tumbling over the edge. In a rush of pleasure and ecstasy, I came in spurts over our fingers.

He disappeared into the bathroom and came back with a warm, wet washcloth and a goofy smile. He threw the cloth to me, then crashed onto the bed beside me, laughing as he covered his face.

I cleaned myself up, though my shirt was a mess. "What's so funny?"

"Ah, holy shit," he said, covering his face. "I just sucked my first dick."

I laughed as I pulled my shirt over my head and lobbed both toward the bathroom door. I settled back on the bed. "I'm honored."

"Was it terrible? Was I bad at it?"

I snorted and took his hand. "Not at all. You were great at it. I just had to clean up how good you were at it."

He laughed but then shook his head. "I didn't . . . I didn't, um. Thank you for warning me. Not sure I'm ready for that."

"Hey," I whispered, squeezing his fingers. "You don't

ever have to be. No pressure, ever."

He pulled a pillow under his head and seemed content to just stare at me with a lazy almost-smile. "We didn't get far with making dinner."

"You had a snack. Are you feeling okay?"

That lazy smirk became a grin. "I feel great."

I laughed. "But you will need to eat."

"Yeah, eventually."

"It won't take long to make dinner tonight. How does lemon pepper salmon with some salad sound?"

"Depends. Do I have to cook it?"

I couldn't help but smile at him. "You can be in charge of finding us something to watch on Netflix."

"Deal."

"I should put on a shirt," I mumbled as I was getting up.

He stopped me with, "Or you could not."

I met his gaze. "Why?" I was so used to hiding my scars . . .

He walked his fingers up my arm to my chest. "I like this. I've never liked a guy without a shirt before. I mean, I've admired, but I've never wanted to touch a man's chest before. Not really. And certainly not in my bed, where I can just touch. Your muscles are . . . well, they're hot."

Of course he wasn't fixated on my scars. I had to wonder if he even saw them. He was simply perplexed at his attraction to a man. He liked what he saw and it fascinated him.

"Okay, no shirt."

His smile was smug and he did that content-to-stare-at-me thing again. "Dinner and Netflix sounds . . ."

"Ordinary?"

He shook his head. "It sounds perfect."

"Not too boring for you? It's not first-class flights to

Paris or five-star meals in Singapore."

He snorted quietly. "You mean takeout in hotel rooms?" He studied my face. "Steve, these days with you here have been amazing. I've never had ordinary or boring. I've never had anything close to a relationship. Dinner and Netflix and napping on the couch with you is the best thing ever." He smirked. "If I'd known it was like this, I wouldn't have taken the mickey out of Maddox and Wes."

I chuckled, my heart thumping against my ribs. "Well, I promise not to tell Maddox that."

He laughed but it faded quickly. He'd obviously just remembered his talk with Maddox earlier. He shook his head. "God. It's been a long day."

"I'll go make dinner." I rolled off the bed and felt the phone in my pocket. "Oh. Speaking of Maddox . . ." I held the phone out. "He wanted us to have this. In case of an emergency. Why don't you call him? Or text him. He'll be on Roscoe's phone. You know he'll be worried sick."

He sighed but took the phone. "I told him I didn't want it."

I took his other hand and pulled him to his feet. "You okay? Not dizzy?"

He seemed to think about it for a second. "I'm okay."

We went downstairs. Me to the kitchen, him to the couch. Dinner took all of fifteen minutes to make. I saw him texting a few times, and I was glad.

Jeremy seemed to want to push them away. With everything going on, he seemed to want to isolate and hunker down, to not burden them.

The truth was, he needed those four guys. Just as much as they needed him.

And maybe there was some merit to Jeremy saying they were a different group of guys now. They'd changed, grown up, and had lives outside of the band. That was also true, to some degree. But they were closer than anyone I'd ever known.

He needed his four best friends, his brothers, not the band.

He was quiet during dinner, his plate almost empty before he spoke. "This is really good, thank you. And you not wearing a shirt was still the best decision of the day."

That made me laugh. "You're welcome." I sipped my water. "How's Maddox?"

Jeremy sighed. "He's okay. Not much we could say via text, especially if someone's reading it." He shrugged one shoulder. "It's a big decision. Whether we call it quits or not. And who knows? Maybe I'm not in the right mindset to be making decisions like that right now. I dunno."

"You'll figure it out. And you'll always have them whether you're in a band or not."

He met my eyes and smiled. "You've never tried to sway my decision. Every time I've talked about it, you never said what you thought I should or shouldn't do."

"It's not my call to make. The only advice I can give is to do what you want. Not what you think others want. Make the decision that's best for you." I smiled at him. "Whatever makes you happy. That's what I want you to do."

He did that staring-at-me thing again, but this time his cheeks blushed pink. He stood up, walked around to my side of the table, lifted my chin, and kissed me. Then he took the plates to the kitchen. "So, I thought we could start watching all the kickboxing and karate movies from the '80s and you can point out all the flaws."

I laughed as I cleared the table. "Sounds good."

When everything was squared away, Jeremy did another prick test. His reading was okay but his fingers were getting sore. "I'm so over this shit," he grumbled. "You know what I need?"

"A new pancreas?"

Jeremy shot me a stunned look before he snorted out a laugh. "Well, yes, that too."

"Sorry." I handed him a bottle of water. "What do you need?"

"I was going to say a cuddle with you still not wearing a shirt, and you can give me back rubs."

I laughed. "I can do that."

I lay on the couch, propped up on cushions, and Jeremy planted himself between my legs, his head on my chest. We started the movie but it was pretty clear he wasn't paying attention. After a while, he looked up, his brows furrowed. "Can I tell you something? I think I've realized something."

"Sure."

"I'm not gay."

*God, here we go again.* "You keep saying that."

"I know. But I've been thinking . . . I don't think I'm completely straight."

I was tempted to smile until I realized he was serious. I thumbed his jaw and gave him time to explain.

"And I don't think I'm bi? I mean, logically I think I have to be? But it doesn't feel right. I don't know. I'm trying to get my head around it. How can I be bi if I've never wanted a guy before you?"

"Being bisexual doesn't have to mean a fifty-fifty split of attraction to men and women" I offered gently. "It can be eighty-twenty or ninety-ten or any equation, to either sexes or genders, if that's what suits you better. There's no minimum or qualifying criteria. There are no gatekeepers. It can be on a sliding scale that changes every day, if that suits you."

His eyes went wide. "It can?"

"Course it can. There are no rules, Jer. Everyone is individual, so it stands to reason that everyone's definition could be too, right?"

He smiled. "I guess. Do you always have to make sense?"

"I try."

"So do you think I'm bi?" He frowned. "I mean, I've always liked women, but then there's you, being shirtless and sexy as fuck, and with your strong arms and hairy chest. And I really liked sucking your dick earlier and I'd really like to do it again. So I'm guessing that's something maybe bisexual guys think about?"

I laughed and leaned up so I could kiss him. "Maybe." Then I looked down at my chest. "I don't have a hairy chest."

"You got more hair than me."

I laughed again and Maddox's phone rang. Jeremy groaned and grabbed it off the coffee table. "Dickbag. I'm trying to—"

He stopped talking and frowned. He looked down at the phone and pressed the speaker button.

It was Maddox. ". . . turn it to the news. It just came on."

Jeremy turned Netflix off and found the news channel. A female reporter stood outside a police station. ". . . according to a statement released by Platinum Entertainment, she was wanted by the FBI and local police in relation to cyber fraud against Platinum Entertainment and threats made against Jeremy Dalton of the band Atrous."

Oh my god. *What the hell happened?*

"Just to recap," the reporter said, "twenty-two-year-old Californian woman, Jacqueline Sosa was found dead at the scene."

# CHAPTER TWENTY-TWO

JEREMY AND I SAT, side by side, staring in horror at the television.

"Jacqueline Sosa had allegedly hacked into Platinum Entertainment's mainframe and attempted to sell all company shares on the stock market. Not for her own personal gain, but it would seem that for no other reason than an attempt to simply seek control of and bankrupt the company. Platinum Entertainment CEO Arlo Kim has said in a statement," the reporter read from her papers, "that the 'transaction would have seen control of the company released to the public.' The illegal breach was caught by authorities before the transaction could proceed."

"Jesus fucking Christ," Jeremy mumbled. He looked at me, bewildered.

"Are you hearing this?" Maddox asked through the phone. "What the actual fuck?"

"Jacqueline Sosa had also allegedly gained illegal access to the phones of each member of Atrous, the band, and threats had been made against Jeremy Dalton."

Then the reporter put her hand to her ear, listening to her producer. Her eyes got wide, excited.

"This just in, we can also confirm, a website has played forty minutes of what appears to be the home security footage of Jeremy Dalton's home."

My pulse pounded in my ears.

The news cut to a black-and-white screen of Jeremy's backyard. Of me in the pool, of Jeremy talking to me. Of me getting out of the pool, of Jeremy touching my scars.

I felt sick.

"Holy fuck," I breathed, turning to Jeremy. I imagine his expression matched mine.

Horrified.

Then the footage cut to the drunk-singing party for a few seconds, and I knew it was coming . . .

Jeremy falling into the pool. Hitting his head. Maddox diving in after him, followed quickly by me.

I could hear Maddox and Roscoe saying something but couldn't quite make out the words over the pounding in my ears.

The room tilted and was suddenly hot.

Then the footage cut back to the reporter. "The site has been removed, the IP address one of many believed to be used by Ms. Sosa."

"Turn it off," Jeremy whispered. He got to his feet and screamed, "Turn it off!" He threw the remote control at the TV. It cracked the screen and the resolution, but the reporter still droned on. Jeremy stomped over and ripped the TV from the wall. It clambered to the floor with a mighty crash, cords pulled from the drywall.

He screamed, hands clawing the air. Then he saw the laptop on the coffee table, picked it up, and threw it at the glass door with such force it shattered.

The sound cut the air like gunfire but Jeremy wasn't done. I'd never seen him this angry.

He grabbed the modem and yanked it from the wall. He trudged through the now-broken door and launched the modem into the pool. He went to the laptop, which was open and upside down on the broken glass, picked it up, and threw it into the pool too.

Then he turned his ire at the security camera. He looked around for something to throw at it, and the closest being only a deck chair, he attempted to hurl it at the camera, but missed. He tried a second time and let out a frustrated growl as he spun it the way an athlete would throw a discus . . . It was a worse shot than the first. He managed to take a chunk out of the wall, though.

"Fuck!" he yelled.

I went to the patio table and took out the sun umbrella, made sure the canopy was closed and secured, and I handed it to him.

Should I have stopped him? Should I have tried to calm him down?

Probably.

But his anger, his fucking rage, was warranted.

He smiled as he took the umbrella. A few good whacks and the camera was on the ground.

Maddox and Roscoe arrived as Jeremy was taking the umbrella to the camera at the front of the house. The red sports car pulled up at the front and Maddox got out of the driver's side and raced up just as Jeremy smashed the camera down.

"Jer, my god," he said, throwing his arms around him. "You okay?"

Jeremy was breathing hard. He was clearly not okay. He

pulled away from Maddox. "Better now," he said. Then he stalked back inside.

Maddox followed and Roscoe gave me a solemn nod as he went in after them. They stopped in the living room, Maddox and Roscoe staring at the smashed door, the damaged wall.

Jeremy, on the other hand, was now trying to look at the bottom of his foot.

Maddox noticed. "Are you bleeding? Jeremy!" Then Maddox shot me a look and gestured to the damage. "What the fuck happened in here?"

I put Jeremy over my shoulder and carried him to the kitchen, sitting him on the counter. "Let me have a look," I said, taking his foot.

It was a small splinter of glass that I easily removed. I wet a paper towel before gently running it over both soles of his feet. "Feel any more in there?"

He shook his head and he gave me a weak smile. "No. Feels okay."

He was lucky it was tempered glass and had shattered into pebbles, not huge shards.

"Uh, Jeremy?" Maddox said, looking a little panicked. Roscoe had his hand on Maddox's back.

"I'm okay," Jeremy said. "Just lost my shit for a second, that's all. Got rid of all the cameras, internet, that kind of thing."

I saw his old phone, still in the container of rice, sitting on the far counter. I took it out and handed it to him. "You forgot one."

He scowled at the black screen so I put him over my shoulder again and walked him out, through the broken glass, to the patio. I turned him around and he laughed as he tossed it into the pool.

But then Wes was there with Special Agent Zielinski. "What the . . . ?" Wes was obviously confused. He pointed his thumb at Zielinski. "I let him in. You need a goddamn phone. Jer, we came over as fast as we— What are you doing? And what the hell happened in your house?"

I set Jeremy on his feet and held onto him for a second, in case he got dizzy. I probably shouldn't have had him upside down over my shoulder.

Zielinski motioned to the back door. "Did something happen? Was there an incident we should know about?"

"Yeah," Jeremy said. "I ripped the TV off the wall. And every electronic device I own is taking a swim. I just had my life broadcast on the internet by some deranged fucking bitch." He pointed toward the shattered door and yelled, "From my own fucking house!"

Zielinski came over and peered into the pool, seeing the various devices at the bottom. "They could have been evidence."

Jeremy snarled and I thought he was going to lunge at him. I grabbed him and held him back. "Zielinski, what are you doing here?" I asked.

"I wouldn't have to be here if either of you were contactable by phone." He looked at us both. "I take it you've seen the news."

"Whose idea was it to release a statement to the press?" Jeremy asked. "Yours or the company's?"

Zielinski put both hands up. "That was your people. I just came here to tell you personally what happened because I had no way to contact you. Because you don't have a phone."

Jeremy grimaced at the pool before he looked back at Zielinski and shrugged. "And there's a very good chance I won't be getting another one. Ever."

And then, because of course, Luke and Blake arrived with Ambrose in tow. They walked out to the patio wild-eyed. "What the fuck happened inside? Jer, you okay?"

"Yeah, I'm fine," he mumbled, though he was clearly annoyed at Ambrose being there.

Ambrose could tell too. "I got here the same time as Luke and Blake," he said sheepishly. "I tried calling . . ."

Jeremy looked at me. "That settles that. I'm never getting another phone."

"Let's go inside," I suggested. I gave Jeremy a piggyback over the broken glass, and everyone watched us. Whether they were looking at me shirtless or at my scars or at the way Jeremy wrapped his arms around me, I didn't know and I didn't care.

*They all know about the stabbing now. Let them see the scars.*

I walked him to the dining table and lowered Jeremy onto a chair. And yeah, when I turned around, everyone was staring at my scars. "I'll just go put a shirt on," I said. I did feel better once I was dressed, a whole lot more professional, anyway.

When I walked back out, all the boys were sitting at the dining table, Maddox near Jeremy, as always. Roscoe stood, leaning against the side cabinet, Ambrose next to him.

I chose to stand by the door.

Zielinski stood at the head of the table as if he was giving some official FBI briefing. I dunno, maybe he was . . .

"We finally got a pinned location on Ms. Sosa, and when we arrived, we found her already deceased. She had four laptops, several smart phones, scramblers, and scanners. All of her computers have been taken into evidence, but there was a lot of stock trading data, from what I could see."

"Was her death self-inflicted?" Jeremy asked quietly.

"There was no obvious outward indicator of the cause of death," he replied. "No sign of a struggle, no disturbances. There'll be a full autopsy."

"Was she really trying to hijack the company?" Maddox asked.

Zielinski gave a nod. "It would appear so, yes. To be honest with you all, I'm not the expert on cybercrimes, and the final reports aren't in yet. From what I've been told, she'd gained access through some encrypted firewalls and was just about to drop one hundred percent of the company onto the stock exchange in a free market."

"Do we know why?" Luke asked.

Zielinski shook his head. "No concrete motives. And given Ms. Sosa now can't tell us, all we can do is put together a chain of events."

"And that website?" Jeremy asked. He looked a little pale. "She had direct feeds from my security cameras. How the hell'd she do that?"

"That drone that connected to your Wi-Fi," he replied. "From what we can tell, she only had footage up until the first password change. Nothing after that."

That still wasn't comforting.

"And," Zielinski said, "she had footage from all your homes. Not just here."

"The fuck?" Blake cried.

"She had them all loaded to go live, but for whatever reason, she never pushed the go button."

Jesus H. Christ.

"For what it's worth," Zielinski added. "If she was taken into custody today, she'd have been charged with piloting an illegal aircraft in California airspace, personal information infringement charges, possible terrorism offenses. That drone she used was a serious weapon. And highly illegal."

"She did all that just to destroy us?" Maddox asked. "I could maybe understand if it was for money. If she had all that technology and the know-how, she could have cleaned us out. All of us, individually and the company. But she just wanted us to lose it all and not benefit from that? I don't get it."

"It's personal," Roscoe said. "There has to be something that ties her to us."

There was.

"Me," I said, still leaning against the doorway. "What did Chase Hystek say? You said he was being interviewed today?"

Jeremy turned in his seat and he gave me a tired but sweet smile.

Zielinski, on the other hand, looked at me like shit on a shoe. "He admits to knowing her. They met through a pen-pal exchange. Denies any involvement, of course. Said he didn't even know you were working for Platinum Entertainment until she told him." He paused. "He said Ms. Sosa was *good entertainment value* and that she was, and I quote, 'unhinged.'"

"So, is it over?" Jeremy asked. He scrubbed his hand over his hair and swallowed hard, and his knee bounced and he did that blink/squint thing I now recognized as a pre-hypo warning. He was pale now. "Uh, Steve?"

I ducked to the kitchen and grabbed a glass of juice and rushed to put it on the table in front of him. He nodded quickly and I patted his shoulder.

"Okay, we've heard enough. Thank you," Maddox said to Zielinski. He put his hand on Jeremy's shoulder. "Jer, you okay?"

Jeremy nodded and drank his juice, his hand trembling.

Maddox looked at me, then at Roscoe, and he shook his head. "Twice today. That's not good."

"Jer, you look like shit. Should we call 911?" Wes said worriedly.

"No," Jeremy said. "Just call Hardwick." He let out a shaky breath. "It just hit me fast, that's all. I'm sorry." He grimaced. "My back is killing me."

I kneeled down beside Jeremy, feeling his clammy palm and trying to get a good look at his eyes. He slow blinked and licked his dry lips. He was not good. Roscoe was already on the phone to Hardwick.

"Jer," I said quietly. "We're gonna get you to the hospital."

He met my eyes and gave a nod. There was no fight in him at all, and that told me enough. He wasn't in good shape.

"No ambulance," he whispered. "It'll be a circus."

I looked up into his face, cupping his jaw. He was still too pale for my liking. "Okay."

"Hardwick's on his way," Roscoe said.

I glanced over at Luke. "Can you get more juice please?" Then I looked at Maddox. "Can you find his glucose meter? I can't remember where we had it. On the coffee table or beside his bed."

Maddox gave a nod and disappeared.

"I'll be going," Zielinski said quietly.

"I'll walk you out," Ambrose said. "And I'll wait for the doctor."

Luke came back with the juice and Jeremy drank half of it, then gave me a nod to signify he was okay.

Drained, but okay.

He was going to the hospital though. If I had to drag him there myself.

I stroked over his cheek, his jaw, his neck. "You'll be fine."

Then Maddox came back with the meter and a packet of strips. "Here," he said, handing them to me.

I took Jeremy's finger and pricked it on the side, knowing his fingertips were a bit sore. I applied the strip to the spot of blood, then to the reader.

I knew Blake and Luke were watching me with him, and I was almost certain Wes had put two and two together.

I didn't care anymore.

I'd leave it up to Jeremy, of course. They were his friends, his brothers. If he wanted them to know, I wouldn't hide it.

The way Jeremy held my hand pretty much told them anyway.

The machine beeped. "It's low," I said.

Jeremy nodded, as if not surprised at all.

I squeezed the back of his neck a few times, massaging, soothing. "You feel okay?"

His gaze lifted to mine, slow and tired. "I hate this."

"I know. We'll get you feeling better soon."

Giving Jeremy some privacy, Luke, Blake, and Wes cleaned up the living room, righting the TV and sweeping up the broken glass. Maddox never moved too far from Jeremy, sitting with him and giving him the occasional squeezy back-hug until Hardwick arrived.

The doctor didn't waste any time.

He came in, put his bag on the table, and shooed me and Maddox away. He sat in the seat next to Jeremy, took his wrist, and measured his pulse while he spoke to him. "I've called the clinic. They're taking you tonight. The mess in the other room? Was that you?"

Jeremy nodded.

"Rage, stress, physical exertion. It's no wonder you crashed," Hardwick said. "You're just damn lucky it happened now and not when you were asleep or you might not have woken up."

Jeremy nodded again.

Hardwick took the glucose meter and looked at the last readings. "What did you intake? Juice, candy?"

"He had about eight ounces of juice," I answered for him. "And his reading didn't get over four. He ate salmon, brown rice, and salad two hours ago."

Hardwick sighed and patted Jeremy's leg. "Well, the clinic's the right choice tonight, huh? You were supposed to take it easy today. I gave you a list of three things to avoid, remember?"

"No stress, sex, or booze," Jeremy said.

"Hm, and? How did that go?"

"Well, I didn't drink alcohol," Jeremy said, trying to smile.

Maddox snorted and shoved me. "Not the bed rest you were supposed to put him on."

I shot him a glare and ignored the glances that Wes, Luke, and Blake exchanged. "Doc, Jeremy said his back's sore."

Hardwick frowned but he nodded. "You're definitely going in tonight. Maddox, can you please pack him a bag? Two to three nights."

"Three days?" Jeremy cried. "No way."

Hardwick clearly wasn't in the mood. "You'll stay for as long as you need. Three days isn't long." He spared me a glance. "It's a secure facility. They deal with a lot of famous people." Then he nodded to Roscoe. "Might want to organize a police escort out of here, if Ambrose hasn't already. There's a lot of media at the gates."

Jeremy sagged. "Of course there is."

And that was what it took. Police to clear the driveway and the road. They had to stand there like some presidential parade to keep the invasive assholes out.

Still, they tried. Camera flashes aimed inside the van as they yelled his name.

The grip of Jeremy's hand on mine only let up after we'd got through the thick of it. He and I sat in the backseat, Maddox and Roscoe in the seat near the door. Hardwick sat in the front. Sayed drove.

Luke, Wes, and Blake had stayed at the house. They'd called to have the glass door replaced and would stay until the company came to install it, so at least it could be locked up. Using Roscoe's phone, I'd called for Robbie, Zoe and Ivan, and we'd left as soon as they arrived.

"You okay?" I asked.

Jeremy nodded but he frowned. "It's sad, isn't it?"

"What's that?" Maddox asked, peering over the back of the seat.

"About that woman. I mean, she died. Clearly she had some . . . issues and she caused a lot of damage. But she didn't have to die. She just needed some help."

I threaded our fingers. This woman had tried to ruin him, almost had. It was hard to know, considering the fallout hadn't even begun yet. Maybe she had. Yet all he had for her was sympathy.

"Don't be worrying about any of that," I said. "You just need to worry about yourself."

He put his head on my shoulder. "Hm."

Maddox must have found his phone by Jeremy's

bed when he went for the glucose meter, because he held it up. "I googled the clinic you're going to," he said. "Says it's the best. It looks fancy. In a hotel-jail kind of way."

Jeremy snorted. "Great."

I gave him a gentle nudge. "It'll be fine. And when you leave, you'll be feeling a hundred percent better."

He mumbled, only loud enough for me to hear. "Hope so."

The clinic had a U-shaped driveway with a front door drop-off area, which meant we weren't afforded the privacy of an underground parking garage with a basement entrance.

Which meant photographers had a clear view of us getting out of the van. They didn't come past the front garden, though, which was good because I didn't think a repeated Hulk Smash would be good for anyone.

Hardwick led the way, Maddox carried Jeremy's duffle bag, Roscoe shielded him from the cameras, and I held Jeremy's arm as I walked him in.

A doctor in a white lab coat met us just inside, and the outside noise cut off as soon as the doors closed behind us. The new doc and Hardwick shook hands and she gestured past an admission desk to a set of doors where a guard stood by.

"We don't get many night admissions," she said. "How about we come through this way?"

What she meant was away from all the fucking cameras.

We filed through, and I noticed the guard was fit and young, armed, and had a reputable security company logo on his shirt. Certainly not some old, pudgy mall-security type.

"Is he there to keep people out, or to keep the patients in?" Jeremy asked.

I snorted. "Undetermined."

The doctor smiled. "It's not uncommon for addicts to assume we hold drugs here. Patients are free to leave at any time."

Jeremy stopped walking. "Oh good."

I laughed. "You can't leave *yet*."

Maddox came and took his other arm. "They might have pudding cups."

"It's a fucking diabetic clinic," Jeremy replied.

Maddox made a face. "Oh. Sorry."

There was a wheelchair in the corridor and the doctor put her hand on it. "Mr. Dalton? I didn't think you'd want us to bring the chair out for cameras to see."

I thought for sure he was going to say no way to using the chair, but he went to it and sat with a tired sigh. He was much more tired than he'd let on. He looked pale, tired, smaller. The scar, his shaved head, and unshaven face didn't help.

He looked a far cry from the superstar singer who modeled luxury labels in magazines.

"I'm driving," Maddox said, dumping the duffle bag on Jeremy's lap. He gave Jeremy's shoulder a squeeze before he took the handles.

The doctor led us to what would be Jeremy's room. It was much like a nice hotel room, but for the hospital bed and machinery. It was big with a private bathroom, a TV.

There was paperwork to fill out to get him admitted, but Doctor Hardwick and manager Roscoe took care of that, leaving just Maddox, Jeremy, and me in the room.

"Here," Maddox said, setting the duffle bag on the floor. "Let's get you into bed."

I took Jeremy's hands and pulled him to his feet while Maddox wheeled the chair over to the corner. Jeremy pulled me in close and slid his arms around my lower back, resting his head on my shoulder.

I held him tight for a long second, then helped him into bed.

Maddox fluffed the pillows, pulled the blankets up, unpacked the duffle bag and toiletries, all while I did no more than hold Jeremy's hand.

He came out of the bathroom, a puzzled expression. "Where am I sleeping?" he asked. "It just occurred to me. There's no couch to pull out."

"You don't need to stay," Jeremy said.

Maddox raised one perfect eyebrow. "You've lost your mind if you think I'm going to let you stay here by yourself." Then Maddox turned the eyebrow to me. "Sorry, Steve. I'm pulling rank this time."

I chuckled, because the truth was, Jeremy needed Maddox. "It's fine."

Jeremy pouted. "You just gonna give in like that? No fight at all?"

I kissed Jeremy's forehead. "You need him." Then I joked, "And anyway, Roscoe asked if he could have a few nights off from Maddox, so I'd be doing him a favor."

Maddox's mouth fell open. "He did not. That is un-fucking-true."

I laughed. "Like Roscoe'd ever say that." I kissed the back of Jeremy's hand. "It's just a day or two."

He pouted. "You know the code to my house."

"I have a home," I replied. "Which I haven't been to in far too long. I should check my mail before the super thinks I'm dead."

Jeremy seemed to think something over for a second

before he frowned. "If the whole security risk thing is over, then you don't have to stay at my place anymore . . ."

The doctors and Roscoe came back into the room. She gave us a bright smile. "Okay, now it's time for everyone to leave so Mr. Dalton can settle in. We have some tests to run tonight."

"I'm staying with him," Maddox declared.

The doctor paused. "Oh, uh . . ."

Roscoe tried. "Maddox . . ." Maddox shot him the perfectly arched eyebrow and Roscoe promptly shut up.

"We normally only allow the parents of younger patients to sleep in the rooms," she added.

"He can be my son," Maddox said, then turned to Jeremy. "You can call me daddy."

Roscoe coughed to cover his laugh, and Hardwick sighed. The nice doctor conceded a smile. "I'll have a cot brought in."

"Perfect," Maddox said. "Thank you."

Then she looked at me and Roscoe. "Everyone else will have to go. I'm sure you understand."

Jeremy's hold on my hand got a little tighter. I gave him a smile. "Get some rest, and I'll see you real soon."

He pulled on my hand, bringing me in closer. I put my forehead to his and he slid his hand around my neck and kissed me, soft and chaste, so perfect.

A minute later, Roscoe and I walked out of the room. The doctors were already talking about BGLs and an A1C test that checked hemoglobin proteins, plus kidney and adrenal tests.

I hated leaving him, even if I knew it was the best for him.

We got to the double doors near the entrance, out of view of the papzz, and waited. "Sayed's bringing the van around now," Roscoe said. "He'll drop us home."

I nodded slowly. "Thanks."

"It's been a helluva day, huh?"

I snorted. "Uh, yeah. You could say that." The last twenty-four hours felt like a month long. I was tired. Roscoe looked tired too. This last week had been hell on everyone.

"He's in the right place," Roscoe said. "The doctors will get his glucose levels on track."

I sighed and gave him a nod. "I think he's a lot sicker than what he lets on. He admitted he's felt off for months and he's supposed to be checking his glucose levels, and of course he hasn't. He needs to be here."

Roscoe's phone kept buzzing. He looked at the screen and rolled his eyes. "It just never ends."

"You know, you could always throw it in Jeremy's pool. I left mine at HQ."

He smirked. "I know. Half of these are update requests on you two."

I grimaced but wasn't entirely sorry. "Sorry."

Roscoe smiled at that just as his phone beeped again. He read the screen. "Okay, van's out front."

We went into the foyer and the security guard pressed a release button to open the front doors. Paparazzi and news cameras flashed and filmed us, calling out our names, but we ignored them and climbed into the van. Roscoe took the backseat, I took the seat near the door, and we both sat with our legs sprawled, leaning against the side of the van.

Roscoe sighed heavily. "Feels weird going home without Maddox. This will be our first night apart. Since we got together."

Oh wow. "He was staying with Jeremy, right or wrong."

He smiled. "They have a unique bond. They're all like

brothers, but Maddox and Jeremy are like twins, in a way. You'll get used to it."

Would I?

Was it something I'd even *have* to get used to?

I had no idea.

"Hm. Yeah. I dunno."

"You don't know what?"

I shook my head. "I don't know what we are. Or where I stand with him. Or what he'll want when he's feeling better."

"I don't think you have to worry."

God, I sounded so whiny. "We got together during a highly stressful time, when he wasn't feeling well. What if he realizes, after some time apart and when he's feeling so much better, that he doesn't need me around?" I banged my head against the side of the van. "Ignore me. I need some sleep."

"Steve," Roscoe said. "How long have you known him?" He didn't give me time to answer. "The better part of a decade?"

I nodded.

"And when have you ever known him to be with anyone in public? To hold hands, cuddle. In all the years, on all the tours, in nightclubs, backstage, parties?"

"Never."

"What he's done behind closed doors is anyone's guess and sealed in NDA's. But has he ever kissed anyone in front of other people before?"

I shook my head. "Not that I've seen."

"He did tonight. He kissed you."

Yes, he had.

"Even Maddox said he's never seen Jer in a relationship. He's more touchy-feely than I thought he'd be." I looked over the back of my seat to see Roscoe smiling at me. "I don't think you have anything to worry about, Steve."

I sat back in my seat and smiled.

His phone buzzed again and this time he groaned. He answered the call. "Arlo . . . Yes, he is. I'll put him on." Roscoe handed the phone to me and mouthed, "Sorry."

I took the phone and let out a deep breath. This wasn't going to be good.

"Steve Frost speaking."

"Steve, Arlo Kim. You not having a phone makes it rather difficult to contact you."

I scrubbed my hand over my face and gave him a report, whether that's what he was calling for or not. "Jeremy's at the endocrinology clinic. The clinic itself has guards and security measures. The police were controlling the crowd of papzz out front. One person was allowed to stay with him so Maddox volunteered. Doctor Hardwick was also there."

"Hm, yes," he said flatly. He already knew all this, obviously, so why was he calling me? "I take it you've heard of the events surrounding the FBI investigation?"

"Do you mean Jacqueline Sosa being found dead? Then, yes. Or that she uploaded private footage of Jeremy to the internet before she died? Because, also, yes."

"The site has been taken down."

"And you're sending cease and desists to every single person who uploads or shares footage on social media, right?"

There was a beat of silence. "Our team is working on it."

I wanted to punch this man.

"And you've heard that Jeremy trashed his house in a fit of rage that caused his sugar levels to crash and we probably should have called paramedics, but he was worried that it would just be another media circus that you didn't need?" I spoke through gritted teeth. "You heard that, right? Or did you need the FBI to tell you to care?"

There was a long, strained pause. "Steve, you're on two weeks' leave. Effective immediately. Full pay, but don't push your luck. And when you do come back, you'll be expected to have a phone so you can be contacted. I won't chase you again. I also won't have a repeat of your attitude. And the next time you're reprimanded for such insubordination will be your last day at Platinum—"

I ended the call and handed Roscoe back his phone. He was a little wide-eyed. "Everything okay?"

"I got two weeks and an official warning. I think? I dunno. I cut him off before he could finish."

"Oh."

I shrugged. "Fuck him. He cares about his company, the money, and the reputation and prestige. He doesn't care about those boys. Not anymore. I'm not the only one to notice it. Even Hardwick mentioned it."

Roscoe nodded. "And Maddox. And Wes."

"Jeremy said he and the boys are gonna talk about the band's future. When he gets out of the clinic. They wanna go up to the cabins."

Roscoe met my eyes. "I know. Remember when we went to my uncle's property in Vermont? When Maddox had his breakdown in New York?"

I nodded. "Sure."

"You asked me then if I thought they'd call it quits. I knew they needed a break, Maddox in particular, but I was sure they'd get through it and the band would kick on."

"But now?"

"Now I'm thinking no. I think they're done."

I ran my hand through my hair. "Same. Jeremy told

Maddox he wanted out. But he hasn't been feeling his best so it might change. I doubt it though. I think he's done. Has been for a while. This whole shitshow just kinda sealed the deal. Or, at the very least, what Atrous is on the other side of this will be different."

Roscoe met my eyes and nodded. "Yeah. And that's not a bad thing."

"No, it's not."

"Ah, Steve?" Sayed called out from the front. "Your stop, coming up."

I looked out the front and saw that yes, we were on my street. The van slowed to a stop. "Will you be okay?" Roscoe asked.

I gave him a tired smile. "Yeah. Will you?"

He smiled right back. "Yeah."

I pressed the button and the door slid open. The night was dark and quiet outside, and I realized without a watch or a phone, I had no idea what time it was.

In the space of a week, I'd gone from living a regimented life, structured and organized down to the minute . . . to now not even caring.

My apartment was just as I'd left it, kinda gray and tiny compared to Jeremy's mansion. His place was so huge, but it never felt sparse or museum-like. It was a home.

My place, on the other hand, felt vastly empty despite it being the size of a shoebox.

I missed Jeremy, which was ridiculous, considering I'd just left him an hour ago.

I cleaned out the fridge. I had a shower. I lay on the couch and stared at the ceiling, still without any idea of what time it was. I was so tired I just couldn't bring myself to care.

Was my job at Platinum over?

As good as.

I wasn't sure I cared too much about that, either.

What I cared about was Jeremy.

I closed my eyes thinking of his touch, his smile, his kiss. I knew he was in good hands. He was being monitored by some of the best endocrinology doctors in the country. He was with Maddox, in a secure facility. The FBI investigation was over. He was safe.

I could finally take a minute to rest . . .

I woke up to sunlight streaming into my living room, a sore back, stiff neck, and a very persistent buzzing noise.

# CHAPTER TWENTY-THREE

IT TOOK me a second to realize the buzzing noise was my intercom. I got up, rubbing my neck, and pressed the button. "Hello?"

"Steve? It's Elsie."

Elsie . . . Elsie.

"From Platinum?" she said. "I have a package for you."

Oh, Elsie, the woman who ran all sorts of errands all over the city.

"Sure thing," I said. "I'll come down."

I went down to the entry hall, squinting at the glare of sunlight coming in through the glass door. Elsie was there by herself, holding a large envelope.

I'd seen those envelopes before. They were Platinum Entertainment signature legal or HR envelopes. I opened the door. "Morning," she said brightly.

"Morning."

She handed the envelope over. "For you."

It was heavier than I'd expected, and sure enough, there was a Platinum Entertainment logo in the corner. "Hey, what time is it?"

She looked at me as if I'd asked her which planet we were on, then glanced at her watch. "It's just after nine."

God, I must have slept for what? Ten or twelve hours?

"Thanks," I said.

She waved and went on her way, and I headed back up to my apartment in dire need of coffee.

I made it strong and black, went back to my couch, and stared at the envelope. Last night, I'd been ready to throw my job away, and now . . . regardless of what was in that envelope, I was pretty sure my time at Platinum was over.

I couldn't work for a company, for a man whose motives I now questioned.

Who I no longer respected.

I considered not opening it, leaving it unread like all my text messages and emails, but with a sigh, I unstuck the seal and pulled out the papers.

The first document was an official write-up, citing my two weeks' paid leave on grounds of attitude and unprofessional conduct unbecoming to the Platinum Entertainment standard, blah, blah, blah.

It was a standard HR bullshit letter for their records to check off all the boxes should my personal issues not be addressed and they fire me. It quashed any hope of me suing them for unfair dismissal.

The second document was a revised employment contract. The cover letter outlined two new clauses added, as they were entitled to amend at any time. And I was expected to return the signed contract upon my return in two weeks.

New clause one, I would agree to keep an attitude and standard of behavior that reflected Platinum Entertainment's world-class reputation.

*What-fucking-ever.*

New clause two, I would hereby agree—while employed at Platinum Entertainment, however not while on leave—to be contactable by the company issued phone at any time deemed reasonable by management.

*For fuck's sake.*

I almost laughed.

But the third document . . . the third document was a new NDA.

A freaking non-disclosure agreement for personal relationships with staff. Me and Jeremy.

I did laugh at that.

Because it was funny as hell to me that Arlo Kim thought for one second I'd do anything to hurt Jeremy. I knew these were standard issue. The rational part of my brain knew that. But *fucking* hell.

I needed to expel some energy. I was either going to punch the living shit out of something or run.

So, I tossed the papers onto my coffee table, put on some shoes, grabbed my keys and wallet, and went running.

And I ran.

I ran until I wanted to puke. I ran until my lungs burned and my legs were as heavy as lead.

And I ran some more.

I thought about Jeremy, wondered what he was doing, how he was feeling, what the doctors had found. I thought about what he'd say when I told him about the NDA, when I told him about the two weeks' forced leave.

I thought about him possibly realizing he *wasn't*, in fact, bisexual and that he'd just felt vulnerable and alone, finding comfort in the only person who was around.

Me.

And that he didn't want to see me anymore. That it had

all been some terrible misunderstanding. That whatever we had was over.

Then I puked.

I was miles from home. *Had I really run this far? Had I not noticed where I was going?* Not really familiar with where I'd even run, I found a store, grabbed a few groceries, and caught a cab home.

I ignored the documents still splayed over the coffee table, took a shower, and made myself a sandwich.

Then, because I still wasn't thinking, out of habit, I picked up the remote control and turned on the TV. I bit into my sandwich before I even realized what I was hearing.

". . . has been admitted to a hospital specializing in diabetes. He can be seen here being escorted in by his bodyguard, Steve Frost, only hours after footage of the two being intimate went viral."

I almost choked on my sandwich.

Footage of Jeremy and me came up on-screen, the security camera footage of me getting out of his pool and him touching my scars. The footage was taken from an elevated angle and it was hard to make out exactly. It looked like we kissed, but it was just him touching my side. He was close enough for us to kiss.

Christ. I thought for an awful second they had actual footage of us on the couch or in bed.

"Jeremy Dalton gave an unscheduled press appearance just yesterday morning," the woman on TV said. "You can see security comes out late, including Steve Frost, indicating they were not informed about the interview. Moments later, when confronted by an angry fan, Steve Frost intercepts and throws the man to the ground in what social media has dubbed Hulk Smash." The woman smiled, reminding me of a horse. "It's been a big week for Atrous, hasn't it?"

The screen cut to a male reporter out in front of the clinic where Jeremy was. "It sure has," he went on. "It sounds like the plot for a movie! First, we have the FBI investigation involving a stalker. We know the target was Jeremy Dalton. We know there was increased police presence. We know the FBI frequented the Platinum Entertainment offices last week. Then Jeremy is taken to the hospital for a head injury, unrelated to the stalking claims. How do we know this? Because footage of private security cameras at Mr. Dalton's house was uploaded onto the internet. We can see Jeremy falling into the pool, hitting his head, and being dramatically rescued by Maddox Kershaw and Steve Frost. Jeremy gives an impromptu press interview, sporting a cleanly shaven head and a very visible scar, a good two inches long. Meanwhile, we learn Steve Frost is actually Steve Hammond, an ex mixed martial arts fighter who was stabbed up to six times in a hate crime attack over a decade ago." The reporter's eyes almost spun, he was so excited.

I slid the sandwich onto the coffee table, my appetite gone.

"Then late, last evening, it was reported that the alleged stalker, a Ms. Jacqueline Sosa, was tragically found dead. Cause of death, still undetermined. And as if all of this wasn't enough, now Jeremy has been admitted to LA's finest endocrinology clinic, where we can assume he's being treated for a diabetes-related illness."

The reporter waved his hand toward the clinic. "No sight of Jeremy or Maddox or any other Atrous member. No statement by Platinum Entertainment either. Social media is in a frenzy—"

I clicked the TV off.

If that reporter was out in front of the clinic right now, I could go down there and shove that microphone right up his—

My intercom buzzed.

Oh my god.

*What if it's a reporter?*

I hit the button, ready to rip someone to shreds.

"Steve? It's Roscoe."

I took a deep breath and hit the button, letting him in, then went to my front door and opened it. He was carrying bags and a . . .

A cardboard cutout?

"What the . . . ?" I helped him with the bags.

He put the cardboard cutout down in my living room. It was, of course, of Jeremy. A life-sized cardboard cutout, just like the one from my office.

Roscoe sighed. "He insisted."

I stared at him. "Who?"

"Jeremy. He called me using Maddox's phone. He didn't want you here by yourself, forgetting all about him. His words, not mine. He insisted, and you know that means threatened, right? He insisted that I go to your office and bring you half the merch. There are Jeremy T-shirts and hoodies with his face on them, a wall poster, and three Jeremy calendars. One for your living room, kitchen, and bathroom. And that—" He pointed to the cardboard version of Jeremy. "—that's specifically for your bedroom. I don't want to know why, to be honest."

I looked at the stupid cardboard cutout of Jeremy, then looked to Roscoe. He was trying not to smile, which of course made me smile. Then we both laughed.

"He insisted?"

Roscoe nodded. "He doesn't want you to miss him."

I palmed my mouth and laughed some more. God, I could have freaking cried. "He's such an idiot."

Roscoe clapped my shoulder. "And you thought time apart would make him realize what, exactly?"

Still smiling, I shook my head. "I'm not putting the cutout in my bedroom." I took out a shirt and rolled my eyes at the huge decal of his face on it. The decal was large. The shirt looked small. I checked the size tag. *Christ.*

Roscoe laughed. "He specifically said to get nothing over a medium. And he wants a photo."

I laughed and tried not to blush, then threw the shirt on the sofa. "Want coffee?"

"Sure."

I switched the coffee machine back on and got the mugs ready. "How was he this morning?"

"He's okay. They ran scans and more tests this morning. Still no visitors. How about you?"

"I fell asleep on the couch last night. Must have slept for about twelve hours, though I have no idea what the time is. No watch, no phone. Went for a run. Ran ten miles and ended up in some suburb I didn't know. I had to ask the guy at the store to call me a cab to get home. I made the mistake of turning the TV on, and you can imagine how that went. And then you arrived." Then I remembered. "Oh, and I had some lovely paperwork from Arlo Kim couriered first thing. Which was what prompted the ten-mile run."

"Oh." His expression was a mix of surprise and eww. "What were the papers?"

"An official warning, a new contract to specify that I must not hurt Arlo Kim's widdle feewings, and that I must have a tracking device on my person at all times. Ooops, I mean a phone. Oh, and an NDA. Because of my *personal relations* with Jeremy."

Roscoe laughed. "His widdle feewings?"

I scrubbed my hands over my face and sighed. "I shouldn't be like that, sorry."

"Maddox was livid when we had to sign new NDAs. And I mean *livid*."

I groaned. "I swear to god, if they send Jeremy papers while he's still in the hospital, I will crack fucking skulls."

Roscoe laughed again. He must have thought I was joking.

*Was I joking?*

I kinda wasn't.

I poured the coffee and handed him a mug. "You know, me having two weeks off right now is probably a good thing."

"I take it Jeremy doesn't know about that either?"

I shrugged. "I'm assuming not. I'll tell him everything when he's better. High blood pressure and low blood sugar isn't a good combination." I sipped my coffee. "I don't want my issues to sway his decision about what he wants for the band."

Roscoe sighed. "You know what we should do?"

"What's that?"

"We should go out tonight. Just to a bar. Watch whatever game is on. Have some buffalo wings and a few beers."

I smiled at him. "That's a really good idea."

"Now, about that photo . . ."

"Absolutely fucking not."

---

"I CAN'T REMEMBER the last time I've done this," I admitted as we walked into the bar.

We'd chosen a place that was obscure enough. Not a

dive, exactly, but not high-end like the band would ever go. It was dark enough, neon beer signs behind the bar, various ballgames on the screens.

We found a booth and I slid into the seat while Roscoe went to the bar. There were other tables, mostly of men, some women—none of them looked like a threat. Bathrooms to the back, plus a fire exit.

I tried to relax.

The first beer helped a little. The second helped a little more. The wings were great too. But more than that, Roscoe was easy to hang out with. We chatted about a whole lotta nothing and it was . . . nice.

I was embarrassed to realize I hadn't done this kind of thing in a long, long time.

It had always been about work or planning trips or training. I'd forgotten there was a life outside of work. A social life, friends, sports, maybe even a boyfriend . . .

Roscoe held up his phone, showing Maddox's name. He rolled his eyes but his goofy smile gave him away. He answered the call. "Yes, my love." He listened for a bit, then he let out a huge sigh. "Awesome. . . . Yeah. Okay. . . . Hang on, I'll put him on."

He put the phone to his chest. "Someone posted a picture of us on Twitter."

"Here? Now?"

Roscoe nodded. "About half an hour ago," he whispered. "Tagged Atrous with the hashtag WhenThe-CatsAway."

*When the cat's away . . . the mice will play.*

"Seriously?"

"Because we're the cat herders. I think. God only knows." Roscoe handed his phone over and I expected to hear Maddox, but it wasn't.

Jeremy's voice was like a balm. "Cheating on me already?"

I snorted, because we all knew that was ridiculous. Not to mention that Jeremy and I had never established what we were, exactly, let alone exclusivity. "He promised me beer and chicken wings."

Jeremy laughed. "You're not even wearing the shirt I sent for you. Not sure which hurt the most, if I'm being honest."

"The shirt's a bit small."

"That was why I chose it. I like tight clothes on you."

I was smiling like a fool and I didn't even care. "How are you feeling?"

"Good. Better. They whacked some pretty good stuff into me. I dunno what it was. An intravenous infusion thing with everything my body needed, apparently. A hundred different tests and scans and more blood tests. And I have an implant now for the glucose readings. So no more finger pricks."

"An implant?"

"Yep. Like Iron Man. But in my arm. And not as cool."

"Does it help?"

"Yeah."

"Then it's cool." There was a beat of silence. I pictured him smiling. "How much longer are you in there for?"

"I told them I want to leave tomorrow. They're running more tests. My kidneys haven't been playing well with the other organs, so we need to—"

"Pardon?"

"It's nothing serious."

"Are you sure? Because last I heard, all body organs need to play well with the other organs? Otherwise it's serious."

"We can talk about it when you come pick me up tomorrow."

"I'm picking you up?"

"Yep. On one condition."

"What's that?" *I had a feeling I knew . . .*

"You wear the shirt."

*Yep. That's what I thought.*

"I'm not wearing the shirt."

"Yes you will. And no more canoodling with Roscoe in public. He's engaged to be married, for god's sake."

I sighed. "Okay."

"I've missed you," he said quietly. "Which is stupid and ridiculous, and I blame you for that."

I grinned. "I've missed you too. And that is one hundred percent your fault."

"Maddox is dying for his phone back."

"Yeah, okay. How will I know what time to get you? We still don't have phones."

"I'll send up a Bat-Signal. And by Bat-Signal, I mean Roscoe. I like not having a phone. Sucks that I can't call you though."

I smiled. Or was still smiling. I wasn't sure. I tried to hide my smile from Roscoe. It was embarrassing enough. "True. I'll see you tomorrow."

"Oh, you gonna sleep with the cardboard cutout in your bed tonight? It's life-size, but the dick is only two dimensional—"

"Goodnight, Jeremy."

I handed the phone back to Roscoe, who listened for a while, his smile wide. "I'd need to measure Maddox's to be sure," he said with a laugh.

I could hear Jeremy yelling something, and then he was obviously talking to Maddox again, so I used it as an excuse to look around. The person who took a photo of us could have been anyone.

Were we really news? I guess anything related to Atrous was news.

"Okay, call me later. Bye." Roscoe pocketed his phone. "Not even gonna look at Twitter."

I drained my beer. "Good idea."

"Should we go? Before anyone else comes in?"

I nodded. "Probably."

We paid the tab in cash and left, and yeah, some folks watched and whispered, some didn't care. We climbed into Roscoe's truck and headed home. No one followed us.

It was exhausting having to be so vigilant all the time.

"Do you think the boys will ever get to live a normal life?" I asked.

Roscoe considered that for a moment. "I sure hope so. But not for a while. Guess it'll depend on what they decide to do. And then even if they disband as Atrous, it'll depend on what they do solo."

I hadn't considered that. "Do you think they'll go solo?"

"Don't know. Maddox hasn't said exactly. I can't imagine him wanting to go on stage without the others. He'd struggle too much with the solo pressure, I think. His anxiety is so much better these days, but it's something he's had to work really hard on." He shrugged. "Whatever he does, it'll be something music related, for sure. Writing, composing, producing? No idea."

"It's hard picturing them doing anything else. And without the five of them doing it together, that is."

"And what are you gonna do?" he asked. "With your two weeks? Or permanently, if you decide to hurt Arlo Kim's widdle feewings again."

"Permanently? I have no clue. These two weeks?" I

sighed. "I haven't really even had a day off in ten years. I wouldn't know where to start." I couldn't think of anything meaningful. "Read a book? Catch up on some sleep."

"Oh man, I gotta say—and don't you dare repeat this to anyone—but last night, being my first night with the bed to myself? I slept so well. Maddox is either sprawled across the bed, or he's clinging to me like a koala. There's no in between. Last night, I had the whole bed to myself. I mean, I missed him, for sure, but yeah."

I laughed. "There is no way in hell I'd tell Maddox that."

"Or Jeremy. Telling Jeremy means telling Maddox."

"Oh, that reminds me. Jeremy wants me to pick him up tomorrow, said he'd have Maddox send you the details. I'm enjoying being radio-silent without a phone or laptop, but honestly I hate that he can't call me if he needs anything. And I didn't want to tell him I can't exactly call for Sayed and the van when I've been suspended."

"I'll organize it," he said. "Don't worry. I can call for the van. We'll pick you up on the way past."

"Thanks. And thanks for tonight. It was good to get out."

"No problem. See you tomorrow."

I went up to my apartment, flipped the lights on, and almost had a coronary at Jeremy's cardboard cutout standing in my living room. I almost took its head off, then laughed at myself, feeling the buzz of three beers. "That's why you're not coming to my bedroom."

Realizing I just spoke to a picture of Jeremy and wondering if I was really losing the plot, I put myself to bed.

I WAS UP EARLY and went for a run. It was good to feel the sun on my face, to burn some energy. I'd missed running. I'd missed a lot of things over the last week or so.

And running was a good distraction because, by god, I missed Jeremy.

He said last night he missed me. He said the other day he wasn't sure what *this* was, this thing between us, but he liked whatever this was.

And as I made my way back home, I realized I'd gone from having all the doubts about him yesterday, to being sure today. It was a seesaw, and it was exhausting. And as I ran, with sweat running down my back, my lungs burning, I knew what I had to do.

I had to tell him how I felt. I had to put it on the line and let him know.

No more doubts.

He had enough to worry about, as did I.

The stalker threat was over, but the future of the band was in doubt. His health. His relationship with Arlo Kim.

And my job was in jeopardy, my future. My financial stability.

There was a list of doubts a mile long, and if there was one thing I was absolutely certain about, it was how I felt for Jeremy.

He should know—regardless of how he feels for me— that he doesn't have to doubt me.

It gave me a fresh sense of resolve.

Maybe my time with Platinum had run its natural course. Change was in the air, and maybe it was something I could be excited about instead of fearing it.

If I had my employment terminated or if I quit, at least I could look back and appreciate the wild ride for what it was. I'd been around the world several times, seen more countries than I could've dreamed of, seen more of America than most people ever would. I'd bumped shoulders with every kind of celebrity and socialite, and I'd spent *countless* hours with the biggest band in the world.

I'd watched them at dance practice, in the recording studio, in rehearsals, on stage in front of a hundred thousand screaming fans. I'd seen them laugh, cry, argue, jump in elation, collapse from exhaustion. I'd been there when they were starting out, their first concerts in small arenas to the world stadium tours, when they were first nominated for major awards, when they won.

Not bad for a kid who had to start his life over at nineteen without a penny to his name.

Perspective.

It felt good to get some.

When Roscoe rang my buzzer, I met him downstairs with a smile. "Happy to be seeing someone?" he asked.

"Could say that."

The truth was, I was fucking excited, ecstatic, and a little nervous. Mostly ecstatic.

I noticed Riko standing by the van door. He grinned when he saw me. "Boss!"

"Hey," I replied, happy to see him too.

Riko opened the van door for us. "I'd just like to say, for the record, that me being the protection detail for you is funny. And redundant."

I snorted. "Hardly. Pretty sure I'm not even supposed to be here."

I climbed into the van and Sayed gave me a wave from the front. "Hello, Mr. Frost."

*Mr. Frost? What the hell happened to calling me Steve?*

"Nah, I'm just here for the ride, Sayed. Ignore me. Please call me Steve."

Roscoe chuckled as he took the seat next to me. "You're a celebrity."

I rolled my eyes. "So what's happening on the ground?"

"Ambrose called a manager's meeting this morning. He said the FBI investigation was still wrapping up, that Jeremy's health was a priority, and that you were taking two weeks' vacation time."

I scoffed. "Right."

"Don't worry. We all know. And Ambrose knows, and he knows we know. He just has to go through the motions for Arlo Kim."

That made me sigh. "Who's in charge of security with me gone?" I whispered.

He pointed his chin toward the front. "Shared, between Riko and Robbie."

That pleased me. "Good choice."

"What did you get up to today?"

"Went for another run. Didn't need a ride home today." Roscoe laughed.

"Came to a realization."

He shot me a look. "What's that?"

"I'm gonna tell Jeremy I love him."

Roscoe's eyes went wide and I laughed. My cheeks were hot and all I could do was shake my head. "I don't know when. But soon, maybe? I dunno. It was a good idea earlier today. Now that I've said it out loud, I'm not so sure."

Roscoe laughed. "Just between you and me, and from what Maddox tells me, I think it will be well received."

I let out a nervous laugh. "Really?"

He put his hands up. "I mean, relationships are never easy, right?"

"I don't know. Last time I was in a relationship, I got stabbed six times."

Roscoe stopped smiling. "Jesus."

"Sorry."

"Christ. Don't apologize."

I wiped my hands on my thighs. *God, where was my head?* "I'm nervous."

It was quiet for a long while. "It'll be okay," he said.

I nodded. I didn't know what he was referring to, exactly. It didn't matter though. No matter what the outcome was of me telling Jeremy how I felt, or maybe quitting my job, if it all went well or even if it didn't, I'd be okay. "Yeah, it will."

Most of the papzz were gone when we arrived at the clinic, but the two police guarding the door probably had something to do with that. I assumed the guard was still inside, which meant it was unlikely anyone was getting in without the proper authority.

I knew, though, as soon as we stepped out of the van, there would be footage of Roscoe and me arriving splashed all over the internet before we could even get to Jeremy's room.

I was grateful for the police presence . . .

"Did something happen to have the cops at the door?" I asked.

"No. It's precautionary, or so Maddox said," Roscoe replied. "I don't think they realized what kind of attention Jeremy would bring."

I nodded. I understood that all too well, and I was glad the clinic saw the issue and addressed it.

We exited the van, ignoring the yelling and calls from the media, and with a nod to the cops, we went inside. The clinic during the day was very different from how it was when we arrived at night.

One woman and one man sat behind Plexiglas at the

front reception desk. She looked up and smiled at Roscoe. "Can I help you?"

"Yes, we're here to see Jeremy Dalton."

"Identification, please." We handed over our IDs and had to sign a digital sign-in screen. The man pressed a button and the double doors we'd gone through last time opened. The woman smiled at us. "Down the hall and follow the noise."

We gave a nod to the guard, a different man this time, and we went in. I didn't have to wonder what she meant by "follow the noise" because a burst of familiar laughter said all we needed to know.

We rounded the corner and found Robbie, Ivan, and Zoe standing in the hall. "Hey, Boss!" Robbie said. They were happy to see me, no doubt. And yeah, it was good to see them too.

But the person I really wanted to see . . .

The door to his room was open, and inside I could see Maddox, Blake, and Wes. I could hear Luke. I could see Jeremy's bed and see he was on it, but everyone stood around.

As soon as he heard Robbie speak, Jeremy looked around Blake and he smiled. Maddox saw Roscoe at the same time and threw himself at him.

But I couldn't take my eyes off Jeremy.

He was sitting up. He'd shaved his face—the scruffy beard was gone. His hair had started to grow back. His eyes looked clearer, less tired.

But the way he smiled at me damn near stole my breath.

"You didn't wear the shirt," he said, still smiling.

"It was like a crop top."

"So, a private showing is what I'm hearing."

"Holy shit, look at them," Blake whispered, looking between us. "You weren't kidding."

"Shut up, Blake," I said, making everyone laugh. *Could Steve, the security guy, say that? No. Could Steve who was here to see Jeremy say that? I just did.*

Jeremy gave me the eye-crinkling kind of smile, and for a few seconds, no one else in the room existed. Then he kind of laughed and looked at the others. "Can you guys give us a second? The cafeteria has a great selection of terrible sugar-free stuff."

They filed out of the room and I very deliberately didn't make eye contact with any of them. But a nurse waited at the door until they'd all walked out before coming in to check his IV.

"Hey Denise," Jeremy said. "This is Steve."

She smiled. "Hello."

"Hi."

She indicated to the IV. "You're almost done."

"Thank god."

"Be back to take it out in a few minutes."

Jeremy waited until she'd gone. "They're giving me a final super juice before I go. I can't get up, so you're gonna have to come over here."

I moved closer, took his face in my hands, and kissed him. Kinda messy, lips and a touch of tongue. It was hard to kiss properly when we were both smiling.

"I've missed you," I admitted quietly. With my hand still at his jaw, I kissed him softly. "How are you feeling?"

"Horny as hell."

I laughed. "That's not what I meant."

"I know. But I've been thinking a lot about what we'll be doing when I get out of here. And being stuck in a room with Maddox for two days who has done nothing but talk about being dicked . . . I'm supposed to be resting."

I laughed and kissed him again. "You look good."

"I feel good."

"I'm glad."

"We have a plan now. I have non-diabetic hypo-glycemia, which we already knew. But they realized my kidneys haven't been great, probably for some time."

"What does that mean?"

"It's not chronic or full-on renal failure. But there were some readings that were really low. Explains the frequent hypos, along with the stress. I just have to eat certain things and take some meds that help it. But I'll need tests every three months or something."

"How? I mean . . ." I shook my head. "How?"

He smiled. "Years of putting my body under too much stress. The exercise, the hours and hours of dance every day, the schedules, the non-stop everything, the hotel room diet. It probably would've been worse if they hadn't shoved those glucogel packs down our throats after every concert. And that 'strained back' I've had physical therapy for? Probably mild kidney pain." He shrugged. "I'm actually pretty lucky. It could've been worse."

I kissed his forehead. "I'm just glad you're okay."

"Oh," he said, excitedly. "Look at my Iron Man implant." He showed me the back of his upper arm, and there was a small, black tab thing stuck there. "It's implanted under the skin and has a transmitter. It'll tell me if my glucose levels start to get low, and it's continuous. No more finger stabbing."

Robbie opened the door for a nurse. It wasn't Denise but Jeremy smiled at her. "Are you here to set me free?"

"I sure am," she replied. She began to undo the IV drip

from the cannula, and doing whatever else she had to do. I didn't pay her too much attention, too busy looking at Jeremy.

He took my hand. "Oh, you should have seen the social media frenzy about you and Roscoe having a date last night."

"It wasn't a date," I said. "Anyway, he's really not my type."

I expected Jeremy to laugh, but he squint-blinked and shook his head. He looked at the cannula in his arm just as Riko burst into the room. "I've seen her face."

I looked at the nurse and my blood ran cold.

She smiled. "Hello, Steven," she said, then Jeremy slumped to his side on the bed.

# CHAPTER TWENTY-FOUR

LILIAN SOSA STOOD on the opposite side of the bed, a needle in her hand.

It was like time stood still, like the world stopped turning. There was no sound, just my heart pounding in my ears. My body was frozen with fear.

"I need a doctor in here!" Riko screamed, taking off down the hall.

Reality snapped back at me, and Lilian seemed to notice the change in me. She put the syringe to Jeremy's arm, threatening to pierce the skin. "Don't try it," she said. "You can't hurt him now. You think he belongs to you? You're wrong. Just like Jacqueline was wrong."

Machines started beeping. Jeremy's arm jerked, and I thought it was a reaction to her touch, but then his leg started. His hands began to shake, then his head.

He was having a seizure.

"Jeremy!" I moved to put my hand on him, but Lilian bared her teeth at me, her eyes wild.

"I said don't touch him!"

The door banged open, a doctor at the front, Riko and

Maddox right behind him. Lilian glanced at them, changing her stance to accommodate the threat. I used the split-second distraction to my advantage. With one hand on the bed, I vaulted the mattress and aimed my body at her.

I connected one knee to her chest and we went to the floor. Riko was there in a flash and we struggled with her, but he recoiled with a hiss. I slammed my elbow into her and something bit into my neck, but I didn't stop.

Rage took over.

I had a fist of her hair and grabbed her wrist, twisting it and forcing her facedown, trying to get up so I could use my body to slam her head into the floor. I wanted to punish her.

I wanted to kill her.

But then there were uniforms beside me. Cops. They took a hold of her, and it took both of them to contain her, even with my knee still in her back. She fought, she screamed, she thrashed, she kicked.

Then big arms pulled me away and more uniforms replaced me. Security, this time. Robbie held me, carrying me as he backed away. I saw a doctor slam a pen-looking thing into Jeremy's thigh while another plunged another syringe into his cannula.

And then I saw Riko sprawled on the floor and a doctor and a nurse hovering over him.

Then a doctor was in front of me. I couldn't make out the words. Everything was too much. Too hot. Too loud. Too quiet. Too fast. Too slow.

How was Jeremy? I needed to get to Jeremy.

Jeremy.

How did I get on the floor?

Why was a doctor peering down at me like that?

Why couldn't I move . . . why couldn't I think?

I tried to fight it. I tried . . .

I tried.

———

THE PAIN in my head woke me. I felt sore all over and nauseous. There was beeping and awful lights. I knew it was a hospital, because . . . because I'd woken up like this before.

Then I remembered.

Jeremy.

I tried to sit up.

"Hey, hold up," a gentle voice said. A familiar voice. "Take it easy."

Ryan.

"Jeremy," I said, trying to sit up again.

Ryan tried to settle me with a hand on my arm. "He's okay. Just lie still. I'll go get the doc."

He's okay . . .

Ryan said Jeremy was okay.

I sagged back on the bed, and after a deep breath, a doctor appeared with Ryan and Roscoe in tow. The doctor asked me a few questions, shined his stupid fucking light in my eyes, and read some machine printouts.

I'd been stuck in the neck with a syringe of insulin, or so he explained. It wasn't a huge dose, but it was enough. And it was directly into my bloodstream.

I'd crashed on the floor within minutes.

I didn't care about myself.

"How's Jeremy?"

The doctor stopped talking. He didn't answer my question though. Roscoe did.

"He's okay. They administered enough dextrose to stop it. Close call, but he's okay. He scored himself a few more days in the hospital though. Just to monitor him. Maddox is with him now. The other guys had to leave but Maddox wasn't going anywhere."

I was flooded with relief. Until I remembered Riko. "And Riko? He was down, right?"

Roscoe grimaced and Ryan gave a nod. "She got him in the lung. One-in-a-million shot, apparently. Needle went in between the ribs. He's okay. Now. But it was close. Lucky it was a diabetic hospital, to be honest."

Holy shit.

"Can I see them? Can I see Jeremy?"

"Riko was taken to UCLA," Roscoe replied.

Jesus.

Roscoe patted my foot. "He's okay."

"Jeremy's here?"

He nodded.

The doctor finished writing whatever he was writing. "You're on bedrest. No visiting anyone."

I sat up despite what the doc said, despite my body protesting. I swung my legs down to the floor and realized in that precise moment I was wearing a gown. And I was attached to a drip and an ECG machine?

"What the hell?" I went to pull the little circle pads off my chest.

"Mr. Frost," the doctor said sternly.

"I need to see him. Just for a minute. Then I'll come back. How long do I have to be here?"

"Overnight. We'll do tests again in the morning and again after breakfast."

I tried looking for any sign of daylight. Or a clock. "What time is it?"

Ryan answered. "9:35 p.m."

Nine thirty . . . that meant . . . "How long was I out for?"

"Four hours, give or take," Roscoe replied.

Fucking hell.

"I need to see Jeremy." I pulled the first ECG pad off my chest, then the second. I put some weight on my feet, seeing if my head spun, and when it didn't, I reached for the IV stand.

Ryan was quick to bring it closer. "Here."

I gave him a smile. "Thanks."

"Mr. Frost," the doctor tried again. "You should be in bed."

Roscoe appeared with a wheelchair. "I'll make sure he's quick."

I got myself into the chair, Ryan helped me with the footrests, I maneuvered the IV stand, and Roscoe wheeled me out.

As it turned out, Jeremy was now in a room right across from the nurse's station. Maddox spotted us through the glass partition wall. "Hey," he said, giving me a long hug in the doorway. "He's sleeping right now."

"No he's not," Jeremy murmured, a croaky whisper. He was smiling at me, his eyes heavy-lidded.

"Jeremy," I breathed, pushing up from the chair and going to him. I took his hand. "God, baby."

"He's only allowed out for a few minutes," Roscoe said.

"We'll give you some privacy." Maddox pulled on Ryan's arm and they left us alone.

I thumbed over his cheekbone and took in every detail of his face. He looked exhausted, a little pale. He was hooked up to all kinds of machines. "I had to see you. How are you?" I asked. "I was so scared."

"Me too." He slow blinked. "Kiss me."

My eyes burned, and with a nod, I leaned down and pressed my lips to his. I caressed his face, needing to touch him, making sure he was okay. I kissed his forehead, his eyelids, his nose, his lips again. Then threaded our fingers and kissed the back of his hand.

"You need to rest," I whispered. "I'm just down the hall. I'll see you in the morning, first thing."

"Steve," he mumbled.

"Yes, baby?"

The corner of his lips lifted, just a fraction. His eyes were closed. "I'm glad I have you."

I had to blink back tears.

"Do I have you, Steve?" he mumbled, barely audible. ". . . I have you?"

I nodded, not that he could see with his eyes closed. "You have me," I whispered. "I'm all yours."

He smiled as he fell asleep, and I didn't know whether to laugh or cry.

After Roscoe took me back to my room and helped me into bed, after the nurse reattached my ECG pads, when the room was dark and I was alone, I did a little of both.

---

THEY TOOK a glucose reading at six in the morning. I ate breakfast and changed back into my clothes, and when I went back into my room, I found Jeremy standing there in his robe, along with his IV stand, getting into my bed.

"Hey," I said. "Sir, I believe this is not your bed."

He lay down and patted what little room there was left. "Your spot."

There was no way I wasn't doing that. I squeezed onto the bed and he wiggled into the crook of my arm. I kissed the top of his head. "How're you feeling?"

"Hm. Better now."

And then the nurse came running in and huffed. It was Denise. She put her hand on her hip. "You trying to give me a heart attack? I was just about to alert security. You're not supposed to be in here."

Jeremy chuckled. "I was sneaky."

"Mr. Dalton," she tried.

He snuggled in closer. "I'm busy."

"Jer," I murmured.

"I'm not leaving. My readings were good. I ate the godawful breakfast and I peed in a cup like a good boy. My Iron Man implant will tell you if my levels drop. And it's been scientifically proven that hugs from Steve lower my blood pressure." Then he propped his head up. "Pleeeease."

Denise came over, threw the sheet up over him, and rolled her eyes. "Two minutes."

I sighed and rubbed his back. Having him safe in my arms now was a very far stretch from yesterday. The memories of him slumping down, the pallid color of his face, him having a seizure. I doubted those images would ever leave me.

"I'm sorry about yesterday," I murmured. "I should have protected you better."

He was quiet for a second. "You know what you're *not* going to do? Is blame yourself for anything that happened yesterday."

I knew he'd say something like that. "I should—"

"You should have what? Personally vetted every staff member of this hospital?"

"Well, yes? Probably a good place to start."

Jeremy sighed. "Please don't. It's no one's fault but the crazy bitch who tried to kill us." He lifted his head, his blue eyes sad. "She tried to kill you too, you know that, right?"

"I know, I just . . . It's my job to keep you safe."

The sadness in his eyes burst into anger. "Your job? Is that all I am to you? A fucking job?"

I tightened my arms around him. "No. Of course not. Whether I'm your bodyguard or your boyfriend, I will always protect you. It's who I am. I need to protect those I care about."

He stared at me, his glare quickly losing its fire. He huffed and put his head back on my shoulder. "That was the correct answer." He was quiet for a few beats and I wondered if my use of the word boyfriend was part of that. Was he going to mention it? Or just pretend I hadn't even said it? "Boyfriend, huh?"

I snorted. "Sorry, it just came out."

He laughed. "Funny, because same."

I laughed too and gave him a squeeze. "Bi and proud?"

"Well, bi and kinda scared, but yes."

I kissed his forehead. "One step at a time. It's all it takes."

He put his head back down with a sigh. "I've never had a boyfriend before."

"Me either."

He chuckled and snuggled into me. "The guys took the news well."

"You told them you're bi?"

"Well, I told them about you."

My heart thumped against my ribs. "Oh."

"Maddox told them I was Steve-sexual. I said I guessed that made me bisexual. Logically speaking. Even though it's only you."

Wow. Okay . . .

I kissed his forehead again. "You're perfect."

He was quiet for a long moment, his breathing deepened. He was almost asleep. "I wanna go home."

"Soon." I drew patterns on his back until he was snoring quietly.

When Denise came back in, I put my finger to my lips in a *shh* gesture. She gave me a *really?* look, took one glance at him, and then she sighed. "Lucky he's cute," she mumbled, walking out.

A few minutes later, Maddox and Roscoe came in. "The nurse said—"

I gave him the same *shh* gesture.

Maddox took one look at Jeremy and smiled fondly. "How is he?" he whispered.

"Okay."

Roscoe looked a little bewildered. "It's a madhouse out there."

"Media?"

He nodded. "Oh yeah. And police and security. Press, papzz, fans."

Instinctively, my hold on Jeremy got a little tighter.

"The hospital advised the band not to visit today," Maddox said. "I told them I will be here as myself and enter through the front door. Or if they'd prefer, I could dress up as a temp nurse with fake ID and just fucking walk in anyway, and we could make it a full press event."

Jeremy snorted quietly. "Have you got a nurse's outfit?"

Maddox kissed Jeremy's cheek. "Morning, beautiful. How are you feeling?"

"Better than I was last night."

Denise came back in and Jeremy latched onto me. "Nooooo."

Maddox laughed.

"Relax. I'm not here for you," she said. She was holding a glucose reader in one hand. "Mr. Frost, hand, please."

Smiling, I gave her my hand and she did the finger-prick. While we waited for the result, Jeremy propped his head up on his arm. "Denise?" he asked sweetly, a little whiney.

"Yes," she replied, probably with more patience than Jeremy rightly deserved.

"Can I go home today?"

She frowned. "I don't know. It's up to the doctors. You've got a few tests scheduled this morning. Which you need to be in your own room for."

Jeremy sighed and dropped his head back onto my chest. "I want to go home."

The glucose reader beeped. Denise held it up to show me. "Good."

Me leaving here without Jeremy was not going to go down well.

Roscoe pulled out his phone and made a call. "Ambrose. . . . Yeah, I'm with him now. He's okay." We all watched him. "I'm gonna need you to pull some strings. We're going to need an on-call endocrinology doctor or nurse at Jeremy's house. I could lie to you and say it's a security issue, because you've seen the news so you know that's a real problem, but I'm just gonna tell you how it is. He *wants* to leave, so that's what we're going to do. He has some more tests to get through this morning, which he will do, but he is leaving today. Make it happen."

Holy shit.

Roscoe ended the call, Maddox grinned at him, and Jeremy got a little teary. "Roscoe, that's the hottest thing you've ever done." I laughed and kissed the side of his head. He scowled at me. "Why couldn't you do that?"

Uhhh. "Well, about that. We should probably have a little chat about my current employment status with Platinum."

## CHAPTER TWENTY-FIVE

THE FIRST THING Jeremy did when he got home was shower. He wanted to wash the hospital feeling from his skin, which I understood. We left Maddox in charge while Roscoe, Robbie, and I did a full check of the house and the grounds.

The rest of the band arrived not long after, with full security in tow, and Ryan, Amber, and Ambrose arrived not long after that, and then Hardwick with the new registered nurse.

They gave a demonstration on Jeremy's new implant and what to do if he had a severe hypo. Truth was, they were confident now with improved kidney health that his hypoglycemia would be easily manageable.

It was all kinds of complicated, but the real simple answer?

More potassium, among other things.

He left the hospital with a health and diet plan, which he'd said looked a lot like my grocery list—whole grains, brown rice, grilled chicken and fish, leafy vegetables, and a shit ton of bananas and avocadoes.

"It'll be easy," Jeremy said. "Steve agreed to cook for me, and he eats all this shit for fun, so . . ."

I walked back to the dining table and gave Jeremy a plate of crackers and grapes. "I absolutely did not agree to cook for you. I'm going to teach you how to cook."

The nurse would be around for a few hours every day for the first three days. Hardwick would come once a day. Jeremy had to take it easy, a lot of dos and don'ts, but at least he was home.

Riko was doing fine and expected to be released from the hospital tomorrow.

"We should go see him," Jeremy said. "Tomorrow morning."

*Another full security issue, but you know what? Fuck it. We absolutely should.* I nodded. "We should."

Next was Ambrose's turn.

"What we know about Lilian Sosa," he began. "She's in police custody. She will undergo a psych evaluation. The FBI think she killed her sister for trying to hurt Jeremy. But the sister was trying to hurt Jeremy to hurt the sister because of how infatuated she was. Her infatuation ruined their lives, apparently. Lilian said her sister befriended the guy that stabbed you, Steve, just to hurt her, and she was going to ruin Platinum Entertainment as revenge." Ambrose shook his head, his eyes wide. "The whole situation is just . . . wild."

"And sad," Maddox said.

We all nodded, because it was sad. It was a whole messed up situation.

"As soon as Lilian heard you were at the hospital, she had an access point. She simply pretended to be a nurse. Hospitals have temp or rotating clinic staff. It's more common than most people realize." Ambrose sighed. "All she had to do was look and act the part. There's footage of her gaining access with the other staff, running in as if she was late. She had the right uniform, the right identification. Not her name, of course. Walked in as if she belonged, big smile, waved to some other random staffer as if she knew them, and simply just walked in."

"Hidden in plain sight," I said. "As if she was *supposed* to be there."

Ambrose nodded.

"That's a huge fuck up," Wes said. "Like huge."

Ambrose nodded. "Oh yeah."

"Bet Arlo's gearing up to sue them into the stratosphere," Luke mumbled.

"No," Jeremy said. "I don't want that. Should there be an overhaul? Probably. Was it someone's fault directly?" He looked right at me and smiled. "No. It's not. The Sosa sisters clearly had some mental health issues they very obviously got no help for. One's dead, one will be in prison for a really long time. It's terrible, and we got caught in the middle. But where does the blame start and stop? The security company? It wasn't their fault. They got hacked. The drone manufacturer? No, it's not their fault the customer did the wrong thing. The hospital? They followed procedure. Lilian Sosa lied and committed fraud and forgery, or whatever it's called. Do we sue the internet for providing fake IDs?" He shook his head and sighed. "I don't know. We can blame them all and achieve what, exactly? No one wins the blame game."

Ambrose frowned. "But if she hadn't—"

Jeremy cut him off. "And if we weren't famous, none of this would have happened. If we weren't on every news channel, none of this would have happened. If we weren't in magazines, or all of the internet, on TV shows in every country on the planet, she wouldn't have become infatuated. If society as a whole didn't glorify celebrities and demand every detail, this wouldn't have happened. Where does it stop?" He looked at his bandmates, his brothers. "If we didn't give ourselves up for public consumption, we wouldn't get chewed up and spat out."

They all stared at him.

No one spoke.

Jeremy took my hand in front of everyone. "Three of us nearly died yesterday," he added quietly. "When is it enough?"

After a beat of silence, Ambrose cleared his throat. "I, uh . . . I just need to say, about the award shows coming up . . ."

Everyone turned to look at him. Maddox shot him a filthy look. "I don't think now's the time to be discussing freaking work, Neil."

Ambrose put his hands up. "No, that's not what I meant." He took a deep breath and let it out slowly. He tried to smile. "What I meant was . . . if you guys are thinking about disbanding, because I'm getting that feeling here, then we need to think of an exit strategy and formal announcements."

Everyone looked around the table, and I squeezed Jeremy's hand.

Ambrose shrugged. "Before the awards? After? One more album? One more tour? Or are you done?"

Maddox let out a long, shaky breath, and Roscoe massaged Maddox's shoulder. He nodded and licked his lips. "We . . . that's something we need to talk about."

Blake gave a solitary nod. "I hate admitting this. I hate even thinking this." He was teary and he cleared his throat. "But I think it might be time."

Wes let his head fall back and he sighed at the ceiling.

Luke frowned, and after a long moment, he nodded.

Jeremy nodded. "Can I ask one thing?" he said. They all looked at him to continue. "I can't do this right now. I can't have this conversation today. I'm tired, and I've been through a lot this week. Right now, today, I'm ready to walk away. I'm so done. But next week or next month, I might feel different." He shook his head and his eyes were glassy. "You guys should know that no matter what we decide, I can't do the schedules, the dance rehearsals, the eighteen-hour days. I can't do that anymore. Physically. Ten years of that did a number on my body. The last tour almost killed me. Literally."

"The last tour?" Ryan asked.

Jeremy nodded. "We got back from a two-month tour and I couldn't regulate my sugars and my kidney function was shit. I can't do that anymore. Not even sure my doctors would let me try. So if we decide to stick it out a little longer, moving forward, what we do is going to be different. We need to decide if that's what we want for Atrous."

"How about next week we go up to the cabins," Maddox said. "Like we said we were gonna. We can just chill, talk about what we want." He let out a shaky breath and stared at Jeremy. "I watched my best friend code out yesterday. I thought he was going to die. I'm not up for making decisions right now."

They each nodded, solemn, teary.

But then Luke laughed through his tears. "We could do one final album. No tour or anything. But a goodbye to the fans. A sequel to *Code Red* but we'll call it *Code Blue*. You know. Medical emergency . . ."

They all laughed, because it was kinda funny.

But then they stopped laughing. They all looked at each

other. Blake raised his eyebrow. Wes shrugged. Luke laughed, and Maddox and Jeremy locked eyes, smiled at each other, and nodded.

Luke clapped his hands, still laughing. "I fucking love us."

They all stood, put their right hands in like they always did before every concert, before every performance. And they all yelled in unison.

"Atrous!"

---

WE'D HAD A BUSY MORNING, which was hardly surprising considering we were in bed asleep by eight o'clock. When everyone had gone, we cooked dinner. And after Jeremy checked his sugar readings and did a potassium reading, he just wanted to go to bed.

He fell asleep in my arms and woke up much the same way. We gave each other slow and sleepy orgasms in the shower. We ate breakfast. His glucose levels were good, but we still packed a little snack pack, just in case. Fruit, some nuts, crackers, two juice boxes. He complained of feeling like a toddler, but it was just what we had to do now.

No big deal.

And we hit the road. We took the Jeep, and I was surprised there were only a few papzz at the gates. Not the numbers we were used to. Maybe it had something to do with the press statement Platinum had released last night.

I certainly wasn't complaining.

First stop was seeing Riko in the hospital. I'd suggested Jeremy wear a disguise or something, but he'd just grinned at me and said, "I don't need a disguise. I have a Steve."

Riko was doing fine. His lung hadn't been too happy

with the puncture or with having insulin directly injected into it, but the doctors were pleased with his recovery. He was happy to see us, itching to leave the hospital, but mostly glad that Jeremy and I were okay.

Next stop was Jeremy's mom's house.

I was nervous going in, though I shouldn't have been. She cried and hugged him, and then she'd cried and hugged me. "Mom, stop squeezing him so hard," he said, pulling her arm away.

She wiped her tears and gave him another hug. "Oh Jer, I'm so glad you're okay. I've been watching the news and I wanted to come visit you in the hospital . . ."

"I know, Mom, but it was a security shitshow."

She shook her head, frowning. "It was all so horrible. I'm so glad Steve's here with you. Having a bodyguard with you is a good idea."

Jeremy smiled at me, then bit his bottom lip. "Ah, about that, Mom."

Oh my god.

"Steve is technically my bodyguard, I guess." The corner of his lip pulled down. "But he's more than that. He's my . . . we haven't really agreed on a term for it yet. The word boyfriend was used once. Lover is just gross. Special friend makes it sound like he licks the windows."

Oh mother of god.

His mom looked at him, then at me, then back to Jeremy. "Oh."

"Don't worry. No one was more surprised than me, Mom."

She covered her mouth, and I wondered if it was going to go horribly wrong, but a smile appeared behind her fingers. "Oh, Jeremy! A boyfriend?"

"Well . . . we haven't—"

She grabbed my hand, excited. "We can go to the Peacock Theater! In West Hollywood. I've always wanted to go."

"Mom, we're not going to the theater."

"I wanted Maddox to take me but he was always so busy."

"Mom, I've told you before, you don't need to be gay to go to those things." He sighed. "But fine. Sometime. I don't know when. We'll take you."

Was this . . . was this even real? Jeremy had said she'd try and make him go to gay theater. I thought he'd been joking.

But then Jeremy's glucose reader beeped. Breakfast had been two hours ago. "You need to eat," I said. The reading wasn't super low, but we weren't playing stupid games anymore.

Jeremy nodded. "Hey, Mom, whatcha got in the fridge?"

While Jeremy ate some leftover roast beef and mustard greens, he told her everything that had gone on with the FBI case, with his Iron Man implant, how it all worked, and what it meant. And finally with the realization that Atrous was coming to an end, and maybe one last farewell album. No tour. No promo schedules.

"It's the right time, Mom," he said.

Her eyes were wide and filled with concern. "What will you boys do? You boys have been Atrous since you were so young!"

He smiled and let out a happy sigh. "Dunno yet. The possibilities are endless. But it's gonna start with a really long break."

"Well, I'm glad to hear that. Does this mean you can come for dinner more often?"

He patted her hand. "Sure does. Once all the craziness dies down, you can come to my place. It's been a while, yeah?"

She nodded fondly. "I'd really like that."

When we were leaving, he gave her a long hug. "It was good to see you, Mom. But I have to get going. I have the nurse coming to check on me this afternoon." He pulled back and looked at her. "And thank you. For being cool about me and Steve."

"Oh, honey," she said. "I only ever wanted someone who would look after you and treat you right. And he's been looking after you for years."

Jeremy nodded and smiled at me. "He has."

Then she hugged me, hard. It was kind of awkward but really nice. He'd just brought a guy home and she'd barely even batted an eyelid.

*If only it was always like this . . .*

When we walked out, a smiling Jeremy put his hand out for the keys. "My turn to drive."

I'd never been in a car with him driving. "Should I be nervous?"

He laughed. "Only when you realize where it is I'm taking us."

Well, that can't be good.

We climbed in and he grinned as he started the Jeep. "I want a normal life. I want to do all the things I've never been able to do. And now that there'll be no more world tours and being gone for months at a time, there's something I've always wanted to do."

We drove along the freeway for a bit before he took an exit that wasn't ours, but he seemed to know where he was going. "There used to be one out here," he mumbled.

"You could enter it into Google Maps."

"But then it wouldn't be a surprise."

I wasn't sure I wanted a surprise, if I was being honest.

But then he grinned. "Aha! Here it is!" He turned into the parking lot . . .

Of a dog rescue center.

"A dog?" I asked.

His grin got impossibly wider. "A dog!"

He parked and jumped out, so excited it was hard not to smile. He opened the front door for me, bouncing with anticipation, and he hurried inside. He got to the front counter. "Hello? I'd like to adopt a dog, please."

The young woman behind the counter took one look at him, recognized him immediately, and lost the ability to speak for a full fifteen seconds. "Holy shit. You're Jeremy Dalton."

He laughed. "I am." Then he read her name tag. "And you're Lizabeth."

Lizabeth had a green mullet, pink-rimmed glasses, and a lip ring. She nodded, getting a little teary. "I am."

I watched this incredibly awkward scene play out and wondered how long they were going to stand there and smile at each other. "Uh, are there dogs for adoption here?" I asked.

Then Lizabeth looked at me. She gasped. "And you're Steve!"

Oh dear.

I nodded. "I am."

Jeremy laughed.

She blinked rapidly for a few seconds, then shook her head. Her brain kicked into gear and she shot out of her seat, rattling off adoption policy and procedure. And then she gave us a tour of the kennels. And she asked a lot of questions about what type of dog he had in mind.

Jeremy didn't mind what breed, small or large, male or female. "I'll just know when I see them," he said.

There were so many dogs. So many. Any one of them would have been lovely. Big dogs, small dogs, bouncy dogs, barking dogs. Every breed imaginable.

I had visions of us leaving with every dog here because I had no idea how he was ever going to choose.

When he stopped at one cage.

This dog was a Pitbull, smaller in size but still had a solid build. It looked young, maybe not fully grown, and it looked scared. It was silver with a white blaze on its chest that ran up under its chin. It had big, round eyes full of love and hope, and Jeremy was staring at it.

"What's this one?"

"She's a Pitty . . . sorry, a Pitbull. Eight months old. She was probably the runt of the litter, but she's pretty and sweet as an angel."

Jeremy whispered. "What's her name?"

"Miss Eleanor Rigby."

Jeremy's mouth fell open. "It is not!"

Lizabeth nodded. "It is."

Jeremy turned to me, his eyes wide. He put his hand on my arm. "Her name is Miss Eleanor Rigby."

"Would you like to meet her?" Lizabeth asked.

Jeremy nodded quickly, and as she unlocked the cage door, Jeremy sat on the concrete floor, one foot under his ass, one knee bent.

Lizabeth had Miss Eleanor Rigby on a leash. "Oh, we normally like to introduce you in the—"

But Miss Eleanor Rigby pulled on the leash and wiggled her way onto Jeremy's lap. He hugged her and she was all but sitting on him.

Jeremy looked up at me, tears in his eyes. "Steve, she's

perfect." He wiped a tear away. "Her name is Miss Eleanor Rigby. How was she not meant for me?"

Lizbeth sniffled and was all teary too. "God. Sorry." She laughed and wiped her cheek. "I think she chose you."

Jeremy nodded, cuddling the little dog that wiggled and smiled in his arms.

And just like that, he'd found his dog.

A bunch of forms and an entire trunk full of doggy goodies later—a bed, a sparkly pink collar and matching leash, toys, shampoo, and a month's supply of dog food—we were on our way.

I don't know who smiled the hardest, Jeremy or Miss Eleanor Rigby.

"Her name," he said.

"I know."

"The freaking Beatles, Steve. It was a sign."

"It was."

He held her on his lap, hugging her the whole way back to his house. He spent the next few hours with her, showing her around her new home, her new bed, her new bowl. She knew some basic commands and Jeremy was so excited to begin training.

"We can take her to classes, and we'll need a vet. Oh my god, Steve, we have so much to organize."

There was an awful amount of *we* in his excitement.

I sat on the sun lounger on the patio and watched them. How they interacted, how they played. I didn't know who was happier.

Jeremy was positively beaming. He ran with her, he laughed, they played with a frisbee.

Miss Eleanor Rigby plonked herself down on the grass in the shade, her tongue lolling, her smile wide. Jeremy fell down beside her. "We need to tell Uncle Maddox . . . Oh man. I don't have a phone."

"Do you want another one? We can go buy one. Or I can call Elsie and ask her to pick one up."

He stared at me. "Call her on what, Steve?"

"Oh."

He snorted and patted his very happy dog. "Maybe we should get one. Now that the case is over. Now that we . . ." He shot me a look. "Oh my god. What if we need to call an emergency vet?"

I chuckled. "We better get you a new phone."

He sighed and sprawled on his back on the shade-dappled grass, his arms out wide. "Do you know how long it's been since I did this?"

"Too long?"

He turned to look at me just as Miss Eleanor Rigby decided to pounce and lick his face. They play-wrestled for a little while, making me laugh, but he soon took her inside so she could sleep on her bed. He'd given her a toy and a blanket to sleep with, which was honestly the cutest thing ever.

He stood and watched her as she slept, frowning and shaking his head.

"What's wrong?" I asked.

"I just love her already. So much," he said. "How is that possible?"

"Sometimes when you know, you just know."

He turned to face me. I wasn't talking about the sleeping dog, and he knew it.

I took his hand and a massive leap of faith.

"I love you, Jeremy."

His mouth fell open. He breathed my name.

I smiled. "I love how you smile and the way you laugh. I love how you smell, how you sleep. I love how you think of other people first, how despite the fame and the money, you're still the same guy you were all those years ago. I love how you sing. And not on stage or in the studio, although that's still great. But nothing compares to the way you sing in the kitchen when you think no one is listening." I squeezed his hand in mine. "I've been in love with you for a long time, Jeremy. But seeing you today, with her . . ." I looked at Miss Eleanor Rigby and back to him. "With your ability to love so freely. Seeing you so happy. I just had to tell you. I don't expect you to say anything back. I just needed you to know. You're amazing, and you're so very loved."

His eyes were glassy and he threw his arms around my neck, hugging me tight. "Steve."

I wrapped him up in the biggest hug, smiling into his neck. I could just hold him forever. And now that I'd said those words, now that he knew, it felt like a weight was lifted.

He deserved to know how loved he was. Not for being the famous Jeremy Dalton, adored singer and performer. But for being Jeremy Dalton, the man when the lights went off, when the cameras stopped rolling.

"Steve," he whispered.

I pulled back, about to tell him not to panic. I didn't expect—

He crushed his mouth to mine, kissing me, trying to climb me like he couldn't get close enough. I hoisted him up and he wrapped his legs around me, only breaking the kiss to smile. "I thought it was just me," he said. "With stupid feelings that I didn't know what to do with."

I chuckled. Stupid feelings . . .

Then I realized what he was saying. He was saying he felt the same.

"Not just you," I said, daring to hope that's what he meant. "Stupid feelings are stupid."

He grinned. "So stupid. What is love, anyway, besides heart palpitations and cold sweats?"

I laughed. "And butterflies."

"So many butterflies," he whispered before kissing me again. Then he pulled back, his eyes fixed on mine. "I've never been in love before. Not with anyone." He swallowed hard. "But you."

My heart felt too big for my chest. "Jeremy."

"Carry me to the couch," he murmured. "Lie on top of me. I want to feel your body—"

A beeping interrupted him. It couldn't have been a phone . . .

He sighed. "It's just my glucose reader."

I laughed and carried him to the kitchen instead. I lifted him onto the kitchen counter. "Food first."

I took out the ingredients to make wholegrain wraps with various salad veggies and sliced turkey. Jeremy stayed sitting on the counter and assembled each one. He chewed the inside of his lip for a second. "Can I ask you something?"

"Sure."

"Will you still feel the same about me when I'm not famous? The days of Atrous are almost done. I won't be on TV or in magazines. No more trips around the world, no more tours. No more sexiest-man-alive titles." He made a face. "You won't always need to protect me from the frenzy."

I held a slice of bell pepper to his lips. He bit into it and I gave him a quick kiss. "Jeremy, I don't care for any of that.

Actually, I'll probably prefer it when it's all over with, when we don't have to worry about any of that. I love who you are when the world's not looking."

He smiled and even blushed a little. "Everything's going to be different now. I've spent so long having every single part of my life scheduled and planned down to the minute, and now, for the first time, I don't know what my future looks like. I've never been me without Atrous. Not really."

"Does that scare you?"

"Yes. But it's also exciting. In a way. I mean, I'm free!"

I grinned at him. "You are."

"What about you? What are you going to do?"

I sighed. "For my contract, I'll request to see you guys finish up. Then I'm done. I won't leave you while you're still under Platinum. But your last day will also be mine. I don't want to work with anyone who's not you."

He smiled and took my hand. "What will you do?"

I laughed. "I have no idea. Maybe start up a protection agency? I have some money saved. I can pay rent for a good while with that until I figure something out. Like you said. It's scary, but it's also exciting."

He hooked his legs around me and pulled me close. "Or you could move in with me."

I stared. "What?"

"You could move in with me," he whispered, vulnerable. "I've loved having you here. Despite you making me cook, which I actually secretly enjoyed, but that's not the point. I got used to having you here. I don't want to live alone anymore, and there's no one I'd rather live with than with you." He pouted. "We could have sex all the time. Like *all* the time. Do you know how good that will be, Steve? And I feel safe when you're here. And now we have Miss Eleanor Rigby. She'll need both her daddies." He rolled his eyes. "So, she's technically my dog. I don't mean to say you're responsible for her financially at all, but I'm absolutely one hundred percent going to spoil her rotten. And you'll need to be the voice of reason, Steve. She's going to need you."

I laughed. "Oh, she is, huh?"

He nodded earnestly. "Yep."

I kissed him. "Can I think about it?"

He nodded, his lips a thin line. He waited all of three seconds. "Have you thought about it?"

I laughed, rolled up the wrap, and handed it to him. He bit into it, chewed, then spoke with his mouth full. "How about now?"

I laughed again. "Do you always get what you want?"

He wiggled, smiling. "Yay!"

"That was not a yes."

He cupped his ear. "Sorry, what was that? I couldn't hear you over that loud and resounding yes."

I laughed, and he pulled me closer with his legs. "Yes," I said. "Yes, yes."

He grinned victoriously, but then his eyes softened. "You just made me ridiculously happy."

"Same. Now hurry up and eat your wrap. You're going to need all the glucose you can get for what I want to do to your body."

His smirk was salacious, filthy. "Hm, yes, please."

But by the time he'd eaten, Miss Eleanor Rigby woke up from her nap.

And ten minutes later, Maddox and Roscoe turned up. Maddox stormed in, waving a new iPhone box. "Where's Jeremy? He's taking this damn phone whether he likes it or not. I had to find out he became a dog-dad when some girl from the shelter posted a photo of him on Twitter. With a dog!"

I smiled. "He took her out to pee," I said. "Come out here."

We went out back, and there was Jeremy in the corner of his yard with his dog. When they spotted us, Jeremy's grin widened. "Come meet your uncles," he said.

Miss Eleanor Rigby bounded over, all uncoordinated legs and goofy smile.

"Oh my god," Maddox whispered. He crouched down and collected a wiggly, happy dog. "She's beautiful. What's her name?"

"Miss Eleanor Rigby," Jeremy announced.

Maddox, still on the ground, looked up. "It is not!"

Jeremy laughed. "It is! That was her name at the shelter. Can you believe that?"

"That's your favorite Beatles song."

"I know!"

Maddox picked her up, somehow easily holding the licking, wriggling dog, showing her off to Roscoe. "Look! I want one!"

Roscoe smiled at me, then at Jeremy. "Thanks *so* much."

Jeremy laughed. "You are *so* welcome."

# EPILOGUE
## ONE YEAR LATER

"UP NEXT IS the number one smash hit from Atrous. From their final album, the title track, 'Code Blue,'" the radio DJ said. "Sad to see them go, but what a gift they gave to their fans! A goodbye album. A thank you album. Does it get any better than that?"

The co-host spoke next. "They sent shock waves around the world when they announced this album would be their last, that their reign as kings of pop was over. But honestly, who can blame them for calling it quits?"

"No one, surely," the DJ said. "Crazy scenes at the LA County Courthouse last week. Lilian Sosa pled guilty to a whole string of charges, including three counts of attempted murder, despite her lawyers citing psychological grounds. And hundreds of fans lining the entrance to the courthouse to protect the band from the paparazzi, in an organized, military-style protection corridor."

"Just shows you how much the fans respect the band who respected them right back. *Code Blue*, the album, is a personal thank you to their fans for a decade of love. And here it is, the title song that broke records all across the globe."

Smiling, Jeremy rolled his eyes. "Turn it off."

We were in the Jeep, heading up to the cabins for a few days with the gang. Jeremy was driving, I was in the passenger seat, Miss Eleanor Rigby was harnessed into the backseat. She was already asleep.

I switched off the radio. "Maddox and Roscoe said to get there around five, right?"

"Yeah. You know what Roscoe's like."

Roscoe would do that dad thing where he spent the day hosing everything down in the communal BBQ area and clearing away cobwebs and dust, while Maddox usually yelled out, "You missed a bit," and Roscoe pretended to spray him with the hose.

If Roscoe wanted to clean the whole place down before we got there, I wasn't going to argue.

It had been an interesting year. It had been a great year.

Arlo Kim almost swallowed his tongue when the boys gave their notice of termination. I thought he was going to try to legally bind them, but when they said they wanted to do one more album, no press shit, no tour, just a goodbye and thanks to the fans, he relented.

Their relationship had been tense since Jeremy's ordeal, and honestly, Arlo Kim knew it. He knew it would get ugly, and no money in the world would pay for the damage he'd do if he held Atrous hostage.

There was no love lost when I told him my plans to finish up with the band. He was, frankly, happy to see me go. By the time the album was done, the year was half over, so the venture into my own protection agency was still very new.

But I had two of the best managers in the business. Robbie and Riko had decided not to renew their contracts with Platinum and had come to work for me. And even though it was only the beginning, things were going well.

*Really* well.

Jeremy and all the boys had spent the last six months, since finishing their last album, having an actual break. A real break. They saw each other all the time, doing all the things they'd missed in the last ten years.

They slept in, they went to the beach, they had movie nights, dinner parties and BBQs, hikes in the canyon, went to museums, and they spent time with their families.

These two days at the cabins had been planned for a while, and I had a feeling it would be a marker of sorts for them to begin thinking about what they wanted to do next.

I had to wonder what Jeremy would do. He'd talked about doing different things, and god knows he had enough money to never have to work again. If he wanted to be a stay-at-home dad to Miss Eleanor, he certainly could. But I'd found him jotting down a few notes and melodies lately and singing unfamiliar tunes around the house. He was starting to get the itch to be productive.

Whatever he did, music would never be far away. I had a feeling he'd lean toward writing and producing, possibly with Maddox, but in the end it didn't matter what they chose.

I just wanted him to be happy.

"Whatcha thinking about, my love?" he asked, taking my hand on my thigh.

"How lucky I am to have you."

"Oh shit, did we bring Miss Ellie's blanket?"

I snorted out a laugh. "Yes. I packed it."

He breathed a sigh of relief. "Phew." He lifted our joined hands and kissed my knuckles. "I'm lucky to have you too."

We eventually turned off the road and went down the long drive to the cabins. I could see four vehicles parked. "Is everyone here already? I thought you said Luke hadn't left yet."

"They were ten minutes behind us." Jeremy pulled the Jeep in close to his cabin, and Roscoe appeared, smiling.

"Hey," I said to him. "Is that Wes's car?"

Jeremy got Miss Eleanor out of the Jeep and set her down. She loved it here and was happy to run around. I waited for Roscoe to answer but he was silent, still smiling. Something was definitely up. "What's going on?"

"Come this way," Roscoe said. The fact he was acting suspicious made us both nervous. I looked at Jeremy, and he shrugged.

The communal BBQ area, which was undercover with a built-in fire pit and bench seats, was now fitted with string lights.

Okay, so that was nothing major.

But Roscoe didn't stop there. He kept walking to the huge barn that had been converted into a recording studio of sorts. It was basically just an open hall for fancy jam sessions that just happened to have recording gear. It didn't look like much, but the acoustics were amazing.

Roscoe slipped in through the doors and we followed, my eyes taking a second to catch up with the dark. But the studio wasn't the studio . . . Gone were the rugs on the floor, gone were the sofas and the gear.

In its place was a makeshift chapel.

String lights hung from the rafters, creating a soft glow.

There were chairs in pretty rows, a small stage, and white flowers everywhere.

Oh my god.

Jeremy gasped beside me. "Where's Maddox?"

Just then, Maddox came walking out from the back with his mom . . . and Roscoe's mom.

Maddox's whole face lit up when he saw Jeremy. "Um, welcome to our wedding."

Jeremy almost burst into tears and they hugged fiercely, and when they pulled back, Jeremy cupped Maddox's face. "You're getting married today? And I'm finding out today?"

Maddox nodded. "Don't make me cry, Jer."

I turned to Roscoe. "You managed to keep this a secret?"

He laughed. "Wasn't easy."

"Oh," Roscoe's mother said to him. "Your father said to tell you there's another car coming."

Luke and Vana arrived with Blake and his new girl-friend of five months, Rebecca. Rebecca was a lovely girl, two years younger than the guys, but she wasn't fazed by who Blake was.

Why wasn't she?

Because she was Luke's sister.

Now *that* had been a conversation. Luke had been pissed at first. Said it was weird and that no, Blake couldn't date his sister. But they'd persisted and stuck it out. The thing was, Rebecca knew everyone already, didn't give a shit that they were famous, and while she absolutely loved her brother, she could also tell him to fuck off when required.

Blake's parents thought it was wonderful, and Luke's parents adored Blake.

Luke wasn't sold on the idea until he figured out that if Blake and Rebecca ever got married, then he and Blake would be legally brothers. It would only be by marriage, but still . . .

They'd be actual brothers.

Then he was okay with it.

Then Wes and Amy arrived. Amy was seven months pregnant and absolutely glowing. Wes was making them all uncles, and Jeremy was over the moon. They all were.

Jeremy had been so scared of change once and what it meant for them. The idea of their group growing and changing had terrified him. Now he loved it. Every new addition, every new thing was something to be celebrated.

Including Maddox and Roscoe's wedding.

Standing in front of their parents and us, and the celebrant, of course, Maddox Kershaw and Roscoe Hall were married. They wore matching burgundy pants and white button-down shirts. Maddox wore his signature black dangling earrings, and they exchanged black wedding rings.

Simple, zero fanfare, no fuss, no media. Just us.

Just perfect.

We toasted the happy couple, we ate, we danced with the string lights over our heads, the moonlight outside. We laughed, and there was so much love in that room. It was fitting that this marked the end of the Atrous road—as adults, in a ceremony for a new beginning.

A ceremony for forever.

As the night got late, after Jeremy had danced with everyone, he slow danced with me. I was never much of a dancer, but Jeremy sure was. He made us dance like magnets. Our bodies pressed together, his arms slung around my back, my hands on his waist.

"Who do you think will be next?" I asked.

"Next for what?"

"Next to get married. Weddings usually have that

effect. I think Wes will ask Amy soon. Surprised he hasn't already."

He looked around at the other couples, all dancing, and he seemed to ponder for a while. Then he looked at me, his blue eyes like azure galaxies. "I think it'll be us."

I laughed, because what?

He smiled and kissed me. "Yes, I'll marry you."

What the actual . . .

"Pretty sure I didn't ask."

He cupped his hand to his ear. "I'm sorry, what was that? I couldn't hear you over that awesome marriage proposal."

I laughed again, because . . . what the hell just happened?

"Umm . . . did we just . . . ?"

"Get engaged? Yep. But let's not tell the others just yet. Don't want to take anything away from Madz and Roscoe." He kissed me soundly, then went back to slow-dancing like nothing had just happened.

He slid his hands around my lower back and hummed like a songbird in my ear, a tune I couldn't quite place.

"What's that song?"

He laughed. "Do you remember, back when I was still trying to figure things out. It was three o'clock in the morning or something and I was playing my piano? You asked me what song it was. I said it didn't have a name."

"I remember."

"Well, the song had a name. But how I felt didn't. I didn't know what to call it or how to make sense of anything I felt."

"Oh, baby."

"It's your song."

I pulled back. My feet stopped moving. "My song?"

He grinned. "Steve's song. Well, it's actually called 'Untraveled Roads' but it will always be Steve's Song to me."

"You wrote a song for me?"

He rolled his eyes. "I have a lot of songs about you."

"You do?"

"Of course I do, silly."

"Sing it for me."

He put his forehead to mine, closed his eyes, and sang.

*I walk when I'm with you*
*Places I've never been*
*Places I can't imagine*
*Places I've never seen*
*Scared of every step I take*
*Can't turn around*
*Don't want to stop*
*Not sure I would*
*Don't know where I am*
*Or what this means*
*But it all feels true*
*When I walk untraveled roads*
*With you*

*I fly when I'm with you*
*Skies I've never been*
*Heights I can't imagine*
*Dreams I've never dreamed*
*Scared of every breath I take*
*Can't turn around*
*Don't want to stop*
*Not sure I could*

*I know now where I am*
*And what this means*
*I know it all feels true*
*When I walk untraveled roads*
*With you*

- Untraveled Roads (Steve's Song)

# SONGS FOR STEVE

# Code Blue

My heart is on the table
Still bleeding, still beating
Come fix me if you're able
Barely feeling, barely breathing


Call the doctor, baby
Code blue, code blue
Call the doctor, baby
I'm so in love with you


Life was never like this
I don't mean to push
I don't want to be alone
I don't remember me before you


Break me, Take me
Heal me, Fix me
Love me , love me


Call the doctor, baby
Code blue, code blue
Call the doctor, baby
I'm so in love with you


I was never like this
Before I met you
But I can't do this without you
I don't remember, baby
I don't remember love like this
I don't know me without you


Code Blue

# Light of Day

Look at me in the darkness
Can't face you in the day
The night makes it easier
To let myself say

Daylight shines too bright
There's nowhere to hide
Don't look at me in the light
I'm a different man at night

It's so much easier in the darkness
To be who I want to be
Where the world can't see
Where it's just you and me
Where the shadows hide Who I might be

Close the blinds
Shut out the light
I'm not sure I want to see
Who I am
Who I really am
What this makes me
Who I want to be

Only look at me in the darkness
Where the light can't see
What this makes me
Who I want to be

# Honest Mistake

I never meant for this to happen
I never planned to let you down
I never went looking
I promised you I'd never

I'm so sorry, baby
I'm so sorry for all of this
Such an honest mistake

When I said I would never
When I promised you I'd never
Such an honest mistake

I don't know how I got here
I don't know what it means
I don't know what this makes me
I only know how it feels

I'm so sorry, baby
I'm so sorry for all of this
Such an honest mistake
I know I said I would never
Fall in love with you

But here I am
So in love with you
Forgive me baby
Such an honest mistake
I'm so in love with you
Such an honest mistake

# Earthquake

You look at me and the ground moves
In ways that don't feel right
You hold me steady while the ground moves
keep me safe inside
when the world shakes
crashes down around me
you stand strong
protect me

You touch me and the ground moves
In ways that don't feel right
Catch me when I fall
Catch me
Stand strong

You touch me and the ground moves
In ways that don't feel right
Tell me this ain't wrong
Touch me, make the ground move
Make it feel right
Look at me, make the ground move
Make it feel right

Hold me
And if I fall,
I'll fall with you

# Love Me

I wish I could tell you how
There's no answer
None of it comes easy
Searching for a way around

I wish I knew what to say
To take this all away
I wish I could tell you

But I don't know how
Baby, there's no answer
Not even I, not even I
Baby, don't you know
I don't even know how to love me

How can you How can you understand
When no one's been here before you
No one's stood where you stand
Not like this
Not like you

Baby, there's no answer
Not even I, not even I
Baby, don't you know
I don't even know how to love me

# ABOUT THE AUTHOR

N.R. Walker is an Australian author, who loves her genre of gay romance. She loves writing and spends far too much time doing it, but wouldn't have it any other way.

She is many things: a mother, a wife, a sister, a writer. She has pretty, pretty boys who live in her head, who don't let her sleep at night unless she gives them life with words.

She likes it when they do dirty, dirty things... but likes it even more when they fall in love.

She used to think having people in her head talking to her was weird, until one day she happened across other writers who told her it was normal.

She's been writing ever since...

## ALSO BY N.R. WALKER

*Blind Faith*

*Through These Eyes (Blind Faith #2)*

*Blindside: Mark's Story (Blind Faith #3)*

*Ten in the Bin*

*Gay Sex Club Stories 1*

*Gay Sex Club Stories 2*

*Point of No Return – Turning Point #1*

*Breaking Point – Turning Point #2*

*Starting Point – Turning Point #3*

*Element of Retrofit – Thomas Elkin Series #1*

*Clarity of Lines – Thomas Elkin Series #2*

*Sense of Place – Thomas Elkin Series #3*

*Taxes and TARDIS*

*Three's Company*

*Red Dirt Heart*

*Red Dirt Heart 2*

*Red Dirt Heart 3*

*Red Dirt Heart 4*

*Red Dirt Christmas*

*Cronin's Key*

*Cronin's Key II*

*Cronin's Key III*

*Reindeer Games*

*The Dichotomy of Angels*

*Throwing Hearts*

*Pieces of You - Missing Pieces #1*

*Pieces of Me - Missing Pieces #2*

*Pieces of Us - Missing Pieces #3*

*Lacuna*

*Tic-Tac-Mistletoe*

*Bossy*

*Code Red*

*Dearest Milton James*

*Dearest Malachi Keogh*

*Christmas Wish List*

Titles in Audio:

*Cronin's Key*

*Cronin's Key II*

*Cronin's Key III*

*Red Dirt Heart*

*Red Dirt Heart 2*

*Red Dirt Heart 3*

*Red Dirt Heart 4*

*The Weight Of It All*

*Switched*

*Point of No Return*

*Pieces of You*

*Pieces of Me*

*Pieces of Us*

*Tic-Tac-Mistletoe*

*Lacuna*

*Bossy*

*Code Red*

*Learning to Feel*

*Dearest Milton James*

*Dearest Malachi Keogh*

*Three's Company*

*Christmas Wish List*


Free Reads:


*Sixty Five Hours*

*Learning to Feel*

*His Grandfather's Watch (And The Story of Billy and Hale)*

*The Twelfth of Never (Blind Faith 3.5)*

*Twelve Days of Christmas (Sixty Five Hours Christmas)*

*Best of Both Worlds*


Translated Titles:


*Italian*


*Fiducia Cieca (Blind Faith)*

*Attraverso Questi Occhi (Through These Eyes)*

*Preso alla Sprovvista (Blindside)*

*Il giorno del Mai (Blind Faith 3.5)*

*Cuore di Terra Rossa Serie (Red Dirt Heart Series)*

*Natale di terra rossa (Red dirt Christmas)*

*Intervento di Retrofit (Elements of Retrofit)*

*A Chiare Linee (Clarity of Lines)*

*Senso D'appartenenza (Sense of Place)*

*Spencer Cohen Serie (including Yanni's Story)*

*Punto di non Ritorno (Point of No Return)*

*Punto di Rottura (Breaking Point)*

*Punto di Partenza (Starting Point)*

*Imago (Imago)*

*Il desiderio di un soldato (A Soldier's Wish)*

*Scambiato (Switched)*

*Galassie e Oceani (Galaxies and Oceans)*

## French

*Confiance Aveugle (Blind Faith)*

*A travers ces yeux: Confiance Aveugle 2 (Through These Eyes)*

*Aveugle: Confiance Aveugle 3 (Blindside)*

*À Jamais (Blind Faith 3.5)*

*Cronin's Key Series*

*Au Coeur de Sutton Station (Red Dirt Heart)*

*Partir ou rester (Red Dirt Heart 2)*

*Faire Face (Red Dirt Heart 3)*

*Trouver sa Place (Red Dirt Heart 4)*

*Le Poids de Sentiments (The Weight of It All)*

*Un Noël à la sauce Henry (A Very Henry Christmas)*

*Une vie à Refaire (Switched)*

*Evolution (Evolved)*

*Galaxies & Océans*

*Qui Trouve, Garde (Finders Keepers)*

## German

*Flammende Erde (Red Dirt Heart)*

*Lodernde Erde (Red Dirt Heart 2)*

*Sengende Erde (Red Dirt Heart 3)*

*Ungezähmte Erde (Red Dirt Heart 4)*

*Vier Pfoten und ein bisschen Zufall (Finders Keepers)*

*Ein Kleines bisschen Versuchung (The Weight of It All)*

*Ein Kleines Bisschen Fur Immer (A Very Henry Christmas)*

*Weil Leibe uns immer Bliebt (Switched)*

*Drei Herzen eine Leibe (Three's Company)*

*Über uns die Sterne, zwischen uns die Liebe (Galaxies and Oceans)*

*Unnahbares Herz (Blind Faith 1)*

*Sehendes Herz (Blind Faith 2)*

*Hoffnungsvolles Herz (Blind Faith 3)*

*Verträumtes Herz (Blind Faith 3.5)*

*Thomas Elkin: Verlangen in neuem Design*

*Thai*

*Sixty Five Hours (Thai translation)*
*Finders Keepers (Thai translation)*

*Spanish*

*Sesenta y Cinco Horas (Sixty Five Hours)*
*Código Rojo (Code Red)*
*Queridísimo Milton James*
*Queridísimo Malachi Keogh*
*El Peso de Todo (The Weight of it All)*
*Tres Muérdagos en Raya: Serie Navidad en Hartbridge*
*Lista De Deseos Navideños: Serie Navidad en Hartbridge*

*Chinese*

*Blind Faith*

Lightning Source UK Ltd.
Milton Keynes UK
UKHW030749180422
401668UK00001B/154